ONYX & IVORY

MINDEE ARNETT

BALZER + BRAY
An Imprint of HarperCollins *Publishers*

Typography by Torborg Davern

Map illustration by Maxime Plasse

19 20 21 22 23   PC/LSCH   10 9 8 7 6 5 4 3 2

❖

First paperback edition, 2019

For Lori M. Lee, friend and champion

PART ONE

The Traitor's Daughter

OUT HERE, DARKNESS MEANT DEATH.

Kate Brighton urged her weary horse ever faster as night crept over the land of Rime. The gelding labored with the pace already, his pants like whipcracks in the air, and his shoulders and neck lathered with foamy white stripes. But they couldn't stop, and they couldn't slow down. They had to make it inside the city before the gates closed.

How much farther? Kate thought for the hundredth time, Farhold still nowhere in sight. The road wound between hills too tall to see beyond, the shadows deep and dark. The swaths of everweeps spilling down the slopes toward them were already drawing their petals closed, while the moon with its pale silvery ring peeked over the crest of the hills to the east like a watchful eye in the bruised face of the sky.

"Come on, Pip," Kate whispered. She stood in the stirrups as she rode, her legs burning from the effort to keep her weight off the horse's back. After so many hours in the saddle, her muscles felt like wood gone to rot.

Pip's sleek ears twitched at the sound of her voice, but his pace remained the same. He had no more speed to give. It was more than fatigue. Even without her magic, Kate could sense the horse's pain in the way his neck dipped whenever his left foreleg struck the ground. When she reached out with her abilities, though, Kate felt the pain as if it were her own, a hot throb running up from the base of the hoof. What must've started as a tiny fracture had only spread and worsened on their long journey.

Fear clutched at Kate's heart. *If the bone shatters* . . . She cut the thought off before it could grow roots and spread.

The guilt was harder to keep at bay, though. If only they'd stayed a bit longer in the Relay tower, where she and Pip had spent the night on their return journey from Marared, a city more than fifty miles to the east. Another Relay rider would've come along to help them. The royal courier service of Rime kept strict protocols about searching for riders who failed to return with the mail they carried. Most riders who went missing were assumed killed by the nightdrakes that roamed the surface of Rime after sunset. The creatures ruled the night in this land, devouring any human or horse they could find. The only safety was behind the fortified walls of the cities and Relay towers or a magist wardstone barrier.

But she hadn't sensed the injury. Pip had left the tower sound, if a little sluggish from the previous day's ride. Then halfway to Farhold—snap. The foot went from fine to on fire. At once Kate had dismounted and wrapped the leg with the cloth bandage she kept in her saddlebag. She wanted to stay put, fearing further damage, but they had to press on. She'd slowed their pace in an effort to keep it from worsening, but that too had been a mistake—one they were paying for now with this hellish race against the encroaching darkness. If she just had the power to halt the sun in its descent . . . but only Caro could do that, and she doubted the sky god was listening.

"We're almost there," Kate said, struggling to convey the complex idea to the horse. Although her gift allowed her to touch the minds of animals, and to even influence their behavior, making them understand wasn't easy. Horses didn't think in words and ideas but in images and feelings, a language much harder to speak in.

Still, for a few seconds she sensed something like relief from Pip, his steps a little lighter, his head a little higher. Then the road began to climb upward, and the horse fell out of the gallop into a trot. Kate resisted pushing him back into a run; Pip needed to catch his breath, and daylight still lingered, if only by a single brushstroke of pink on the sky ahead. *Farhold can't be much farther,* she hoped. They'd been in the hills that formed the city's eastern border for more than an hour now. But this was only her second time taking this route, and she couldn't be certain. The Marared route, with its lengthy distance and taxing pace, was reserved for veterans, and Kate had only just made three years as a Relay rider for Farhold.

Nevertheless, her instinct proved true. When they finally crested the hill, she spotted Farhold's towering stone wall less than a mile ahead. In the deepening darkness, the wardstones set in the embrasures at the top of the wall glowed bright as starlight. The magic inside each stone served a single purpose: to repel the nightdrake packs. No one knew where or how the drakes passed from under the earth to the surface, but they always appeared at dark and terrorized until dawn.

Kate ran her gaze over the cornfields on either side of the road, which started at the base of the hill and stretched all the way to the city. The green stalks, high as Pip's knees, swayed in the breeze, making gentle *whish-whish* sounds. At least, Kate prayed it was the breeze. In the weak light, the stalks offered enough cover for the nightdrake scouts to venture out without fear of being burned by the sun. The smaller, more timid drakes of the pack, scouts always appeared first to spy for prey. With teeth like knives and claws like razors, a single scout could bring down a horse with little effort. The drakes came in every size. Some small as pigs, others large as horses. All of them deadly.

The path ahead appeared clear for now, and she allowed Pip to slow to a walk as they descended the hill, the pressure in his hoof too great for anything faster. Each step sent needling pain through both horse and rider. Kate wanted to withdraw from it, the agony making her dizzy, but she didn't dare. Sharing the pain with Pip was the only way he would endure this final stretch. The horse had great heart, but even the strongest spirit couldn't push a broken body forever.

With her nerves on edge, Kate kept her eyes on the fields, flinching at each twitch of the stalks. She retrieved the bow tied to the back of her saddle and held it crossways over her lap. The quiver on her back contained twelve arrows, half of them fashioned with ordinary steel tips and the other half bearing tips enchanted with mage magic, same as the wardstones. Piercing a nightdrake's hide was no easy task—only arrows imbued with mage magic could do it from a distance. Pistols could as well, but they fired a single shot, which made them next to worthless against a pack. The remaining drakes would be on the shooter before she had time to reload.

Kate closed her legs around Pip's sides, asking for more speed. He snorted and tossed his head in protest, the bit jangling in his mouth. She couldn't blame him; the pain was more tolerable at this pace. For a second, she considered letting him stay at the walk, but then two sounds reached her ears. The first was the clang of Farhold's evening bell, calling for the gates to close. The second was the distinctive screech of a nightdrake from somewhere behind them. Both had the same effect. Digging her heels into Pip's side, Kate sent him a vision of an attacking drake. The horse had no trouble understanding the concept this time, and he charged into the gallop.

Turning in the saddle, Kate spotted a pair of bright, glistening eyes peering out from the stalks just behind them. The scout gave chase, flanking them on the left but staying hidden beneath the cover of the corn. *For now.* With her heart thrumming, Kate grabbed an arrow, nocked it, and loosed it, all in the span of a second. She missed, but it didn't matter. Scouts spooked easily, and it backed off.

But there would be others. There always were.

Turning back around, Kate heard the wind shriek in her ears even louder than the bell. Ahead she saw the teams of oxen hitched to the insides of the gates, pulling them closed.

"Wait!" she shouted. "Wait!" Once the gates closed, they wouldn't reopen until dawn—not for one lowly Relay rider. There was another way into the city, through the hidden mage door, but only mage magic could find and open it. Hers was wilder magic, outlawed and secret and good only for influencing animals.

If the men driving the oxen heard her, they didn't respond. She urged Pip even faster, but the horse was failing by the second as the pain in his foreleg spread. She heard the rustle of corn behind her, louder than before. In the distance, the rest of the pack began to screech, closing in. Kate spied the Farhold guards waiting atop the wall with arrows nocked to repel the beasts should they approach the gate before it closed.

Come on, Pip. Gritting her teeth, Kate closed her eyes and went deeper into the horse's mind until she found the very center of him, his essence. All animals possessed it—a glowing brightness like a burning candle that she could see and feel only through the eye of her mind and the magic that gave it sight. She found the brightness and wrapped her magic around it, shielding the horse from the pain. She took that pain into herself instead, gasping at the sensation. The ploy worked, and the horse shot ahead, his strides lengthening.

Moments later they charged through the narrow space between the gates and into the safety of Farhold. The gates thudded closed, sealing them in. Kate resisted the impulse to let go of the horse's mind, fearing what the shock would do to him. She eased back on the reins and brought him to a halt. Then she slid from the saddle and slowly withdrew her magic. Immediately the horse began to tremble, struggling to stay upright with only three legs able to bear weight now.

Ignoring the curious looks from the Farhold guards, Kate led the horse forward, one slow, hobbling step at a time. The Relay house wasn't far from the eastern gate, but it was like miles to poor Pip. Now that she'd withdrawn from his mind, he bore the pain in full, but she couldn't risk maintaining the connection. There were magists in Farhold, same as in every city in Rime, and all of them carried enchanted stones designed to detect wilder magic. If they ever discovered what she could do, she would face imprisonment and execution, a fate she feared for more reasons than the obvious. Not that she would even be able to use her magic much longer today, with true night descending. Wilder magic worked only during the day. Like the everweeps on the hills outside, the power closed up inside her and would remain dormant until dawn.

Still, Kate did what she could to help the horse. Halting him, she removed both saddle and mailbag, slinging them over her shoulder despite the weight and her own weariness. She tried to find comfort in knowing that at least they'd made it into the city, but she couldn't stop the tears stinging her eyes. She had done this. Broken this horse to save her own life.

By the time they arrived at the Relay house, the ringed moon had risen high overhead, drenching the cobbled street below in silver light. Irri, the goddess whose nightly charge it was to spin that shining orb, was hard at work. Kate wished for darkness, if only to hide her guilt. The iron gates into the stable stood closed and barred from the inside. She started to shout for entry when the door into the main house opened and a young man stepped out.

"You're late, Traitor Kate," Cort Allgood said in a mocking, jovial tone.

Kate ignored him. He used the name far too often for it to bother her like it once had.

A grin twisted Cort's lips. "We thought you died. Even started making bets on it. You cost me more than a few valens."

Clenching her teeth, Kate adjusted the mail pouch across her shoulder. Of all the people to be here now, why did it have to be him? *The gods must hate me.*

"Open the gate. Pip is lame."

Cort examined the horse, cocking his head so that his blond curls bounced foppishly. Instead of his usual Relay rider uniform he wore a green tunic over breeches and tall black boots. The sight of his dapper appearance made Kate regret her own state of disarray. She smoothed down the front of her soiled tunic and brushed back raven-black hair from her face, where it had escaped the neat braid she'd plaited this morning.

"That horse isn't lame," Cort said, finishing his examination. "He's good as dead."

Kate's hands balled into fists around the reins. *Open the gate.*

"How'd he get like that anyway?" Cort cocked his head in the other direction, his curls doing another ridiculous bounce. "You ride him off a cliff? Could've sworn they trained us not to do that."

Turning to the gate, Kate opened her mouth to shout for someone else but stopped as Cort made a quick retreat. A moment later he appeared on the other side of the gate and swung it open.

"Come on, Pip. Just a little farther." Kate tugged the horse forward.

"Poor thing." Cort slapped the gelding on the rump, making him flinch. "But that's what happens when you're forced to carry a traitor." Cort touched a mocking finger to his chin. "How does the Relay Rider's Vow go again, Traitor Kate? The part about protecting the horse at all costs?"

She kept walking, head up and lips sealed, but her blood heated with every word he spoke. She had reason to hate Cort Allgood. He was the one who had first discovered who she really was: Kate Brighton of Norgard. Daughter of Hale Brighton, the man who tried to kill the high king of Rime.

The traitor's daughter.

After her father was executed for his crimes, she'd come to Far-hold hoping to escape her past, to start over with a new life and a new name. For the first ten months she'd managed it, but then Cort had seen an illustration of her in the *Royal Gazette*, a new monthly newspaper published by the royal court and sent to all the city-states that formed the kingdom of Rime. The story that accompanied the illustration marked the one-year anniversary of Hale Brighton's attack on the king. Within days of its publication the anonymous Relay rider Kate Miller became Kate Brighton once more. She was lucky not to have been dismissed from the position.

"Then again, Traitor Kate," Cort said, catching up with her, "if you had kept the vow, you would've ruined your reputation." He paused, frowning. "You know, I've always wondered why it is your father did it. None of the stories ever say. Do you know why he did it?"

Kate ignored his question as well as the same one that echoed deep inside her. No, she didn't know. She never would. *The dead tell no truths,* as the priests were fond of saying.

Spying a stable boy ahead, Kate waved him down. "Fetch Master Lewis."

The boy looked set to argue, then changed his mind when he saw Pip stumble sideways, struggling to maintain his awkward three-legged balance. While the boy made a dash for the foreman's quarters, Kate continued on, guiding Pip toward the eastern stable.

Cort started to follow her, another cutting remark on his lips, but someone shouted his name from across the way. He shouted back a response, then turned and addressed Kate.

"Well, I'm off, Traitor Kate. Good luck saving that doomed horse."

"Shut up," Kate said, her hold on her temper finally slipping. "He's not doomed."

Cort barked a triumphant laugh. "I'd say let's make a wager on it, but there's no sport in a fixed game." He winked, then turned and jaunted off without another word.

I hope you choke on your own spit, Cort Allgood, she thought after him.

By the time Kate managed to get Pip inside the stable, the foreman had arrived. Small and lean as a tree branch, Deacon Lewis looked fit enough to still outride any of the riders in his charge, despite his years. Short-cropped black hair, tinged with silver, framed his angular face, his brown skin leathered with age. He was intimidating on a normal day, but in this moment, Kate could barely bring herself to look at him for fear of his judgment. Over and over again, she ran her hands down the front of her tunic, trying to make it lie flat, trying to give herself the shield a good appearance could bring.

At first, he stood examining the horse from a few feet away, acknowledging Kate with a glance. Then he came forward and ran his hand down Pip's injured leg. The gelding hopped sideways, protesting the touch.

Sighing, Deacon let go of the leg and straightened up. "I'll summon a healer," he said, and his doubtful tone felt like a punch to Kate's gut.

"I might be able to mend the bone," the magist healer said sometime later. "But I doubt he'll ever be sound for hard work again." He straightened from his hunched position and smoothed his green robes, the mark of his order. The magestone he'd used to diagnose the horse's injury remained fastened around Pip's pastern on a piece of leather. It glowed bright red, pulsing like a heartbeat.

Kate stared at the green robe, frustrated that she couldn't read his expression behind the mask he wore and despising his matter-of-fact tone. All magists wore masks, the cut and coverage of them signifying rank. This one's covered his whole face, marking him a master, the very best of his order—and the most expensive.

"How much?" Deacon said, his face as expressionless as the magist's. Nevertheless, the way he kept rubbing his fingers along the four scars on his left forearm betrayed his concern. The scars ran so deep, they made the muscles beneath look permanently twisted in a cramp. There weren't many riders who survived a nightdrake attack, but Deacon had come through two in his long years with the Relay.

"Seventy valens," the magist said.

A wrench went through Kate's stomach. That was nearly as much as it would cost to replace the horse, and she knew what Deacon's answer would be.

Forgetting her position, Kate touched Deacon's arm. "Please, Master Lewis, let me pay for it. If you hold back my wages this month and the next, maybe—"

Deacon brushed her off and raised a hand for silence. He turned to the green robe. "Thank you for your services. We'll pass on further treatment."

The green nodded, then stooped to untie the piece of leather around Pip's injured foot. The glow in the magestone faded the moment it was removed.

Once the green robe had gone, Kate wheeled on Deacon, unable to stay silent a moment longer. "Please reconsider. Please. I'll do anything. I'll give up a month's salary. I'll do extra rides for free, muck out the stables for the next year. Anything. Please, Master Lewis."

Deacon turned to Kate, meeting her gaze for the first time, it seemed. "I'm sorry, Kate, but I can't let you."

"But, sir . . ." Tears burned in her eyes, making her cheeks flush. If she didn't stop speaking she wouldn't be able to hold them back. "He's a good horse, and it's my fault. I didn't mean—"

"Hush now. There's no place for such foolishness here." Deacon folded his arms, fingers worrying at his scars again. "I know he's your favorite, but Pip's a working horse and only as good as his legs. If he were a mare, it would be a different story, but a lame gelding is worth more dead than alive."

"But, sir, given time he could be sound again. He's still young. If you just let me buy him, then maybe—"

"I said no, and that's final." Deacon glared down at her now, his dark eyes sharp enough to cut. "How would you feed him? Where would you keep him? He can't stay here, and don't tell me you're paid so handsomely that you can afford to be wasteful with your coin, because I know better. No, I won't let you sacrifice for nothing."

Kate flinched at every point he made, each harsh truth laid bare. He was right. She couldn't afford the coin, and a part of her even understood the practicality of his reasoning. Saving a lame horse was more than pointless—it was wasted space, a great selfishness in a city already overfull with humans and animals both. There wasn't room for anything that didn't serve a purpose. Even the elderly were encouraged by the priests and priestesses to give their lives in sacrifice to the gods. But the rest of her had touched Pip's very essence, had caressed his soul with her magic. That part couldn't bear the idea of his death. A piece of her would die with him.

But she couldn't tell Deacon any of that, not in a way that he would understand and accept. Although Deacon always treated her fairly, even after he learned who she really was, he wouldn't tolerate her wilder magic if he ever found out. Wilders were outlaws, subject to the Inquisition.

Sagging in defeat, Kate swallowed. "Yes, sir." She reached for Pip's lead. He was her charge, and it was her responsibility to take him to the slaughterhouse. She'd never had to take a horse there before, and her fingers shook as she untied the rope.

Deacon took the lead from her, his expression softening. "Go home, Kate. I'll see it done."

Kate looked up at him, torn between what she knew she ought to do and what she wanted to do. But in the end, she couldn't refuse his kind offer, the escape too welcome, too easy a path to choose any other.

She turned to Pip and ran a hand over his sleek neck, wishing she could touch his mind one more time, to give him the peace he deserved. He leaned into her touch, burying his muzzle in her belly. She stroked his nose for a moment, whispered good-bye into one velvety ear, then turned and walked away.

Shame and regret dogged each step she took on the way to her rented room, a few miles from the Relay house. Cort's taunts echoed in her mind, taking on weight. It was true—as a Relay rider, she had vowed to always bring Pip back safely, to hold his life equal to her own. But she had broken that vow tonight, an act of betrayal as sure as any other.

Have I become my father? Did oath breaking run in her blood? She was so much like him. Even her magic was inherited from him. Hale Brighton had been master of horse to the high king, a position he'd earned with the help of his secret, forbidden gift. He'd been the king's friend and liegeman, and yet he had tried to kill him. Kate didn't know why, but there was no denying her father's guilt. *Just as there's no denying mine.* Traitor's daughter. Traitor Kate.

Once again, she had lived up to her name.

THE MORNING CAME TOO EARLY, as it always did, night slipping away like a thief afraid of discovery. Fingers of sunlight pressed against Kate's eyelids, and she rolled over out of their reach. It was more comfortable on this side, cooler, though the bed remained hard, nothing like the beds she used to sleep in. Memories disguised as dreams—of feathered mattresses wrapped in silken sheets and long luxurious mornings spent dozing only to be awakened by the smell of sugar-glazed sweet rolls—started to lull her back to sleep.

Then a more recent memory slid through her mind—of Pip, and the disaster of the night before. Kate groaned, coming fully awake. She forced her eyes open, breaking apart the crust of dried tears that had sealed her lashes together. The urge to renew that crying rose up in her, only to be shoved aside by a sudden jolt of alarm. The sun beyond the narrow window shone too brightly and too high in the sky, more than an hour past dawn. *But the dawn bell didn't ring!* She was sure of it. She never slept through the loud gong that signaled the opening of the gates.

Panicked, Kate scrambled out of bed just as the door swung open and her roommate stepped in, carrying with her the faint, sweet stench of barberry wine.

"You're still in bed?" Signe's pale eyebrows climbed her forehead, almost disappearing into her golden-blond hair. "What happened?" Yawning, she gestured to Kate's unmade bed. She wore a sleeveless jerkin and breeches, both disheveled from whatever activity had kept Signe away all night from their shared room.

"I don't know." Kate stooped and picked up the clothes she'd discarded on the floor the night before, their presence there, instead of carefully folded and put away, a telling sign of her distressed state of mind. Scowling at the soiled state of her Relay rider's tunic—*whoever thought light blue and horses was a good pairing should be drawn and quartered*—she slid it on over her shift. "What time is it?"

"Nearly eight." Signe stepped in and dropped onto the bed nearest the door. There wasn't much room for standing and the two narrow beds were the only places for sitting. "If you hurry, you should make it to roll call." Signe was a Relay rider too, and both of them knew the consequences of a late arrival. Fortunately for Signe, it was her day off.

"Gods, let it be so." Kate pulled on the rest of her uniform of black breeches and overskirt, wishing she had time to rebraid her hair and wash the dirt from her face.

"Did you hear?" Signe asked, a gleam in her voice. "There's a royal in the city."

"What?" Kate's hand stilled in the act of fastening her belt over the tunic.

Signe nodded, raising one leg to pull out the knife tucked inside her boot. She leaned back on the bed and idly began to toss the knife in one hand. "I don't know who, but it must be someone important."

"Obviously," Kate said, breathless. A royal was in the city. A Tormane. *But who?* She shook the thought from her head. Whoever it might be was not her concern anymore. She'd left that life behind. "That explains it, though. The dawn bell doesn't ring when there's a royal in the city."

"It doesn't?" Signe cocked her head, birdlike. Even with her gaze fixed on Kate, she didn't stop juggling the knife, catching it absentmindedly. Although they'd been friends for more than two years now, Kate had no idea where Signe had learned such a skill. She was from the Esh Islands and never talked about her life there or what had brought her to Rime, but Kate often suspected she'd either been a circus performer or a thief. "If I'd known that," she continued, "I would've come home sooner to wake you. Why doesn't it ring?"

Kate made a face. "Because royals don't like to have their sleep disturbed so early." That wasn't precisely true, but she didn't have time to explain the political nuances involved. Although there were kings in Esh, there weren't sealed city gates. All the islands were free of the nightdrakes that plagued Rime after sunset.

Why did you ever leave? Kate wanted to ask, the memory of Pip ambushing her again. If the horse had been reared in Esh, he would still be alive.

She shoved the regret down deep inside her and headed for the door. "I've got to go."

"Wait," Signe said. "I brought you a gift."

Kate turned back automatically, unable to resist her friend's infectious enthusiasm. She gaped as she saw the object in Signe's hand, a silver chain with a series of small colored stones fastened between the links. The magestones glowed faintly, the enchantment on them strong and new. "A moonbelt?"

Signe grinned. "I swore I would find you one." She thrust out her hand. "Take it. And learn to enjoy life. Like I do."

Against her better instincts, Kate accepted the moonbelt. The very hint of its purpose made her insides squirm like she'd swallowed a jar full of worms. It was indecent for an unmarried woman to possess one, let alone wear it.

"Uh, thanks, Sig, but I enjoy life enough already." Kate tried to hand it back.

Signe brandished a finger at her like a whip. "Working all the time is not enjoyment."

"It is if you're me." There was nothing Kate liked more than riding, and—last night aside—she loved working for the Relay. "Besides," she added, "you know I've no need for it."

A suggestive smile stretched across Signe's face. "Yes, so now you must choose a nice boy for a plaything and create the need."

Ignoring the blush creeping up her neck, Kate shoved the moonbelt into the single outside pocket on her overskirt, making sure it was hidden from view. She would put it on—or not—at the Relay house.

"I've got to go."

Signe shooed her toward the door. "Yes, yes, may the luck of Aslar be with you."

With a determined bent, Kate hoisted her overskirt and trotted down the narrow hallway to the even narrower staircase. If she was late to morning roll call, she would get bumped from her route by one of the other riders to either a less lucrative one or a more difficult one. The latter was the last thing she wanted, especially after the tragedy with Pip.

Grease hung thick as smoke in the air as Kate descended, the walls and railing slick with it. She would be slick with it too by the time she made it outside. A greasy face and hair were an inevitable consequence of renting a room in the Crook and Cup. So was the stench of boiling meat and ripe onion (a smell she despised) that lingered on her clothes nearly as strong as the ever-present scent of horse (a smell she loved). She and Signe would've preferred staying at the Relay house, but there wasn't a bunk for women riders, only the men, who vastly outnumbered them.

Turning right into the kitchen, Kate darted between a cook and a serving girl on her way to the alley door. The cook shouted that she wasn't supposed to be in here, but Kate batted her eyes at him and smiled before heading outside. She turned left down the alley, her boots splashing mud over the hem of her overskirt with each step, and soon reached Bakers Row.

"Oh hells," she muttered at the congestion in the street. Always a little crowded, this morning Bakers Row looked like a fisherman's net after a good catch, full of flailing, chattering people piled one next to the other. There were women in brightly colored gowns embroidered with lace and with long gaped sleeves, and men sporting velvet or silk tunics and boots polished to a high sheen. Jewelry hung from belts and around necks, some glowing with mage magic designed to enhance beauty or hide disfiguration, others merely glinting in the sun. Kate clucked her tongue in dismay. Such finery had no business in a marketplace as common as Bakers Row.

One man, a merchant by the looks of him, wore a sash made

from the carcass of a small nightdrake. The reptilian head hung over the man's shoulder with its fanged mouth fastened to the scaly tail, and its body wrapped crossways over his back and chest. Shiny black stones had been placed in the eye sockets, making it look alive. Kate suppressed a laugh at the absurdity of such a person wearing such a trophy. No one would believe this portly, gray-bearded man had actually killed the drake.

She pushed her way into the crowd, elbowing sides and stepping on toes without care. *The royal is to blame for this,* she realized. Why else would everyone bother with such finery if not with the hope of impressing whichever of the Tormanes was here? *Not that they're likely to be seen right now.* In her experience, the nobility preferred to breakfast late in the quiet comfort of whatever palace or stately home was grand enough to host them.

With her agitation building, Kate couldn't keep the glare from her face. Some of the people stepped out of the way at the sight of her blue tunic with the silver galloping horse on the left breast, but most did not. A Relay rider uniform commanded respect only from atop a horse and with a full mail pouch in tow—the contents of those pouches too important to impede, containing everything from personal missives to newsletters to royal decrees.

Booths and vendor carts lined both sides of the streets, some beneath canopies, some leaning with off-angled sides, but all displaying savory wares like sweet buns, pumpkin-glazed crumpets, or flatbreads slathered with butter and honey. The smell of yeast and sugar filled Kate's nose, making her stomach quiver. She'd been too distraught last night to eat, and hunger sabotaged her now when there was no time to assuage it.

As she reached the end of Bakers Row, turning onto Copperfield, Kate began to silently curse the royal for all the congestion. Nothing brought out a crowd as quickly as the chance to ogle one of the Tormanes, especially way out here in Farhold, where they so rarely journeyed. She wanted to scream aloud how foolish everyone was being, that they were wasting their time—and hers.

But when she reached the intersection with Main Street, she realized she might be the foolish one. A row of city guardsmen standing at parade rest blocked the road ahead. In the distance Kate heard the trill of trumpets, sounding the approach of a royal procession.

Damn them all, she thought, picturing every member of the Tormane family in her mind. Well, not everyone. There was one she refused to picture. One she chose to believe did not exist.

Kate glanced behind her, weighing her options. Nearly everyone towered above her, and they were all pushing forward, vying for a spot near the intersection. The only option was to sneak across Main Street somehow, and her short stature would be an advantage. She ducked under the arm of the woman in front of her, then jostled her way forward until she reached the guardsmen. They stood with their backs to her, their cloaks so dark a shade of green they were almost black. Kate couldn't see beyond to determine how far the procession still was, but it didn't matter. She refused to be late, especially after last night. Taking a deep breath, she dashed between the guards onto the empty street.

"Stop!" someone shouted, but Kate plunged on, counting on her size and quickness to keep her from being caught.

Once again, her assumption proved wrong. Whether motivated by the approaching royal or perhaps just favored by the gods, one of the guards managed to grab the end of her braid. The sudden jerk against her scalp yanked her off-balance, and she landed hard on her rump, a shock arching up her spine and into her neck. Her teeth clanked together, catching her bottom lip, and the iron taste of blood filled her mouth.

"Get her up," one of the men yelled. "Prince Corwin is almost here."

Prince Corwin.

The sound of that name struck Kate like a cattle whip. She clambered to her feet, ready to claw and bite her way free if she had to. Anything to get out of here before the procession reached them.

But it wasn't to be. The guard still had hold of her braid, his fingers twisted cruelly around her black hair. "What were you thinking?" He gave the braid another jerk. "And you, a Relay rider. You ought to know better."

"Let me go." Kate craned her neck, pulling uselessly against his hold.

"Get her off the street!" another guard called. "They're here."

Kate stopped fighting and let herself be dragged off to the side, where two of the guards stepped in front of her, shielding her from view.

"Please let me go," Kate said, hating the plea in her voice but desperate for escape. "I didn't mean to cause trouble. I'm going to be late. I'm—"

"Be quiet." Another tug on her braid, this one hard enough to make her yelp.

She bit back the sound, her heart sinking as she realized it was too late anyway. The procession had reached them. As always, the prince rode up front, flanked by a dozen men on horseback. Some wore the livery of the governor of Farhold and some wore that of Norgard, the home city of the royal family. Kate's home city.

No, not anymore.

Dropping her gaze, she fixed her eyes on the prince's warhorse, a tall bay with a white strip on its face. An ache squeezed her chest at the sight of it. The horse had been sired by Shadowdancer, her father's prized stallion. She would've known the breeding anywhere. Looking away, she told herself she would be all right once they passed.

The discordant clop of steel-shod hooves striking the cobblestones halted. Again, Kate refused to look up. *Dear gods, make me small. Sweet Farrah, goddess of night and shadows, make me invisible.*

"What's the commotion here?" It was the familiar voice of Governor Prewitt, the most powerful person in Farhold. "You there, step forward and explain."

Kate braced as her captor pushed her out of the shadows of the intersection and onto the cobbled street once more.

"Apologies, lord governor." The guard bowed low, forcing Kate to do the same with another harsh tug on her braid. "This Relay rider tried to break through our line."

"Ah, yes, the riders are always in such a hurry," a new voice said. This one familiar, too. It was deeper, more mature than the last time she'd heard it, but still unmistakable.

Prince Corwin. The sound stirred emotions long buried inside her—anger aged to bitterness, and something else she refused to name.

"But surely," the prince continued, "no harm has been do—"

Looking up was a mistake, but Kate couldn't help it.

Corwin stared down at her, his mouth falling open and his eyes widening in shock.

Kate stared back. Her heart had become a separate living creature inside her body. It thrashed and quaked. There were so many things she wanted to say. *You let my father die. You ruined my life.*

You broke my heart.

She shoved the last away. That thought didn't belong to her. Not anymore.

"Do you know this girl, your highness?" Governor Prewitt asked.

The prince didn't answer. His pale-blue eyes, like winter sky, remained fixed on her, and his jaw worked back and forth as he took in her appearance. Kate's stomach roiled at what he must see—dirty tunic, mud-caked skirt, hair in disarray. She'd imagined this scene a hundred times before, the day her path crossed his again, but she always pictured herself with an impeccable appearance, the undeniable air that she was fine, that she had triumphed over the hardships he'd helped bring down on her. Instead she looked one step above a beggar wallowing in the gutter.

Belatedly she realized there was blood on her lips, and she wiped it off. With her confidence shattered, Kate looked away, her eyes refusing to be still in her growing nervousness. She swept her gaze over the crowd, which was pressing in for a better look, voices murmuring as someone recognized her.

Traitor Kate . . . Traitor Kate . . .

"Your highness?" Governor Prewitt prodded. "Do you know this young woman?"

Kate glanced back, her gaze on Corwin. He was as handsome

as ever, with his dusky blond hair and a tanned face chiseled by the gods—each angle and plane designed to complement the other, from the high cheekbones to the angular jaw. All except for his nose, which was more crooked than she remembered, and the thin, white scar across his chin. The source of these injuries was a mystery no one had solved. The newspapers out of Norgard had nicknamed him the Errant Prince, thanks to the way he had vanished for nearly two years. He'd returned some few months ago, to wild speculation as to where he'd been and what he'd done. To Kate's dismay, the scars only added to his attractiveness. *Damn him.*

"No," Corwin finally said. "I don't know her."

The words were a slap, and Kate lowered her gaze to his horse. Temptation called out to her. One little push with her magic and she could fill the horse with an inescapable desire to dump its rider. A poor vindication, but better than none.

"But neither would I begrudge her a livelihood," Corwin added. "Let her go."

"As you wish." The Governor cocked his head toward Kate's guard, and he released her braid at last.

She dropped into a quick bow, then started to turn, ready to run.

"Wait a moment, rider," a new voice called. "You've dropped something."

Against her better judgment, Kate stopped and glanced behind her. The speaker rode beside Corwin, atop another of her father's horses. A hunting falcon perched on the man's shoulder, its head covered in a black hood. Kate didn't recognize the nobleman, with his black hair and bronzed complexion. His tunic of soft, slick wool dyed red and trimmed in gold piping bore no insignia. He was pointing at the ground in front of the horses with an amused expression.

Kate's gaze shifted to the glow rising up from the cobblestones. *The moonbelt.* She touched her skirt pocket, hoping she was mistaken, but only fabric met her hand. A blush heated her neck, inching upward.

"Is that yours?" the nobleman asked.

Kate stooped to retrieve the moonbelt, returning it to her pocket with fingers gone clumsy. Whispers from the crowd reached her ears, coaxing her blush to spread. Trying to ignore them, she stood up straight and raised her head.

She had nothing to be ashamed of. She was no longer the kind of girl who needed to worry about reputation. So what if she might have a "plaything," as Signe put it. So what if she might seek physical comfort and pleasure. This was who she was. Kate Brighton. Rider for the Relay.

I am Traitor Kate, she thought, drawing strength from the name for once.

"Thank you, my lord." Relieved at how steady she sounded, Kate bowed again.

The man's grin widened. To her annoyance, he was every bit as handsome as the prince. A magestone glistened in his left ear, and she wondered what the magic in it was concealing.

"You're welcome," he said. "And best of luck to you on all your endeavors—both work and leisure."

Several in the crowd laughed at the innuendo, and the falcon on the man's shoulder shifted nervously at the noise. Kate risked a glance at Corwin. His expression was inscrutable, but cold fire seemed to burn in his eyes.

Once again Kate considered using her magic. She could spook all the horses, reducing this band of noblemen to a gaggle of fools trying to stay astride. No one would know. Horses spooked all the time, for all sorts of reasons.

Then she spotted the master magist riding at the back of the procession, his face obscured behind the full white mask. His blue robes marked him a member of the defensive order, one of the most powerful and dangerous. Like all the magists in every order—blue, green, brown, red, white, and gold—he carried a mace, its head embedded with magestones, including one that would flare into life in the presence of wilder magic.

Fear doused her anger as quickly as cold water on hot steel. *Never use your gift where someone can see, Katie girl*, she heard her father saying as clearly as if he were standing beside her now. She couldn't believe how close she'd come to doing it. If she had, this disaster of a day would've turned into something much worse.

As if to emphasize this truth, the loud clang of the bells sounded, chiming the arrival of the eighth hour. She was officially late. Kate allowed herself one last dark look at the prince, then turned and walked away, feeling as if something inside her had broken.

Yes, this morning had indeed come too early. She wished it had never come at all.

PRINCE CORWIN SIGHED IN RELIEF when he and his escort arrived at Farhold's southern gates without further incident. Two massive owl statues, the symbol of Farrah, patron goddess of Farhold, perched atop either side of the gates, their wings raised toward one another to form an archway through which visitors would exit. The wall of this remote city was among the most impressive in all of Rime. Fifty feet tall and ten feet thick, it boasted iron reinforcements at every measure.

Even more impressive than the size of the wall was the number of wardstone embrasures built into it. Hardly more than four feet existed between each one and its neighbor. Farhold's forefathers had taken the defense of the city against nightdrakes very seriously. *If a bit optimistically,* Corwin thought. There might be an abundance of embrasures, but only one in three currently bore active wardstones. The enchanted rocks glowed with varying levels of intensity, some bright as the full moon and others hardly visible in the morning sun. He wondered if the city had ever possessed enough wealth to keep an active wardstone in every embrasure. The sight would be something to behold, the entire place luminescent with magic.

He wished for that distraction now—anything to block the memories intruding into his mind. Kate Brighton was here, in Farhold. The knowledge made him tense. He'd never dreamed he would see her again, no matter how many times his thoughts had turned to her over the past three years—questions of where she was, how she was faring.

Does she ever think of me?

It seemed he finally had his answers, to at least some of those questions.

Traitor Kate, they call her. A terrible mix of regret and guilt squeezed his chest. She was as beautiful as he remembered—raven-black hair, skin sun-kissed to a golden hue, and large, large eyes, the color of amber. But older. *Aged.* She'd been sixteen the last time he'd seen her, himself just a year ahead. *She is nineteen now,* he realized, *a woman.* He remembered the vivacious girl she'd been before, quick to laugh and to speak her mind, with the swift temper of a sudden summer storm. Now she seemed thin and worn—hard. Like leather boiled until all the soft suppleness was leached from it.

Doubtless the years had not been kind to her. Once, her prospects had been guaranteed. She'd been born into the gentry: those of the lesser nobility who possessed no title, only land. With her father being master of horse to the high king, her family had both wealth and respect. Until the day Hale Brighton tried to murder Corwin's father. Now Kate's prospects went no further than her next ride. Being a Relay rider was a respectable profession, at least, if a dangerous one.

Or maybe the years have not been that hard, he considered, remembering the moonbelt. It was an expensive piece, one bestowed on her from some wealthy lover, perhaps, maybe even a husband. Jealousy prickled inside him, and he shoved everything out of his mind once and for all. *Kate Brighton is not my concern.*

Corwin turned his attention to the fine, bright morning. Now that they were outside the city, a faint breeze kept the heat at bay. And it was blessedly quiet, the noisome trumpeters left behind at the gate. Of all the annoyances he had to endure during this peace-keeping tour his elder brother had forced him on, the trumpets were the worst. They were so piercingly loud and pretentious, he could barely stomach even the idea of them. And yet he had to endure it. Everywhere he went, there they were, ready to give proclamation of his presence. *I'm lucky they don't announce my trips to the privy.*

It was all so absurd. These people looked on him like he was someone who mattered, who could change their lives. He wasn't. His brother, Edwin, was the prince who could do that, a fact they would come to accept in time, as he finally had.

Farmland lined both sides of the main road leading away from Farhold. To the left, rough, sturdy fences marked individual fields, penning in cattle, sheep, or goats. The animals would graze through the day, until the shepherds herded them back into their pens and stables inside the city shortly before dusk. The next morning they would return to graze again. To the right of the road, neatly partitioned plots held crops of every kind—soybeans, corn, wheat, even cotton.

Corwin had seen similar fields when he arrived at Farhold, but it had been nearly twilight, and he was too concerned with trying to make it into the city before full dark to be impressed by the diversity of this area, one he'd never visited until now. Most of the city-states of Rime relied on one primary export. For Andreas it was coal; for Aldervale, lumber. His own city, the capital, Norgard, produced livestock—mostly horses to support its military strength.

Corwin turned toward Governor Prewitt. "I've always heard rumors that Farhold is completely self-sustaining. I see now that might be true."

Prewitt smiled, broadening his already broad face. His wide, flat nose huddled between ruddy cheeks. "Indeed it is, your highness. We have meat, crops, clothing. There's even an open iron pit a few miles west, right at the foothills of the Ash Mountains."

"Impressive." For a second Corwin almost added that he would like to see it, but he changed his mind. If he said it, the governor would make it happen, and that would mean another day in Farhold. As interesting as the city might be, he'd been here long enough already, and he was due to visit three more cities of the western province before making the long journey home. He tired of the slow pace and the constant decorum. Even now he felt the urge to loosen his grip on Stormdancer's reins and touch his heels to the warhorse's sides.

As if Corwin had spoken the desire out loud, his friend, Dallin Thorne, leaned over in his saddle toward him and whispered, "Shall we ask the good governor to let us ride ahead? Such a wide-open road begs for a race."

Corwin grinned. For a moment, he wanted nothing more than to indulge in the diversion. But then he remembered that his brother's spies were among the guards, eagerly waiting to inform Edwin of Corwin's every misstep on this tour. There'd been several already, such as in Eetmark when he overindulged in wine during the farewell banquet and ended up calling the high chancellor a worthless ass. Never mind that it was true—what else could you call a man who decided that rather than rebuild the orphanage that burned down, he would erect a new temple to Eetolyn in its place? Surely, any goddess worthy of worship would value caring for children more than some new shrine, but then again, the sex rites practiced by the Eetolyn priestesses no doubt swayed him. *He's still a worthless ass,* Corwin thought, but nevertheless, he didn't want to give his brother any more material with which to berate him upon his return.

"Or," Dal said, his voice dropping to the level of conspiracy, "would you prefer to wait and race with the pretty rider we met in the city? The one you claimed not to know?"

Corwin's fingers tightened around the reins as Kate's face appeared in his mind once again.

Dal clucked his tongue at Corwin's silence. "No one believed you, you know. They were just too mindful of your station to contradict such an obvious lie." He spoke more freely now, as their Norgard warhorses had already outpaced the others on their shorter-legged, lesser-breed mounts. Dal winked. "But no mind. I will get the truth out of you sooner or later, I promise."

Corwin rolled his eyes. "I don't doubt it." Dal had become his closest friend in the years since Kate was exiled, but he'd known Kate much longer. His relationship with her began as a childhood friendship, one built on rivalries over who could ride faster, fight better. Later, that friendship grew intimate, stolen kisses and secret touches. Then her father had nearly slain his and changed things between them forever.

Ended things.

"And I think I will enjoy the telling," Dal added as he raised his gloved right arm to his shoulder, encouraging Lir to step onto it.

He removed the falcon's hood, then stretched out his arm, releasing Lir's jesses as the falcon launched into the air. Dal watched Lir's progress for a moment before returning his gaze to Corwin. "She might've been a dirty little thing, but still pleasant to gaze upon, and with a mouth made for kissing."

Corwin hid his prickling nerves behind a dry cough. "You would do best *not* to think about that one's mouth. Seems to me the girl didn't appreciate our presence much. Or did you not notice?"

"Me? Of course not. Unlike you, I don't know her." Dal paused, running a hand over the stubble on his chin, its presence a poor attempt to disguise the too-perfect hue of his skin on the left side of his face where the magestone in his ear hid his scars. "So you do have an acquaintance with her mouth then. This is good news. It seems to me the girl is willing for such a diversion as kissing, given the moon—"

"No." Corwin cut his friend a hard look. "I have no acquaintance, and I don't care about her diversions."

"Oh yes. Clearly." Dal winked again, no doubt delighted that he'd finally gotten a rise out of Corwin. Such reactions were not easy to provoke in him. But Dal would not be Dal if he didn't try. Corwin both loved and hated him for it. Without him, Corwin feared he would spend far too many days brooding inside his own mind. Dal had a way of smoothing Corwin's rough edges.

"Why did I bring you along on this again?" Corwin said, cocking his head.

"Self-preservation." Dal placed a hand over his heart. "You would die of boredom without me."

"If I recall, you were the one who begged me to come. Something about adventure and amusements."

Dal gave a mock bow. "Whatever version of the truth your highness prefers."

Shaking his head, Corwin slowed Stormdancer until he once again rode side by side with Prewitt. "How long before we reach the Gregors' manor, lord governor?"

"Quarter of an hour, I would guess." Prewitt frowned. "Is your highness sure you don't wish to send a rider ahead to announce your arrival? Showing up like this is a great discourtesy."

"Yes, I daresay it is," Corwin replied. He would've loved not to be doing it at all, but attempting to discover why Marcus Gregor, former governor of Farhold and one of his father's greatest supporters, suddenly chose to withdraw from public life was part of what had prompted Edwin to include a stop in Farhold as part of this peacekeeping tour. The tour was to be Corwin's recompense for the trouble he'd caused by disappearing these last few years. His punishment came in the form of endlessly facing all the duties he'd avoided in his long absence. *Duties like trying to smooth the ruffled feathers of some pompous old man too proud to voice his complaints directly to the high king.*

Then again, he didn't like to think what his punishment would've been if the truth of where he'd been was ever made known. Instinctively, his gaze dropped to the vambrace he wore around his right wrist, hiding the tattoo beneath.

Corwin forced his eyes up again and sighed. "However, as Lord Gregor has refused to commit to seeing me, I'm afraid springing on him unannounced is the only way forward."

Prewitt cleared his throat. "Yes, of course, but as Gregor no doubt has his reasons for staying away, I wouldn't expect a warm welcome."

Corwin didn't. Faith in the high king was low throughout all of Rime. Orwin Tormane had never fully recovered from the assassination attempt. The wound he'd suffered at Hale's hand lingered, a festering corruption that had robbed him of his health, both in body and mind.

Dal slowed his horse to join them. "I don't see how anyone would dare such disrespect toward the royal family."

"That is because you were born in the time of high kings, my lord Thorne, and you come from the east." Prewitt laughed, the sound guileless and surprisingly pleasant, the kind of laughter one felt inclined to join in. "Things are different in Farhold. Before the Sevan Invasion, we were not a people used to bowing to kings."

Dal's brow furrowed. "But the invasion was fifty years ago, and we've had a high king ever since."

Prewitt laughed again. "I'm sure it seems an awful long time to someone so young, but remember that before the cities united under the high king, we ruled ourselves for more than a thousand years. That's a long time to forget."

"Oh, I remember my history lessons," Dal said drily. "A thousand years of war and bloodshed. No wonder the cities are so reluctant to serve the high king."

Corwin shot Dal a look, sick of the subject already. For weeks now, all he'd heard was how there was unrest in the west, protests in the cities over the high king's rule, tax strikes among the merchants, and the growing threat of the Rising. He wanted to cover his ears and hum a tune just for a moment's peace.

Prewitt shrugged, his expression placating. "Not that we aren't learning to appreciate the new way of things. High King Orwin is a worthy ruler, and every day we reap the benefits of our united cities. Such as the bridge he's commissioned for the Redrush."

Corwin made a mental note of how easily Prewitt changed the subject, a mark of a skilled politician. *Edwin would hold him in high esteem.* Especially as it was Edwin and not their father who had commissioned the bridge. Orwin ruled in name only these days.

"Yes, the bridge is a marvel of engineering and an industrious decision as well," Prewitt continued, nodding. Despite the breeze, beads of sweat dotted the top of his bald head. "It will make the journey to Andreas easier for the entire realm and free us all from reliance on unreliable ferrymen."

And it will bring in a hefty sum to the royal coffers, Corwin silently added, *once Edwin levies the toll.* He wondered what Prewitt would make of that when he found out.

"The Relay riders will appreciate it most of all, I believe," Dal said. He waggled his eyebrows at Corwin. "Wouldn't you agree, highness?"

"For certain," Corwin said, ignoring the implication.

They turned off the main road, following a narrower path through a copse of trees dense enough to be called a wood. A strange smell on the air teased Corwin's memory. He tried to determine the source but couldn't with the sweet scent of everweeps so strong here, dozens of the colorful flowers growing wherever sunlight reached the ground. Nevertheless, something about that underlying smell made him uneasy.

When they emerged from the trees a few minutes later, Corwin's unease turned to alarm. Ahead, the Gregor manor house sat in the middle of a wide clearing. Three stories high and half again as wide, the house was nothing but a charred husk. Smoke still billowed up from several of the gables.

Fire, Corwin thought, his mind finally connecting the memory to the smell—*and burned flesh.* His stomach threatened to rebel, and he turned his breathing shallow. For a second he was sixteen again, surrounded by terrified shouts as fire raged through the central marketplace of Norgard. He heard his mother screaming, ordering him to climb the roof, to save—

No, don't go there now, he told himself and, with an effort, pushed the memory away.

Governor Prewitt's mouth fell open, his jowls quivering. "What happened here?"

"Death and destruction," Dal said on a puff of air.

"But who? And how?" Corwin moved his eyes off the house to examine the wall surrounding it. The fine hairs on his neck stood up as he saw that every wardstone set in the wall had been smashed to pieces. This wasn't an accidental fire—the place had been attacked. Although the wall here stood easily fifteen feet high, that wasn't nearly tall enough to keep out nightdrakes. Only the wardstones could do that, and someone had deliberately destroyed them. Corwin swept his gaze over the destruction to see that the gate had been blasted apart.

Several of the men riding with them exchanged looks and whispers. "Was it nightdrakes that done this?"

"No, couldn't've been. They don't really breathe fire, you know."

"They used to."

"That's just superstition."

"Wilders must've done it."

The Rising, Corwin thought, tension spreading through him.

Governor Prewitt silenced the chatter with a wave of his hand. "You four, sweep the perimeter. The rest of you head in to investigate. We need to see if anyone is yet alive in there."

Corwin doubted it. The house looked gutted, every visible surface charred and every window shattered. *Wilders.* It seemed the only explanation. These last few months, the high council had received dozens of reports about so-called Rising attacks from all across Rime. But they were mostly small skirmishes, raids on caravans or personal assaults on members of the Mage League. He'd never heard of them striking so big and neutral a target as this freeholding. On the contrary, from what he'd gleaned, the Rising was little more than a disjointed idea, one picked up here and there by wilders living in fear of discovery by the Inquisition, not a true underground movement. Even their symbol—a lion haloed by a rising sun, left painted on walls or carved into trees—varied widely in its depiction from city to city.

Spying a hole in the ground a few feet ahead, Corwin guided Stormdancer toward it. The horse crow-hopped nervously as Corwin tried to steer him near enough to see into the hole. In seconds he understood the horse's reluctance—the hole went so deep he couldn't make out the bottom.

"It must be the Rising," Dal said, bringing his mount to a halt next to Corwin. His voice held a note of awe. It was like the ancient stories come to life—wilders who could rain down fire, summon winds and lightning, even rip the earth asunder. Some of the stories claimed that during the War of Three, a conflict that preceded the Sevan Invasion by more than two hundred years, the wilders cut holes so deep that the first nightdrakes were able to rise up from the three hells themselves.

"Why would the Rising attack the Gregors?" Corwin said.

"As an affront to the high king," Prewitt said, almost matter-of-fact. "Lord Marcus is your father's greatest supporter in the west."

Was, Corwin thought, *not is.* He turned Stormdancer toward the opened entrance into the manor, scanning the charred wood for the sign of the sun lion in any of its variations but finding nothing.

"Um, your highness," Governor Prewitt said. "Would it not be best for you to stay out here until we determine all is safe?"

Corwin pulled his sword free of the scabbard belted at his waist. He held it up, steel glinting in the sunlight. He wore a pistol too, but he could carry only one weapon and still steer a horse. The pistol held a single shot—the sword could be used many times. His buckler he left hanging from the side of his saddle, at the ready should he need it.

"Maybe," Corwin said, "but I'm not going to."

"But your highness. You've no armor, no—"

Corwin rode forward, ignoring the governor's protests. If wilders were responsible for this, it was his duty, both personal and public, to bring them to justice. He saw his mother's face again, the fear etched across her brow just as the crowd swept over her, trampling her in their mad need to flee the fire—one set by a wilder determined to harm as many people as he could. And that was before the wilders began to organize into this Rising. No, Corwin would not stand idly by now.

Dal joined him at once. "Thank the gods. Thought I might expire from curiosity." He pulled free his sword as well. Although he wore an eager, boyish expression, he carried his weapon with the surety of a man who knew how to use it. Which he did, all too well. Both of them did. It was a skill that had bonded them together during their adventures away from Rime.

The smell worsened as they passed through the gate into the bailey. Corwin blinked the sting of smoke out of his eyes and breathed through his mouth, trying not to focus on the stench of burned flesh. Stormdancer snorted in protest, nostrils flaring. Bodies littered the bailey, scattered here and there like desecrated statues. It was impossible to count their numbers. Several of them had burned together, loved ones clinging to each other through the end. Corwin couldn't understand why so many were caught in the fire. With so much stone in the house's structure, surely there would've been ways to escape before the fire spread. Then the explanation came to him—*it must have been more wilder magic.*

Corwin and Dal headed to the right, with the rest of the Tormane guards following behind them, while Prewitt's men swept the left. Dal stared down at the bodies as they passed, but Corwin kept his gaze up and forward, paying as much attention to Stormdancer's ears as he did to everything else. If there was danger ahead, Storm would give him early warning. The warhorse was uneasy, his neck arched and back tense, each step punctuated by a snort.

They rounded the first corner only to find the destruction continued on. More bodies were scattered about, charred to unrecognizable husks. In the distance, what remained of the postern gate hung open, three-quarters of it blown away. The attackers must have surrounded the house.

Hearing a noise beyond the gate, Corwin tightened his grip on his sword and steered Storm toward it. Once on the other side, he spotted a bonfire burning ahead. A man knelt beside the fire, but the moment he spotted them, he leaped up and bolted.

"Stop!" Corwin dug his heels into Storm's sides and reined him after the stranger, who disappeared down a narrow path through the woods. Giving pursuit, Corwin swept his gaze through the trees on the lookout for other enemies. His knees brushed tree trunks and bushes, branches scraping through his hair like grasping fingers. Still, Stormdancer made ground on the man easily. They were almost upon him when the path opened up into a clearing.

Reaching the man, Corwin leaned over in the saddle and grabbed the back of his tunic. Corwin kicked his feet free of the stirrups and tackled the stranger to the ground. Storm halted at once, as he'd been trained to do. Corwin quickly stood and pointed his sword down at the man lying facedown in the grass.

"Roll over slowly and look at me."

The man obeyed, shifting awkwardly onto his back. Corwin held the sword steady, his gaze unmoving even as Dal and the others arrived. Out of the corner of his eye, Corwin watched Dal fetch Stormdancer for him, securing the horse's reins.

"Who are you?" Corwin said.

The stranger shook his head, which was as bald as Governor Prewitt's. Pockmarks and dirt spotted his face while blood and char covered his tunic. His right sleeve had been torn away at the elbow, exposing a muscled forearm rimmed with a blue tattoo.

Corwin brought the sword closer to the man's throat. "I won't ask again: Who are you and what are you doing here?"

In answer, the man opened his mouth, but only a garbled sound came out, a red pit where his tongue should've been.

"What in the three hells is going on?" Dal said, joining Corwin.

Corwin stepped back, giving the man room to stand. "Get up."

The man did so, limbs trembling. Corwin frowned, surprised by the depth of his fear. Surely he knew that if Corwin was going to kill him, he would've done it already.

"Watch out, Corwin!" Dal shouted, making a grab for the man, who had reached into his pocket for a weapon. His hand came out empty save for a puff of smoke. For a second, Corwin thought the stranger was summoning fire, but then he saw it was magic of a different kind entirely. Just what, he didn't know, but he stumbled back from it in fear.

The smoke transformed into two long black tendrils like snakes. They slid into the man's mouth, disappearing down his throat. He began to scream as black lines spread over his face and down his arms, following the flow of his veins. Those veins swelled until they burst, breaking through the skin with blood blackened to tar. The man's screams abruptly ended, and he fell to the ground in a messy pile.

Covering his mouth, Corwin turned away from the sight. Around him, the others gasped and shuddered, several of them gagging. At least one man vomited.

Governor Prewitt and the rest finally arrived. "What happened?" Prewitt said. He dismounted, feet striking the grass with an audible thud, and handed his horse's reins to one of the guards before approaching the body. Corwin relayed the story while around him the guards made warding gestures.

After several seconds of examination, Prewitt announced, "This man was from Andreas."

Taking a steadying breath, Corwin forced his gaze onto the body. "How do you know?"

"This tattoo." Prewitt indicated the blue ink wrapped around the man's forearm, barely visible on the ruined skin. "It's a miner's mark. All who work in the mines in Andreas receive one. The ink glows in the dark, making their bodies easy to find if there's an accident or they lose their way."

Across from them, Dal wrinkled his nose. "That's rather unpleasant." He picked up the magestone whistle around his neck and blew it. No sound came out, at least none that the men could hear, but somewhere overhead, Lir let out a cry in answer to the silent summons.

"But what sort of magic was that smoke?" Corwin said. "I've never seen something like that. I thought wilders could only manipulate the elements . . . fire, earth, air, and water."

"And sometimes spirit," Prewitt said. "That's what the oldest tales say."

"No wilder born with spirit has been seen for centuries." Dal stretched out his arm to catch Lir as she landed.

"Quite right, Lord Thorne," said Prewitt with a bob of his head. "They haven't been *seen*."

Corwin considered the implication. It was true that wilders lived in hiding. The eradication of their kind was one of the Mage League's primary purposes, one they'd grown even more successful at these last three years since the inception of the Inquisition and the formation of the gold order. Before it, wilders were condemned only once they'd been discovered performing wild magic. Now, the League actively searched them out. Every city and freeholding in Rime was bound by royal decree to allow the gold robes to examine their citizens, regardless of age. Could it be that there were those with spirit abilities who had simply managed to avoid being caught all this time? Corwin didn't know. But with magic like he'd just seen, he supposed anything was possible. He knew a dozen men or more who would give their right hands to possess such a weapon.

"Lord governor," one of the guards shouted, bursting into the clearing to join them. "The fire that man was tending had a night-drake corpse in it."

Corwin, Prewitt, and Dal followed the guard back to the fire. Corwin fixed his eyes on the charred pieces. The guard was right—there was a drake corpse among the debris. Still, he couldn't make sense of it. Drakes couldn't have done this. So why were there corpses here? Nightdrakes scavenged their dead. Why burn them? It was like trying to solve a puzzle with misshaped pieces.

"What would you have us do, your highness?" Governor Prewitt asked.

Corwin didn't answer at first, uncomfortable with the question and the responsibility that fell to him. "I suppose we should take the miner's body back to Farhold and have the magists examine it. They might know more about the magic that killed him. And we need to complete a thorough search of the house and grounds."

Prewitt nodded. "Will you be prolonging your stay in Farhold then?"

Corwin considered the question, his unruly thoughts turning to

Kate once more. If he did stay, it was possible he might run into her again. He could even orchestrate the meeting, if he dared.

But only heartache lay down that path.

"No," Corwin said. "I will not prolong my stay. If the man was from Andreas, then that's all the more reason for me to keep on with the tour." *That and the fact that Lord Nevan of Andreas is one of my father's biggest detractors,* he thought but didn't say. "I was scheduled to head there next," he added. "I'll be leaving tomorrow."

"Beg pardon, your highness," replied Prewitt, "but given that this attack might have been an act against the high king, surely someone from your party should stay to learn what the magists have to say."

"I'll stay," Dal said before Corwin could respond. Corwin shot his friend a suspicious look, and Dal shrugged. "Should take only a short while. I'll be able to catch up to the tour easily."

Corwin resisted an eye roll, understanding Dal's motives clearly—by delaying his departure, he could avoid the slow pace they were forced to keep with the royal caravan. *Should've volunteered myself instead.*

Corwin sighed. "If you're sure, Lord Thorne."

"Quite sure." A hint of a smile curved the edges of Dal's mouth. "It will give me time to do a bit more exploring of this lovely city. I'd very much like to visit the Relay house."

Corwin looked away, hiding a scowl. Dal was free to do what he wanted, as was Kate.

It's not my concern, he told himself.

No matter how much he might wish it were.

BY THE TIME KATE REACHED the Relay house, roll call was over. The other riders were already coming out of the meeting room when she crossed the threshold into the office building attached to the main stable. Their boots made heavy thuds against the wood floor. For a second, she tried to duck into one of the staff rooms, but true to the theme of her life recently, she was too late.

A familiar voice called out to her, "Late again, Traitor Kate!"

She braced, ready for a repeat of last night's torment as she watched Cort heading toward her. *He will not get a rise out of me this time,* she silently swore.

Cort stopped in front of her, blocking her way. He slid the saddle he was carrying off one hip to rest it against the other. He'd been the only rider carrying one. Most preferred to keep their saddles in the tack room, conveniently located in the stable. Not Cort, though. This saddle was too valuable to leave in the care of anyone else—or so he claimed. And it was indeed valuable. Custom crafted from the finest calfskin leather, brass fasteners, and gold-laced thread, it was a saddle made for nobility. Kate knew it well—it had belonged to her father.

The sight of it in Cort's arms brought emotions surging to the surface, as it always did, only worse after her run-in with Prince Corwin. It was as if the past were stalking her this day. The saddle was one of the few of her father's possessions she'd been allowed to keep after his execution. She'd given it over to the Relay to cover her apprentice fee. It was worth three times as much as that, but it was all she'd had. Through a cruel twist of fate, bad luck, and Relay politics, it belonged to Cort now. She forced her eyes away from it and onto his face, a glare heating her gaze.

"What was the holdup this time?" Cort said. "You look like you took a tumble in the gutter." He sniffed at her, then grimaced. "Yuck. What'd you do, spend the night at the slaughterhouse with Pip?"

Kate balled her hand into a fist, wishing she could punch him.

"Well, never mind," he said, then with mock apology added, "but thought you should know that . . . unfortunately . . . you've been bumped." He grinned, leaving no doubt that he'd been the one to do it.

Kate started to go around him, pushing her way between the other riders still departing, but Cort grabbed her arm with his free hand, stopping her.

She yanked out of his grip. "Don't touch me."

The grin on his face twisted into a sneer. "Believe me, I've no interest in touching you. Who would? Treachery might be contagious."

Do not respond, do not—oh hells. She flashed a cold smile. "Well, that's great news for me, then. Now I won't have to worry about catching stupidity from you."

Cort snorted. "Stupid, am I? At least I know how to be on time."

"Oh yes." Kate rolled her eyes. "Because it's so difficult to do that when you live in the Relay house. You just roll out of bed and here you are."

Cort's eyes narrowed. "You're welcome to bunk with the boys. Like I said, a traitor like you wouldn't have to worry about any unwanted advances."

Mutinous tears stung Kate's eyes—her deeper emotions betraying her. Corwin's face swam into her mind once more. He had looked on her like she was a stranger, someone unknown and beneath his notice or care. Someone who didn't matter.

But she had. Once. Once she had been wanted.

She forced the thoughts away, holding off the tears with a will forged by years of hardships. "Like any girl would be safe with you, Cort. One look from you and—"

"Kate Brighton!"

Flinching, she turned to see Deacon Lewis standing in the doorway of the meeting room. The foreman's gaze was fixed on her in an expression so displeased, it chilled the heat of her anger in an instant.

"I need a word," he said, and stepped back into the meeting room.

Swallowing, Kate headed for the door.

"Have a nice ride to Andreas, Traitor Kate," Cort called from behind her. "Hope you fare better than poor Eliza."

Dread began to thud in her chest at this news. She'd known she would be bumped, but she hadn't realized it would be to the Andreas route. Deacon had forbidden female riders from taking the route after Eliza Caine failed to complete her ride a few weeks ago.

No one knew for sure what happened—other than that the nightdrakes had taken her and her horse. All they found afterward were the remnants of the saddle, mail pouch, and bits of clothing.

Speculation was that she'd run into trouble with the ferrymen of the Redrush. Ever since High King Orwin had commissioned the bridge, the ferrymen went out of their way to delay riders, often forcing them to wait until nearly dusk before letting them cross. Especially the female riders. The Redrush ferrymen considered themselves Andrean above all else, and most held the belief that women had no business in a profession that required them to ride horses, carry weapons, and wear breeches beneath their skirts.

Deacon was waiting next to the podium at the front of the room as she entered. Behind him, the massive blackboard held the details of this week's rides. Kate scanned it, quickly finding her name next to the Andreas route, surrounded by telltale smudge marks. She glanced at the Aldervale route—the one that should've been hers—and to her complete lack of surprise saw Cort's name there instead. He wasn't the most senior of the riders, but he'd earned the most honor points, giving him first dibs at bumping. Of course, just how Cort, son of the Relay master, earned those points was a different matter.

Kate stopped a few feet from Deacon and reluctantly met his gaze.

His expression was no less displeased than it had been a moment before, and he was already worrying at his scars. "How many times have I told you not to engage in arguments with Cort or any of the other riders?"

"Hundreds." Kate resisted the urge to squirm. "I'm sorry. I was already in a foul temper, and he does his best to provoke me."

Deacon shook his head. "I don't care. Your best is better than his. You must stop taking the bait. If he complains to his father about you, I won't be able to save your job."

Kate huffed. "No chance of that. He enjoys tormenting me too much to get me fired."

Crossing his arms over his chest, Deacon let out a sigh. "I suppose you might be right." His eyes flicked to the board. "At least the Andreas route won't be as bad as you're expecting."

She arched a single eyebrow. "How so?"

"The Relay council has decided to add an extra day to the route, giving you time to compensate for any troubles with the ferrymen."

Kate bit her lip, judging her response carefully. The last thing she wanted was to sound disrespectful. "That's great for dealing with ferrymen, but it doesn't help us avoid the nightdrakes. I mean, the sun keeps setting same time as always."

"I have something to help with that, too." Deacon headed for the desk in the far corner where he did most of his work. He had a private office nearby, but he detested small places. This room was large enough to hold thirty people comfortably, but Kate suspected Deacon would work outside in the stable yard, beneath the open sky, if he could. They had that in common.

He opened a bottom drawer on the desk and pulled out three fist-sized wardstones, glowing with fresh enchantments, and set them on top of the desk, which was littered with parchment and maps. Then he opened the drawer in the center and withdrew a large key. He held it out to her. "This will unlock the Relay tower half a mile east from the Redrush crossing. Do you know the one?"

Kate accepted the key, frowning. "Sure, but it's been closed for years. Is it even usable?"

"It should be fine. I had Henderson take a look at it when he returned from the last Andrean run. The well is still good and the walls are solid. These will be enough to keep you safe inside for a night if need be." Deacon motioned to the wardstones. "They'll be in your mail pouch before you leave. You're scheduled to depart at noon."

"Thank you," Kate said, trying to put as much gratitude as she could into her voice. The wardstones and key to the tower were the first bright point in her day. And a noon departure gave her time to get cleaned up and then drop in on her friend Bonner, a necessary stop whenever she returned from a ride.

"You're welcome, but it's not as generous as it sounds. I need you to inspect the horses this morning." Deacon rubbed at the scars on his forearm. Kate wondered if he would one day smooth them away entirely.

She nodded, unhappy at the request. Inspections weren't her job, but Deacon had learned early on that Kate Brighton had inherited her father's ability for judging horseflesh. Usually, she could tell when one was in danger of pulling up lame or was off in some other way that might affect the ride. *But not always,* she thought, remembering Pip.

There was the risk involved, too. She didn't think Deacon suspected the truth—that she was a wilder capable of communicating with horses—but she had to be careful. If she was too insightful, detecting a problem without any physical indication to go along with it, then Deacon, or someone else watching, might guess. Someone like Cort might be too stupid to see her insight for what it was, but the magists weren't. They didn't often visit the Relay house, but she had no idea how close they needed to be for the magestones to detect wilder magic. She had no plans to find out.

"I wouldn't be asking you again so soon," Deacon said, "but we've gotten some extra scrutiny from the Relay council of late. What with Eliza's death and all."

Kate bit her lip. "Are you sure you want me to do it? I didn't realize Pip's injury until it was too late."

"No one's perfect, Kate. I'm sure if there'd been warning to find with Pip, you would have." The foreman's confidence in her made Kate feel better, if only by a margin, and she stowed the key in her pocket, where it clanked against the moonbelt.

Then, summoning a brave smile, she said, "I'll do it right now."

Later that morning, Kate left her room at the Crook and Cup once more, this time cleaned and dressed in a fresh tunic, breeches, and overskirt. At Signe's insistence, she'd even put on the moonbelt.

"Don't be such a prude, Kate," Signe had said. "Even if you have no one to play with yet, it will still stop your monthly flows. How can you say no to such a boon?"

Kate couldn't, and so had conceded. At least it was safely hidden beneath her clothes and in no danger of falling out of her pocket anymore. Still, the feel of it around her waist made her nervous as she walked along, certain every person she passed could tell she was wearing it. She knew she was being foolish—her virtue didn't matter now that she was no longer a part of the gentry—but the trappings of childhood morals were not so easily cast off.

She found Tom Bonner standing over the forge in the back of his father's blacksmith's shop, his face red from the fire and glossy with sweat. He'd stripped out of his tunic, wearing only trousers and a thin undershirt with the sleeves rolled up, exposing his massive arms.

A broad smile lit his boyish face when he spotted her. "I didn't think you were going to make it."

She pulled her saddlebag off her shoulder and set it down on a nearby chair. "When have I ever not made it?" she said, grinning back at him.

He snorted. "More times than I would like."

"We can't all be as perfect and punctual as you, Tom Bonner."

"I know. It's too bad. The world would be a better place if everyone were like me."

Kate didn't doubt it. "I can't stay long."

"I know that, too." He pulled out the horseshoe he'd been heating in the forge with a pair of iron tongs and dropped the hot metal into a nearby water trough. Both the water and the metal protested the convergence with a loud hiss.

Bonner set down the tongs and then came around the forge to Kate. Even though they were the same age, almost to the day, he towered over her by a foot and a half and was at least twice her width. He pulled her into a hug that squeezed all the air from her lungs.

She giggled breathlessly and patted his back. "It's only been four days since I've seen you." He squeezed harder. "I missed you, too, but I'm about to pass out."

"So fragile." With a sigh, he let her go. He stood to his full height and gazed down at her with moss-green eyes. He wore his auburn hair in a short ponytail at the nape of his neck. He was handsome like a bear was handsome—large and intimidating but with an alluring gentleness. "It's why I worry you won't come back one of these days."

Kate poked him in the chest—it was like jamming her finger against solid rock. "I am not fragile. And you of all people know how unlikely it is that I would fail to come back."

He cast her a dark look. "Just because you can read horses doesn't mean nothing bad can happen to you out there. I worry about you, Kate."

She shrugged, dropping her gaze to the floor. He didn't know how right he was, but she knew better than to tell him about Pip. Aside from Signe, Bonner was the only person she'd ever told about her magic, and only because Bonner was a wilder, too—an earthist. He could control minerals and ores, with a particular affinity for metalworking. It was an ability she'd spotted in him by accident—and with a bit of carelessness on his part—when he'd visited the Relay house to shoe some of the horses and had used his ability to smooth out a bent horseshoe without a hammer. Most people probably wouldn't have noticed, but Kate had been paying particular attention that day. Later, she'd admonished him for using his gift so openly, but only after she'd confided in him her own.

A smile crested her lips. "I'm glad you worry. I wouldn't trade it for the world. I mean, between you and Signe that makes two whole people who would miss me if I died tomorrow. It's some kind of record." She spoke glibly, but after her painful morning, this truth struck her hard, and the smile slipped from her face.

Fortunately, Bonner had already turned away, heading for the cabinet on the far side of the shop. Swords, knives, spears, maces, morning stars, and various other weapons adorned the walls beside the cabinet. "Better to have two people whose love is true than a whole city of fair-weather friends," he said over his shoulder.

"You sound like your father," Kate replied, then winced at her blunder when she saw Bonner's spine stiffen. "I'm sorry, I didn't . . . I meant that as a compliment." She cleared her throat. "Is he doing any better?"

Bonner pulled out a wooden box from the cabinet and set it on the table, his movements careful, gentle, like he was handling a babe. "No."

Kate let out a low sigh. For months now, Bonner's father had been bedridden with a sickness the healers had been unable to cure. In truth, Kate had begun to doubt there was a cure. She'd seen the effects of a wasting disease before, and Master Bonner showed clear signs. Not that she would dare say it aloud to his son.

She crossed the floor to Bonner and gave his shoulder a pat. "I'm sorry."

"Don't be," he replied, optimism brightening his voice already. "He's going to be fine any day now."

Kate managed a meager nod; then, searching for an easier topic, she motioned at the box. "Did you finish the latest model?"

An eager grin broke over his face. "Just last night, and this time, Kate, I'm certain I've made a breakthrough."

"You've said that once or twice before." She touched a finger to her chin. "Wait, make that six times."

Bonner huffed, puffing out his chest in indignation. "All new inventions take time and refining. Anyone will tell you."

He raised the lid to reveal the pistol inside. Except the gun was unlike any other in all of Rime, in all the world. It was breech-loading instead of muzzle, with a circular chamber to hold the bullets. A revolver, Bonner called it, based on the way the bullet chamber rotated with each press of the trigger. For months now, Bonner had been obsessed with creating a gun that could fire multiple rounds without reloading, enough shots to take the place of the mage-enchanted arrows the Relay relied on. Enchantments did not come cheaply, and Bonner wanted to give Kate a better way to protect herself from nightdrakes. In truth, he wanted to give all of Rime a better way, although he rarely spoke of the ambition out loud. Like most wilders, Bonner hated the Mage League. Only for him, it wasn't about the injustice of their persecution, but rather the cost of their magic. The green robes might be able to heal his father, if only Bonner could afford their price.

Pulling the revolver from the box, he handed it to Kate. "Same one, better design."

The weight of it tugged at her hand, but the hilt fitted easily in her palm. She aimed it at one of the swords on the wall, cocked the trigger, and pulled. Not loaded, it made only a faint pop, but the action on the gun worked smoothly. She cocked it again, marveling at the easy way the cylinder rotated.

"Okay," she said, lowering the gun. "I accept that it's a better design, but you're sure it won't jam this time?"

"Yeah, I'm sure. The trick was in the new bullets. See." He pulled one of the bullets out of the pile in the box and held it before her. With a wave of his hand, he dismantled the bullet with his magic.

"Bonner," Kate hissed, "don't do that. What if a magist walks in?"

"I'll use him for target practice."

She shook her head, flustered by his bravado. The risk of using magic inside the city was greater than ever these days, with more and more golds turning up at every turn, on the hunt for wilders. Kate blamed the influx on these rumored Rising attacks. She wished they would stop. Such violence could only create more support for the Inquisition, making it harder for wilders like her and Bonner to go on living in secret. *And here Bonner is, courting the danger,* she thought. The Mage League wished to purge all of Rime of wilder kind. The Rising was just helping it along.

With the bullet's innards spread across his hand, Bonner launched into a complicated explanation about how the cartridge case needed to be copper, the soft metal better suited to seal the barrel and prevent it from backfiring. Kate made a face, knowing all too well what that backfiring entailed. She'd nearly lost a hand "testing" his designs. She was no less leery about this one.

"Well, to be honest, changing the casing was Signe's idea," Bonner said, "since she's the one who knows how the black powder works, but I'm the one who decided on copper, what with my understanding of metals."

And your ability to manipulate them, Kate thought. That was the irony of Bonner's quest to create these weapons—they still required magic to manufacture. Modern tools would never accomplish it, though few who enjoyed Bonner's wares knew it.

"Well," Kate said, "I hope you're both right this time." Bonner and Signe had been in on this together from the start of their friendship. Black powder, the substance crucial to the firing process in all pistols, was made only in Esh but could be bought in most stores in Rime. But for some reason the regular mixture wouldn't work with

Bonner's design—something to do with the rate at which it burned. Signe had had to modify it somehow. The secret of mixing black powder was known only to the Furen Mag Sisterhood, a mysterious and secret order of Eshian craftswomen, and—for some reason she'd never divulged—Signe Leth. She was far too young to have learned the trade, even if she once had been an initiate in the order. Both Bonner and Kate had tried to get the truth out of her, but Signe refused to tell. Nevertheless, it was their secrets, both shared and not, that bonded the three of them together in such a tight friendship.

"So will you test it?" Bonner asked, brows raised in an eager expression.

"I suppose I must," Kate said with a resigned air.

Beaming, Bonner slid his arms around her waist and spun her around. "Thank you. It's going to work this time, and I'll finally be able to stop worrying about you."

"I hope not," she said as he set her on her feet again. "A little worry feels nice." Her voice broke over the words, memories of Corwin ambushing her again.

"What's wrong?" Concern creased Bonner's brow.

"It's nothing. Just an unpleasant morning."

"What happened?" he insisted, hands on hips.

Biting her lip, Kate debated whether or not to tell him. But then the story came spilling out of her. That was how it always was around Bonner—openness like an impulse. It helped that he already knew about her past with Corwin. For some reason, it was a story she'd shared only with him and not Signe. Kate managed to tell the story without crying, but only barely. Not that she could fool Bonner.

He pulled her into another bear hug. "Forget about him. He doesn't matter."

"I know. I'm just being silly."

"No, you're not. It has to be hard to be confronted with your old life like that." He took the revolver from her hands and slid it into a holster. "But you've got a new life now. And I swear to take care of you forever." He held out the holster to her like a promise.

An ache squeezed Kate's chest at his words. He'd said such things before, but he didn't mean it. Oh, he loved her, for certain, but not in the way that would last forever. Not in the way she wanted to be loved. Their love was like that between a brother and sister. But someday he would find someone who stirred the deeper parts of his heart, the way Corwin had once stirred hers. For a second, she wished it were different—that Bonner felt that way about her, and she him. But no amount of wishing could change their hearts, and desire could not be mined, only ignited.

Swallowing regret, Kate accepted the holster and stowed it in her saddlebag along with a case of bullets. "I've got to go or I'm going to be late."

"Safe ride, quick return." He planted a chaste kiss on the top of her head and pushed her toward the door.

She hurried outside, trying to force her mind anywhere except on Bonner and the future that she knew waited for him. A wife and children to claim his devotion. Any woman would be lucky to have him. There was no such future for her. Who would want a traitor's daughter?

Trying to escape her own head and the image of Corwin's face, Kate hurried faster, soon arriving at the Relay house. Deacon was waiting for her, holding the reins of a bay gelding called Darby. Kate quickly fastened her saddlebag to the back of the saddle, then mounted.

"The wardstones are in the pouch," Deacon said, checking Darby's girth. "And I added some extra valens for you to help sway the ferrymen to let you cross—if you need to."

"Thanks." Kate adjusted her grip on the reins. Darby was eager for the ride, his hooves shifting beneath her. She was eager, too, if only to escape Farhold and the troubles it had brought her today. No matter how much time she spent here, this city never felt like home. It was a place to stay, not belong.

Deacon patted the gelding twice on the neck. "May the luck of Farrah be with you."

Kate headed out of the stable yard and into the street. Passing through the city gates a short while later, she gave Darby his head, allowing him to run off some steam. The wind shrieked in her ears, tugging at her braid as they picked up speed. As Kate fell into the rhythm of Darby's stride—horse and rider becoming one—she felt her spirits soar. For a little while, with the scenery blurring by, she was no longer Traitor Kate. No longer the girl despised by a kingdom. No longer the girl cast aside by the friend and prince she had once loved.

In moments like these, atop a horse and flying over the ground, she glimpsed her old life. She became Kate Brighton again. Daughter of Hale Brighton, master of horse to the high king. She was free. A girl with a future. Someone who mattered.

LETTING DAL STAY BEHIND WAS a mistake, one Corwin regretted less than an hour after he departed Farhold the next day, ahead of a long ponderous train of wagons and mounted men. A ponderous *slow* train. The journey to Andreas from Farhold was a little less than fifty miles, a distance a Relay rider could cover in two days. It would take this caravan, comprised of five wagons, fifteen armed guards, six servants, three magists, and one cook, easily twice that.

The journey would've been bearable with Dal around to distract him, but as it was, there was no one to talk to. He could exchange a few polite words with Captain Morris or even Master Barrett, his royal adviser, but neither was willing to talk loosely with him or tell jokes—the type of conversation Corwin needed to distract him from the tempest of his thoughts.

Even though he tried to keep his mind focused on the intrigue at the Gregors' house and the dead miner, it kept returning to Kate. He replayed their chance meeting in his head, imagining all the better ways it could've gone, if only he'd had time to plan and if there'd been no one around to overhear. But their relationship was cursed. It always had been, it seemed. He'd said as much to Dal when he finally told him about her last night.

Kicking his feet free of the stirrups, Corwin let out a groan at the ache in his knees. That was the worst of riding slow—joints frozen from so many hours stuck in the same position. He could've ridden in one of the wagons, spending the time in relative comfort, but his mind couldn't take it. At least outside, the view offered occasional distractions. He dismounted slowly, letting the blood flow back into his legs.

They'd managed to reach one of the caravan campsites along the road to Andreas—a wide circular clearing that offered several permanent fire pits with nearby racks loaded with wood for burning, a gift from the high king to the travelers of Rime. While the servants and guards began to make camp, Corwin took his time unsaddling Stormdancer. He refused to let a servant do it for him, although four of them tried. It was the one chore he was permitted to perform himself, prince or no. Even Edwin couldn't complain. For the people of Norgard, the care of a warhorse was considered a noble endeavor.

Thank the gods, Corwin thought, wishing that Stormdancer were twice as dirty as he ran the hard-bristled brush over the warhorse's sleek, muscled back. Although night crept toward them over the horizon, it would be hours before he was ready for sleep. While he worked, he caught himself watching the three blue-robe mages—a master, journeyman, and apprentice—as they set the wardstone barrier. The apprentice wore a black mask, just a few shades darker than her skin, which covered only the right side of her face. The journeyman's was black as well, but it covered the top half of his, the contrast striking against his paleness. The master's was full faced and bone white.

The three of them gathered in the center of the campsite, facing one another in a circle. Cupped in the palms of their hands, each held a wardstone the size of a human head. In unison, they spoke the word of invocation, the magic in the wardstones alighting. Then they turned around and began to walk away in a straight line, following the three points of an invisible triangle. The apprentice passed nearest Corwin, and he watched her reach the edge of the campsite, where she stopped and set the wardstone on the ground. The magical barrier went up a moment later, the only hint of its presence a faint shimmer around the campsite like sunlight catching on a smudge in a piece of glass.

Corwin returned his attention to Storm, finishing a short time later. He considered retreating to his tent, but his restlessness remained. Ordering his meal to be served outside, he sat down at a small table near one of the fire pits, which offered an unobstructed view of the land beyond. He ate slowly, with his gaze wandering over the surrounding hills cloaked in everweeps and witchgrass and a million insects chattering in the night.

Not long after Corwin finished eating, the master magist approached him. "Do you mind if I make use of your table, highness?"

Corwin blinked up at him, caught off guard by the request. The fire cast a troupe of dancing shadows across the man's bone-colored mask, his eyes glistening black points inside it.

Recovering quickly, Corwin motioned to the empty chair across from him. "By all means. I would welcome the distraction." He supposed of everyone present, the magist might make for the most interesting conversation, if not the most comfortable. There was something disquieting about talking to a masked person.

But to Corwin's relief and further surprise, the master magist took off his mask as he sat down and placed it on the table beside him. The skin of his face was nearly as white as the mask, except for a dark-red birthmark that spread over the top of his nose and beneath both eyes. *He's Shade Born,* Corwin thought, recalling the old superstition. There were some who believed people born with such marks were claimed for service to the Shades, those hellish minions of the gods whose sole purpose was to thwart and torment mankind for the entertainment of their exalted masters. All nonsense, of course, and yet Corwin found himself uneasy. He couldn't quite place the magist's age; older than himself, certainly, but younger than his father.

"I'm doubtful what distraction I can provide," the magist said, pulling out a deck of cards from a hidden pocket in his robe, "but I will do my best. My name is Raith."

Corwin arched his eyebrows. It was odd enough to have a magist remove his mask, but to give a name as well? That went against the usual front of faceless unity the League preferred to maintain. There were some magists high enough in their orders to be publicly named, but not many. The only ones he knew of were Grand Master Storr, head of the League, and Maestra Vikas, head of the gold order. Both of them served as advisers to the royal council in Norgard, although neither held a seat. By ancient laws set forth in the League Accords, no magist could hold political position. They couldn't even own land aside from their freeholding in the north, site of the League Academy.

"So tell me, Master Raith," Corwin said, watching as the magist began to lay down the cards in a game of solo, "did you hear about the attack on the Gregors?" He noticed the man's fingertips were tinged black as if from some disease or trauma, the nails thick and grayish.

"Indeed, your highness. I was there."

"You were?" Corwin cocked his head, mouth open in surprise. He'd asked the question merely to make conversation, and really, what else was there to discuss with a magist? But learning Raith was there opened up new avenues to explore. "In that case, what do you make of the magic that killed the man?"

Raith flipped over the first card in line, a six of flutes. "You mean the magic he used to kill himself?"

Corwin slowly nodded. Yes, that did seem true, and he gave a shudder as to what desire could drive a man to that extreme. It wasn't the first time he'd witnessed such, though. The wilder responsible for his mother's death had been determined to die as well—and to take as many innocent lives with him as he could. "Was it wilder magic then?" Corwin asked. "A spirit gift, like Governor Prewitt claimed?"

Raith looked up from the cards, where he'd overturned a ten of stones, a bad draw so early in the game. "That is a difficult question. I'm afraid I can't answer, not even to speculate."

"Why not?"

"There's not enough information. The man might not have had any magical ability at all."

"But that's absurd. I saw him use magic." Corwin leaned back in his chair and folded his arms over his waist.

Raith shrugged. "All the people who buy the charms and spells the League sells use magic, your highness. Like these cards, for instance." Raith picked up the queen of candles he'd just over-turned and muttered the word of invocation. Orange light spread through the card, starting with the candle the woman held in her right hand and ending in a halo around her crowned head. A faint smell of burning incense drifted up from the table.

Corwin stared at the magic, a simple trick, really, whose main purpose was to seal the card in play so that a player couldn't cheat and replace it. But he saw Raith's point well enough. Ordinary people did do magic, of this type. But the spells the League sold in their order houses across Rime were mundane, preset tasks imbed-ded within various stones and other trinkets. In addition to cards, there were necklaces that would enhance the wearer's allure, rings that gave courage or strength, parchment that would hide ink until someone spoke the words to make it visible.

He gestured to the still-glowing queen. "Spells like these are harmless, frivolous indulgences. Not death traps."

"True enough." Raith removed the spell with another word and returned the queen of candles to the deck. "But they still contain magic, same as any other magist spell."

"Are you suggesting it was mage magic that tore that man apart from the inside?" Corwin asked, remembering the way he'd reached into his pocket for something.

"No," Raith answered at once with a quick shake of his head. "At least, it was no spell approved by the League."

Corwin's eyebrows drew together. "What do you mean?"

Raith turned over another card. "Surely your highness knows that all the orders work to invent new spells, improvements on our trade, as it were. And those spells are submitted for review and acceptance."

"For sanctioning." Corwin nodded. "Yes, I know."

"Well then, that means there are spells that do not receive League approval, but that still exist, nonetheless."

"Hmmm." Corwin pressed his lips together. Again, he saw the man's point, an unsettling one. He knew from his history lessons that the League did sometimes sanction spells that could harm and kill. They'd created dozens of such during the Sevan Invasion fifty years ago, but the use of them was outlawed once the Sevan forces had been defeated. Corwin's grandfather, King Borwin, the first high king of Rime, did not want his people to live in fear of their own magists.

"But surely no magist would have reason to invent such a spell now," Corwin added. "We are at peace." *Not counting the Rising,* he reminded himself, but the threat of wilders wasn't new, just the notion of them banding together. Even still, he couldn't see their threat being the reason a magist would invent a spell that could kill so quickly. Wilders weren't to be executed on the spot but taken prisoner for the Purging, a ritual designed to rid the world of their magic once and for all.

"The League never assumes peace will last," replied Raith. "Seva remains a threat. The Godking will attack again. It's only a matter of time."

"True enough," Corwin said. He knew better than most the bloodthirsty nature of Seva's monarch.

With a loud exhale, no doubt at the sad state of his hand of solo, Raith gathered the cards on the table and looked up. "Would your highness like to play a game of peril?"

Corwin supposed he ought to say no, but after the long, boring day, he couldn't refuse such a diversion. With a sly smile, he reached for his coin purse at his side. "Only if we make it a true game."

Raith retrieved his own coin purse in answer. They flipped a valen to determine the deal. Corwin won, and Raith activated the magic on the whole deck before handing it over.

The cards seemed to vibrate against Corwin's palm as he dealt. For a few moments, neither man spoke, their attention focused on building their hands. Raith played a three of jars first. Matching him in the low-power gamble, Corwin played a four of flutes. They made their wagers, then moved to the second round. Corwin won the hand with a last-minute draw of the shade card, trumping Raith's full court.

Moving on to the next hand, Corwin said, "Given what you said earlier, do you believe the spell could've been unsanctioned then? One made by a . . ." He searched for the word. "A rogue magist?" It seemed incredible anyone would dare. The League was the most powerful force in all of Rime, quick to find the guilty and swift to punish them.

Raith glanced up. "We are all human, your highness, whether we're possessed of magic or not. And any human is capable of treachery."

Yes, they are, Corwin thought, remembering Kate's father. Once again, the memory of that terrible incident and its aftermath rose up in his mind. Kate had come to him that morning, bursting through the door into his bedchambers with the castle guards quick on her heels. She screamed his name and fell at his feet, begging for him to intercede for her, to convince the high council to stay the execution. *Exile,* she had begged. *Let us go into exile!* He'd told her no. That he couldn't. Wouldn't. Hale Brighton was guilty—he'd seen it with his own eyes. The law was the law.

Shaking his head to chase off the memory, Corwin glanced at his cards and played a jester of flutes. "Even if it was mage magic, wilders must still have been behind the attack." During the search they'd found what looked to be a hastily drawn sun lion etched in ash on a piece of the fallen wall.

"Yes, the Rising. It certainly seems that way." Raith picked up his bag of coins and upended it onto the pot.

Corwin stared in surprise at the bold wager. He resisted glancing down at his hand, where another shade card waited next to four kings and a pair of sevens, the hand as good as any he recalled having recently. The shade card lay on top, revealing the figure in a black cloak with a horned crown wrapped around its hooded head.

"Then again," Raith continued, seemingly unconcerned about how much money he stood to lose, "in these uneasy times it's difficult to be certain of anything. Nothing has been the same since your lord father was wounded. It's your wager, highness, shall you call or fold?"

"I never fold." Upending his own purse, Corwin kept his eyes fixed on the magist. "How have things changed?"

Giving the bid a passing glance, Raith replied, "Well, the Inquisition, for one thing. Some blame its inception for the Rising. And there was also the year of the drought, followed by two years of flooding. Disease in the north felling livestock in record numbers. And of course the increasing number of nightdrakes."

"Increase?" Corwin frowned. He'd heard the other rumors before, superstitions among the people that the king's ailment affected the very land itself, but the drakes were news to him.

"Why yes. Surely you're aware the League keeps count." Raith shifted the cards in his hand, and Corwin caught the faint smell of rain in the air—it seemed the magist held a fair amount of jars. "Grand Master Storr presents the numbers to the high council regularly, I believe."

Corwin sat back in his chair, sensing the rebuke in the man's words clearly. It wasn't that he wasn't aware of his own ignorance; it was that normally he could avoid situations where it was pointed out to him.

"That's very interesting," Corwin said drily. "I wonder how you magists can tell them apart well enough to keep an accurate count. Who's to say you aren't just counting the same packs over and over again?"

"We have our ways." Raith raised his hand, palm up and fingers splayed in the universal sign of magic.

Corwin smirked—magic was a magist's answer to everything. "Well, have no fear, Master Raith. I'm sure my brother is already concocting new and clever ways to deal with all these troubles."

"Ah, so it's true then," Raith said, nodding to himself.

Corwin narrowed his eyes. "What's true?"

"That you've decided not to challenge your brother for the throne."

The words hit Corwin like a slap. The impertinence of it, the presumption. "There's been no sign of *uror*," he said, knowing full well that this magist must be aware of it already. Hardly a week went by when some newspaper didn't speculate on its absence. In Norgard, the right to rule did not pass from father to eldest son, but from father to the son most worthy to succeed. Determining that worthiness was done through the trials of uror, but only once the sign appeared. It should've appeared the year Corwin came of age at sixteen. Only it hadn't. And here he was, four years later, and still not worthy enough for the gods to initiate uror.

"Oh, my apologies then." Raith touched a hand to his left breast. "I am not from Norgard. I can't say I fully understand how this uror works."

That's because it doesn't work at all unless both heirs are judged to be equal, Corwin thought. He forced his jaw to relax, feeling an ache in his teeth.

"Yes, that's a common enough difficulty. Few outsiders truly understand it." Uror was a belief peculiar to his people, although some born of Norgard struggled with the concept as well, those too young to have lived through the last uror, when Corwin's father, Orwin, earned the right to sit on the Mirror Throne over his twin brother, Owen. The word itself meant both "fate" and "self-determination," two forces that seemed fundamentally opposed.

Corwin cleared his throat. "It's your play, Master Raith." He was ready for the game—and this conversation—to end.

"Yes, of course." Raith laid down his remaining cards. "But what happens once your father moves onto the next life if there never is an uror sign?"

Corwin stared at the play before him, his lips pressed in disbelief at the five jar cards and two shades—a nearly unbeatable hand. Sighing, he conceded the game. "Nicely played, Master Raith.

But—" He broke off as a strange sound echoed in the distance, raising the hairs on his arms and neck.

Wordlessly, he and the magist stood and approached the ward-stone barrier as the loud keening sounded once more, closer now. Just beyond, a pack of nightdrakes swept down the side of the hill toward them like a gray tide. Moonlight glinted off bared fangs and set dozens of beaded eyes ablaze. Drawn by the smell of live meat, the drakes raced toward the camp, their clawed feet tearing up the earth with each stride.

Corwin laid one palm against his sword hilt and the other against his pistol, instinct urging him to pull them free.

"Do not fear, your highness," Raith said from beside Corwin. "The barrier will hold."

Corwin didn't respond. The truth of that claim would be determined soon enough.

Seconds later, the leader of the pack reached them. The size of a bear, the nightdrake was covered in corpse-gray scales from its reptilian head to its long, spiked tail. It leaped toward Corwin and Raith, spreading out its stunted wings to soar the short distance. Corwin held his breath, knuckles flexed over his weapons. If the barrier failed, the beast would be on him in a second.

The nightdrake struck the invisible wall with a sound like a thunderclap, and the magic flung it backward into the rest of the arriving pack. Several more hurled themselves at the barrier only to be repelled as well. Soon catching on, the pack began to swarm around the perimeter in a frenzy of snapping jaws, beating wings, and writhing bodies. Over and over again, they tested the barrier, as if probing for a weakness. It was always the largest that attacked, the ones as big as horses and oxen, while the scouts and other small ones kept making that awful keening sound.

The other people in camp had arrived by now, drawn by the noise. "Look!" one of the guards shouted. "There're more."

Corwin glanced where the man had pointed, lifting his gaze from the pack out into the distance, where a second pack was moving in, easily another dozen drakes. Then came a third, charging down at them from the opposite direction.

"What would you have us do, your highness?" Captain Morris asked.

"Kill them," Corwin replied. *That should help thin the numbers.*

"We'll run through all our enchanted arrows doing that." Captain Morris glanced at Raith. "Will your blue robes be able to provide more on this trip?"

"To be sure," Raith replied. "I doubt Prince Corwin's purse will cover it, but we can settle with the crown when we arrive back in Norgard."

Corwin sighed. Edwin would not be pleased at the added expense. Then again, this tour had been his idea from the start. *Let him deal with the consequences.*

"Make it so," he said, and moments later the twang of bowstrings filled the air, followed by the cries of wounded drakes.

With his stomach twisting at the sound and the gore, Corwin turned to Raith, who still stood beside him. "To answer your question, Master Raith: when my father dies, Edwin will rule after him."

Raith arched a single eyebrow, the mark of the Shade Born on his face a striking contrast to his white skin. "You mean only if there is no sign of uror before the high king's death?"

There won't be, Corwin thought. The last few years he'd spent away from Rime had shown him that beyond doubt.

Turning away from the magist, he spoke the assertion again, one he reminded himself of daily: "Edwin will rule."

The next day dawned bright and bloody, the stench of burning drake corpses on the air. Corwin had passed the night in fitful sleep, spending most of it in that halfway place between waking and dreaming. His resulting fatigue made the slow pace even more unbearable. Before long he began to formulate a speech about why he and a few of the men would be striking out ahead of the caravan. *We must get to Andreas soon,* Corwin reasoned. *These troubling events cannot wait.* The speech sounded good in his mind—believable and, most importantly, inarguable. But just as he was about to approach Master Barrett, doubt set in. As usual, it came in Edwin's voice. *So irresponsible, Corwin. Always thinking of yourself first and never of your duty.*

Corwin groaned inwardly, hating the debate and the way it paralyzed him. Trying to appease the divided parts of his nature, he decided to wait until after they'd crossed the Redrush.

Again, the hours slowly ticked by. But today, unlike yesterday, Corwin managed to hold a tighter rein on his thoughts, keeping them away from Kate and focused on more important matters. That was, until he spotted a Relay tower standing on top of a hill in the distance, far from the main road. It was a small one, narrow but still two stories high. He wondered if Kate ever stayed there. He doubted it, given the weathered, ill-used look of the tower. The stone blocks that formed the walls had been windswept smooth, except for the places where they were beginning to crumble.

Still, the idea of it—of her alone, locked inside that forlorn place with prowling nightdrakes just outside—consumed his thoughts. The danger she placed herself in, and the reasons for doing so. If only Hale hadn't been responsible. He and his family had led a good life in Norgard. They didn't want for anything.

Then why did he try to kill my father?

The question haunted Corwin. Hale's actions made no sense—both during the attack and afterward, when he refused to offer any explanation for it. But neither did he deny it. Maybe if he had explained, Corwin could've done something about Kate's pleas for the mercy of exile.

Damn the man, Corwin thought, teeth clenched. *He—*

The thought died in his head as a strange movement caught his eye. He turned toward it, back twisting in the saddle. Although his eyes saw clearly, his mind couldn't make sense of the black-bodied creatures spilling over the hill that lay in between the road and the larger hill occupied by the Relay tower.

"What is that?" someone shouted from behind Corwin.

"Nightdrakes!" someone else answered.

No, it can't be—it's daylight. And yet they most certainly were drakes, Corwin realized with a jolt of shock. They didn't look exactly like the nightdrakes he was familiar with; instead of pale gray, these were black as tar. But they bore the same dragonish heads, the same fangs and claws, and sinuous bodies with flightless wings fanned out behind them. And that same awful keening.

Stormdancer snorted and started to shy, tossing his head in the instinct to flee, but he stood no chance outrunning them at this distance. Reining the warhorse under control, all further thought fled Corwin's mind, and his own instinct took over. He yanked the pistol from its holster and fired. The shot struck one of the scouts, and it went down. With the pistol's usefulness expended, Corwin stowed it and reached for his sword.

A moment later the pack was upon them. Storm jumped sideways as one of the black creatures leaped. Bringing his sword arm in range, Corwin reined the horse hard to the left. He swung, but the blow glanced off the nightdrake's toughened hide. Still, the hit was strong enough to deflect the beast momentarily. It fell to the ground but circled and came again. Moving impossibly fast, it became a dark blur before Corwin's eyes. Before he could raise his sword, the beast struck him full force, knocking him from the saddle.

Corwin landed hard on his back, starbursts arcing across his vision. He'd managed to keep hold of his sword, but it didn't matter. The nightdrake was on top of him, jaws spreading wide. It closed its fangs around his left shoulder, and Corwin cried out, the sound lost in the commotion around him. Chaos had erupted over the caravan, men and horses screaming.

The pain paralyzed Corwin, stealing from him the will to fight, to survive. But only for a moment. Then he lifted his right hand, sword still clutched in his fingers, and brought the hilt down on the creature's head, smashing its eye like a grape. The drake's jaws loosened, and it let out a howl of pain.

Summoning his strength, even as he felt its poison burning through his veins, Corwin raised the sword again and thrust it into the beast's opened mouth and out through the back of its head.

Corwin lay there, panting for several long seconds. Then he pushed the heavy weight of the drake corpse off him and struggled to his feet. A few feet away, he saw Storm sprawled on the blood-soaked ground, the stillness of death already lying like a shroud over the warhorse. A wrench went through his chest at the sight. He and the horse had been through so much together, survived so many trials and threats. *This is the end for both of us, my friend,* Corwin thought, his vision blurred from poison and the fire burning inside his wounded shoulder.

For a second, the will to fight almost went out of him again. *No.* He pulled his eyes away from the dead horse. There were others still alive. He would do what he could to protect them for as long as breath remained in his body. Raising his sword once more, he charged the nearest drake. *If I'm to die today, I will die fighting.*

SOMEONE DIED HERE.

The thought slid through Kate's mind unbidden, and for a moment she wasn't even sure where it had come from. Ahead the hard-packed road looked undisturbed, tranquil almost. No dust from hooves or wagon wheels clouded the air. To either side of the road, the grass grew long and wild, strewn with everweeps. It was beautiful, a welcome sight after her long argument with the ferrymen of the Redrush. They'd delayed her for hours on her return journey from Andreas, enough that she would have no choice but to stay in the abandoned Relay tower tonight.

So where did that thought come from?

The smell on the air—but not one she could detect. Rather it was Darby smelling it, reacting enough that Kate sensed it with her magic without meaning to. She reached toward the horse with her power and soon saw a distorted image of a nightdrake. To his equine mind, the dragonish creature was more monstrous than in real life. He made it the size of a wagon, with fangs as long as daggers, claws like scimitars.

Kate frowned, trying to process the image. It made no sense. The sun shone too brightly for a nightdrake to survive it, dusk an hour away at least, and there were no shadows for them to hide beneath. *There must've been an attack last night,* Kate reasoned. She sent reassurance through the link, convincing the horse there was no threat.

Kate urged Darby onward, and soon they crested the hill. In the valley below, the ruin of a caravan lay sprawled across the road. Overturned wagons, the long, rounded bodies of dead horses, and the thinner, frailer bodies of dead men were easily distinguishable even from a distance. *Those poor people and horses,* she thought, mouth hanging open in dismay.

She steered Darby away from it, meaning to bypass the scene altogether and head on to the Relay tower. This was not her business or responsibility. The reek of death was strong enough now that she could smell it, too; Darby pranced beneath her, anxious to move away. Kate was just about to let him have his head when movement drew her eye to a flag fluttering atop the only remaining upright wagon. The sight of the familiar white horses in a rearing pose on a dark-blue background made her stomach clench. The royal sigil of Norgard . . . House Tormane . . .

Corwin.

She wheeled the horse about and pressed her heels to his sides, sending him forward. Darby protested, each step short and choppy, until Kate took hold of his mind and bent his will. *There is no danger,* she insisted. *The drakes can't survive the sun.* Only, even as she pressed this truth onto Darby, doubt rose inside her. Something wasn't right. The caravan hadn't been encamped when the attack happened, and the destruction felt fresh, as if it had occurred only hours before instead of last night. *And why did the drakes leave so much meat behind?* They never did that, but as she drew nearer, she saw that one of the men was still alive.

He lay flat on his back in the middle of the wreckage, not far from the upright wagon, and was struggling against the weight of some creature lying on top of him. At first Kate thought it was a nightdrake—it had the right shape—but the color was wrong, black instead of pale gray.

As Kate scanned the area, steering Darby forward with her legs, she saw several of these black creatures and no recognizable night-drakes at all. A surge of alarm went through her, heightening all her senses.

She turned her gaze back to the man struggling to free himself. Her breath caught as she realized it was Corwin. Smears of blood and dirt marred his face, but still she recognized him. In a sudden panic, she heeled Darby forward. Corwin's eyes turned to the sound of pounding hooves, and she saw the delirium on his face. He'd been wounded, that was certain, but she couldn't tell how badly.

How am I going to get him out from under that thing? The strange creature was close to horse size and probably twice as heavy. At least it was dead, the tip of a sword protruding from the juncture where its neck met its shoulder.

Corwin peered up at her. "Kate," he said in a voice weak as a kitten's mewling.

She started to dismount, but stopped as movement off to her right caught her eye. She turned to see a black beast, about a hundred yards away, charging toward her at full speed. In an instant she knew it was a drake, despite the color. Its movement was unmistakable, powerful like a charging bull, but also sinuous like a cat. Even more unmistakable was the sound that issued out of its opened, snarling mouth. Impossibly, the daylight did not affect it, as if those black scales were sun-block armor shielding the nightdrake beneath.

Nightdrakes who do not fear the sun.

Daydrakes.

A shudder passed through Kate's body even as panic seized Darby's mind. The horse reared back on its haunches, ready to spin and flee. Kate wrestled for control, forcing Darby to remain still. Then she dropped the reins and grabbed her bow off the saddle. Reaching for an enchanted arrow from the quiver on her back, she quickly nocked it, the magical tip dazzling her eyes.

She inhaled deep, willing her nerves to calm, her focus to center. Then she exhaled and released the bowstring. There was a sharp twang as the arrow launched forward, the tail wavering for a second before straightening out. Her aim was a little off, as it always was on the first shot. Still, the arrow struck the daydrake in the shoulder, the enchanted tip penetrating the hardened scales and sinking deep. At least these new beasts weren't immune to magic, as they appeared to be to the sun.

But the daydrake didn't even break stride. She pulled another arrow from the quiver, nocked it, and released. Again, her aim was off, but it didn't miss—this one sinking into the beast's chest a few inches below its long neck. Still the daydrake didn't slow.

Darby pranced sideways, but Kate stayed centered in the saddle, her legs working as anchors. *Breathe, focus, aim.* Instinct and training took over. She pulled the third arrow free and launched it. This time it found its mark in the creature's jugular. The daydrake's nostrils flared and its wail turned from threat to pain. She loosed the fourth arrow, striking the neck again. The creature continued its charge—pain now becoming rage.

The fifth arrow struck the same, a third shaft protruding from its neck. *One arrow left.* The creature was slowing, but it wouldn't fall in time. Not without a killing blow. It was close enough now that she could smell the scorched stench of the air around it.

She pulled the last enchanted arrow from the quiver and nocked it. Inhaling, she centered her aim over the arrow, willing the shot to be true. Darby's panic pressed against Kate's control. Distantly she heard Corwin calling for her to flee. If she failed to kill this creature now, they would both die.

She pulled the bowstring as taut as her reach would allow. Then she let it go. The arrow flew hard and true, sinking six inches deep into the daydrake's eye socket. The creature loped forward two more strides, then stumbled, going down on its knees. The hind legs rose up over its head and it flipped, landing in a broken heap less than a yard from Darby.

The horse snorted and began to back away. Kate let him, her breath coming in frantic gasps now that the threat was over.

She'd done it, survived her first nightdrake attack. And during the day. She—

The thought stopped dead in her mind as the sound of more wailing reached her ears. Kate jerked her head to the right to see three more daydrakes bearing down on her.

Three drakes, and she was out of enchanted arrows.

THERE WASN'T TIME TO THINK, only react. Kate drew another arrow, this one without an enchanted tip. Aiming again, it flew true, better than all the ones before, but to no avail. The moment the tip struck the daydrake's hide, it glanced off, as harmless as a pebble tossed at a boulder.

Hissing between her teeth, Kate dropped the bow and reached for the sword sitting in its harness by her left leg. She had it halfway free of the sheath when she remembered Bonner's revolver. There was no time to worry if it would jam or not. Kate plunged her hand into the saddlebag and yanked it out.

Aiming at the nearest drake, she pulled back the hammer with her thumb, then pressed the trigger. The bullet struck the drake square in the head, felling it at once. She pulled the hammer again, aimed for the second drake, and pulled the trigger. The first bullet went wide, but she fired again a second later, and this one hit it in the throat.

With another bullet already in the chamber, she fired a fourth time, and a fifth. The second daydrake went down. She aimed for the third, but Darby reared up, breaking free of her hold on his mind. By the time the horse fell back onto all fours again, the daydrake had reached them. The creature leaped from a crouched position, soaring so high that for a moment it looked like it was really flying, its membranous wings extended out around it like a ghastly cloak. The beast struck her, wrenching her out of the saddle.

She landed hard on her back, her head smacking the ground. But somehow she'd managed to hold on to the gun. The creature's weight crushed against her legs and torso, and its claws raked the ground beside her as it fought to get at her. She pulled back the hammer, struggling to point the barrel toward that jaw opening before her. Jagged teeth glistening with venom filled her vision. Its foul breath burned her nose and throat. With shaking hands, Kate pulled the trigger. Fire burst out from the end of the gun, the noise so deafening she felt that someone was using the inside of her skull for a bell.

But the bullet flew true, crashing into the creature's mouth, through its brain, and out the back of its head. Death came instantly. It fell onto her, pinning her to the ground.

Kate gasped, desperate for breath as the daydrake's weight crushed the air from her lungs. Dropping the revolver, she reached up and tried to push the drake off her. Blood, sticky and hot, flowed over her hands and down her arms from the hole in the creature's head. She pushed and pushed, teeth gritted with the effort. She was barely aware of the tears sliding over her cheeks. It was no good. She wasn't strong enough to free herself from such a weight.

Kate heard Corwin call her name again, but she ignored him, craning her head to find Darby. She spotted the horse in a flat-out run, heading away from the death and terror.

"Stop!" Kate screamed at him, putting all the force of her mind and magic behind it. For a second she thought the distance too far, but then Darby stumbled to a halt. His nostrils flared as he snorted

in protest of her command, the opposite of what his instincts demanded.

Come back here, Kate thought, projecting the image of what she wanted. *I am your herd. Stay with me.* Hesitantly, the horse obeyed. He returned slowly, cautiously, upset by being forced closer to the thing that had nearly killed him.

Kate fought hard to keep the horse under her spell, her magic wrapped tight around his glowing center as she bent his will. Her head spun from the effort, the dizziness made worse from the struggle for each breath. Finally, the horse reached her. She willed him to lower his head so she could grab the reins and pull them over his neck. Sweat darkened the horse's brown coat to black, and he trembled with every movement.

"Easy, boy." Kate ran her hand over his nose. "Now come on, and pull me out of here." She sent the image, guiding him with her magic. Eager at any chance to put more distance between himself and the daydrake, Darby began to back up. It didn't matter that the drake was dead, only that it was still here, fouling the air with its stench.

When the reins grew taut, Darby paused at the uncomfortable pressure of the bridle against his poll. He pinned his ears and stomped a foreleg.

"Go on. I know it's hard, but you'll die without me." She sent him an image of night falling and what would happen then. The horse dug in his back feet, his head reared high as he pulled her free of the daydrake's crushing weight.

"Good boy. Good wonderful, handsome boy." Kate lumbered to her feet and stroked his face. The horse snorted in response, spraying her with gunk. She laughed, light-headed with relief. "Extra grain for you tonight."

Now Darby pressed his head into her chest and gave her stomach a push with his lips. Of all the times not to have a sugar cube tucked away in a pocket. "Soon, I promise," she said, moving his head aside.

"Kate."

The soft cry made her flinch, and her relief gave way to fear. They weren't out of danger yet. Giving Darby a firm command with her magic to stay put, she strode over to the prince, stopping only long enough to retrieve the revolver and reload it with fresh bullets. Then she tucked it into her belt, determined never to be without it again. Bonner would have a treat coming to him, too. *A lifetime's supply of his favorite chocolates.*

Kneeling beside Corwin, Kate surveyed the damage. It was worse than she'd feared. Gashes ran up and down his arms, and four puncture wounds rimmed his shoulder, blood oozing out, sluggish and dark. It made a shocking contrast to the bright red of his face, a sign of the venom burning him from the inside.

"Kate," he said, reaching toward her. "Kate."

"Shhhhh, don't talk." Each time he said her name, her heart lost its rhythm. She needed to concentrate. There was no telling what other damage he might've suffered, and the sun was already dropping toward the horizon. "I'm going to pull you out."

Corwin nodded, and she hoped that he wasn't as far gone as he seemed.

Kate blew out a breath, trying to summon her courage at the idea of touching him. Then she slid her hands beneath his arms, bringing her face alarmingly close to his. Closing her eyes, she tugged. He slid maybe half an inch but no more. Kate leaned back, pulling harder, but it was no use.

She didn't bother trying to move the drake; it was too big. She went in search of rope, finding some in the nearby wreckage. Returning to Corwin, she fastened an end around his chest and the other to Darby's saddle. Then she guided the horse forward. Corwin cried out when the rope squeezed around his injured torso. Kate bit her lip, hating the sound of it but not stopping. *Pain is better than death.*

When it was finally over, Corwin lay panting on the ground, his eyes closed and his sweaty face shining in the fading sunlight. Hesitantly, Kate approached him, her gaze sweeping his body for more damage. Most of his wounds seemed confined to his upper torso, but it was impossible to assess the damage to his legs. There was no blood or visible sign of injury, but that didn't mean the bones hadn't been crushed.

Kate cleared her throat. "Your highness, do you think you can stand? We have to get out of here before dark."

Corwin shifted his legs, drawing them close to his body for leverage. *Not broken, then.* But when he tried to sit up, his trembling arms gave way at once. More blood trickled out from the puncture wounds, and a sweet, noxious smell came with it, like milk gone sour. He needed a healer. He needed a squadron of soldiers. He needed someone who could take care of him and get him away from here.

But he has only me.

Hardening her resolve, Kate set to work. Never in her life had she been quite so thankful for her magic. Without it, she never would've managed to get Corwin in the saddle. She willed Darby to lie down beside the prince. She worried Corwin might remember this later and wonder how she'd made the horse do it, but there was nothing for it. She had to get him out of here. Once the horse was down, she grabbed Corwin under the arms and pulled and pushed and shoved him up, using all her strength.

"You just had to get bigger in the last few years, didn't you?" she whispered, struggling beneath his weight. Then she shouted in his ear, "Please, your highness, you've got to help. We're not going to make it if you don't."

Corwin made some unintelligible noise in answer. Then, with visible effort, he raised his arms, grabbed hold of Darby's saddle, and hauled himself up. With Kate bracing him from behind, Corwin managed to swing a leg over the horse's back. The moment he was in place, Kate willed Darby to stand, urging the horse to be gentle. Even still, Corwin nearly plummeted over the side. It was all she could do to keep him up there.

Once the horse was upright, Corwin slumped forward, leaning awkwardly against Darby's neck. The gelding pinned his ears, but Kate willed him to stay still as she climbed up behind Corwin. Once she was mounted, she pulled Corwin upright until he leaned against her, his broad back as warm as a brick oven and just as hard. In seconds her arms and back began to ache from the effort of holding him in place. Gritting her teeth against the discomfort, she urged Darby forward.

Anything faster than a walk proved impossible. Corwin was too weak to keep his balance, and she was barely strong enough to hold him upright completely on her own. He wavered somewhere near unconsciousness, often muttering under his breath or making soft noises.

Night stalked them, as dangerous as any predator. Kate scanned the horizon again and again, fearful of drakes. The abandoned Relay tower loomed in the distance, but no matter how long they rode, it never seemed to get any closer.

Dusk arrived, quickly turning to twilight. Darby's ears shifted at every sound, the horse on alert for danger. The normal night noises of crickets and birds seemed ominous, each one a possible drake in Kate's imagination. She felt her magic weakening by the second. Any moment now and she would lose her ability to control the horse. But it seemed for once the gods were favoring her—or more likely they were favoring Corwin—for they reached the Relay tower just as full dark set in. There was no hint of drakes about, but Kate didn't waste time. She urged Darby inside, then dismounted.

"Hold still," she said, speaking as much to the horse as to Corwin. The former listened, but the latter, she couldn't be sure. She doubted he was conscious. For the last half hour he'd been utterly silent.

She swung the heavy wooden door closed, then slid all three slats into place. Not that the wood would stop a drake. She needed to set the wardstones and activate them. But first she had to get Corwin out of the saddle before he fell and broke his neck. With her luck, she would be accused of murdering him if that happened.

With her magic gone for the night, she had no choice but to pull Corwin from the saddle herself. She positioned Darby in one of the two stalls filled with old straw. Then she grabbed Corwin about the waist and pulled him toward her. She crumpled beneath his weight, and he landed halfway on top of her. Scrambling out from beneath him, she moved Darby into the other stall, pulled off the saddlebag, then raced up the narrow stairs to the second floor.

The three wardstone embrasures were set around the circular room, forming the three points of the sacred triangle. Kate placed the stones in each one, whispering a prayer that the magic on the embrasures would still work. Any shift in the tower's foundation could cause the enchantment to fail. When she slid the third one into place, she spoke the word of invocation and waited, breath held. A moment later the shimmer of the barrier appeared, and for the first time in hours she breathed easy. They were safe from outside threats.

Now to deal with the ones from inside.

Fighting off a wave of fatigue, Kate made her way back down the stairs. Corwin lay in the same awkward heap he'd landed in.

"Please don't be dead," she whispered, approaching him.

Kate hauled him over, wincing at how roughly she was handling him. Not that she could help it. He was so heavy, as if the drake poison were taking on weight inside him. His forehead burned with fever when she laid her fingers against it. His eyes slid open for a moment, before falling closed again. His breathing deepened, and she hoped he was truly asleep now. She didn't want him awake for this next part.

Steeling her courage, she set about removing his belt and unfastening the buttons on his outer tunic. Once it was undone, she pulled his arms free one at a time. He wore short leather vambraces around each wrist. She unlaced them, pausing for a moment when she saw the tattoo on his right wrist: a hawk with a shield clutched in its talons. Recognition tugged at her mind but she couldn't identify the symbol. Nevertheless, its presence sent a strange flutter through her stomach, a reminder of all the years that had passed since she'd last seen Corwin. He never had the tattoo when she knew him.

He's a different person now, she reminded herself. *As am I.*

His under tunic proved a bigger challenge. She had to pull it up and over his head. He groaned as the fabric grazed his wounds, some of it stuck to him with dried blood. Once it was off, she tossed it aside. Then she looked down on him, trying to ignore his nakedness and focus only on the wounds that needed cleansing. Even still, a flush spread over her skin at the sight of his body, his skin smooth and perfect save for his injuries and the thin line of dark, coarse hair running down from his navel to the waist of his breeches.

Next she retrieved water from the well and set about cleaning the wounds. Her fingers trembled as she ran a wet rag over the gashes. For the puncture wounds, she poured water straight into them. Corwin flinched and came awake enough to cringe. But just as quickly he faded again.

With the wounds finally as clean as possible, she retrieved the jar of salve from her saddlebag. It was meant for horses, but she didn't think it would harm him. At least it couldn't be worse than the drake poison. Gently, Kate began to apply it. His skin was fire against her fingertips. When she finished with this, she would have to wet more rags and drape them over him to fight the fever. She herself was starting to get chilled, but there would be no fire tonight.

Kate became so focused on the task that she failed to notice when Corwin awoke.

"That tickles," he said, capturing her hand where it hovered an inch over his bare chest. His fingers were listless, but his touch was heavy. It sent tingles down her arm.

She stared at him, startled to see he was close to lucid, more than he'd been so far during this long, horrible day. She dropped her gaze, a flush heating her skin once more. "I'm sorry."

"Don't be, Kate, sweet Kate, Traitor Kate. . . ."

She sucked in a breath at his use of her hated moniker. She raised her gaze to his face, for a second believing he'd meant to hurt her with those words, but he wasn't as coherent as he'd momentarily seemed. She waited to see if he would say more. When he didn't, she returned her focus to applying the salve.

Sometime later she heard him draw a ragged breath. "You are so beautiful, Kate Brighton. Did I ever tell you that?"

Once, she thought, her heart beating too rapidly for speaking. *The first time you kissed me.* She stole a glance at him, only to find his blue eyes opened and peering at her. They were bloodshot and bleary, but as alluring as ever, like the sky on a clear, summer day. She looked away.

"I should've told you that every day," he said.

Old memories stirred in Kate's mind, and for the first time in years, they were good ones.

"And your sideways smile. I haven't seen it in so long. Not outside of my dreams."

Now Kate gaped down at him. His words had been slurred together, and one look at his face told her the truth of his delirium, but what he said made her heart wrench. It was cruel to remind her of something that was no more, that could never be again.

"But then your father . . . he had to . . . had to do what he did and ruin everything."

She went still, her emotions churning hard. He was delirious, she knew, maybe worse than before, but he was speaking of things that she had longed to know. Things she had once begged him to tell her. Temptation seized hold of her. She'd waited so long to learn the truth of that night, to hear what he had seen. When they arrested her father, she was forbidden to see him. Corwin was her only hope to understand. Years ago, he'd refused to tell her anything.

"I don't want to hurt you with the truth, Kate," he had said. "Your father attacked mine, nearly killed him. Can't that be enough?"

No. Because the truth is the only way to put the torment to rest, Kate thought now, staring at Corwin's face. His eyes were still open but his gaze wavered, never quite focusing. She knew she shouldn't. It was wrong to press him for truths he'd refused to give before, when he was too weak to tell her no now. She also knew that everything he said might be exaggerated or false in his venom-weakened state. But she would never again have this chance.

I have to know, she thought. *I need peace.*

"He did ruin everything, didn't he?" Kate allowed a smile to curl the side of her face, her sideways smile, as he used to call it. "But I've never understood what really happened. Will you tell me, your highness?"

"Corwin," he said. "I'm always Corwin to you, my sweet Kate."

She bit her tongue and drew a breath deep enough to temper the tremors sliding through her stomach.

"Corwin," she said, the sound of his name in her mouth an exquisite sort of pain. "Please tell me what happened that night. Tell me everything."

THE JOURNEY INTO THE PAST didn't last long. And in the end, Corwin told her little she hadn't heard before, if only as rumor. Her father attacked the king, stabbing him several times with a dagger. He wasn't crazed or possessed, but a man in full control of his faculties. If anything, it was King Orwin who had been crazed that night. Corwin described the way his father had screamed, flailing about, yanking the hair from his head. Afterward, the green robes speculated that the blade Hale had used was tainted with some kind of poison they were never able to identify.

When Corwin finished the story, Kate felt an emptiness expanding inside her. She had allowed herself to hope for more, some insight into the inexplicable. She never denied her father was guilty; she just wanted to understand why. He must have had a reason. But it seemed that was a secret he'd carried with him unto his execution. *The dead tell no truths.*

Biting her lip, Kate stared down at Corwin, whose eyes had closed again. She couldn't tell if he was still conscious or not. "Why didn't you let me see him?"

Corwin's eyes fluttered open, his long, dark lashes a striking contrast to the blue. "He . . . he didn't want to see you. He asked for you to be kept away."

Kate gaped. It was impossible. Her father had known he was to be executed—he never would've stopped her from saying good-bye. He loved her too much to betray her like that.

Like he betrayed the king?

No, she refused to believe it. They were too close, as alike as petals on an everweep flower.

Corwin shifted restlessly on the straw, his eyes closed again. "But he had a message for you."

"What?" Kate leaned over him, her heart beginning to race. "What was it?"

"He said . . . go to Fenmore."

Kate's brow furrowed as she mulled the words over in her mind. Fenmore was a distant land far to the west, across the treacherous Fury Sea. Stories described it as a place so wondrous and strange that those who ventured there never wished to return. Of course, those same stories failed to speculate that perhaps people simply perished in the attempt to find it. It might've been where Kate and Hale would've fled, if he'd been granted a sentence of exile, as she had begged Corwin to make happen.

Her confusion turned to anger. "Why didn't you tell me this before?" When Corwin didn't answer, she shook him, unmindful of his injuries. "Corwin, why didn't you tell me this before?"

His eyes remained closed, and he sounded far away as he answered, "I was so angry at him for hurting my father . . . and at you and Edwin."

"Edwin?" Kate gasped.

She hadn't thought about Corwin's older brother in ages. Growing up, the three of them had sometimes played together, but they weren't close. The rivalry between the two brothers never allowed for it. The last time Kate spoke to Edwin was the night before her father attacked the king. They were in the gardens playing Scouts in the Bailey—Corwin the drake and Kate and Edwin the sheep in hiding. Kate chose her favorite spot, a little cove between the rose-bushes where Corwin would know to find her. She waited with her heart fluttering in anticipation of the kiss Corwin would steal when he caught her. He appeared just moments after he finished count-ing. The ringed moon was waning that night, making it so dark that she couldn't see his face through the shadows when he pulled her into his arms and pressed his lips against hers. Still, she sank into the kiss, her mouth hungry for his. Only it wasn't Corwin, but Edwin—a fact she realized moments later when the real Cor-win found them. Kate had never seen him so furious. She tried to explain, but he stormed off. He stormed all night, it seemed. Why else would he have been awake and roaming the castle at dawn, only to find Hale trying to kill his father?

And I never explained what happened, that I thought Edwin was him, she realized. The mistaken kiss had seemed meaningless in light of her father's crimes, a cruel prank played by a jealous brother.

Kate wanted to press Corwin for more, but he'd fallen asleep, and she couldn't wake him. His stillness frightened her. His skin was still afire, and she wet rags and laid them over his brow, arms, and chest. She spent the night afraid to leave his side. Every few hours a fit would come over him, and he would thrash about, deliri-ous. She held him down as best she could, afraid he would injure himself further.

The moment dawn broke, she saddled Darby. Castle Gilda, the nearest freeholding, was only a few hours up the road. She could get there, entreat Count Gilderan for help, and get back to the Relay tower before sunset. She couldn't risk leaving Corwin alone long enough to make it to Farhold, a whole day away at a quick pace.

When she was ready to go, with Corwin's outer tunic stuffed into her saddlebag as proof of her story, she knelt beside him and shook him awake. "Your highness . . . Prince Corwin."

His eyes fluttered open. They found her face, but she couldn't tell if he was seeing her this time or not.

"There's water and food here for you. I'm going for help. I'll be back before nightfall." She paused, resisting the urge to shake him again, harder this time. "And don't you dare die." *Dear Noralah, please make it so.* It was the first time since her father's death that she'd prayed to the patron goddess of Norgard, but if any of the gods were to help her in this, it would be her.

Kate kept the pace easy at first, well aware of the gelding's fatigue. They hadn't ridden any harder than usual yesterday on the return journey from Andreas, but it was still a lot of miles, and the stress of the drake attack had taken its toll as well.

For the first three hours, nothing moved on the road except for them. It was as if the entire land was holding its breath, perhaps out of fear of the daydrakes, this newest threat in a world already overflowing with danger. *How will we survive when both the night and day are so perilous?*

Kate kept her eyes in a constant sweep, alert for any movement. Only the presence of Bonner's revolver—now fastened to the front of the saddle in its holster—brought her any comfort. She was in such a heightened state of awareness that she spotted the group of riders in the distance long before they saw her. They were little more than specks on the horizon, but a dust cloud heralded their movement, dozens of shod hooves pounding the road. As they drew nearer, she caught the glint of steel. Whoever they were, they rode armed and ready for battle. There was no flag bearer among them, their pace too quick for the burden of it. They could be mercenaries or bandits, but she doubted it. That ilk wouldn't ride so brazenly in the open.

She heeled Darby into a gallop toward them and didn't slow until she saw several of the men draw their bows, arrows nocked.

Reining Darby to a halt, she called, "Good sirs! I need your help!" She pulled Corwin's tunic free from her saddlebag and raised it over her head. "In the name of the high king."

At once, the group moved forward, but they didn't lower their weapons. For a second Kate thought ill fortune had found her again and that they were bandits after all, but then she saw familiar Norgard uniforms and that the man leading them was the same nobleman who'd been with Corwin that day in Farhold. Her spirits lifted. Riding with them were three blue robes and one green, a master healer.

"Kate Brighton!" the nobleman said, reining his horse to a stop. "Is that you? What are you doing here? Where is Corwin?"

"How do you—" she began, then shook off her surprise. "The high prince is alive, my lord, but only just. His caravan was attacked by drakes—ones that moved in the day, un—"

The man cut her off with a raised hand. "We know about the drakes, but you say Corwin's alive? Where?"

"A Relay tower, three hours' ride from here."

"Then let's make it in two." The nobleman waved her on. "Show us the way."

Once they were on the move again, the nobleman introduced himself as Dallin Thorne of Thornewall. "But you may call me Dal. Tell me, though, were there any others left alive?"

"No, my lord," Kate replied. "Not that I found." She brushed hair back from her face, scanning the hills ahead but seeing only a rainbow growth of everweeps swaying in the breeze. "Excuse me, my lord, but how did you know about the attack?"

Dal motioned to the blue robe riding silently beside them at the head of the group. "Master Raith was with Corwin's caravan. He managed to escape and come for help."

Kate frowned, questions crowding into her mind. "Do you know what these creatures are, then?" She addressed Dal, but her gaze lingered on the magist, face hidden behind his mask. The man's fingers were blackened at the tips, bent at a stiff angle around the reins.

"We know only as much as you do. Nightdrakes that attack in the day."

"Daydrakes," Kate said.

"Yes, that's a good name, I suppose. Only I hope you're wrong. If these creatures breed and spread like nightdrakes . . ." Dal trailed off.

Master Raith turned his masked face toward Kate. "Please, Miss Brighton, describe Prince Corwin's injuries. Was he bitten?"

"Yes," she replied, a little breathless at the idea of talking to a magist. She couldn't forget for a second who she was and what she could do. Not in front of this man or the other magists present. If they detected her magic, she would be the next target of the Inquisition. "A single bite in the shoulder, but I cleaned the wounds and applied some of the salve we riders carry for our horses. He was still feverish when I left him this morning."

Raith nodded. "He's lucky to have survived so long, and that you came along when you did. I believed all had been lost."

"How did *you* survive?" The question escaped her lips before good sense could stop it. The magist couldn't have outrun them. No horse could, and drakes loved a moving target.

Dal gestured to the sky, palm up and fingers spread. "With magic, of course."

"And luck," Raith added. "Only one chased after me. I blinded it with a flash stone, one of my own inventions. But tell me, Miss Brighton, how do you know these drakes moved in the day?"

"Oh, um, there were . . . two . . . still alive when I came upon it," she lied. She didn't want these men knowing she had felled four when only one had been killed with enchanted arrows. They would want to know how she managed the other three, and—with a gun fashioned by wilder magic—that wasn't an answer she wanted to give. The very thought of Bonner being taken by the Inquisition was enough to freeze the blood in her veins. It wasn't just death he would face, but the Purging.

Dal gaped at her. "And you survived?"

"Yes," she said, feeling the hot stench of that breath against her face again. Now she understood why these men had been riding ready for battle. It could happen again, at any time.

"Impressive," Raith said.

"I think we call that understatement." Dal eyed her with new-found interest.

Kate looked away from both men, swallowing a ball of nerves rising up her throat. "They train us well at the Relay house."

"Indeed they must," Dal agreed.

They made it back to the Relay tower in less than three hours, their horses lathered with sweat and heads drooping. But each second was precious to Corwin's life. Kate didn't know much about drake venom—so few people survived attacks, let alone escaped after being close enough to get bitten—but she knew it was bad. The fever it caused could go so high it wrought permanent damage. But the magists would know what to do, she reassured herself. Their spells were vast and powerful—*and expensive*. Corwin was lucky he'd been born rich enough to afford such treatment.

Dal charged into the tower first, Raith and the green robe following. Kate stayed outside with the soldiers and remaining blue robes. Despite her fatigue, she couldn't remain still as she waited for word on Corwin's condition. She busied herself removing Darby's saddle and fetching him water, her eyes drifting to the closed door into the tower again and again. Corwin had been alone close to six hours now.

Minutes later, Dal and Master Raith remerged.

"He's alive," Dal announced.

Kate took a deep breath and leaned against Darby's sweat-slicked shoulder, light-headed with relief. If Corwin had made it this long, he would surely survive, and this would all be behind her soon.

"We need to make camp," Raith said. He motioned to the other magists. "First set the wardstone barrier in a wide perimeter around the tower. Then report to me. I'll need help seeing to the prince."

With orders given, activity burst around her, but Kate just stood there, unsure what to do with herself now. It was too late to head for Farhold, and Darby was much too spent. Neither could she go into the tower and make herself at home with the magists at work in there.

Dal approached her moments later. "I'm afraid you'll have to stay the night out here, Miss Kate. But I see you have your bedroll. Is there anything else you need from the tower?"

Kate shook her head, the motion making her dizzy. Exhaustion had caught up with her now that the stress of caring for Corwin was someone else's responsibility.

"When was the last time you ate?" Dal eyed her with open concern.

"I don't recall."

"Well then, come sit down over here, and we'll get you taken care of. Can't have the savior of the high prince expiring on us." He steered her toward the edge of the tower where the land rose in an easy slope.

"My horse . . ."

"I'll see to him. You've done enough." Dal smiled broadly at her, but there was a command in his voice that she dared not argue against. She grabbed her bedroll off her saddle, spread it out, and sat down. "I'll have someone bring you food," he continued. "And don't you waste a moment worrying about Corwin. He'll be fine. We both know he's got a lot to live for." Dal winked, as if this were some private joke between them, then turned and led her horse away.

Kate leaned back on the bedroll, vowing not to fall asleep, but less than a minute later, she drifted off into oblivion.

When she woke it was full dark. She noticed the stars first, a thousand bright points above her, as if the gods had punched holes in the fabric of the sky to reveal a universe of pure light beyond. So few times in her life had she ever seen the stars like this, near enough to touch, it seemed, and without the haze that so often blanketed the sky above the cities.

Lured by the sounds of camp, Kate sat up slowly and looked around, taking in the sight of Norgard soldiers gathered around the fire, eating and drinking. She was lying in the same position in which she'd fallen asleep, near the tower. Not far from her, Dal sat atop his own bedroll, cleaning his sword.

"She wakes," Dal said, spying her. "Welcome back to the realm of the living. I've never seen a woman sleep so soundly before."

Kate rubbed her eyes. "How long have I been out?"

"Nearly six hours, I would say. But rightly earned." He motioned to her. "Have some food and drink, and when you're finished, you can tell me all about this." Dal set the sword down beside him and picked up Kate's revolver.

Her heart gave a lurch. "Do you make a habit of stealing other people's things?" she said, forgetting for a moment that he was the noble and she the peasant.

To her surprise, though, Dal laughed. The black magestone in his ear winked in the firelight. "A mouth indeed. Well, you can't just leave a weapon like this in plain view and expect a man to ignore it. Especially one like me."

Kate cursed inwardly. How could she have been so stupid? Of course he would be curious about such an unusual pistol. She could see that he had removed the bullets from the chamber, each one spread in a careful line before him.

Worried how she could safely explain her way out of this, Kate reached for the plate of food and began to eat. She did it slowly, hoping to delay the conversation about Bonner's revolver.

"Oh, in case you were wondering, Corwin's already on the mend," Dal said, handing her a cup of wine. "Master Raith says it will be a long recovery, but he's safe to move. We already have a litter built to carry him back to Farhold in the morning."

Kate took a long, deep drink, the wine finer than any she'd tasted in years. "That's good news. I will be leaving come morning as well."

Dal's eyebrows rose. "On your own?"

"I need to get back to the Relay house as soon as possible. I can move faster than a caravan."

"That is certainly true." Dal fixed a penetrating stare at her. His eyes, despite their intensity, sparkled with some unknown mirth. "Only, will you stay long enough to speak with Corwin in the morning? If he's coherent, I mean. I'm sure he will want to see you."

"I doubt it." She took another quick swallow of wine. *And I certainly don't want to see him.* Now that she knew he would live, her anger at him had returned in force. *Go to Fenmore,* her father had said. Was it because of the danger she faced as a traitor's daughter? Or was there some other meaning in the message? Try as she might, she couldn't come up with an explanation.

Dal smiled but didn't press the issue, allowing her to finish her meal in silence as he set the revolver down once more and resumed cleaning his sword. He seemed to be doing it out of either bore-dom or compulsive habit. The sword was already immaculate, the steel smooth and glistening. The ivory hilt, carved in the shape of a hawk with two rubies for eyes, glowed white.

Kate turned to look at the soldiers near the fire as one of them began to sing an old, familiar song. "The Ride of Adair," the story of the first king of Norgard. Kate's father used to sing it to her every night, trying in vain to settle her down for sleep, but the story the song told was far too exciting for that. It made young Kate want to jump up and down on her bed while she slew invisible dragons atop her warhorse.

As she listened now, older and far different from that little girl, longing for the past filled her chest, squeezing the air from her lungs. She drew a deep breath and tried to tune the song out. It was like trying not to feel the wind on your face at full gallop.

"Tomorrow," Dal said, his voice breaking into her thoughts, "Master Raith and I will return to where the caravan was attacked. We need to learn more of these daydrakes. I know you're eager to get back, but would you like to accompany us? It shouldn't take long, and your experience with them might offer some insight."

Kate bit her lip, uncertain if this was a request or a command veiled as one. She didn't know him well enough to tell. She had never heard of Thornewall but guessed it was a minor house and holding.

"You don't have to if you don't wish, of course," Dal continued in her silence. "I imagine the visit will be unpleasant."

"You're right about that." She didn't want to guess what a day left out in the summer sun had done to those corpses. "But I must decline. I have to get back to Farhold as soon as possible. The Relay riders need to be warned of this new threat."

The thought chilled her. Signe would have left for her next ride already. What if she was attacked? Would the Relay even be able to continue if these daydrakes proved as big a menace as their night-time kin? It was a possibility too horrible to consider. Kate needed this job. There was nothing else she was fit for, nothing else she wanted to do. She stood little chance of marrying, and she couldn't fathom a life where she didn't get to ride.

"If you're finished eating now," Dal said, resting his sword atop his crossed legs, "please tell me more about this remarkable pistol." He picked it up and rotated the cylinder. "I've never seen its like before, but if I'm not mistaken, it can fire multiple rounds without reloading."

Kate nodded, her lips pressed together. She tried to come up with some passable lie, but failed. *The partial truth then.*

"It's called a revolver. My friend made it. He's a blacksmith in Farhold. Gunsmithing is his hobby."

"Indeed." Dal turned the revolver over in his hands, examining it with a strange intensity. For the first time, Kate noticed the scars on his arms, several long, thick lines, surely the result of some bat-tle. She wondered where he'd gotten them. He was far too young to have fought in the Sevan Invasion, the last war on Rimish soil. And there was the magestone in his ear as well, the kind that usually held spells to hide disfigurement.

Dal looked up. "Does it work as well as a pistol?"

Kate hesitated, but only for a moment. "For the most part."

"Your friend must be truly remarkable," Dal said with a note of awe in his voice. He began to slide the bullets back into the chamber. "There are gunsmiths who've spent years trying to create something like this. I would like to fire it and see how it works for myself." He made as if to get up.

Kate felt herself pale. "Excuse me, my lord, but now doesn't seem the best time. It's late and guns are loud."

Dal made a face, the gesture turning his handsome features boyish—although no less handsome. "You're right, I suppose. And I wouldn't want to disturb Corwin. He can be quite grumpy when woken up early." Sighing, he handed the revolver to her.

Kate smiled, relieved to have the gun back in her possession—now if she could just get Dal to forget that he'd seen it. "When the prince was small, his mother called him her little bear for that precise reason."

"Did she now? I didn't know that. Little bear." Dal laughed. "Maybe it's time to resurrect the moniker."

"Please don't," Kate said quietly, her eyes dropping to her lap. "I shouldn't have told you that. Corwin can be touchy about his mother's memory. Or at least he used to be."

"Don't worry, I won't repeat it. He's still that way about her." Dal shook his head, smiling again. "It's so strange to be around someone who knows him better than I do."

Kate frowned. "I *used* to know him, my lord. But not anymore."

There must've been something more in her voice than she intended, for Dal's expression turned apologetic. "I'm sorry, Miss Brighton. I didn't mean to stir up bad memories. Please forgive me."

She shrugged. "It's fine. I shouldn't be so sensitive about it. The past is the past."

Dal gave a skeptical cough, as if this was in doubt, but he didn't comment on it.

They passed a few minutes in silence, listening as one of the guards began to sing a new song, this one a crude ballad that Kate had only ever heard since becoming a Relay rider.

Finally, she worked up the nerve to ask, "Where is your home? I've never heard of Thornewall."

"That's not surprising," Dal said with a snort. He picked up his sword and returned it to its sheath. "It's a small freeholding on the eastern cliffs overlooking the Penlaurel River. My father is Baron of Thornewall. Thankfully I am not the heir. One of the many advantages of being the sixth-born son."

Kate didn't quite believe him. His tone reminded her of the way Corwin used to sound whenever they discussed the long-absent uror sign.

"How is it you know the high prince?" she asked, curiosity getting the better of her.

"Ah, now that is a story." Dal leaned back on his bedroll, head cocked toward the night sky. "But sadly, not one I'm permitted to tell."

"Why not?"

"Because I met him on my travels. Or his travels, as it were."

"Oh." Kate's eyes widened in surprise. "You mean during those years he disappeared from Rime."

Dal cracked his knuckles. "It's a secret every newsman would give his right hand to print."

As if I would tell, Kate thought, crossing her arms. She had no love for newsmen. She knew she shouldn't be offended—Dal didn't know her, after all—but part of her irritation was from disappointment. She would like to know what Corwin had been doing in those missing years. She remembered the hawk and shield tattoo and once again felt she ought to have recognized it, but still she couldn't.

"Not that I believe you would tell," Dal said, sounding somber now. "But it's not my right to share his secret. Corwin might never forgive me if I did, and his good opinion matters more to me than anything else in the world."

Kate stared at Dal, her curiosity mingling with a hint of jealousy. She'd once felt the same about Corwin, and the reminder of that lost friendship stung. All their lives, they'd been the best of friends, comrades in mischief and mayhem. So many times they'd gotten caught running midnight races on the training fields or filching sweets from the kitchens the night before some important ball. Once, they'd even set fire to a castle storeroom on accident, both refusing to tell the truth about what happened for fear of getting the other in trouble.

I am not that carefree, reckless girl any longer, she thought, trying to bury the memory deep inside her. She wondered if the same was true of Corwin. Given the way Dal talked about him, she thought it must be.

"Have no fear, though," Dal said. "I wouldn't be surprised if Corwin tells you all about it one day soon. Just make sure you listen with a skeptical ear to anything he says about himself that makes him seem less than heroic. It's not true, and I will enjoy explaining why once I'm allowed."

Kate raised her brows at this cryptic message, her curiosity spiking even higher. Then the implication of what he was saying struck her, and she shook her head. "I doubt very much I'll ever speak to him again."

A smirking and altogether irritating grin rose on Dal's face. "We shall see, my dear Kate. We shall see."

"IF YOU DON'T GET OUT of that bed soon, I will surely expire from boredom."

The voice, amused, lighthearted, and familiar, called out to Corwin through a haze of sleep so deep he thought it was a part of the dream. But then a loud, obnoxious yawning sound reached him next, and he knew it was real. Slowly, the prince opened his eyes and blinked against the light.

Dal sat on a chair beside the bed, his feet propped up on a lace-covered end table. His expression looked far from bored when his gaze met Corwin's. "He lives!" Dal clapped his hands. "Alert all the maidens in the land and let them rejoice. Or maybe just one maiden in particular."

"What are you going on about?" Each word felt like gravel in Corwin's throat, and he started to cough.

Dal slid his feet from the table and stood to pour a glass of water from a nearby pitcher. He held the glass out to Corwin. "Don't you remember?"

Corwin stared at his friend, his thoughts clouded at first, then slowly parting into clarity. "The caravan was attacked by night-drakes, only it was in the day." He sat up, his aching body barely a match for the thick, soft mattress that seemed to drag him down again. "Kate was there."

Dal tsked. "You're sorely behind the times, my friend. We're calling them daydrakes these days. And that attack was more than two weeks ago."

"Two weeks?" Corwin gaped, his dry, cracked lips protesting painfully.

"Just drink this already." Dal shoved the glass toward Corwin again. "You sound like a toad."

Corwin accepted it and took a long drink that burned down his throat and into his belly.

With his duty accomplished, Dal resumed his seat. "The green robes have been keeping you asleep with some potion or other. They claim it was necessary for your recovery. Something about the way drake venom lingers in the blood. It made no sense to me." Dal shrugged. "But then again, I'm not a healer. How's the shoulder?"

It took Corwin's sluggish mind a moment to catch up to Dal's rapid chatter. Then he remembered a drake had bitten his shoulder. He raised his left arm and felt the twinge of flesh not quite healed beneath a thick bandage.

"It's more bearable than your nattering. How did I get here, anyway?" Giving the room a glance, Corwin recognized it as the same one he'd stayed in before when he visited Farhold. Green curtains trimmed with golden tassels hung around the large canopied bed, all drawn back at the moment to let in the breeze coming through the opened window across the room.

"Nattering indeed." Dal huffed, then launched into a story about Kate coming upon the caravan not long after the attack and rescuing him. Images, broken and confused, spun through Corwin's mind. He remembered her being there, and how his fear for her had surpassed the pain of his injuries. And yet, she survived. *She saved me.* More memories came to him, of the bleary journey to the tower. Then of the way she had tended his wounds, her fingers on his skin. Tingles rippled down his body at the recollection.

"Where is Kate now?" Corwin said, cutting Dal off in the middle of another rambling sentence.

A sly grin slid over his friend's face. "In the city. I've been keeping an eye on her for you. She's been grounded from making any Relay runs. All the women riders have been, with the threat of these daydrakes."

Corwin frowned. "I bet she's not happy about that."

"My informant tells me she's as friendly as a half-starved rattlesnake." Dal assumed a deep, gruff voice. "'It's a very good thing that young lady doesn't have sharp teeth or she might bite someone.' That's a direct quote."

"Yes, you can see my surprise, I'm sure." Corwin took another drink, hiding a smile. Perhaps Kate hadn't changed so much after all. "Tell me the rest. I remember the Relay tower, but little beyond that."

"Well, after your sweet damsel rescued you and carried you off to safety, she went for help. I was already out looking for you, thanks to Master Raith, who, gods be good, managed to escape the attack with his life. We came upon her around midday. She led us back to the tower and the magists got to work fixing you. We brought you back to Farhold, and you've been stuck in this bed ever since."

The notion turned Corwin's stomach. It reminded him too much of his sickly father. Despite the fatigue weighing him down, he swung his legs over the side of the bed, determined to get up. *Just not yet,* he thought as a dizzy spell struck him. He squeezed his eyes closed until it passed.

"How did Master Raith escape?"

"He's a wily one, that one," Dal said. "He used something called flash stones. They're newly sanctioned, apparently. They blinded the creatures long enough for him to get away."

Corwin scooted to the edge, planting both feet on the thick carpet. "Have there been other attacks?"

Dal shook his head. "Fortunately, no. There haven't been any sightings of these daydrakes."

"None at all?" Nothing about this made sense. Looking back, Corwin didn't think there'd been more than nine or ten of the beasts that had attacked the caravan, less than in a typical nightdrake pack, and yet it had been more than enough to destroy them. *We weren't ready.* They hadn't restocked the enchanted arrows before setting out that morning. Corwin hadn't believed there was a need, and he'd been impatient to get moving.

"I've not even seen one yet." Dal crossed his arms and gave a huff.

"What?" Corwin clutched at the bedpost as he tried to summon the strength to stand.

Dal stepped forward and offered him a hand. "It's true. Master Raith and I visited the remains of the caravan. All the drake corpses were gone."

"Gone?" Getting to his feet, Corwin swayed a moment, gripping Dal's hand hard for balance.

"Yes, gone. And that hurts, by the way."

Corwin let go, locking his knees into place as Dal continued.

"All we found were signs of something heavy having been dragged away. It didn't even look like a drake attack. All the dead horses and men were still there, just lying in the road."

Uneaten, Corwin heard the implication. He shuddered, guilt twisting his insides as he pictured Master Barrett, Captain Morris, Stormdancer, the guards. All dead. He was their prince. *And I failed them.* Corwin glanced down at the tattoo on his wrist, the hawk and shield symbol mocking him, as always—reminding him of the other men he'd failed.

"Don't you do that," Dal said, catching him in the glance. "How many times do I have to tell you that what happened wasn't your fault? There's no way you could've—"

Corwin cut him off with a raised hand, uninterested in the old argument. "Will you please fetch me a robe?"

With a loud grunt, Dal spun away to grab the robe from the wardrobe just beyond. He returned a moment later and helped Corwin into it. Corwin would've preferred to get out of the dressing gown he was wearing, but he didn't feel up to it just yet, and he had no wish to call for a servant. In the two years he'd been gone from Rime, he'd learned to live without such things. He preferred it that way, finding freedom in simple tasks.

Fastening the cord around his waist, Corwin turned and walked over to the sitting area, where he dropped onto one of the sofas. The effort left him panting. Parts of his body hurt that he didn't even know existed.

"I've been wondering," Dal said, following after him, "if the attack on the caravan is connected to what happened at the Gregors'." He took the chair opposite Corwin.

"Why would you think that?" Corwin slowly rotated his neck, bones popping and muscles screaming.

"Because of the disappearing drakes. That Andrean miner was burning a drake corpse, presumably to hide its presence. We assumed it was a nightdrake, but what if it wasn't? And surely whoever removed the daydrake corpses had similar motivations—to hide their existence."

Corwin drew a deep breath, confusion muddling his thoughts as he tried to make sense of it. Drakes were wild beasts, deadly and unpredictable. But Dal's speculation made it seem as if the attack on the caravan had been deliberate, same as the attack on the Gregors, as if someone was controlling these drakes and using them like weapons. *Highly effective weapons.* The Gregors were all dead, or presumed to be. Perhaps someone wanted him dead as well. *But why?* As it stood now, Edwin would become high king and not Corwin. He hardly mattered by comparison.

Corwin waved the thought away. "I think that's a bit of a leap at this point."

"Perhaps." Dal stretched his hands high above his head, yawning. "I suppose it doesn't matter anyway considering we've been relieved of all obligations to investigate these daydrakes. Oh, and your peacekeeping tour is officially over. We are to return to Norgard as soon as you've recovered."

"Let me guess," Corwin said, rolling his eyes. "Is that another direct quote? From my brother?"

"Indirect. The word came signed from the high king."

"Of course it did." Corwin leaned back on the sofa and rubbed his temples. He should be relieved, thrilled actually—he was finally free to do as he wished, and the gods knew he had no desire to deal with such evil tidings. And yet, he didn't want to just let it go. The mystery nagged at him, demanding to be solved. *And the dead avenged.*

Corwin sat forward again. "What does Edwin say about the Gregors?"

"Very little." Dal pulled a dagger from his belt and began to clean beneath his fingernails with the tip. "Officially, it's been declared a terrible tragedy, and that was that. No mention of the Rising."

"Of course not. Edwin wouldn't want to alarm the public by blaming wilders." Corwin paused, thinking it over. "He's probably glad of it. With Marcus Gregor dead, there's one less dissenter among the nobles." Several choice curse words rose up in Corwin's mind, but before he could voice them his stomach gave a loud growl.

Snickering, Dal said, "Think I'd better call for some food."

"Yes, I suppose that's wise." Except Corwin didn't feel hungry in the slightest, despite his protesting stomach—it was anger at his brother's presumption with ordering him home that pulsed inside him. While he'd vowed to obey, to finally submit to Edwin as the next high king and heir, he struggled against his own independent nature at every turn. Especially now, with this puzzle set before him.

Dal disappeared, leaving Corwin alone with his thoughts. Forcing his mind off Edwin, he soon found himself thinking about Kate, remembering fragments of their time together in the Relay tower. They'd spoken about her father and why he never delivered Hale's message to her—his childish anger at the kiss she'd shared with Edwin, one his brother claimed later had been an accident,

Kate mistaking him for Corwin.

The truth shamed him now, but back then her actions had seemed almost worse than Hale's attack on the high king. He'd never had a chance to confront her about it, but he couldn't quite believe it had been accidental. It had looked so willing. Seeing her in the arms of someone else had driven home the terrible truth he'd been trying to deny—that she could never be his. He was the high prince, destined to marry a princess or someone from a noble house. Not the daughter of the master of horse.

Sighing, Corwin forced his thoughts elsewhere. He struggled to recall all he could about the daydrake attack. He'd managed to slay several of them, but it hadn't been enough. There were too many, the creatures too powerful and relentless in their attack. The luck of Redama, goddess of fortune, must've been with him when he took down that last drake. It landed on top of him, hiding him from the view and scent of the others. But it forced him to lie there while he listened to the shrieks of dying horses and men, helpless to stop it. He must've passed out for a time, but then Kate arrived. She'd been attacked herself, by three—*no, four*—drakes, he remembered with sudden, certain clarity. The panic of seeing them bearing down on her was enough to drive off what remained of his delirium. The first she took down with enchanted arrows. But the remaining three . . .

"Food will be here shortly," Dal said, returning. He flopped down on an armchair and swung one leg over the side, as if the effort of calling for food had been taxing.

"Did you talk to Kate yourself?" Corwin asked, a part of him dreading the topic.

A grin split Dal's face. "Why, yes, I did. She was far too cordial with me though. I only got a glimpse of the feisty thing you described. I believe she reserves most of that for you."

Corwin shifted in his seat, unsure if he was annoyed or pleased. "Did she tell you about the attack?"

"A little. She claimed to have killed two drakes." Dal winked. "Like I said. She is your damsel in shining Relay tunic. Although personally, I'm keen to see her in a dress and with her hair combed and face washed."

Corwin ignored the comment, tame by Dal's standards. "She didn't kill just two. She killed four. I saw it. She took down the first with enchanted arrows, but the other three she slew with a single pistol."

Dal jerked upright, eyes widening. "The revolver!"

Corwin winced at his shouting. "The what?"

"The revolver, she called it." Excitement strained Dal's voice. "It can hold six bullets at once. She said her friend made it, a blacksmith here in Farhold. But you say she killed three drakes with it?"

With the memory growing sharper in his mind, Corwin nodded.

"Holy mother of horses," Dal said, his mouth hanging open. "I think I might need one for myself."

"You and me both, especially if there are more of these day-drakes out there. Did she mention the name of this blacksmith?"

"Afraid not. She didn't seem keen on talking about it much." Dal scratched at his cheek. "One might even say she was cagey about it."

Corwin sat forward in his chair, his excitement over a gun that could fell so many drakes tempered only by his nervousness at seeking out Kate to learn more. It was one thing to have talked to her in the state of delirium he'd been under; it would be quite another to face her now that he wasn't under duress.

Still, it must be done. A weapon like that was the kind of invention that could change the world—the way the steam engine was slowly transforming countries like Endra and Rhoswen that didn't have magic to rely on as they did in Rime. With enough of those weapons in enough hands, they might even be able to slay all the drakes and free Rime from a life behind walls and wardstones.

"You say she's been grounded?" Corwin asked.

Dal slowly nodded. "She's spending every day at the Relay house though. You can find her there right now, I'm sure."

Corwin shook his head. "Not today. I can barely stand, let alone sit a horse."

"I see. But this means you will go see her then?"

"Yes, eventually."

Dal pressed his lips together, stifling a smile, while his eyes sparkled with amusement. "I'm coming with you. I'm dying to meet the feisty Kate you spoke of."

Corwin sighed "Let's just hope she doesn't decide to bite me."

"On the contrary," Dal said. "That's exactly what I'm hoping for."

EVENTUALLY PROVED TO BE NEARLY a week. That was how long it took for Corwin to regain some measure of strength—and to deal with all the other business pressing for his attention. Governor Prewitt had been in to see him at least twice each day, always with an air of sincere concern over his welfare. Corwin knew better; the governor was just eager for him to depart. Corwin was, too.

There'd been no news on the Gregors. In the weeks since the attack on the freeholding, no one had seen or heard a word about the entire family. Officially, they'd been declared dead. Corwin didn't doubt it, given the utter destruction of their home. It had also been confirmed that wilder magic was responsible for the fire and other damage. The two magists who'd examined the body of the dead Andrean miner finally identified the magic that killed him as a form of spirit magic. Their authority on such matters was absolute. One was a white robe, whose order dealt in the high arts, those spells too complex for everyday application. The other a gold robe, the order in charge of detecting wilder magic and the running of the Inquisition. The confirmation made Corwin uneasy, especially given Dal's speculation that the two attacks were connected. At a minimum the Rising was gaining in power.

"Do you think wilders could have created these daydrakes somehow?" Corwin had asked the magists. "Like how they were supposed to have unleashed the nightdrakes upon us?"

The gold robe made an exaggerated motion with his hand. "Anything is possible with wild magic, your highness. All the more reason it must be eradicated."

Such was the mantra of every magist. Corwin didn't know what to make of it, except to feel certain that if there were answers, they lay in Andreas. Despite his brother's command, he planned to head there before returning to Norgard. Dal had already commissioned an artist to draw the miner's face so they might learn his identity.

But first Corwin had to talk to Kate. It felt a little like preparing for battle. He forced food down his gullet as often as he could and took to walking up and down every flight of stairs in the governor's mansion. When he was finally able to make it all the way to the top floor without feeling faint, he declared himself ready—despite his lingering certainty that he would never be ready.

The next morning, Corwin and Dal headed for the Relay house. Although he wanted to go without escort, Governor Prewitt insisted on sending four guards with them. Corwin reluctantly agreed but ordered them not to carry the royal banner—and no trumpeters either. The royal tour was over, after all.

Not that it made a difference. Everyone still recognized him. Even though he'd dressed in a plain tunic, forgoing the royal sigil anywhere, his likeness had been posted in every newspaper across Rime far too often of late for anonymity. What with his disappearance and sudden return, he was a mystery that kept the press in print. Doubtless, some of the servants in the governor's household had been paid handsomely to provide notice of the high prince's movements as well. The moment Corwin appeared on the street, the crowds converged.

It made for slow going, the four guards a weak force to part the crowd. Halfway there a woman dressed in rags and smelling like a tavern privy managed to get past the guards and race up to Corwin's borrowed horse. The mare shied away, snorting, but the woman grabbed onto the reins.

"Mercy, your highness!" she shrieked, unmindful of getting trampled. "Mercy!" The guards seized her at once and started to haul her away. "Mercy for my husband! He's been banished!"

Corwin gritted his teeth, a muscle ticking in his jaw. Banishment was the cruelest of sentences handed down by local judges. Execution was arguably kinder than the uncertainty of being sent outside the city walls without protection. By nightfall, the condemned would become drake fodder. Corwin wished he could just ignore the woman, but there were too many eyes on him, including Dal, who watched with a mouth half opened in dismay.

"Stop," Corwin commanded the guards. "Let her speak. What is your husband's crime?"

The woman dropped her head in some semblance of a bow. "They say he killed a man, your highness, but my Joe couldn't have done. He's a good man, your highness. A kind man. Mercy!"

Corwin took in her tear-streaked face and the brittle, hopeful look in her eyes. Pity swelled inside him, and he wished for the power to end her suffering.

"Her husband was a drunk, your highness," one of the Farhold guards said. "He killed a man in a tavern brawl."

Corwin sighed. It was a common enough story, and he knew without asking that banishment was always the sentence for such a crime in Farhold, same as it was in many of the cities of Rime. Violence could not be tolerated. Life behind these cities' walls was too confining to allow the possibility for panic or mayhem. Punishment must be swift. *But it should also be absolute,* Corwin's father insisted, which was why banishment was not employed in Norgard. Loved ones of the condemned needed the closure of a certain death so that they would not spend the rest of their lives in futile hope that their relative had survived and might one day return.

If only Norgard laws were Rimish laws.

"When was the man's punishment carried out?" Corwin asked the guard who'd spoken.

"Nigh on a week ago, your highness."

And there it was, although Corwin knew there would be no convincing this distraught woman of the truth. Instead he relied on the advice Edwin had drilled into him before he'd come on this tour: to avoid any political entanglements. "I'm truly sorry, but the high king is not above the law. What the judges of Farhold have decreed must stand."

The woman's mournful tears turned to anger, and she spat at him. "Coward. Coward! What good's a high king who won't rule and do right? What good? What—" The guards covered her mouth, silencing her as they hauled her away.

Relief swept over Corwin once it was over, but the woman's words continued to echo inside his head. *What good, indeed. A prince without power. That's who I am.* If only the rest of the world would finally come to accept it. Although he would never wish his father dead, he wanted it to be over, for Edwin to be named heir and for him to be free of the expectation at last.

When they arrived at the Relay house, the Relay master welcomed them in with palpable enthusiasm, an expression exaggerated by the way his eyes seemed to protrude from his head. "Please come in. The grooms will see to your horses."

"Thank you," Corwin replied, handing over his horse's reins to one of the stable boys who approached them. "We are here to see Miss Kate Brighton."

The Relay master seemed to deflate a little. "Miss Brighton? Oh, yes, she is here, but I'm afraid she's due to run a trial any moment. We're holding qualifications today, you see. Our current riders have to requalify, and the new hopefuls will be tested this afternoon."

"A trial?" Dal arched his head, sounding delighted. "I'm sure his highness would like to see that, if we may."

Corwin nodded, and again the Relay master looked disappointed. Rubbing his hands together, he gave an awkward little bow, his foppish white curls bouncing. "As you wish."

The man led them through the stable yard to the training fields situated in the back of the complex. A grandstand resided at the side of the field, more than half the seats occupied. "The trials always draw spectators," the Relay master explained over his shoulder.

For a moment, Corwin hoped the crowd would allow him to blend in and go unnoticed, but as always, the gods were working against him where Kate was concerned. Astride a stocky chestnut with a white blaze running down his nose, she was facing the fence that ran in front of the stands when he arrived. As if by some magnetic force, her gaze caught his at once. The color blanched from her face, and she jerked her head to the side, steering the horse away from the stands. Corwin winced, hoping that his presence wouldn't interfere with her trial.

She seemed unaffected, however, as she asked the horse for a trot, then a loping canter. Keeping his attention centered on Kate, Corwin climbed into the stands and sat in the second row, a place opening up for him at once as the people realized who he was. Excited murmurs echoed all around him.

Dal let out a low whistle. "The girl can ride."

"Did you expect something less?" Corwin shot him an amused look. "Her father was master of horse at Norgard. Not a position easily won."

"Maybe so," replied Dal, "but he might've required his daughter to study more womanly pursuits."

Corwin laughed. "Not Hale." The sudden affection he felt for the man took him by surprise. It had been years since he'd thought of Hale Brighton with something other than hatred. But once, he'd loved him like a second father. "He always encouraged her where horses were concerned," Corwin added. "If she'd been a boy, you would've thought Hale was training Kate to take over as master of horse."

"Didn't her mother object?" Dal glanced at Corwin, frowning.

Picturing the small, wispy woman, Corwin grimaced. "Lynette Brighton never went against her husband's wishes. At least not directly. You've never met a more passive person. She's the opposite of Kate in every way, meek and decorous."

"You mean boring." Dal wrinkled his nose. "I would say you're lying, but I know better." Craning back his head, he peered up at the bright sky. "Thank you, sweet gods and goddesses, for not dooming us all to become our parents." Lowering his head once more, he added, "I'll bet the woman isn't happy her daughter is now a Relay rider."

"I doubt she knows," Corwin replied. "After Hale's death she returned to her father's house in Kilbarrow. Lady Brighton is the fourth-born daughter of Baron Reece."

Dal scratched at his unshaven face. "It's hard to believe Kate was once part of the gentry." The magestone in his ear looked dull this morning, a sure sign it was beginning to fade, and Corwin made a mental note to have it replaced before they left Farhold. It was his fault Dal had to wear it, after all.

"I know what you mean," Corwin said, thinking about the Relay master's reaction when they'd asked for her. "When Hale was condemned, Kate refused to renounce him and lost any such claims to land or station. Her lady mother, however, did not. She returned to Kilbarrow, leaving her daughter to her own means."

"She sounds like a peach." Dal leaned over the edge of the grandstands to spit in emphasis.

They fell silent as Kate's trial began. She lined up her mount in front of the starting pole on the far side of the field, her gaze fixed on the flag bearer at center. Two judges stood next to the flag bearer, one holding a pocket watch to record Kate's time and the other carrying parchment and pen to record errors. The field was divided into three lanes, each designed to test a particular skill—arrow, lance, and sword.

When the flag bearer lowered the standard, Kate sent her horse forward and drew her bow, heading down the farthest lane. She pulled an arrow from her quiver and let it fly in one quick, seamless movement. It slammed into the first archery target only an inch outside the bull's-eye. Before it had even landed, Kate twisted her body to the left, aiming at the next target, one set lower than the first. This time the arrow hit dead center, and in moments her quiver was empty and all her targets were marked.

Arriving at the end of the lane, Kate slid the bow onto her back and grabbed the lance protruding up from the ground just ahead, yanking it free. She wheeled the horse around and headed down the middle row; this one was comprised of jousting rings and ground targets. She raised the lance to shoulder height while the horse ran steady and straight beneath her. Aiming for the first ring, Kate missed it by a hair's breadth, but she snagged the second one and the next, making the difficult task look easy.

Dal whistled low again. "She's good. I think she's better than you are. Hells, she might even be better than me."

"She always was better." Old memories tumbled through Corwin's mind. So many nights they'd snuck their ponies out of the stables and ridden them onto the cavalry yards, where they challenged one another to races or mounted duels with wooden swords. Their childhood competitions had been fun but fierce, each trying to best the other. Kate usually lost the duels but never the races. When it came to riding, she was untouchable. *She is as good as her father ever was.*

Clearly her fighting skills had improved, too. She snared the last jousting ring, completing the line, then bore down on the ground targets just ahead. Most riders slowed their horses for this part, the tent pegging, as it was called, but Kate kept the horse at full gallop. With easy effort, she lowered the tip of the lance just in time to stab the wooden peg sticking up from the ground. She yanked up, pulling the target free with a mighty heave. Raising the lance once more, she launched it over her shoulder and into the straw dummy crouched at the end of the lane.

They were moving so fast, the horse looked ready to crash into the fence. Kate sat back, pulling on the reins, and the crowd let out a collective gasp as the compact animal set his haunches and slid to a stop mere inches from collision. Then Kate spun the chestnut around once more, drawing the sword from the scabbard at her waist at the same time. She headed down the last lane, this one rimmed with burlap sacks shaped like men posed in attack stances. She slew the first one easily.

Dal whistled through his teeth. "Is the Relay training riders or soldiers?"

"A little of both, I suppose," Corwin replied. "The Relay has ancient military roots. It was formed during the War of Three."

"It's as old as the nightdrakes?"

Corwin nodded. "During the war, the cities needed a way to communicate with their allies quickly and without risk of exposing secrets. One fast horse with a skilled warrior proved the most effective way." He wondered what Rime would be like now if that war had never been fought. Its official name made it seem like some minor conflict, when in truth every city in Rime had been involved, all of them aligned in opposition on three fronts—eastern, western, and northern. The fighting nearly destroyed Rime. Ironically it was the unleashing of the nightdrakes that eventually wrought peace. The cities couldn't afford to fight one another when faced with this greater, more devastating enemy.

Leaning forward in his seat, Corwin focused on the final leg of Kate's trial. The targets were spaced so close together that she barely had time to pull back from one swing before launching another. They were set high, low, and in between, and she managed to hit each one, demonstrating a flexibility Corwin felt certain neither he nor Dal could've managed. Corwin watched her with his mouth hanging open in awe. She rode and fought with her whole body, her face a hard mask, eyes blazing.

Kate crossed the finish line a moment later. Corwin and Dal both raised their hands in applause, but their claps were met with silence from everyone sitting around them. All except for the only woman rider in the stands.

"I don't understand," Dal said, speaking loud enough that everyone could hear. "Why wouldn't you applaud a performance like that?"

"Because silence is the coward's favorite tool," the woman said, in the accent of an Esh Islander. She cast a glower over the crowd, but most refused to look at her.

It's because of who she is, Corwin thought. *Traitor Kate.* The truth struck him hard. It wasn't his fault—Hale had attacked his father—and yet he felt the blame as if it were his own.

The Eshian shook her golden-haired head, then stepped off the stands and disappeared around the corner.

Corwin clasped a stunned and speechless Dal on the shoulder. "Come on. We better find Kate now before she has a chance to run away."

They hurried off the stands and headed toward the gate. Kate was leading the horse, having dismounted the moment the trial was over. She walked fast, her head down in a bid for a quick escape, but before she could make it, the judge with the pocket watch called out to her.

She stopped and faced the man as he approached. A wary but respectful expression rose to her face. From the sigil on the man's tunic, Corwin guessed he was the Relay foreman. He and Dal hung back, not wanting to intrude.

"Well done, Kate," the man said. "That was your best time yet, and you had only one error."

Kate scowled at the compliment. "Does this mean I'm finally ungrounded then?"

The foreman rubbed his fingers over a line of pale, twisted scars on his forearm, vivid against his brown skin. "We'll discuss it later." The finality in his tone told Corwin that Kate's chances of riding again were slim. *What a waste,* he thought, although secretly he didn't mind the idea of her not being outside the city walls again anytime soon.

The foreman retreated to his post, and reluctantly, Kate turned her gaze onto them at last. "Your highness," she said, giving him a stiff bow.

"Nice to see you again, Miss Brighton." Corwin smiled, wishing he had some way to set her at ease.

"What are you doing here?" She glanced over her shoulder, as if afraid someone would notice them talking. Her worry was pointless—everyone had noticed.

Corwin cleared his throat. "I wanted to talk to you about what happened on the road to Andreas."

"Oh." Her gaze fell to the ground. "Can it wait? I need to take care of Trooper." As if in emphasis, the horse sucked in a breath, then blew it out in a loud snort.

"We'll come with you," Dal said before Corwin could respond.

Kate's lips formed a thin line, but she didn't argue. Leading the way, she headed into one of the stables. Fortunately, few people lingered about. *As good a battleground as any,* Corwin thought, then chided himself for it. This wasn't a battle. He refused to let it become one.

Kate led the horse into a wash stall in the back and pulled off the bridle, trading it for a halter. Then she snapped the crossties into place before stepping past the gelding's shoulder to the saddle, her hands raised to undo the girth.

"That was a fantastic ride, Miss Kate," Dal said, patting the horse's neck. "I was just telling Corwin that you're even better at cavalry games than he is. However do you manage to be so accurate with the targets?"

A smile ghosted across Kate's face. "It's not so hard. I just imagine I'm slaying my enemies."

Although she didn't look at Corwin as she spoke, he couldn't help but wonder if *he* was among those enemies. Then again, perhaps it was best not to know. He clasped his hands in front of him to keep from fidgeting. Gods, this was hard.

Dal cleared his throat, not quite concealing the sound of suppressed laughter. "Speaking of slaying things, his highness is here to thank you for saving him."

Corwin inwardly groaned, feeling like a fool. *I should be doing the saving.* He pushed the thought aside, letting his gratitude come to the forefront. He bowed his head toward Kate.

"Yes, thank you. I would be dead if not for you. I am in your debt."

"You're welcome." She glanced at him with her large, large eyes. Then she added in a low breath, "If only I had earned such before now."

Corwin winced at the blow. *Save him. He's my father,* he heard her beg again. *Stop the execution, give us exile!* And he hadn't. At the time, he'd believed there was no alternative, that such an offense must be paid by death, lest someone else believe they should attempt the same and perhaps succeed. But in the years that followed, he'd begun to wonder if he'd been wrong. The time he'd spent away from Rime had taught him that the world was rarely so black and white. He wrapped his fingers around the vambrace on his right wrist, hiding the tattoo beneath.

"Well now," Dal said with a nervous laugh. "We're also here to find out more about that marvelous revolver your friend made."

Pulling the saddle from the horse's back, Kate glanced at them both, her expression guarded. "Why?"

"You used it to kill three of those four daydrakes," Corwin said, holding out his hands to take the saddle from her.

Ignoring the offer, she stepped past him and slid the saddle onto a rack just out front of the wash stall. "I . . . I didn't think you would remember any of what happened."

Dropping his hands back to his sides, Corwin hid a wince at his blunder. Of course she would hope he hadn't remembered. Especially after all the intimate things he said to her in his delirium. If only he could take it back—but somehow he doubted telling her he'd been crazed out of his mind and hadn't meant a word of it would go over very well. *Denial then.*

"I remember very little aside from that. But seeing a weapon kill so many drakes so easily is impossible to forget."

"There was nothing *easy* about it." Kate picked up an empty bucket at the front of the stall and crossed the aisle to the water trough, where she dipped out a bucketful. "What do you want to know?"

"Well, to start," Dal said, stepping forward to take the bucket from her. To Corwin's chagrin, she allowed the help this time. "Are there any more?"

"I . . ." Kate bit her lip, then seemed to realize she was doing it and schooled her expression into a neutral mask. "There is only the one. My friend Tom Bonner made it special for me. To keep me safe on my rides."

Corwin's fingers clenched, halfway toward making fists. *Who was this Bonner? Was he the one who gave her the moonbelt?* For a second, the image of another man with his hands at her waist, pulling her into a kiss, flashed in Corwin's mind. It wasn't one his imagination needed to conjure. Memory of her and Edwin would suffice.

"That's very nice," Dal said, shooting Corwin a wary glance. "But surely if he made the one, he can make others."

Corwin nodded his agreement while he wrestled the jealousy beast back into its cage. Kate's life was not his business anymore. Who she was friends with, who she loved . . . *who loved her.*

Fetching a dry rag off the front of the wash stall, Kate dipped it into the bucket and doused the horse's neck with it. The gelding snorted a protest, raising his head in a vain attempt to avoid the water.

"Oh, stop it, you big baby," she chided. "This should feel nice."

The horse shook his neck, spraying them all with water. Kate bent toward the bucket once more. "Yes, I suppose he could make more."

"Excellent." Dal clapped his hands once. "When can we meet this Tom Bonner?"

Kate rolled her eyes as she ran the wet rag along the horse's back. "Seeing how I've no real work to do anymore, I suppose I can arrange a meeting." She made a point of addressing the offer to Dal.

He grinned. "Perfect. Should we come back later today?"

She shook her head. "Bonner will want time to prepare. Tomorrow would be better. Meet me here at seven o'clock."

"The moment the bell tolls." Dal placed a palm over his heart and stooped into a theatrical bow.

That sideways smile appeared on Kate's face then, stealing Corwin's breath away for a moment. It always made her look like she had some secret, one you would give your right eye to possess, if only she would tell you.

Emboldened by the smile and the warm memories it provoked, Corwin said, "Thank you again, Kate."

The smile vanished, and she fixed a cold stare at him. He wished he could know what she was thinking at that moment.

Then again, maybe not, he thought, imagining his face on one of her targets.

After a few seconds, she asked, "Is that all you wanted from me then, your highness?"

It was a dangerous question, a multi-edged sword forged to cut no matter which way he answered. "Yes," he finally said, guessing it was the answer she wanted to hear.

WHEN THE BELL TOWER TOLLED the seven-o'clock hour the next evening, Kate stepped through the Relay house main gate and onto the street. She'd been waiting just inside for more than ten minutes now, worried Corwin would turn up early. The riders and workers in the house kept giving her strange glances, but they were easier to ignore than the people on the street would've been. Out there, she would've felt like a beggar, despite wearing her nicest clothes and with her hair in a tidy braid. In here, she just felt like an outsider, same as always.

And a traitor. She couldn't forget that. Only it wasn't a title she inherited from her father this time. She had betrayed Bonner, even if he insisted otherwise—as he'd said over and over again when she went to confess her guilt not long after her meeting with Corwin yesterday.

"It's not your fault, Kate. You couldn't just let him die. If you hadn't used the revolver, you'd be dead too, and believe me, that would be worse. Besides, I made the gun hoping there'd be interest in them."

"You are a fool, Tom Bonner," Kate said before she could stop herself. "You used *wild* magic to make that gun, and now the high prince of Rime wants one for himself."

"You worry too much, Kate," Signe said, from where she sat reclining in a chair with her legs propped up on one of the work-tables in the Bonner shop. "As I'm always telling you."

"Worry too much?" Kate folded her arms over her chest. "Wilder magic is outlawed. If they find out he's a wilder, the gold robes will imprison him, purge him of magic, kill him, then bury his body where no one can find it."

"Why do they hide the body?" Signe cocked her head in a charmingly fragile gesture that belied her fierceness.

Kate huffed, annoyed at Signe's disconcerting habit of always focusing on the wrong point. "So that it can never be burned with holy fire."

"I don't understand this need to burn flesh." Signe pinched her nose. "It smells awful."

Yes, it did, Kate had to agree, even with all the scented oils the priests applied to the corpse, but the stench didn't outweigh the purpose. "The holy fire is needed to free the spirit, allowing the de-ceased to cross the barrier from this world to the next. The buried remain dead forever." Some believed they became Shades, their spirits bound in slavery to serve the whimsy of the gods.

Signe scoffed. "That's not what my people believe. We bury our dead. The spirits of our ancestors don't depart. They are *Aslar.* They remain with us, watching over us, guiding us. Anything else is barbaric."

No, Kate thought, what was barbaric was how the nightdrakes dug up the dead and consumed them.

She waved her hand impatiently. "The burial or burning is

beside the point. Death is the point, Sig."

"I'm not going to die," Bonner said, his tone annoyingly carefree. "I'm not going to work magic right in front of him. Prince Corwin just wants to see the revolver I've already made."

"No, he wants you to make more," Kate said, hand on hips.

"But I *want* to make more." Excitement lit Bonner's boyish features, and he stood up from the workbench. "And here's my chance. The high king might commission hundreds of them. Thousands."

Kate glowered, her eyes narrowed so much it blurred her vision. "Are you listening to yourself? How are you going to manage that alone? You can't work magic at night, and it'll take you forever trying to sneak it in during the day. Not to mention the risk of getting caught by the magists." That risk would be greater than ever here in Farhold if the rumor that the Rising was behind the attack on the Gregors was true. Even if it wasn't, there were bound to be more golds on principle alone. She wondered how bad it would have to get before the Rising realized their folly.

"I'll figure it out." Bonner shrugged. "Now that I know copper is the key, I might be able to find a way to create the bullets without using magic, and I'll make molds of the revolver parts that any blacksmith could use."

Kate pressed her lips together to hold back a curse. She'd been around Bonner enough to know that his optimism about such accomplishments rarely played out.

"Don't forget me." Signe slid her legs off the table and stood up. "Only I can make the special black-powder mixture that will work with your revolver, and nothing will change that."

Bonner smirked. "How could I forget when you remind me every day?" He waved his hand in front of her ear, transforming the gold hoop she wore so that it dangled in a straight line, blending in with her golden hair. She laughed, flicking it back and forth with her finger like a cat at a ball of yarn.

"And you wonder why I worry." Kate cupped her forehead.

"Aw, poor Kate," Signe purred. "We must have something for her to do, too, when all these kings and princes come seeking our genius."

"Don't worry, Sig," Bonner said, fixing her gold hoop with a flick of his hand. "We'll put Kate in charge of demonstrations. She's already done such a good job of it."

Bonner reached out and tickled her side. Kate slapped his hand away, but that only encouraged him. In seconds he had her pinned and tickled her until she laughed and begged him to stop.

But when the laughter died down, Kate begged him once again. "Please don't agree to make these revolvers for him. It's not worth the risk it'll place you in."

A battle played out in Bonner's expression. Then he finally gave a reluctant nod. "If it's that important to you, Kate, I'll find some way to say no." He paused and smiled. "All I really want is you happy and safe."

Now, as she waited for Dal and Corwin, Kate clung to his promise, but she couldn't keep her doubt at bay. Letting anyone examine the revolver risked discovery of his magic. Corwin was no fool about weaponry, and given Dal's battle scars, she doubted he was either.

Despite Dal's promise that they would be here promptly at seven, he and Corwin didn't appear until some twenty minutes later. They dismounted when they reached her, and Kate was dismayed to see the crowd following them. Rumors were already swirling in the Relay house about his visit yesterday. If she wasn't careful, the newspapers would start printing about it. That was the last thing she wanted.

Bowing, Kate listened with only half an ear to Dal's explanation for their late arrival.

"We need to hurry," she said, cutting him off. "Bonner's father has been ill for some time now. He will want to close the shop before dark."

The walk to the blacksmith's shop took less than ten minutes. Corwin ordered the guards to stay outside while Kate led him and Dal inside. As always, the place felt like an oven, warm air smothering them when they stepped through the door. Bonner looked up from where he stood in the back of the room near the forge, a low railing separating the work area from the small reception up front. Bonner wore his outer tunic for once, and his face was clean, if not his hands. The place looked tidier than she'd ever seen it.

To her dismay, Signe was present as well, still dressed in her Relay tunic. Kate had asked her not to come for fear she might say something untoward, given her habit of always speaking her mind, regardless of her audience. There might be kings in Esh, but nobility didn't seem to matter to Signe. But failing to listen was one of her regular shortcomings. *I am powerless to resist the call of curiosity*, she would often say as an explanation. Kate didn't doubt that was a factor now.

She motioned to her friends. "Your highness, this is Master Tom

Bonner and Signe Leth of Esh."

"It's just Bonner please, my lords. My father is the master here still." Bonner bowed, and Signe reluctantly followed suit, though she didn't stoop quite as low.

"It's a pleasure to meet you both," Corwin said. "And yes, let's dispense with all formalities. This is Dal, and you may call me Corwin."

Kate sighed. It seemed some things hadn't changed after all. Corwin always did dislike titles. She used to agree with him on the lack of need for them, but not anymore. Titles served their purpose in creating necessary boundaries, reminding people of their place in life. Once she hadn't realized how vast the chasm was between the highborn and lowborn, but she'd spent the last few years learning better. It was a vast chasm indeed, uncrossable.

"I'm sure the lovely Kate has already told you why we're here," Dal said, giving her a wink. The gesture disarmed her, and she felt a smile tug at the edges of her lips.

"She has." Bonner folded his impressive arms over his equally impressive chest. "You're interested in my revolver."

"And my black powder," Signe added.

Dal cocked a brow. "*Your* black powder?"

She nodded, her chin raised to a haughty angle. "Bonner's gun fails without my special mixture of black powder for his special bullets."

"Interesting." Dal eyed her with an appreciative gaze. "But I must say you're far too young to be a Sister of the Furen Mag. How did you learn the secret of it?"

A mischievous smile spread across Signe's lips. "I stole it from the grave of the king of Skaar, and when his kinsmen found out, they sent twelve warriors to bring me back, but I killed them one by one, the first with a hunting knife and the last with a kiss."

Shock registered on Dal's face, and Kate laughed. "She's kidding, my lord. It's a secret she refuses to tell anyone and instead makes up absurd stories." Kate had heard over a dozen versions so far.

"What a delightful mystery," Dal said with a glint in his eyes.

Corwin cleared his throat. "Yes, well, the more pressing mystery is the revolver. May I see it?"

"Of course, your highness." Bonner clasped his hands together with suppressed excitement. "I just finished a new one yesterday. It's the same as Kate's in every way." He retrieved a box from a nearby shelf, removing the lid with theatrical exaggeration. Then he lifted the new revolver out of the box, handling it with showy, delicate care, like something made of glass instead of metal. He passed it to Corwin. "Careful now. It's already loaded."

Corwin examined the weapon with naked wonderment on his face, his attention focused on the cylinder, which he pushed open to reveal the bullets tucked inside. "It doesn't misfire?"

"Never once," Bonner said. "Not this version at least." Then he launched into a detailed explanation of how it worked and why. Kate listened, stiff with worry that he would reveal too much, raise too many questions about the intricacies of its creation. But by the end of it, neither Corwin nor Dal seemed suspicious in the slightest. Instead they appeared even more wonderstruck than before. Bonner's delight in their reaction saddened Kate. He deserved to be so proud, and yet he had to hide the nature of his genius at every turn.

She wondered what the world would be like if wilders like him were able to practice their gifts openly, same as the magists.

"This is beyond impressive," Corwin said. "So much so that I have no choice but to ask if you'd be willing to make more." He motioned to include Signe. "Both of you, and for a nice commission, of course."

"How many do you mean?" Bonner said.

"As many as you can make," Corwin replied, a handsome, irresistible smile appearing on his handsome, perfect face.

Bonner shook his head, his expression apologetic. "I can make you two or three, but I can't commit to more than that. It takes so much time, you see, and with my father sick, I'm too busy just keeping up with the shop."

"Yes, I understand." Corwin shifted his weight from one foot to the other. "Governor Prewitt tells me Bonner-forged steel is the stuff of legends. It's a wonder you can keep up with even half of the demand."

"Yes, they say it's fit for royalty," Dal added, charm oozing out from him. It was all Kate could do not to roll her eyes.

Bonner beamed, standing up even straighter so that he seemed to tower above everyone else. "Thank you. I do the best I can."

Using your illegal wilder magic! Kate thought. If they knew, the praise would turn to condemnation.

Corwin ran a thumb over his chin in an old habit Kate recognized, a sign that his stubbornness was preparing to make an appearance. Only the gesture was different now, thanks to the scar. He traced the line of it. "What if you had help? Could you teach others how to make these revolvers?"

Bonner sagged a little beneath the question. "It's the same problem as before. I don't have time for it."

"What if you no longer had to worry about this shop?" Corwin gestured to the room.

His words set Kate's nerves on edge as she guessed what was coming next. Only, this couldn't be happening. Bonner was her friend. She couldn't lose him. *Don't you dare!* she wanted to scream at Corwin. *You've already taken enough from me.* Desperately she searched for a distraction, finding it in the slight disarray on a nearby worktable. She set to straightening the tools at once, the simple act keeping her calm.

"What I mean to say," Corwin continued, "is will you come and work for House Tormane in Norgard? As royal blacksmith—and gunsmith."

Bonner's mouth fell open in astonishment, and Kate's heart sank, her knuckles bone white around the hammer she'd just picked up. It was a generous offer, and far more tempting than any they'd speculated about earlier. A position in the royal house meant a lifetime of wealth and security. Most of the royal smiths were born into the trade.

But Bonner would still be a wilder, in the capital city of Norgard.

"What about your father?" Kate said, gently setting down the hammer and forcing herself to move away from the table.

Bonner flinched, the hopeful look in his eyes dimming. "Kate's right. I can't leave Farhold. Not with my father so ill."

Guilt washed over Kate, smothering her relief at having volleyed the danger of his leaving.

But Corwin wasn't just any opponent. He nodded, his expression grim. "I understand the burden of a sick father all too well."

Kate stared at him, realizing he was referring to his own father. Rumors circulated in some of the less-reputable newspapers that High King Orwin suffered a lingering illness. She'd never believed it could be true until now.

Corwin ran his thumb over his chin again. "Would you change your mind if I were to have your father tended to by the magist healers? I don't know what ailment affects him, but their magic is powerful. With their care, he might soon recover enough to join you in Norgard."

All the air evacuated from Kate's lungs, the weight of defeat pressing down on her. Next to her, Bonner's eyes filled with sudden, bright hope.

"Do . . . do you really mean it?"

"Yes, he means it." Dal slapped Bonner on the back. "He's the high prince, and wealthy enough to afford the League's prices."

Don't do it, Kate prayed. *Pick me.* But she bit her tongue to hold back the protest. Bonner loved his father more than anything. Same as she had loved hers. She would've done anything to save him—include risking her own life. She couldn't get in the way of letting Bonner do the same.

"Yes," Corwin pressed. "Your revolver is important enough that I must do everything in my power to see that you make more." He turned and motioned to Signe. "And you with your black powder. You can become royal alchemist, or whatever title you wish, if you'll come to Norgard."

He turned back to Bonner. "Just think of it. Your revolver let Kate kill three drakes in a matter of moments. If we make enough of them, put them in enough hands, imagine how many drakes we could slay. Maybe even enough to rid the world of them. That would be a feat to make any father proud—and yours will live to see it."

Kate closed her eyes and drew a deep breath, accepting defeat. There were a million things she wanted to say to Bonner, reminding him of the risk of the Inquisition, the reality of his magic when it came to his invention. The gold robes were based out of Norgard, for Shades' sake. But she couldn't. Even worse, she didn't think it would matter. Saving the kingdom? Getting his father the help he needed? Those were risks Bonner would be willing to take.

She opened her eyes and touched Bonner's arm, needing the reassurance of him for as long as it would last. "It's too good an offer to refuse."

Bonner turned his head and looked down at her, a muscle working in his jaw. He covered her hand with his before turning his gaze back to Corwin. "Very well. I will accept, but only if Kate may come with me."

Kate's fingers tightened around Bonner's forearm automatically, her fingernails digging into flesh. *What are you doing?* she tried to shout with her eyes, but Bonner ignored her completely, not even flinching at the assault on his skin.

"I didn't spend so much time and energy keeping her safe to just leave her behind unprotected," Bonner continued.

Scowling, Kate pulled her hand free. "I've no need of your protection, Tom Bonner. Or anyone else's." She shot a glare at both Corwin and Dal for good measure. "I can take care of myself."

"Oh, that's not in any doubt," Dal said, grinning. "Not after your performance yesterday. Or considering you single-handedly slew all those daydrakes."

"Yeah, thanks to me," Bonner pointed out, his grin as broad as Dal's.

The only person not smiling now, aside from Kate, was Corwin. She could guess why—he didn't want her in Norgard any more than she wished to come.

Dal must've sensed Corwin's reluctance, too, for with a wicked glint in his eyes, he said, "I'm sorry for not mentioning this earlier, Kate, but I'm afraid you really have no choice about coming to Norgard, at least for a little while."

"Why is that?" Kate said while Corwin shot his friend a dark look.

"Because of your heroics in saving our high prince, of course," Dal said with an exaggerated frown. "The high king insists on rewarding you for such. How could he not?" Now it was Dal shooting the dark look—at Corwin.

Corwin drew an audible breath, then addressed Kate. "Dal is right. You are to be honored for your deeds. The . . . high king commands it."

Kate knew he was lying, but she didn't know why. She considered calling him on it, but Bonner spoke before she could. "You've got to offer her more than some reward or you can count me out. The number of guns you want is going to take a long time, and I'll need Kate's help."

"With what?" Dal asked, sounding genuinely curious.

"She's our weapons tester," Signe said with a fox-like grin.

Dal clapped his hands. "Oh, that sounds like a job I might sign up for as well." He waved at Corwin. "I'm sure we can devise something for Kate. Yes, your highness?"

Corwin was silent several seconds before slowly nodding. "I might be able to arrange a place for you in the royal stables. You've certainly the skill for it."

It was a cruel jab, even if he didn't mean for it to be. He surely remembered that had been her wish once—to follow in her father's footsteps, training Norgard horses day in and day out, year after fulfilling year.

She couldn't keep the bite out of her voice as she replied, "You forget, *your highness*. I'm a traitor's daughter. They won't welcome me there."

"They will if I make it so," Corwin said with a hint of anger in his voice. Then he abruptly calmed. "You saved my life, Kate. That makes you welcome anywhere in Rime. I give you my word that you will be well treated if you decide to return."

Your power is not so great, Kate thought. People would obey the decree, but only when there was someone around to enforce it. When there wasn't . . .

Still, she had saved him. The high king was in her debt and that had to count for something. *Go to Fenmore,* she remembered once again. She had no idea what her father had meant by it. If she returned to Norgard, there was a chance she might discover his intention. Maybe someone he'd been close to would know what he'd meant.

Kate turned her gaze to Signe, "Are you going to go?"

Signe bared her teeth in a smile. "I never walk away from a new adventure."

Then I would be here alone, Kate thought. For a moment she let herself picture Norgard, with its outer wall of white stone rising up over rolling fields of grass, green as emeralds. On any given day, more than a thousand horses roamed those fields. And beyond that white wall stood the castle itself, home to the finest horseflesh in all the world. *My father's horses.*

But it was also home to the executioner's block, the place where her father had died.

Why? Why did he do it?

Go to Fenmore.

Kate stood up straight, feigning courage she didn't feel. "All right, I'll go."

PART TWO

The Errant Prince

THEY LEFT FARHOLD A WEEK later, heading for Andreas. Half a dozen people met them at the gate to bid farewell to Bonner and Signe. For Kate, only the Relay foreman came out. Corwin was grateful to the man, but also sad to see it. He wondered what kind of life she must've been living here.

Riding at the head of the caravan, Corwin couldn't keep himself from looking back at his new companions with a sense of wonderment and dismay. They made for a strange party—the Eshian, the blacksmith, and the traitor. It sounded like the start of some mythic journey. Or a bad tavern joke. To make things even more unusual, Master Raith was riding at the back of the pack, having volunteered for the travel duty.

"My order has a deep interest in rooting out the source of these daydrakes," Raith confessed. "I have volunteered to take lead."

Corwin had been pleased by the appointment even though he wasn't sure he entirely trusted the man. Still, the magist's resourcefulness when it came to defending against the daydrakes dispelled any reservations he had. Raith provided the entire party with his flash stones in the event of another attack. Corwin also commissioned some hundred enchanted arrows, a fortune that would have Edwin pulling out his hair when the bill came due. Corwin didn't envy the page who delivered it. But ensuring Bonner and his revolver arrived safely in Norgard would be worth the expense. Even Edwin, with his excessive concern about maintaining the wealth of the crown, would have to agree.

At least the caravan was smaller this time, a single wagon and just a dozen riders. The group followed the main road leading east from Farhold toward Marared until they were out of sight of the city watchtowers. Then while the wagon and the remaining Norgard soldiers continued on, Corwin and the rest turned south toward Andreas.

The ruse was an attempt to allow Corwin to enter the city without being recognized. They would rejoin the wagon and soldiers in Thace, the central city equidistant from the others. Keeping his identity secret was the best chance he had of learning anything about the Andrean miner involved in the attack on the Gregors. People would talk more openly with a group of common travelers than they would with the prince of Rime. Corwin also wished to avoid meeting with the Andrean ruler, Lord Nevan, as he would surely be expected to do if his presence were known.

They made the journey in three days, spending both nights on the road, beneath wardstone barriers. They didn't see any nightdrakes or daydrakes this time, and the absence of the former, like a lull in a deadly storm, made Corwin uneasy. Of the latter, he didn't want to speculate.

Corwin had never been to Andreas before, and the sight of it in the distance filled him with a kind of nervous awe. The city resided in a narrow, rocky valley at the base of three mountains. Unlike most of the freestanding walls in the other Rimish cities, the wall here rose out of the sides of the mountains like stone arms on a giant—the kind that would like nothing more than to gobble up unsuspecting humans. Barren scrubland filled the valley. The only sign of life aside from the always-present everweeps was the smoke rising up from the chimney of the gold-order house, a freeholding to the east of the main gates. The golds were formed only recently, and with space inside the cities so limited, they'd built their houses outside the walls in all the cities. Corwin once heard his brother claim the isolation was a good thing, for it kept the public from overhearing the unpleasantness of the Purgings. Corwin didn't know if that was true or not, but he didn't plan on going near enough to ever find out.

The royal castle of Andreas, a forbidding fortress carved into the central mountain itself, kept watch over the town below. The city looked impregnable even without wardstone magic. It *was* impregnable, as proved during the War of the Three when the northern forces broke their army against Andreas' wall after the western forces had retreated behind it.

Or maybe it's inescapable, Corwin thought as they entered the city. He'd never seen a place so filled with people in the middle of the day. They swarmed down the streets like bees over a hive. Then again, the congestion made sense. There were no fields to tend and even fewer herds to flock here. Andreas relied on the coal and precious metals it produced for its livelihood—and the people who labored inside its walls and mountain caves day after day.

"We will need to stable the horses," Kate said once they'd made it through the gates. "They're not allowed on the streets here."

Corwin glanced at her, making sure he'd heard her right. The cowl she wore over her head, mouth, and nose muffled her words.

They were all wearing them—Signe's idea to help them remain anonymous. The small, shoulder-length hoods were common in this city, where the dust and grime from the mining hung in the air, coating the streets, buildings, and people in a gray film. The peasants passing by them were dressed in gray and brown, adding to the overall dingy feel. Their stark garb surprised Corwin. When the Andreas nobility visited Norgard, they wore bright, garish costumes bedecked with the precious gems harvested by the cartload here.

They stabled the horses in the livery next to the Relay house, then gathered outside on the street. Raith excused himself with plans to check in with his order's house.

Once he was gone, Dal turned to Corwin and said eagerly, "Where should we go first?"

Corwin motioned to Kate. "What do you think? You and Signe know this city better than the rest of us. Where is the best place for information?"

Kate's brow furrowed. "No idea. Women riders aren't welcome here, no matter what the Relay's rules are. We hardly left the Relay house."

"*You* hardly left the house," Signe said, scowling. "I wouldn't let these men make me unwelcome. I go where I wish."

Dal grinned. "I'll bet not a one of them complained."

"Where do you suggest then, Signe?" said Corwin.

"The Boarbelly Inn," she answered without hesitation. "It's the biggest gaming house in town. The innkeeper is a friend, and he knows everything there is to know about his city."

Corwin supposed it made sense. Gaming houses were often

hubs of gossip. "All right, we'll try there."

"If you don't mind, your highness," Kate said, "I would rather not venture any farther than this. May I get the rooms rented instead? I recommend that inn over there." She pointed to a faded sign that read "The Guided Torch." A single curved-handled torch framed the sign, the symbol of Andre, patron god of Andreas.

"I can go with her to help," Bonner offered. He looked road weary, with dark circles under his eyes and a telltale stiffness when he moved.

Corwin took in Kate's expression, trying to read her thoughts as always. Their journey here had been uneventful, aside from the Redrush ferrymen charging them double for the crossing, but tension hung thick in the air every night they stopped for camp. Kate never seemed to stray far from Bonner's side. At first Corwin mistook it as a sign of intimacy between them, only their interactions spoke more of friendship than of love. Even if Bonner did have an annoying habit of touching her every chance he got—tickling her sides, patting her head, hugging her. Corwin was forced to conclude then that Kate simply didn't want to be caught alone with him. The feeling was mutual. Having her around made him restless. Try as he did to ignore her, he kept obsessing over her every move and gesture. It was like having an itch that couldn't be reached for scratching.

Corwin gave his blessing to the plan, and once Kate and Bonner had departed, Signe led the way. The congestion in the city grew the farther in they went. Twisting, narrow roads drew them deeper and higher, the constant incline soon making Corwin's legs ache. He supposed the return journey would be a relief, but for now it daunted. At least it wasn't terribly hot, with the buildings casting long shadows as they rose up several stories high on both sides of the street.

The Boarbelly Inn occupied the farthest corner of the town square, the highest point of the city aside from the nobles' houses and the castle itself. Above the entrance perched a carved wooden boar, reared up on its stubby hind legs. Signe hopped up and patted the boar's foot on her way through the door. Corwin could see from the worn wood it was a common act, probably done for good luck.

The interior of the inn was dim and smoky, but considerably quieter than it had been outside. More than a dozen round tables filled the place, half of them occupied. Some of the patrons were eating and drinking, but most were absorbed in games, everything from cards and dice to elaborate board games played with stone pieces, like Kings in the Castle and Five Fates.

Signe's boast of being welcome here proved true, as several of the patrons and even more of the workers called out to her in greeting as she removed her cowl. She waved back to each in turn before approaching a table occupied by the fattest man Corwin had ever seen. Yards of belly spilled down from his triple chin to a nonexistent waistline. When the man raised his goblet in greeting, the fingers holding it resembled bent sausages.

"Signe Leth!" he said in a voice as big as his stomach. "My eyes haven't looked on your pretty face in weeks. Come give the fat man a kiss."

Grinning, Signe stooped and brushed her lips against one plump cheek. "I have not missed your fat face nearly so much as your belly." She gave his gut a hard pat, and the man howled with laughter.

Corwin and Dal exchanged bemused looks. It seemed no one was a stranger to Signe.

"Sit down, you beautiful girl, and introduce me to your friends," the fat man said.

Signe pulled out the chair next to him and sat down while Corwin and Dal took seats opposite.

"This is Gordon Bombasi, innkeeper here," she said. She motioned to Dal, then Corwin. "And this is Ronan Dorn and Clash Farley."

They'd both chosen their false names before entering the city. Corwin had worn his before, during his years spent away from Rime. He hoped the name, along with the cowl and the beard he'd been letting grow, would keep him from being recognized.

"Welcome to the Boarbelly, the crown gem of Andreas," Gordon said, his voice still booming loud enough to make Corwin wince. Of all the people to seek information from, surely this man should be the last choice. Everyone in the city would soon know their business.

"Thank you," Dal said. "But that welcome would go a lot farther with something wet to cool our tongues."

"Of course." Gordon brought his meaty hands together in a clap. A serving girl soon appeared, carrying a wine tankard and goblets. Another followed behind her, bearing bread and bowls of broth for dipping. "Eat and drink as much as you want, but be aware that we have no vacancies tonight." The man shook his head in emphasis, and Corwin noticed he wore magestones in both ears, each emblazoned with the symbol of the spell it contained. The left one held a truth spell for detecting deceptions. Fortunately for Corwin—or

Clash Farley—it wasn't active. The one on the right was the same as Dal wore, a concealment spell to hide scars or blemishes. *His business must do well to afford such trinkets.*

Dal leaned forward, eager. "Is there some special entertainment planned?"

Gordon smiled, revealing teeth white as porcelain. "There is always special entertainment at the Boarbelly. But tonight we play the Death Bones."

"Ah, yes. That will draw a crowd." Dal placed a palm against his chest. "Not a game for the faint of heart."

Corwin silently agreed. Death Bone cards were imbued with far more powerful mage magic than a normal deck, each one bearing a spell that players might incur during game play. Decks came with different intensity levels, some so dangerous players risked pain and even death. The worst Corwin had seen was a man who drew the poverty card only to discover he had been pickpocketed, but he'd heard tales of far greater tragedies. Then again, he supposed the rewards of winning—wealth, luck, good health—could be worth it to some.

"It is not any game though, young man." Gordon wagged a sausage-like finger at him. "For tonight we host royalty."

"Royalty?" said Signe with a birdlike cock of her head. "From where?"

Corwin frowned, surprised by this news and interested in the answer, if only to have some tidbit of gossip to pacify his brother with when he returned to Norgard.

Gordon picked up his goblet and took his time drinking it down before answering, purposely drawing out the suspense. "Why, the royal is none other than Eryx Fane, prince of Seva. Although sadly he is only the last-born of some six brothers. The heir would've drawn an even bigger crowd. More than my poor inn could hold."

Corwin nearly choked on the piece of bread he'd just placed in his mouth. The timing proved fortunate, preventing him from saying something rash. Seva, the massive kingdom to the southeast, had been the most hated and feared enemy of Rime even before the invasion.

Next to him, an uncharacteristically dark look crossed Dal's face. He and Corwin both had personal reasons to hate Seva and its Godking, Magnar Fane. The kingdom was like a plague of locusts, ever spreading, ever consuming. Only four of its neighboring nations had yet to fall to its conquests—Endra, Rhoswen, Esh, and Rime. *Rime shall never fall,* Corwin silently vowed, fingers curled around his goblet. It almost had during the invasion, some fifty years ago when Seva sacked the port city of Penlocke. Instead, Corwin's grandfather had united the cities and driven the Godking's forces back across the sea.

"Why is a prince of Seva being welcomed here?" Dal asked, running an idle finger over the rim of his cup. "Especially given his father's crimes."

Gordon dismissed the comment with a wave. "He has been granted amnesty by Lord Nevan. In Andreas, we do not hold grudges."

Corwin bit back a humorless laugh. Lord Nevan could give lessons in grudge keeping, as his continued opposition to the Tormane family proved. When the Rimish forces finally defeated Seva, Lord Nevan had wanted to become the first high king, but the cities chose Norgard's might over Andreas's riches in selecting their leader. The presence of this Prince Eryx was troubling news, and Corwin filed it away to examine later.

"Would you care to make a wager on the game?" Gordon extended his hand palm up.

Signe gave the man's belly another pat. "We did not come for beds or gaming, fat man."

Gordon craned his head to look at her. "What else is there in life worth having?"

"We are looking for a man." Signe cut her eyes to Corwin.

"Actually, we're looking for information about a man. This one." Corwin reached into his pocket and passed Gordon the portrait bearing the miner's likeness.

The moment Gordon unfolded it, his eyes widened. "You could not have seen this man."

"Why not?" Corwin glanced at the picture. It looked exactly the same as the man he remembered that day at the Gregors' house.

"Because that is Ralph Marcel," Gordon said on an exhaled breath, "and he was taken by the gold robes nearly a year ago."

Corwin frowned. "Are you saying he was caught by the Inquisition?"

Gordon inclined his head, his expression sober. "Yes, and no wilder has ever escaped the golds."

It was true, at least none had ever been heard of before—until now. But it fitted the puzzle all too well. If this wilder had somehow managed to escape from the Inquisition, what else would he do but join the Rising?

Taking back the picture, Corwin asked, "What was his magic?"

Gordon raised his hand palm up, fingers splayed. "I don't know. Marcel didn't make a fuss when he was captured, and it was never said afterward. Although—" Gordon paused and scratched his cheek, several deep strokes sure to leave red welts. Only when he dropped his hand away a moment later, the skin remained unmarked. "There were rumors that he had a strange affinity with animals. Some fifty cats and dogs living in his house."

"An affinity with animals," Corwin repeated. The stories claimed that was a spirit gift, too. *Are these daydrakes animals?* Corwin wondered. He supposed so, though, like their nighttime kin, they felt more like monsters, something too dark and dangerous to share the same nature as a cat or dog. But if a wilder could control them, that would strengthen Dal's suspicion about the connection between the two attacks.

Seeming to grow bored with the conversation, Signe pulled out the throwing knife she kept tucked on her belt and began to toss it overhead, juggling it with mindless ease. "I don't understand this Inquisition. Why do your people fear each other so? In Esh, we fear no one. Not even our enemies."

"That's because there is no magic in the islands, pretty one, nor anywhere else besides Rime for that matter," Gordon said, his eyes moving up and down as he followed the knife's movement. "No one not of Rime has been born with the ability to manipulate the unseen world, not for centuries. And our magists are forbidden to ever leave our shores."

Corwin tapped a thumb against the table. "That's true enough. And wilders are something to be feared. No man should have the power to level cities at will."

Signe caught the knife and held it, point up. Her gaze fixed on Corwin. "What cities have they ever leveled? The only magic I've seen is used for good. Like the wardstones that protect us. Or your truth stones, fat man. Oh, and the moonbelts."

A devilish grin danced across Dal's face, and he wagged his eyebrows. "Yes, those are definitely for the good."

"But wilder magic is often used for great harm," Corwin said. *Like the kind that killed my mother.*

Gordon smacked a fist on the table. "Good or evil, the only thing certain is that magic causes strife. Take our high king, for example. The Tormane family is bound by a most terrible magic. One that often pits brother against brother."

"You mean the uror," Corwin said before he could stop himself.

Gordon bobbed his head, setting his chins to wiggling. "It creates chaos when there is more than one possible heir. No one knows who will rule. No one knows where to place their loyalty."

"How do you know that?" Dal said, speaking the exact question Corwin wanted to ask but didn't dare for fear of revealing too much. "You're not from Norgard."

"I've heard the stories. High King Borwin Tormane only claimed the right to the Mirror Throne after he slew his two brothers in the name of uror."

My grandfather did not kill his brothers, Corwin longed to reply. One died during the uror trials, yes, but it wasn't murder. The very idea of kin slaying was unthinkable. The other brother lived to old age.

"What is this uror?" Signe tapped the edge of her blade against the table.

"It means fate," Gordon replied.

"Not quite," Corwin said, unable to stay quiet on this point, at least. "It means a calling of fate or sometimes a call for trial. In Norgard, the right to rule doesn't always pass from father to firstborn son. If there is more than one heir, the sign of uror will come and the brothers must prove to the people their worthiness of succession through trials and deeds."

Signe nodded as if this made perfect sense to her. "In Esh, if a king or queen is weak, others will challenge their rule. Only the strongest and wisest should lead."

"Yes, gorgeous girl." Gordon put a hand on Signe's shoulder, dwarfing it completely. "But in your country, the challenge isn't foretold in signs and portents."

"What signs?"

"The first is always the appearance of a uniquely colored animal," Dal said. "The last uror sign was a wolf, I believe."

Murr, Corwin thought, nodding. He remembered the animal clearly even though she had died when he was just a boy. "And the coloring is always the same—half white and half black."

Signe frowned, as if she were trying to picture a creature like that but failing. Corwin didn't blame her. Such coloring didn't exist in nature. Only the gods could make it so.

She started to ask another question but broke off, her head cocked to the side as if she was listening to something. A moment later, the rest of them heard it too—the sound of a commotion outside.

"What is that?" Gordon demanded, searching the room for someone to provide an answer, but his employees were already heading for the door. Corwin, Dal, and Signe followed.

Outside, the town square had become an ocean of bodies, the source of the disturbance impossible to see. Not to be delayed, Signe climbed onto the porch railing in front of the Boarbelly, grabbed hold of the roof's edge, then hauled herself up onto the low-sloping shingles with remarkable ease, unhindered in the breeches she always wore.

Dal and Corwin quickly followed suit. Once up, Corwin spotted the trouble—a group of magists, including a white robe, a blue, and two golds, were gathered out front of a flower shop across the way. A skinny boy stood in the center of them. Gangly limbed and with ears still too large for his face, he looked ten or eleven at most. An Inquisition collar encircled his throat, marking him a known wilder. *So young,* Corwin thought, a sick feeling rising in his stomach. The glowing stones set into it served a single purpose—to keep a wilder from using their magic.

It wasn't the boy causing the stir though, but his mother. She was screaming at the magists, begging them to release her son. Corwin couldn't make out her exact words over the noise of the crowd, but there was no mistaking her desperation. Her arms and hands shook, and tears glistened on her cheeks.

Signe made a strangled noise. "Why are they arresting that little boy?"

"He must be a wilder," Dal said, sounding dubious.

Corwin bit his lip, distraught by the woman's cries. He'd heard of the Inquisition taking children, but this was the first time he'd borne witness to it; the golds did not generally hunt among the nobility. He wanted to step in, to question why they were taking the boy. He seemed harmless, and far too young to be put to death. But there was nothing he could do. High prince or not, he had no authority over the League. That was the price of the League's service to the kingdom—they did not interfere or make policy, but they were not under the crown's command either.

The magists began to haul the boy away. For a second, Corwin thought the woman would collapse. Andrean guardsmen in orange and black had stepped in to hold her back, but instead they seemed to be holding her up. Then without warning, she wrenched free of them and raised her hand at the nearest one, a look of rage transforming her features. Corwin's breath caught in his throat as he watched the guardsman stiffen as if some force held him in its grip. A red haze appeared around his body. No, it was coming *out* of his body. *Blood*. The woman was a wilder, too—a hydrist, with command over water.

The skin on the guard's face began to draw in on itself, like an apple left to dry in the sun. Then his whole body began to do the same until there was nothing left of him but skin dried to leather and the bones beneath nothing but dust. It was over in the space of a breath, stunning in speed and destruction. Utterly terrifying.

A second later, the crowd began to scream and scatter in panic. Even the guards were retreating. The magists turned toward the woman, maces raised with the magestones in them aglow. Water burst forth from the hydrist's hands, but it vanished before reaching the magists. Refusing to give up, the woman tried again, the water flowing harder this time, as if she meant to drown them beneath it. But again it was beaten back by the wardstones.

She screamed her outrage, oblivious of the danger coming at her from behind. One of the guards had conquered his fear, drawing his sword. He plunged it into the woman's back, ramming her all the way through to the other side. The water magic vanished as the woman's face slackened into shock. Then the guard yanked the sword free, and the woman fell. Her son, so silent and still before, began to shriek and struggle. But whatever his power, the collar rendered him harmless.

The magists hauled the boy away, bound for the gold house and the Purging. They picked up his dead mother—for burial. A terrible mixture of pity and fear swirled inside Corwin as he watched them depart, knowing that soon the child would be laid in the ground beside her.

THE MOMENT THEY ARRIVED IN Andreas, Kate was ready to leave. She despised this city, crammed full of people both day and night. The two days they ended up spending there were nearly unbearable, even though she understood the need for it. The attack on the Gregors unnerved her, especially learning for certain that wilders were indeed behind it. With the violence escalating all around, she could almost feel the collar around her neck. Even if she never used her magic again, the magists had ways of knowing what she was. And death by the golds' hands wouldn't be quick, but long and torturous. *The Purging.*

At least Corwin had quickly identified the miner involved, although he'd needed another day to track down his family—only to discover Ralph Marcel had left behind no kin.

"But he did seem to have some gift with animals," Signe reported back to Kate and Bonner the night before their departure. Signe had accompanied Corwin and Dal on every visit they made, insisting she be included.

She could insist the sun not set, and it would probably listen, Kate thought, bemused at the idea of her best friend spending so much time with Corwin.

"That's what got him into trouble," Signe continued. "We found the man who reported him to the golds, and he told us how Marcel could always predict when one of the canaries they use down in the mines was soon to die."

Bonner's brow furrowed. He was leaning near the window of the room Signe and Kate were sharing, a far larger one than they'd rented back in the Crook and Cup. Even still, he seemed too big for it, his head lurking near the ceiling. "And the man told on him for that?"

"It makes no sense," Signe said. "I thought when those birds die, it means the air is poisoned. They should've been grateful for the warning."

Kate shook her head, wishing the room were a mess so that she could put it right again, just to relax. Instead she sat on the bed, legs tucked to her chin. Occupying the bed across from hers, Signe had already pulled out her knife to juggle, her own relaxation exercise. *Maybe I should get her to teach me how,* Kate thought.

Aloud she said, "People are raised to fear wilders, no matter how harmless or useful. It's always been so."

"Yes, well, I suppose they might have a little reason to fear us, after the attack on the Gregors. Not to mention what that woman did outside the Boarbelly," Bonner said, running a hand through his long hair, still wet and hanging loose after his bath. Neither he nor Kate had been there to see the hydrist use her magic, but everyone in the city was discussing it, in all its gruesome detail.

Fear us. The implication in Bonner's words didn't sit well with Kate, the idea that she and Bonner were like that woman in the square. As if being a wilder was the extent of who they were instead of one aspect of themselves. Other than Bonner and her father, she'd known no other wilders, and certainly none who had used their power to kill. She certainly couldn't kill someone directly with her magic, and she'd never been tempted to compel some animal to do it for her.

Signe fixed a scowl at them both. "They were taking her son to be executed. If I were her, I would have fought back with whatever weapons were at hand."

Her hands were the weapon—that's the problem, Kate thought. *A sword could be taken away. Magic is a part of us.* But neither Bonner nor Kate bothered to argue. Not when Signe had that look in her eyes, the one that spoke of how her understanding of the world was the only right one. Kate envied her the ability to see things in such clear shades of black and white. For her, there was always so much gray.

"This Ralph Marcel might've been like you, Kate," Bonner said, bringing the conversation back to its point.

"Yes, a wilder who can control animals," Signe said with a bob of her head. "Corwin thinks the Rising might be controlling the daydrakes. That this is what Marcel was doing." She turned a questioning look on Kate. "Is that possible? Could you control a drake with your power, like you do horses?"

"I . . . I don't know. I've never thought of trying." Kate rolled the idea through her mind, both intrigued and alarmed at the possibility. Could she have stopped those daydrakes attacking that day with her magic? If so, then Corwin would never have seen the revolver, and they wouldn't be here now. Still, the idea of touching the mind of something so foul made her cringe. "It might be possible, though. I used to use my magic on all sorts of animals when I was little. Before my father made me swear to only use it on horses and only when necessary."

"So Corwin may be right." Signe caught the knife and returned it to its sheath. "I wish we could tell him."

Kate sucked in a breath. "Are you mad? He would hand me over to the golds before you could blink."

Signe wrinkled her nose. "I don't believe Corwin would do such a thing. I've seen the way he looks at you. All the time."

Heat filled Kate's cheeks. For a second she wanted to ask for more, to ply Signe with questions about those looks as if she were some silly girl in a romantic tale. But no, this was Corwin. "He doesn't feel that way about me. Not anymore."

Bonner made a noise of dissent, but didn't comment after Kate threatened him with a glare.

She turned back to Signe. "You can never tell Corwin or anyone else about me and Bonner, Sig. You understand that, right? You must promise not to."

Signe managed a haughty scowl, the sort of look only she could pull off. "Of course I won't. But if you ask my opinion, you should."

"No," Kate said, "what we should do is turn around and head straight back to Farhold before we all end up collared."

"Why would they collar me?" Signe asked, cocking her head.

"For being insane," Kate replied.

But joking or not, there was no going back, and they all knew it. *We might be as good as caught already.*

The closer they drew to Norgard, the tenser Kate became. The days were long and tedious as they journeyed from Andreas to Thace, where they met up with the soldiers and wagon, then headed on to Carden. They spent only a single night in each city, barely long enough to appreciate the unique flavor of each.

In Thace, a city built on a marsh where many of the streets were water instead of road, Signe and Dal sacrificed an entire night's rest to roam the city in a rented boat. They'd come back wet and exhausted, but full of adventurous tales involving a capsized boat, a daring underwater escape from the city guardsmen, and a run-in with either a mermaid, a seafairy, or some other such mythical creature. Kate knew not to believe the half of it, although she found it amusing that Dal was so willing to play Signe's tall-tale game.

In Carden, a city renowned across Rime for its distilleries, Corwin and Dal overindulged so badly that neither could sit a horse the next day.

"We didn't know there was bourbon in the chocolates and whiskey in the apple pie," Dal insisted.

"Oh, you knew," Signe replied, smirking. "You just thought yourselves strong enough to take it."

Kate felt sorry for them, even if their suffering was self-inflicted. Corwin always did have a sweet tooth.

Still, despite the pace, every minute felt more like ten, the miles endless. If only she could ride at a Relay pace; then she could outrun these nerves plaguing her at every step. She almost wished for a daydrake sighting, just to distract her. But there'd been no sign or rumor of them since they left Andreas.

When they finally entered Jade Forest, some several weeks after their journey began, her anxiety grew to a fever pitch. The forest bordered Norgard from the west, close enough that its thick, towering trees were visible from the city itself. Kate supposed even more than the worry about Bonner being discovered, it was this sense of homecoming that bothered her so much. Her heart ached at the sights and smells, at once so familiar and yet so long forgotten. The three years she'd been away felt like both an eternity and no time at all. She feared Norgard. Feared the past even as she hoped to uncover it, and she feared the present, too. In Norgard, she would be Traitor Kate to everyone, the wound of her father's crime so much deeper here.

When they stopped for the night more than halfway through the forest, Kate busied herself making camp as best she could. But the activity didn't last long. They had reached one of the caravan campsites, the kind with permanent shelters carved into the bases of the massive trees that formed Jade Forest. There were even wardstone barriers carved into trees as well. This was the same site she'd stayed in the first night after her voluntary exile from Norgard. The straw covering the ground inside the trees made for comfortable bedding, but she doubted she would be able to sleep much, any more than she had that night long ago.

Kate looked up from unrolling her bedroll, her eyes finding Corwin easily. She always seemed to know where he was. He'd selected the tree across the way from hers, his bedroll already spread out inside it. As if he sensed her gaze, he glanced up, and for a moment their eyes met before they both looked away. Kate's heart skipped inside her chest. For just a second, he'd looked like the Corwin she used to know, the boy who could make her pulse race at just a glance, his eyes full of mischief and his mouth curved into a sensual promise.

Her reaction unnerved her, and she scrambled to her feet. "I'm going for a walk," she said to Signe, who'd just come in, carrying her own bedroll. "I'll be back before dark." There was enough light still in the forest to see by, and she had her revolver holstered to one hip if there was trouble.

Signe waved her away. "Go off and make yourself tired so you finally sleep still tonight."

Kate sighed, wishing it were that simple. "You could always sleep somewhere else, you know. Then I won't keep you up with my restlessness."

Signe flashed a suggestive grin. "I would if only you would do the same. That moonbelt is going to waste."

Kate didn't dignify the comment with a response, but slipped out the back side of the tree and into the forest. The magists had already set the barrier around the camp, but she wasn't worried about nightdrakes just yet. There'd been a rumor of daydrakes spotted not far from Marared, but no official word of an attack. Kate doubted the creatures had migrated so far as Norgard. *Unless Corwin is right and the Rising are controlling them.* She prayed it wasn't so. If only the other wilders were more like her and Bonner—careful in using their magic and never doing harm—then maybe the League would stop hunting them, the people stop fearing.

She followed a narrow path through the trees. They grew so tall here that little brush survived, making it easy for her to move without making noise. It was a game she used to play as a child—trying to be as silent as a wild animal. The existence of such creatures had always been a wonder to her—that they could live and thrive outside the city walls despite the threat of drakes. She'd asked her father why the drakes didn't kill all the deer and other woodland creatures, and he'd told her that the drakes hungered for human flesh.

"Then why do we bring our horses and cattle inside the city at night?" she'd asked him.

"Because the drakes are drawn to the human scent we leave on our domesticated animals. They will always hunt those touched by humans first. Anything else does not satisfy their hunger."

"But why?"

"That is their nature, Katie girl. It is mankind's punishment from the gods."

What they'd supposedly done to deserve it, she'd never asked.

The farther Kate walked from the campsite, the more she wanted to reach out with her magic and touch the minds of the animals she sensed around her. She'd barely used her gift at all these last few weeks, not daring to with Master Raith and his blue robes always about. The abstinence was getting to her. It was like not being able to take a full breath for hours on end. Still, she resisted the temptation, as much for Bonner as for herself. If she were ever caught, it would risk exposing him—just because he would doubt-less fight to protect her, like that woman in Andreas. She wondered how many of these Rising attacks were actually that—a loved one defending another.

The path ended in a wide clearing dotted with everweeps and wildflowers. She walked several steps into it, then stopped and breathed in, savoring the sweet smell. She chose a seat in front of a log on the edge of the clearing. Dozens of white daisies grew there, and before she knew it, she had picked a handful and begin weaving them together in a garland. This too was a game she hadn't played since childhood. It took her several tries before she remembered the trick of threading the stems together. As she worked, the wind began to pick up, the storm that had been threatening all day finally drawing close. But Kate liked the song it played through the trees, the leaves rustling, and the creak and murmur of shifting branches.

She became so engrossed that she failed to realize when she was no longer alone.

"I didn't know you could still do that."

Giving a start, she dropped the garland and looked up to see Corwin standing at the head of the same path she had followed. She sucked in a breath, willing her heart to settle.

"I'm sorely out of practice."

"Doesn't look that way to me." He stepped toward her, then stooped to pick up the garland. He held it out to her. "Will you wear it like you used to?"

"No," Kate said at once, and Corwin flinched at her harsh tone. His reaction made her soften, and she took the garland from his hands, adding in a gentler voice, "I would feel too foolish."

Corwin stared down at her, unspeaking.

"Is there something wrong at camp?" Kate said into his silence.

"No, I've just come to fetch you back. It's getting dark and a storm is coming."

"Right." Kate moved to get up, but stopped when Corwin sat down on the log next to her.

"But it's not night yet, and this place is lovely."

Uncomfortable with sitting beneath him, Kate joined him on top of the log, brushing the petals and twigs from her breeches.

Corwin stared up at the sky, swollen with gray clouds. "Do you remember that time when we convinced the master of that traveling circus that we were orphans needing work?"

Kate blinked, taken by surprise. "Of course," she said, tentative toward the subject as she was toward all things from the past. She would never forget it. That night was the first time they'd fantasized about running away together, both of them knowing that the life they dreamed of could never be. He was the high prince, destined to marry someone politically advantageous for Rime—the choice wasn't any more his than hers. *And I was so in love with you,* she thought, the admission more painful than she could've imagined after so long.

She cleared her throat. "He hired us on the spot. You to lunge the horses and me to perform the acrobatics. I always thought he'd gotten that backward."

Corwin smiled. "Me too. You were the best with the horses."

"Yes, and you would've looked better in those tight outfits the acrobats wore."

"Oh, I wouldn't say that." His gaze slid down the outline of her legs visible in the breeches. After much badgering from Signe, she'd stopped wearing the overskirt outside of the cities. A blush crept up Kate's neck, and she focused her gaze on the garland, turning it over in her hands.

Corwin sighed and leaned back, crossing one leg over the other. "I sometimes wish we'd gone through with it. Our lives would be very different now."

"Yes, I suppose they would," Kate said, but without any conviction. It wouldn't have lasted even if they had been brave enough to run away. *Look at us now. Barely able to talk to one another.*

"Signe would be good in a circus," Corwin added, breaking the sudden tension with a grin.

Kate returned it. "I think she was part of one. At least for a little while. But you never know with her. She tells so many stories, then contradicts them by turns."

"She might be the most interesting person I've ever met. Though to tell the truth, her never-ending questions can be a bit tiresome. That's half the reason I came out here, just to get away from them."

Kate rolled her eyes, understanding the sentiment perfectly, despite her undying affection for her. "What is she on about now?"

Corwin ran a palm down his face. "The Inquisition. She can't seem to grasp why it is we let the golds take children from their mothers."

"She doesn't understand. Or maybe she chooses not to." Kate kicked at a rough patch on the ground, uncomfortable with the topic. "Although I can sympathize with her struggle, on that point at least."

Corwin shifted toward her. "How do you mean?"

Tread carefully, Kate told herself. "The League holds a lot of power over people, more than I think they ever had before. Now they can come and go as they please, invading homes, destroying families. I was surprised when your father sanctioned the Inquisition."

"My father didn't." Corwin kicked at the ground too, unearthing an everweep, this one with blue petals, glistening with the constant moisture that gave them their name. "Edwin did. He's responsible for all the changes of late. Even the bridge over the Redrush was his idea."

Kate gaped, feeling a stab of anger. Edwin had always been

arrogant, but she couldn't believe he would attempt to rule with his father still alive. That stupid bridge had gotten Eliza Caine killed. He had no business making such decisions from the lofty towers of Norgard.

"It's my father, you see." Corwin swallowed, the cords in his throat flexing. "The rumors about him are true. He's sick. Something festers inside him that the magists can't heal. It affects both his body and his mind. They don't know what it is, but it came on after the attack."

But that was years ago, Kate thought. A sickness festering this long sounded unnatural, like magic. Her old tutor once told her that during the Sevan Invasion, the green robes had applied their healing arts to create spells that could cause sickness—fever, boils, watery bowels. That was magist magic, though, nothing like what her father could do. Not that she could explain this to Corwin.

"He goes weeks without speaking sometimes," Corwin continued. "And when he does speak, it makes little sense. We've hidden the truth as much as we can, but someone has to make decisions in his stead. Someone has to rule."

Why not you? Kate wanted to say, but she already knew the answer. There'd been no sign of uror. Surely by now, odds were there never would be.

"You sound uncertain," she gently pressed.

Corwin sighed. "That was the first time I'd seen the golds arrest a child. What his mother did was horrible, make no mistake, but Signe has a point. The woman was provoked. My mother would've reacted much the same if it had been Edwin or me. I probably would too, with my own son."

His admission surprised Kate. The first few months after his mother's death, his grief and rage had been so great he couldn't even hear the term *wilder* without needing to hit something. His knuckles still bore the scars. But now he seemed sympathetic to one.

"But then again," Corwin went on, "it really wasn't Edwin's decision to support the Inquisition. It was my father's plan to sanction it before he . . . fell ill." Corwin paused and looked at Kate, his expression suddenly guarded. "I overheard them fighting about it the night before, my father and yours."

Kate stared back at him, not daring to speak or react at all. Of course her father would've objected to the Inquisition if he'd known about it. But if he'd been worried about it, why didn't he tell her? Even afterward, when he'd been imprisoned, he'd refused to see her. He could've given her warning. Maybe she would've gone to Esh instead of Farhold. Then again, maybe he'd tried to tell her, but Corwin never delivered the message.

Go to Fenmore.

"You're so quiet, Kate," Corwin said. "Are you all right?"

She slowly nodded. "It's just I know so little about what happened that night."

Corwin scratched at the stubble darkening his cheek. He'd started shaving again since they'd left Andreas, but not every day. "You know more than you did before." At her sharp look, he made an apologetic face. "Yes, I remember you asking me about it. And I'm sorry I didn't tell you when I had the chance. You had a right to know sooner."

"Yes, I did," Kate said, flustered that he remembered more about that night in the Relay tower than he'd let on. She stood, and in a too-harsh voice she said, "Is there anything else you haven't told me about that night?"

He leaned away from her, brows drawn over his eyes. "No, you know everything now."

Not everything. She stared down at him. "How can I believe you when you held back so much?"

Anger flashed in Corwin's eyes. "How dare you make me feel guilty when it was your father who tried to assassinate mine? Especially when whatever he did left my father a shell of a man."

"Are you accusing my father of sorcery now?" Glaring, Kate raked a hand across her face to push the hair out of her eyes where the wind had begun whipping it about.

"No, of course not." Corwin stood, his superior height giving him an unfair advantage in any argument. "But . . . when I confronted Hale after the attack, he told me he was sorry. That if he'd only known what would happen to my father, he never would have done it."

"Done what? Attack him with a dagger? Like he wouldn't know what would happen if he did that? It makes no sense, Corwin."

"I know. I've thought the same a hundred times, but it's what he said, Kate. I was there."

"And you didn't ask him for an explanation? For more?" She balled her hands into fists, angrier than ever that she'd been kept from her father.

Corwin rubbed a thumb over his chin. "I did, but he refused to tell me. He refused to tell anyone why he did it. We don't know if he was an assassin working for some rival to my father, or whether it was a personal grudge, or something else entirely."

She clenched her teeth. Her father, an assassin? It was absurd. But—"I want to know why he did it," she said, the words coming out of her in a rush. "That's the only reason I agreed to come back to Norgard. I need the truth. Can you understand that?"

A strange look passed through Corwin's eyes, and the anger drained from his face. "Yes. It must've been torture not knowing all these years." He touched her arm and held her gaze, unblinking. "And I promise, Kate, I'll do whatever I can to help you learn the truth."

She examined his expression, probing it for any insincerity but finding none. Then she understood, and immediately, her own anger subsided. This was the Corwin she'd known before. This was a peace offering, his way of calling a truce. They hadn't fought often when they were younger, but when they had, the battles had been epic. Stubbornness was a trait they shared, neither of them willing to admit defeat or wrongdoing, to compromise. For some reason this echo of the past didn't frighten her like the others. Instead she felt her nerves grow calm for the first time in days. Once upon a time, she had trusted Corwin more than any other person, save her father. She hoped he was someone she could trust again.

With a smile curling one half of her face, she said, "Do you swear with both hands?" This was yet another game they used to play.

With a glint in his eyes, he raised his hands and made a cutting gesture over both palms, following their old ritual with ease. But before offering his palms to her, he stopped and said, "On one condition."

"What?"

He stooped to pick up the garland. "That you wear this." He reached toward her and dropped the garland over her brow. His warm fingers brushed the sides of her face, sending a shiver down her neck. He leaned back to examine the effect. "There now. Not foolish at all, but enchanting."

Finally, he held his palms out to her, waiting for her to complete the ritual.

With her sideways smile, she made the slashing gesture against her own palms, then pressed her hands against his, their fingers entwining automatically. More shivers slid through her, and these had nothing to do with the chill in the wind and the raindrops starting to bead her face.

They lingered that way for a moment, hand to hand, but then a loud crack of lightning echoed around them.

"Time to get back to camp." Corwin turned and pulled her toward the path. In seconds they were running through the trees while the thunder rolled and the clouds overturned barrels of rain on them. It plastered Kate's hair to her head, destroying the garland in an instant. Now more than ever she was glad not to be encumbered with a skirt.

Something was wrong at the camp. Kate sensed it even before the sound of the horses' screams reached her. *Drakes?* With her hand on the revolver, she burst through the trees into the campsite after Corwin.

The horses were in a panic. Lightning had struck one of the trees nearby, setting it on fire. All the horses were tied to the same picket line, making the situation even more perilous. One horse was already down, thrashing to regain his feet while the ground turned to mud. Two others were tangled in each other's ropes, legs threatening to break and necks to snap.

Dal and the others were trying to free the horses, but no one could get close enough to get them undone, and they couldn't just cut the rope either. Not with the horses so panicked and straining to run. They would be food for the drakes if they got away.

With the horses' fear invading her mind, Kate acted on instinct. She reached out to the entire herd with her magic. It was easy, her neglected ability hungry for the use and nightfall still far enough away not to impede the magic. She'd only rarely compelled so many horses at once, but it wasn't any harder than shouting to a crowd, a matter of projection. With a single thought she calmed them enough to get them free of the ropes.

The whole thing took no longer than a moment, and so it was only later, once things had settled, that Kate noticed the strange way Master Raith kept looking at her, the expression obvious without his mask to conceal it. With a jolt of fear she understood her mistake. A single lapse, made on instinct, and yet it was enough to condemn her.

For Raith's penetrating look, so sinister in the flashes of lightning, could only mean the magist had seen what she was.

CORWIN HAD NEVER BEEN SO glad to see Norgard. Not even after the two years he'd spent away from it. The last night on this return journey had been far from idyllic. Although they managed to get the horses freed before any suffered permanent damage, and the magists had eventually put out the fire, the rain lingered all through the night. Corwin barely slept, and when he finally woke, he was damp to his bones with a stuffy nose and aching head.

The ride through the rest of Jade Forest and into the countryside on Norgard's western border was subdued. Despite the bright, cloudless day, no one felt much like talking. Foolishly, Corwin had thought things might be better today between him and Kate, after their private conversation, but she seemed even more withdrawn than before. He wasn't sure what had possessed him to seek her out last night, other than a desire to dispel the weary tension between them. If she was to live in Norgard again, they needed to make peace, for both their sakes. But the only notable difference was that she had opted to ride next to him at the front of the group for once.

When the city at last came into view, Kate drew a loud breath and let it out with a rapturous exhale. "Gods, I'd forgotten how beautiful it is."

Corwin took in the sight as well, trying to see it through her eyes. It wasn't hard to feel that same sense of awe. A gleaming white wall, festooned with round turrets capped in pale-blue marble, surrounded a chaotic sprawl of colorful buildings and streets, each one like a wrapped present set about with streamers and ribbon. At the center, Mirror Castle seemed to nest amid the splendor of colors like a giant, rose-gold-hued dragon guarding its treasure hoard. The castle claimed its name from its seven towers, each with a conical roof made of obsidian so polished it reflected the sun like a mirror, setting each point aglow. That and it was home to the Mirror Throne, of course.

"It is at that," Corwin said. The air tasted better here, light and fresh when he sucked in a lungful. The grass was richer, tall and green among the everweeps, and the sky bluer than anywhere else in Rime. *Than all the world.*

But the best sight of all was the horses in the pastures that covered the land beyond the wall, mile after mile of split-rail fencing. Grays, chestnuts, bays, blacks, spotteds, they feasted on the grass, stopping only long enough to drink from nearby streams or water troughs or to pin their ears at the foals and yearlings who played around them, snorting, bucking, and kicking in youthful merriment.

Beside him, Kate seemed to drink in the sight of the horses, her eyes lingering on each one they passed. He wondered what she saw, which ones caught her attention and which she passed over with less interest.

Soon they reached the opened city gates. Two massive horse statues stood, one on either side of the entrance. They weren't identical but asymmetrical complements of each other. The left one, carved in sleek ivory, was leaned back on its haunches, just coming up to a rear, muzzle pointed skyward. The right, carved from glistening onyx, black as pitch, was in full rear, its head curved downward, forelegs striking.

Signe let out a whistle as she stared up at them in awe.

"They are named after the horses of Noralah, the goddess who founded the city," Kate said, glancing at her friend. "Niran and Nalek."

"Magnificent," Signe replied in a breathy voice.

Corwin flashed a grin at Kate. "Remember when we changed their names to Pie and—"

"—Pig," she said with a nervous titter. "We should've been struck dead for blasphemy."

"Not at all. The gods have a sense of humor—a wicked one, in my experience."

It was strangely quiet as they approached, hardly any shepherds or farmers in sight. But the moment the guards standing in the watchtowers realized it was Corwin at the gate, they sounded the bells and shouted down onto the streets, "Prince Corwin has returned!"

The cry was soon picked up by others in the city, until it became a collective roar. "Prince Corwin! Prince Corwin!"

Kate reined her horse back almost at once, moving to the middle of the pack as if she feared being recognized as well. He couldn't blame her wanting to go unnoticed here.

Despite the crowd, they traveled quickly through the winding streets on their way to the castle. Unlike those in Andreas, the paths here had gentle slopes, some up, some down. The buildings weren't nearly so tall either, allowing for plenty of light and an open feel. They were also more pleasant to look upon, that wrapped-present appearance still maintained up close. They came in all shapes, some squat and short with shutters painted in fanciful patterns and awnings trimmed in tassels or ribbons, others sleek and refined in contrasting, complementary colors.

Corwin smiled and waved at the people calling his name, but he wondered at the fervency of their greeting. It was nearly as great as when he'd returned from his long absence. But that time he'd been gone two years, not just a matter of weeks. The people in the street were pressing in to touch him, fingers brushing his boots or his horse's sides. It brought luck to touch a returning prince, but it was a gesture normally reserved for times of war. Then again, maybe the people believed he had been at war, of a kind. By now, every newspaper in Rime had carried the story about his brush with death on the road to Andreas. He wished he could've kept it secret same as he had his time spent away. At the thought, he glanced down at his vambrace, making sure it remained in place. How foolish it had been to get that tattoo. *I never thought I was coming back here.*

His hope had been to enter the castle quietly, not drawing attention to his companions until after he had a chance to discuss things with Edwin. He'd sent word ahead that he was bringing guests with him, but he'd been vague on the details. He knew any objections Edwin or the high council might have about Kate would fade once they learned that she had saved his life and introduced Corwin to the revolver; but it was something he wanted to explain in person, the pen too cold a medium for expressing such events.

But by the time they reached the castle gates, he saw that there would be no quiet entrance. A squadron of royal guards in their blue uniforms awaited their arrival. Captain Jaol stood at the head of the guard, his gaze fixed not on Corwin but somewhere behind him. *On Kate,* Corwin suspected. The chief duty of the royal guard was to ensure the king's safety, and Jaol had been captain of it for nearly twenty years. He'd been there when Kate's father had nearly killed the king, and every line on his face spoke of his animosity toward the traitor's daughter.

Determined to deflect it for now, Corwin waved in greeting. "Captain Jaol, how nice of you to greet me personally."

Jaol bowed, revealing the bald patch on the top of his head. He was a tall man, slight of build and with a nose like a twig snapped in half. "Welcome home, your highness," he said, coming up from the bow. "We received word of your arrival, and I'm glad to see you are well and whole again."

"Thank you. It's good to be well and whole."

Jaol didn't smile at Corwin's poor attempt at cheek. He motioned behind him. "Your brother is in the courtyard. There's been a bit of excitement this morning."

Excitement? Corwin arched an eyebrow but didn't ask for more. Not when he could hear the commotion from here. He dismounted and handed his horse to one of the grooms who had rushed up from the stable the moment they'd arrived in the bailey. The others in the company followed suit.

Master Raith, who'd been riding at the back of the procession, led his horse to the front and bowed to Corwin. From behind his mask he said, "Your highness, with your permission, I will give my fee summary to the clerk, then be on my way. I've business at my order's house."

"Of course," Corwin said. "Thank you for your service. If I may ask, would you mind keeping me informed of any news you hear about the daydrakes?"

Raith inclined his head. "And I would ask you the same. My order is the most at risk from these attacks."

"Yes, I understand." As the defensive order, the blues protected all the caravans. Corwin clapped the man on the back, surprising himself by the ease of the gesture. It seemed he'd grown fond of this particular magist. "The moment I hear anything, so shall you. I'll send word to your house if you're not presently in the city."

"Thank you." Raith bowed again, then handed his horse off to a groom. Before departing, he said good-bye to Signe, Bonner, Dal, and finally to Kate, who had drifted slightly away from the group, as if she hoped to make a quick escape. He whispered something into her ear that made her eyes narrow and her lips press into a thin line. Corwin wondered what it was, but the noise in the courtyard beckoned to him once more.

He turned and strode across the bailey, through the main archway between the east and west wings, and into the cobblestoned courtyard. A large circular fountain, bearing another set of statues honoring Niran and Nelek in its center, occupied the middle of the courtyard. On a normal day, the place was quiet and empty save for a page scurrying to fulfill some duty or a wagon or carriage delivering goods or guests. But today it was full of people;

courtiers, nobles, and servants crowded around the edges, all of them with their attention fixed on the group of men standing near the fountain.

Corwin spotted his brother among them, along with all the members of the high council: Minister Rendborne, master of trade; Knox, master of arms; Porter, master of coin; Fletcher, master of the hearth; Nell, master builder; and Alaistar Cade, master of horse, who had once served as second under Kate's father. If it hadn't been for the location, Corwin would've thought this was a council meeting. Grand Master Storr, head of the Mage League, and Maestra Vikas, head of the gold order, who were not part of the council, were present as well.

What are they doing out here? he wondered, but then his eyes fell on the thing lying in their midst. He recognized the black scales and the dragonish shape of the body.

A dead daydrake.

Corwin passed through the crowd, which parted at the sight of him, and stepped up beside his brother. "Where did you get that?" he said.

Edwin turned his head toward Corwin, the look of surprise on his face quickly giving way to annoyance. "And a welcome home to you, too, brother."

Corwin was too intrigued to feel guilty about his lack of diplomacy. This was the first time he'd been able to examine a daydrake closely, and although dead, it was no less intimidating. This specimen was roughly the size of a small bear. It lay halfway on its side, mouth opened to reveal the sharp teeth, and with its right foreleg extended out in front of it, the claws spread like curved daggers set up in a row. Its neck had been partially severed from its body. Corwin covered his mouth as its putrid stench reached him.

"What happened?" Corwin turned his gaze fully on Edwin for the first time. Surprise struck him at Edwin's unkempt state. Blood and dirt smeared his tunic and breeches, and fresh scratches lined his forearms. Nevertheless, Edwin still cut an imposing figure. Tall and elegantly handsome, he sported a lighter shade of blond hair than Corwin's and his eyes were their mother's hazel. Sometimes when Corwin looked at them, all he saw was her.

"I came across that thing when I was out riding," Edwin replied. "It's the same as what attacked you on the road to Andreas, yes? A daydrake?"

Corwin nodded, a sick feeling rising in his stomach. Some of the travelers they'd passed on the road spoke of daydrake sightings around Marared. That city was a little farther east than Andreas and Farhold, but not much. But this one had made it all the way to Norgard already. "Where were you riding?"

"On the road toward Penlocke."

South then. Only—"There was just the one?"

"Yes, and a good thing, too, or I might not have come through it at all." Edwin rubbed his hands together as if trying to clean away the blood. "My pistol shot only wounded it, but when it jumped at me, I was able to use the force of its leap to cut its throat with my sword."

"You did well, your highness," Minister Knox said. The large, burly man looked elderly with his gray hair and skin like crumpled parchment, but Corwin knew from experience he was still fit enough to pummel men half his age—as he did often in his arms lessons.

Several of the people around them echoed the sentiment, and Corwin reminded himself that whatever was said and done here would be discussed and passed along until the entire city knew the story, or some version of it.

"I'm glad you're all right, Edwin, but I'm surprised there was only one." Corwin stooped nearer the daydrake for a closer look. "They seem to run in packs, same as nightdrakes." Still, one could be dangerous enough. *And it attacked my brother,* Corwin realized. First the Gregors, then him, and now Edwin. If the Rising was behind this, then their purpose was clear—to unseat the power of Norgard.

Nervous chatter broke out all around them, several of the courtiers daring to come closer.

"How can we be safe with these creatures terrorizing the daytime?" someone asked. The question was repeated in a dozen different variations as it swept through the crowd.

Minister Rendborne raised his hands, the right one bearing a large magestone ring that glowed dully in the sunshine filling the courtyard. Whatever vanity the magic allowed him, Corwin couldn't guess, but the master of trade was easily the most dashing member of the royal council, with striking eagle eyes, golden hued and sharp. He was also the most comfortable with public speaking.

In a loud voice he said, "Have no fear. The Tormane family has always kept us safe and will continue to do so. Have faith in the high king!"

The speech had little effect, despite Rendborne's enthusiasm and charismatic manner. Most of these people lived in the castle, and either they knew firsthand of King Orwin's sickness or they suspected it strongly. How could they have faith in a king so infirm that he was rarely seen outside his personal chambers?

The realization of their doubt spurred Corwin into action. He walked over to the fountain just beyond the drakes' body and climbed onto the edge.

"What Minister Rendborne says is true," Corwin said in a raised voice, commanding immediate silence. He drew a breath and plowed on. "In my travels I have discovered a weapon that will change the face of Rime forever, one so powerful it may one day end the plague of the drakes, both in the night and the day."

He paused and turned back the way he'd come, scanning the crowd for Bonner, Signe, and Kate. He spotted them lurking on the edge of the courtyard with Dal. "Miss Brighton, Miss Leth, Master Bonner, please come here," Corwin called.

A look of horror came over Kate's face, and Corwin guessed that if he'd been near enough, she might have murdered him where he stood. But she couldn't refuse him, not in front of so many watching eyes. With Bonner leading the way, the three approached the fountain.

The silence from a moment before shattered as the people recognized Kate. Corwin heard her name spoken over and over again in worried, hostile tones. *Kate Brighton . . . the traitor's daughter . . . Traitor Kate.* He heard his own unofficial title uttered as well, *the Errant Prince.* Anger churned in his stomach. He'd promised Kate he would protect her from this very thing; he'd assured her she would be welcomed back.

"And I mean to see it done," he said under his breath. Although she might indeed kill him for it later, Corwin called for Kate to come stand beside him on the fountain.

Once Kate was up and visible to the entire crowd, Corwin spoke again in the loudest, most kingly voice he could muster—a voice that no one would dare contradict or disrespect. "Kate Brighton, daughter of the traitor Hale, saved my life on the road from Farhold to Andreas when my caravan was attacked by an entire pack of these daydrakes."

He paused to sweep his gaze over the crowd. Dozens of eyes stared back at him—ladies in elegantly embroidered day dresses with parasols over their shoulders, noblemen with clean-shaved faces and bejeweled daggers at their waists, servants and guards in their uniforms. He held them all as equal in his gaze.

"I owe her a blood debt great enough to have canceled out any transgressions she herself can be held accountable for." *None of which were hers to begin with,* he added in his mind. "Let it be known to everyone assembled here and throughout all of Norgard that Kate Brighton is no longer an enemy to the high king."

Corwin stopped speaking and waited for the crowd to respond, but only silence and icy stares met his proclamation.

That was until Edwin stepped forward and said, "I, for one, am proud to welcome her back." He took hold of Kate's hand, and she stiffened, lips pinched tight as he raised her knuckles to his mouth to kiss them. Corwin gritted his teeth at the sight of it and the bad memories it invoked.

"Thank you for seeing my brother returned safely," Edwin told Kate with a warm smile on his face. "You are welcome in Norgard, Miss Brighton. Now and forever."

This time the crowd broke into applause. It was reserved, not quite enthusiastic, but a start. Edwin had developed the knack for swaying their opinion in the years he'd secretly worn their father's mantle.

When the crowd quieted once more, Corwin said, "It was Miss Brighton who brought a new weapon to my attention. She used it to kill three daydrakes at once!" He pulled the revolver out of the holster at his side and held it up. "This weapon is what I bring back to Norgard from my travels. It is no ordinary pistol. It's called a revolver, an invention of Master Tom Bonner from Farhold, created with the help of Miss Signe Leth of Esh. Both have traveled to Norgard to make more of these weapons for us. Master Bonner has done what no other gunsmith in the world has managed. It is a firearm that can discharge multiple rounds without reloading."

Corwin turned and pointed the revolver at the dead drake. "Stand back," he commanded.

Edwin and the high councilmembers obeyed, several of them going so far as to cover their ears.

Corwin cocked the trigger and fired, to the shock of the crowd. Then without pausing he did it again and again, discharging all six bullets. The drake's body rocked back and forth at the impact, blood and scales spraying out as each one tore through it.

When it was over, the crowd broke into cheers. He heard his name shouted in ecstatic tones, the title Errant Prince forgotten. Even Edwin clapped, although the gesture was perfunctory, his expression aloof. Corwin ignored the disappointment he felt at such a tepid response. He should've known better than to hope for his brother's approval.

With the demonstration now over, Corwin stepped down from the fountain.

Edwin turned at once to Signe. "Welcome to Norgard, Miss Leth. But what, may I ask, is your part in this endeavor?"

"May the blessing of Aslar be upon you, your highness." Signe made a quick bow. "I am honored to be welcomed here. I hold the secret of the black powder used in the bullet casings, my own special formula that makes the revolver possible."

"I see." Edwin beamed at her. "That is surprising and excellent news." He gestured to Bonner. "And it is a pleasure to meet you, Master Bonner."

Grand Master Storr approached them then, introducing himself to Bonner and Signe with a bright smile. He wore no mask, a privilege of his rank, and the only indications of his own importance were the magestone mace hooked at his belt and his black robe. A thick multicolored band of stripes ran down the robe's front, representing all the League orders and marking him as grand master. The largest stripe was white, indicating the order from which he'd been raised. He was handsome in an understated way, with wavy brown hair threaded with silver that hung to his shoulders. He had a way of making everyone feel as if they were the most important person in the room regardless of rank or station.

Storr kissed Signe's hand, then did the same to Kate. "Welcome to you all. Now, I for one would love a closer look at this remarkable revolver."

A nervous smile appeared on Bonner's face as Corwin handed Storr the gun. The moment it was in the grand master's hands, the rest of the high council crowded in for a better look. Soon they were plying Bonner with questions about how it worked.

Corwin slowly retreated, allowing them the chance to fuss over Bonner, who seemed to be enjoying the attention. Signe was enjoying the same as several of the councilmembers speculated that surely her special mixture of black powder was the key to keeping the mechanism from misfiring.

"Are you one of the Furen Mag?" Minister Rendborne asked, and Corwin turned away, not wanting to laugh at whatever ridiculous answer Signe would give him.

Spying Kate on the other side of the group, Corwin moved to join her, but before he could, Edwin appeared at his side. "Congratulations, brother. This round to you then."

"Round?" Corwin cocked his head. "Whatever do you mean?"

A cool smile parted Edwin's lips. "Surely someone has told you by now."

"Told me what?" Corwin placed his hands on his hips, annoyed at Edwin's patronizing tone. Not that his brother could help it. Ever since they were little, he'd had that tone whenever he addressed Corwin, as if such were a requirement from an older brother to a younger.

The smile retreated from Edwin's face. "To be honest, my only regret is that Mother didn't live to see it."

Corwin flinched, struck as he always was whenever Edwin mentioned their mother. Although he'd spoken the words in a pleasant, conversational tone, Corwin didn't miss the barb, the never-ending blame Edwin placed on him for her death.

"See what?" Corwin said through gritted teeth.

"The uror, brother. The sign has finally appeared."

At Edwin's words, the ground seemed to shift beneath Corwin's feet, and he widened his stance, steadying himself. All at once the enthusiastic greeting of the crowd outside made sense. They weren't welcoming home the second-born prince of Norgard but the next possible heir, the man who could be the high king.

Only uror would tell. It was finally here.

THERE WAS MUCH TO DO. A dozen decisions to make and words to be spoken, but in the hours that followed his arrival at Norgard, only one thing occupied Corwin's thoughts.

The uror.

He'd been convinced it would never come. The first year after his sixteen birthday, he'd woken every morning expecting it to be the day the sign would appear. He'd been told since birth that it would come, that he and his brother would have to prove their worth to follow in their father's footsteps.

But day after day came and went with no sign of it. And as one year became two, he would go to sleep each night with the weight of his unworthiness pressing on his chest. By the time the third year came, he began to accept in his heart that it was never going to happen. That acceptance was half the reason he left Rime. There seemed no point in staying. Not with all his failures.

I failed as a son.

When the panic started that day in the marketplace, the wilder burning everything in reach, Corwin's mother had ordered him to climb the rail outside the seamstress shop, but he'd argued with her. He wanted to help, not flee. She'd insisted, and he'd finally obeyed, climbing all the way to the roof. But when he turned to help her up after him, it was too late. All he could do was perch there on the edge and watch while the frenzied crowd crushed her beneath their feet.

I failed as a brother.

"Why did you let her die?" Edwin said that night. "Corwin, why didn't you save her?" They were questions he couldn't bring himself to answer. He didn't need to. All of Norgard bore witness to his shame. He heard them whispering about it when they laid the queen's body on the pyre and anointed her skin with holy fire.

I failed as a friend.

"Dal!" he had screamed, searching for him among the black-ened, smoking debris. "Dal!" When he finally found him there'd been so much blood, so much damage. "I'm sorry, Dal. I didn't mean for this to happen. I didn't know."

I failed . . . Kate.

"Please let him go, Corwin," she had said, falling to her knees before him. Shudders wracked her body, her voice hoarse from screaming. "Mercy, please. Send us into exile. If you ever loved me, please do this. Don't let him die today. Don't let him die."

With sheer force of will, Corwin stopped the flood of memories. He couldn't handle them right now.

While the soldiers loaded the dead daydrake onto a cart to send to the League Academy for dissection and study, Corwin led his companions into the central wing. He needed to get them settled into their new quarters. *Or old ones,* he reminded himself, taking a quick glance at Kate. A stoic expression sat across her features and her spine formed a rigid line, but he could see the fragility beneath that hard exterior.

Doubt rose up in him. When he'd sent word to the castle of

their impending arrival two days ago, he'd made an impromptu decision to request the old Brighton quarters be prepared for Signe and Kate. The three-bedroom suite had been unoccupied since Hale's arrest and execution, no other courtier willing to reside in the home of a traitor. Although the Brighton family had owned a house in Norgard's Glentrove district north of the castle, Hale and his wife and daughter had resided primarily in the castle. Hale's duties as master of horse required him to spend so much time in the royal stables, and the quarters had been Kate's home. But now Corwin wasn't sure that his decision had been wise. Suppose it was too painful for her?

Damn, he inwardly cursed. He'd failed again. *Why didn't I ask her?* It was too late to take it back it now, though. The castle housekeeper, Mrs. Paden, approached them the moment they stepped through the door.

Bowing stiffly to Corwin, she said, "I have both the Brighton quarters and the bachelor suite adjacent ready for your guests, your highness. I will escort them there myself, if you wish."

Corwin heard Kate's sharp intake of breath from behind him and winced. "Yes, that would be fine. Thank you, Mrs. Paden."

The woman made an abrupt turn and motioned for them to follow.

Corwin spoke a quick good-bye to Signe and Bonner, promising to check in on them later. Then, he touched Kate's arm and said in a low voice, "If you don't wish to stay here, I can make other arrangements."

She stared back at him for several seconds while a tempest of emotions churned in her eyes. Finally she offered him a timid smile. "I'll be fine."

He nodded and dropped his hand from her arm. He wished he could go with her, to help combat the demons she would face returning to her childhood home three years after her father's death.

But Corwin had his own demons to battle.

For the next three days, Corwin did nothing but provide accounts of his travels and prepare for the uror ritual that would officially mark the beginning of the trials. He spoke openly about what he had learned of Ralph Marcel in Andreas—much to Edwin's annoyance at his disobedience—and his speculations that the Rising was behind the daydrakes, but whenever the subject of the uror came up, he found himself tongue-tied.

In the two-hour session covering the history of the uror that he had with Master Weston, his old tutor, Corwin failed to ask so much as a single question. The realization that there was an uror sign in the city, some animal bearing the black and white marking of the gods, had left him paralyzed. *There must be some mistake.* He hadn't even asked what kind of animal it was—and so far no one had volunteered the detail, as if speaking about it were taboo.

Fortunately, he had a few pressing matters to distract him. He spent several hours discussing the presence of Prince Eryx Fane of Seva with Minister Knox. The old master of arms was an expert strategist, able to anticipate enemy moves with uncanny skill, but after a long debate, they both decided the prince's visit was little threat. Knox couldn't see any advantage Seva might press in Andreas. Lord Nevan might envy House Tormane's rule, but his city was strong only in physical defense, not offering the Godking anything he would need to conquer Rime where he'd failed before.

To do that, he would need magist magic and nothing less. No army could survive here long without the magists to protect them from the drakes.

There was also the follow-up business with Ralph Marcel. Before leaving Andreas, Master Raith had inquired after the wilder with the gold robes, but they said that no such person had ever been claimed by the Inquisition. Although Master Raith didn't state it outright, Corwin had gotten the impression that Raith wasn't surprised they would deny it. Losing a captured wilder would reflect poorly on them and might even give other wilders ideas. But Corwin wasn't ready to give up so easily. Too many people had seen Marcel taken. Although he doubted it would lead anywhere, he spent an entire afternoon drafting a letter to the head of the gold order house in Andreas, asking for them to send the official record of all the people taken by the Inquisition in their city in the last year by order of the high prince. He delivered the signed and sealed missive to the Relay house in Norgard himself.

On the night of the ritual, Corwin stood in his quarters with his back rigid, waiting impatiently for a servant to finish buttoning the black tunic down his front. Fine silk piping of sky blue trimmed the front of the tunic and the edges as well as his black breeches. In the quarters adjacent to his, Edwin was donning the same somber outfit. The two of them would enter the Temple of Noralah side by side, mirror images of one another in solemn solidarity of the quest they were embarking on together.

And against each other.

"You look nervous," Dal said from where he sat lounging in a nearby armchair. He held a glass of wine in one hand, his third by Corwin's count.

Corwin rolled his eyes. "Sure you're talking about me? They say wine is courage in liquid form."

"Indeed they do." Dal stood and held the glass out to him. "And I feel ready to slay giants and shame gods. Care for some?"

Temptation called to Corwin, but he ignored it. If the priestesses smelled wine on him, they would be forced to stop the ritual. Neither prince was permitted anything to help dull his senses. They'd also been required to fast all day. The sacrifice, in both the hunger now and the pain that would come later, would be a measure of their worthiness.

On second thought, maybe I should drink the whole bottle.

But the servant was finished, and it was time to leave.

As they stepped out into the corridor, Corwin said to Dal, "Is she coming?"

"I think so," Dal replied, knowing exactly which "she" he meant. "Signe plans to drag her along regardless of her wishes."

Corwin suppressed a sigh. He'd barely glimpsed Kate these last few days, but every time he did, he could sense her unhappiness like a cold breeze seeping through an icy window. He'd sent her several messages asking if she would like new quarters, but she'd ignored them. *Once this is over, I will seek her out in person,* he swore to himself for at least the tenth time.

The two princes were to ride at the head of a procession from Castle Norgard to the Temple of Noralah. The high councilmembers, Grand Master Storr, along with the head of each order, and a squadron of soldiers led by Captain Jaol were to act as escort. Their horses were already saddled and ready when the brothers arrived in the courtyard. Corwin climbed aboard his new mount, wishing it were Stormdancer. He liked Nightbringer well enough so far, but they'd had little chance to bond. *It will be trial by fire for us both tonight,* he thought as he guided the horse through the gates and out into the streets, where every citizen in Norgard had assembled to watch the princes meet their fate.

Nightbringer pranced and crow-hopped, tossing his head at the noise. It took years to train a warhorse, and Nightbringer had been in training less than two. Corwin steadied the animal with his legs and kept his eyes fixed ahead, trying to ignore the crowd.

Astride his own horse, Edwin eyed Corwin and gave him an approving nod. "I was half worried you would disappear again."

"Worried or hopeful?" Corwin replied, returning his brother's jab more out of habit than true defensiveness. It was an old conflict between them. Although Edwin was older, Corwin had always been the favored son. Their father valued Corwin's bold and fearless nature over Edwin's caution and cunning. Once King Orwin had all but declared outright that given the choice, he would pick Corwin to succeed him.

I doubt he would say the same now.

The Temple of Noralah stood in the middle of the main square in the Valeo district. Surrounding the temple were five of the six order houses, each painted its respective color, with only the gold absent. Same as in the other cities, the gold house resided outside Norgard's walls. The temple itself was long and rectangular, made of massive stone blocks with pillars set across the raised front entrance. The crowd had surrounded the building but left a clear path to the steps. No one save the priestesses, the princes, and the high king were permitted inside for the ritual.

With Nightbringer finally settling, Corwin allowed himself to gaze at the people. Almost at once, his eyes fell on Kate, standing off to the side with Signe and Bonner. Her presence gave him a brief moment of comfort. When they were younger, the two of them had often discussed what the uror would be like, what it would mean. Kate always knew what to say to make him feel better. The memory of the last time they'd discussed it came to him now.

"Just think how exciting it'll be, Cor. It will make our races and duels seem like child's play," Kate had said while the two of them lay sprawled on a blanket, letting the food from their picnic settle in their stomachs. "You're sure to win."

Corwin reached out and brushed a strand of black hair back behind her ear, his hand lingering to cup her face. "What if I don't want to win?"

"Whyever not?" She smiled that sideways smile, her large eyes veiled in dark lashes.

"It'll mean . . . giving you up." He tried to kiss her, but she pressed a finger to his mouth.

"Don't think about that. When you're king, you can set your own rules. You must win and enjoy every moment of it. We'll find a way to make it fun and exciting together."

"If it ever does come," he had said. "If ever."

How wrong she'd been. It wasn't excitement he felt now but dread, heavy and pressing.

I don't want this. Maybe once, when he was young enough to still believe he was worthy, before he'd proved without doubt that he wasn't. He glanced at his vambrace, making sure the tattoo was hidden from view. It would've been easier to keep it hidden with a magestone, but he didn't want the speculation such would draw.

The darkened entrance into the temple seemed to leer at him like the snarling mouth of a predator. But there was no backing out. To deny the uror was anathema, a sacrilege so great that he would be accursed by the gods. Only one of the Tormane line had ever done it before—the brother of Corwin's great-great-grandfather, Morwen. The name of that brother was unknown, stricken from all record and memory. The accounts referred to him only as the Nameless One.

Edwin and Corwin dismounted and left their horses with their escorts. The sound of drumming greeted them as they entered the temple. Priestesses in shimmering, iridescent robes stood along both sides of the dimly lit sanctuary, playing the drums in a hypnotic harmony, the sound like galloping horses. They wore blindfolds and played with their faces tilted up toward the mural-covered ceiling. At the front of the sanctuary, the high priestess stood in a similar pose before the altar. Her headdress was made to look like a horse head, its coat a fiery chestnut with black diamonds for eyes. They sparkled in the light of the torches on the walls and the glowing coals scattered across the top of the altar. Three statues reared up behind the high priestess—Niran and Nelek on the right and left, with the carved likeness of the goddess Noralah between them.

Sitting in a chair adjacent to the altar, High King Orwin watched his sons approaching. Only there was no recognition in his gaze or pride in his expression. There was nothing but the same emptiness that had been there for the last three years. A magestone glowed at the base of his throat, held there by a leather cord. Corwin didn't recognize the spell on it, but he could guess it was something to keep the king calm and as close to lucid as possible. Gray, wrinkled skin hung loose over Orwin's gaunt cheeks. He was leaned back in the chair, slumped to one side. His tunic drooped about his stooped shoulders and sunken chest. Seeing him like that, unable to forget the strong, robust man he'd been before, Corwin wondered if death would've been better than this half life.

Pulling his gaze away from his father, he focused on the high priestess as she began to speak. She told the story of Noralah, who had tamed the first horses, then about the first uror and the early kings of Norgard. They were stories Corwin had heard before, and he found his mind wandering, as the never-ending beat of the drums thrummed inside his skull. He thought about Hale and the attack on his father. He thought about Kate and his brother and mother, Dal, and every way in which he had failed and all the ways he would fail again.

When the high priestess came to the end of the stories, she leaned toward the altar and picked up the branding iron. Its tip glowed bright orange from where it had sat nestled among the coals.

She approached Edwin first. "Hold out your right hand, first-born son of Tormane." Edwin did as she bade, and the high priestess pressed the brand to his palm, searing it with a dreadful sizzling sound. Edwin flinched but he didn't scream, not even when the smell of his own burning flesh filled the temple. Watching and waiting his turn, Corwin felt the sweat break out on his body. He thought he might vomit if he opened his mouth.

When she finished with Edwin, the high priestess returned the brand to the fire, heating it once more. Corwin counted all the breaths he took, forcing them to be deep and slow. *I will not flinch. I will not scream.* He widened his stance and held out his hand when the high priestess approached him. She jammed the glowing tip against his palm, and he clenched his teeth to keep from crying out. The pain tore through him like something alive and ravenous. His legs went weak, heart hammering against his breastbone. Nausea clenched his stomach and climbed his throat, and he swallowed back bile.

It was over in a moment, but the pain seemed like it would never end. He wrapped the fingers of his left hand around his right wrist, trying to squeeze the sensation off like a tourniquet. He couldn't open the palm on his injured hand, but he knew the skin beneath was blistered in the shape of the brand—a wheel with eight spokes set inside the holy triangle. The symbol of choice and of fate.

The uror mark.

Praying it was almost over, Corwin forced himself to count his breaths again, his mind focused on something other than the pain. He felt Edwin's gaze on him, judging his every reaction.

The priestess raised both her hands and said in a loud, ringing voice, "Bring forth the uror sign."

For a moment nothing happened, but then Corwin heard it— the sound of hooves striking stone behind him. Was it a stag? A boar? But then the animal made a noise of the kind that Corwin had heard a thousand times before. A sound so familiar it wouldn't have even registered to him if he were any other place besides the Temple of Noralah. But no. It couldn't be.

Corwin turned and let his eyes behold the impossible.

The uror sign was a *horse*.

It was young, but not a foal, two years at least. Later he would learn that the colt simply appeared in a pasture a few weeks after he left on his peacekeeping tour. One half of his body was inky black, the other white as ivory. The shaded line dividing the two followed the length of his spine in a gray-colored dorsal stripe. A priestess held the colt by a halter and lead, the muscles in her arms taut from trying to keep control of the animal. The colt arched his neck and pranced sideways, snorting and tossing his head. His eyes rolled with skittish excitement, one pale blue and one black.

Corwin had never before beheld something so beautiful or terrifying. Tears burned his eyes at the sight of it, and fear rippled through his chest. He both loved and hated it. *A horse. The uror sign is a horse!*

He tried to force his mind to accept the truth but failed. There had been only one horse as an uror sign before, more than two hundred years ago during the War of Three, when the nightdrakes first appeared in Rime. It was a dark time, one of great turmoil and upheaval, and the goddess sent the most powerful and sacred of signs to hail the new king, a man strong enough to rally Norgard against the nightdrakes long enough for the wall to be built around the city.

And now the daydrakes have appeared, and the Rising is gaining strength, Corwin thought. Dark times had come again.

He bowed his head, unable to look upon the horse a moment longer. A voice whispered in his mind that he should just concede now and let the worthy brother win.

If only he could.

THE FIRST YEAR OF KATE'S exile from Norgard, she'd been plagued by homesickness. It would strike at random moments, triggered by a familiar smell or sound or a common phrase spoken by a stranger. Then all at once tears would prick her eyes and breathing would become a struggle. She'd dealt with it then the only way she knew how—by moving forward, staying busy. That was the best part of her work with the Relay; the pressure of the rides helped her outrun the ghosts. On the road, there was no one around to see her cry, and eventually the longing for home passed until she was certain she would never suffer it again.

But since returning to Norgard, her homesickness had returned worse than ever and with few ways to combat it. She didn't understand how it could be so when the very home she longed for surrounded her now. Every piece of furniture, every painting and statue, every mark on the marble floor was familiar. Nothing had changed. It seemed since her father's death, no one had wanted to inhabit the quarters of a traitor, not even long enough to clear it out. Then at last Kate understood that it wasn't the physical space her heart wanted, but the past she could never return to.

It didn't help that the present had become so tense as well. When she wasn't being ambushed by memories of the past, her mind kept returning to the parting words Master Raith had spoken to her the day they arrived at the castle.

I know what you are.

He'd whispered it into her ear so no one could hear, then walked away without another glance. There'd been no sign or word from him since—nearly a week now. She couldn't understand it. Why make the threat and never follow through with it? All she could think was that he was waiting for the right moment to reveal her secret, some opportunity that would best serve him in some way.

Or maybe it wasn't a threat at all.

But no, she couldn't believe that. Not from a magist. Not when she was a wilder—*and he knows!*

She was trapped. She couldn't leave, not with Bonner and the task he faced of making the revolvers. He'd run into trouble already—the first molds he created cracked the moment one of the royal blacksmiths tried to use them. Kate had a feeling Bonner didn't fully realize just how much he relied on his magic to accomplish what he did. Sometimes the magic was so instinctual, the wielder wasn't even aware of using it. She feared things were only going to get worse. It was why she hadn't told either him or Signe what Raith had said. Kate didn't want them to panic and do something foolish, like try to get her to leave the country. *I need more time to discover the truth about my father.*

It was past time she got started.

Mustering her courage, Kate flipped back the sheets and climbed out of bed. She dressed quickly, knowing that if she hesitated even for a second, she might change her mind. She'd barely left her rooms these last few days, but today she would visit the royal stables. Surely there were still some of her father's friends there, people who knew him well enough for him to have shared his secrets with them. *Since he wasn't sharing them with me.*

Go to Fenmore. She still had no idea what it meant. But someone must. She hoped that Alaistar Cade might help. He was master of horse now, but for the first seventeen years of her life, Alaistar had been her father's second—and her uncle by proxy. She had no other family, not counting her mother, who was never around enough to be counted. But she didn't know what to expect from Alaistar now. On the day her father was executed, he'd been away on an expedition to Rhoswen in search of new horses to add to the bloodlines. Kate fled Norgard before his return. When she saw him in the courtyard the day of their arrival, he'd glanced at her several times, but always with a guarded expression.

Leaving her bedroom, she headed down the hall to the main room. The place was quiet, Signe still asleep after a late night out with Dal. For a moment as Kate passed her father's study, a large ebony desk tucked in the far corner of the main room, she could almost see him out of the corner of her eye. With a hollow ache in her center, she headed through the door.

Dim light filled the corridor, the sun just starting to show its face beyond the stained glass windows, these depicting the Ride of Adair in a series of frames. The sound of footsteps reached her ears and for half a moment she considered retreating back to her room long enough to let whomever it was pass. But then she raised her head and carried on. She was done being a coward, or at least behaving like one.

Keeping to one side of the staircase, she headed down, only to stop a moment later when she saw Corwin climbing up. He held a napkin in his left hand, the smell of cinnamon and lemon wafting toward her. His right hand was still wrapped in gauze from the uror branding. This was the first time she'd seen him since that night.

A smiled crested his lips when he spotted her. "Oh good, you're awake."

She eyed him suspiciously. "Did you bring me sweet rolls?"

"What, these?" He held up the napkin, his expression turning impish. "Whyever would you think I'd bring you something so delicious?"

Against her better judgment, Kate closed her eyes and inhaled the smell of them. A smile curled the side of her face. "Because you know I have an unholy obsession with the way they taste."

"Unholy indeed." He held out the napkin. "I'm glad to see your tastes haven't changed."

Kate snatched one of the rolls and took the biggest bite she could manage. She'd eaten well since arriving at the castle, decadent meals shared with Signe and Bonner and comprised of every food imaginable—except for sweet rolls. Those were a treat considered appropriate only for children, it seemed.

And the high prince of Norgard. Corwin took the second roll on the pile and devoured nearly half of it in one bite. They shared an icing-smeared grin.

He wiped his mouth with the back of his hand. "Where are you headed this morning?"

Her stomach did a somersault. Maybe such a sugary confection wasn't a good idea just now. "The stables."

A look of surprise crossed Corwin's face. "That's fortunate. I was coming to ask you to visit the stables with me today, actually."

"You were?"

Corwin nodded, his gaze shifting nervously away from her face, then back again. "I had a talk with Bonner yesterday. He mentioned that you were . . . ah . . . a bit restless and spending far too much time inside."

Kate put a hand on her waist. "You two were talking about me?"

Corwin ran a thumb over his chin, tracing the line of the scar. "He was worried about you, and . . . and so was I. I thought I'd made a mistake placing you back in your family's old quarters." He motioned to the hallway behind her.

It was a mistake, she thought. *You should've asked me.* And yet, it wasn't. She knew that no matter how much it hurt, she needed to face down these restless ghosts if she ever hoped to find peace. She drew a deep breath.

"I'm fine with the quarters. What is it you and Bonner decided about me during this little talk you had?" she said, her tone biting.

"I thought it was time for me to honor my promise to find you a position in the royal stables. I know it was always your dream and—" He broke off, clearing his throat. "And so I've arranged for you to audition with Master Cade."

Kate's heart did a strange jilting dance in her chest. *An audition?* It seemed impossible to believe after years of wanting to follow in her father's footsteps. Even more than that, if Master Cade was receptive to the idea, then maybe he would be open to answering her questions, too. Hope bubbled up inside her, and she forced back a giddy smile.

"I suppose I would be okay with that. Gods know I'm dying to ride."

Corwin bowed his head, then motioned to the steps. "All right, let's be off then. Although it seems a shame I didn't need these to bribe you to come along." He held up the remaining sweet roll, and Kate snatched it out of his hand. Her churning nerves were no match for her love of such sugary goodness.

"Your instincts weren't wrong, though," she said around a mouthful. "For this kind of bribe, I might do anything."

A suggestive smile teased his lips. "Anything?"

Kate rolled her eyes, which only made him laugh in response. She wasn't sure what to make of him. Yes, they'd formed a fragile alliance on the road here, but she didn't know if she was ready to be so casual around him. It felt too much like how it used to be. *Be careful,* she thought, distrusting the lure of those old feelings.

The stables occupied the entire west half of the castle grounds, a sprawling single-story building that housed more than a hundred individual stalls. The horses here lived better than most common folk, their stalls bedded with fresh straw, their water buckets emptied and refilled twice each day, near-constant grooming. They never wanted for food or care. That wasn't to say that they didn't earn their keep, though. The warhorses were ridden several hours each day, their training as rigorous as any soldier's. Some days they were worked over obstacles, some days it was flatwork or endurance training. All days they were exposed to battlefield conditions. The horses produced here were expected to be as fierce as the riders they carried.

"I'm sorry I haven't been around much since we arrived," Corwin said as they headed into the barn, toward the main office. The grooms and stable hands they passed watched them with poorly veiled interest. "But I've been a little preoccupied with the uror."

"I understand." Kate longed to ask how he felt about it. She'd witnessed firsthand how much he struggled when the uror sign failed to arrive when it was supposed to, watching as it slowly shattered his once-solid certainty that he was meant to rule. "Is it true the sign is a horse?" she asked.

"Yes, it is." He halted midstride and faced her. "Would you like to see it?"

At Kate's nod, Corwin turned left down one of the smaller aisles. Ahead, two armed guards stood outside a stall. They stepped aside at Corwin's approach. He stopped in front of the barred window and peered in. Kate did the same, her breath catching in her throat at the sight of the horse, marked by the goddess in black and white.

The uror colt was still finishing his breakfast, but he raised his head from the grain bucket and peered back at them. With wide, wild eyes, one black and one blue, he stretched his neck to the bars and sniffed Kate's fingers where she gripped the edge of the window. She longed to touch the horse, her gift humming inside her, but she didn't dare.

That was, until Corwin said, "You can go in, if you'd like."

Kate's fingers trembled as she slid open the stall door and took a step inside. The colt retreated, tossing his head nervously. Then curiosity got the best of him, and he stretched his nose out to Kate. She let him sniff at her fingers again, then touched the soft velvet of his muzzle. For just a second she dared to use her magic, touching his mind as well—but she couldn't read anything from him. It was as if a black veil hid him from her sight.

She ran a hand down the front of his nose, and he leaned his mouth toward her chest. Worried he might nip, she started to push him away, but then he snorted, blowing snot over the front of her tunic.

She grimaced. "Aren't you the naughty boy?"

He snorted again—less messily this time.

"It's strange how normal he is, isn't it?" Corwin said, watching the exchange from outside the stall. "If you didn't know better, you would think he was an ordinary horse. That is, if you only went by his behavior."

"What do you mean?" Kate said at his peculiar tone.

Corwin shrugged. "The horse makes me feel . . . strange. When I'm around him, it's like this buzzing in my head."

Frowning, Kate turned back to the colt and reached out to him with her magic once more, a gentle probe against that black veil. She felt something respond, but then it skittered away, behind the curtain once more. Nevertheless, she sensed the horse's intelligence, his vibrant energy.

Withdrawing her magic, she ran her hands down the colt's sleek neck. "What are you?" she whispered, and for a second she experienced a buzzing like Corwin described, a tingle like the magic in a magestone once invoked.

"Prince Corwin," a voice called from down the corridor. "You're early."

Kate turned her head, spying the newcomer through the bars on the front of the stall. Age had marked Alaistar Cade in the last few years, spreading liberal amounts of salt through his red hair and painting a spiderweb of wrinkles around his eyes. But the crooked smile he turned on her now was exactly as she remembered.

"Welcome back, Miss Brighton."

She stepped out of the stall, closing the door behind her. "Good day, Master Cade." The title tasted strange on her tongue. She used to call him Uncle Alaistar but couldn't imagine doing so now. That name came from another time and place—one she couldn't go back to, no matter how close it might seem.

Alaistar must've sensed the distance, too, for his manner turned more formal. "Are you ready for your audition then?"

"Yes, sir." She swallowed back a tremor of nerves.

Master Cade turned and led the way out of the stables to the cavalry field, where several of the horses in training were already saddled and waiting to be worked. Kate eyed them with a heart both full and hungry. She sensed her father's hand in the making of each one. Here was his true legacy. The one he should be remembered for.

"Do you mind if I stay and watch?" Corwin asked, but before Kate could respond, a page arrived. He bowed low before the prince and handed him a folded card. Reading it, Corwin made a noise of disgust. "Tell the council I'm on my way." The page bowed again, then ran from the stable, eager to deliver his message. Corwin touched Kate's shoulder. "I'm sorry, but duty calls." He smiled, but it seemed weak around the edges. "Good luck, and I'll come by to see you later if I can."

Then he was gone, leaving her alone with Alaistar Cade. She turned to him, expecting to see that same smile again, but his gaze as he looked on her now was cold as a midwinter wind. She shivered, fearing the worst.

Alaistar folded his arms over his chest. "Now that the high

prince is gone, we can be done with the charade. There is no need for you to audition, because the last thing I would ever allow is for that traitor's daughter to ride one of my horses. I've better things in mind for you."

Kate stared at him, openmouthed with shock. It quickly gave way to anger. *Your horses? These are my father's horses! His legacy!* A dozen curses slid through her mind, but she was still too stunned to say them. It was just as she'd warned Corwin—the moment he was gone, they would turn on her. Only, a part of her had thought, had hoped, that Alaistar Cade—Uncle Alaistar—would be the one exception.

She was wrong.

Cade turned on his heel and headed back into the stable. He hadn't ordered her to follow, but she'd understood the command just the same. With tears burning her eyes, she followed after him. She breathed shallowly, teeth gritted. She refused to cry in front of this man.

Once inside, Cade pulled a pitchfork off a hook on the wall and held it out to her. "You can muck out the stables. Start here and work your way down the line. I'm sure you remember where to dump the manure."

Kate took the fork without speaking, outrage and betrayal forming a hot lump in her throat.

"And don't you dare touch any of the horses. If a stall is occupied, skip it until the horse is let outside for the day." Cade didn't wait for confirmation this time, but turned and marched away, his boots making hard clicks against the floor.

Several seconds passed before Kate was able to shake off the daze that had seized her. A part of her wanted to quit right there, but the rest of her knew that would only make Cade happy. He wanted her to quit, and she wouldn't give him the satisfaction. Retrieving a wheelbarrow, she set about her task.

It was hard, back-breaking work, but not unfamiliar to her. Her father always said that those who wanted to ride needed to earn the right by caring for their mounts first. Wishing more than ever that he was still here, Kate worked with her head down and shoulders set. She didn't look up, not even when a groom or stable hand passed by. That was, until one of them knocked over her nearly full wheelbarrow, spilling piss- and shit-covered straw over the concrete floor.

"You bastard," she shouted at the groom's retreating back.

The boy looked over his shoulder at her. "Better a bastard than a traitor." He made a rude hand gesture, then marched off.

The abuse continued throughout the day—half a dozen spilled wheelbarrows, her pitchfork going missing the moment she set it down, then finally, the last straw—when one of the stable hands dumped a forkful of steaming fresh manure over her head while her back was turned.

Kate's anger burned in her cheeks and tears of outrage stung her eyes. She threw down the fork, ready to pummel the stable hand, but the boy was already running down the aisle out of reach.

Drawing a deep breath, Kate forced herself to walk serenely to Master Cade's office. She felt the manure hot and wet against her scalp, but she didn't shake it off. Not yet. To her satisfaction, she saw Cade sitting at his desk through the window.

She pushed the door open and stepped in. Cade looked up, his expression first surprised, then stormy. But he didn't scare her. Not anymore. She leaned over the desk and shook her head, dislodging the manure right on top of the breeding registry he was working on. It slopped against it, ruining hours' worth of work.

Cade leaped out of his chair with a curse.

"I'm glad he's dead," Kate said, hands on hips and sides heaving with rage. "So that he didn't live long enough to see the kind of man you really are, *Uncle Alaistar.*"

Cade flinched but seemed too furious to respond.

Kate turned and marched to the door, pausing just long enough to say over her shoulder, "I'd rather be dead, too, than work for you. I quit."

She made it all the way back to her quarters before finally breaking down into tears. To her relief, Signe was gone, allowing Kate to express her grief and shame in private. With her eyes blurred from crying, she drew a bath, grateful that the castle had running water, which allowed her to stay in her rooms instead of fetching a bucket from the kitchens. Enough people had noticed the state of her on the trip from the stables back to the castle as it was. All of Norgard would learn of the incident before long, she didn't doubt. It would make for an amusing illustration in one of the newspapers.

Trying not to think about it, Kate washed the manure from her hair and body, scrubbing until her skin and scalp felt raw. Then she dried herself off and dressed in fresh clothes, throwing the old ones into a pile to be washed later. But still the pain had not subsided.

She wandered back to the main room and sat down behind her father's desk. Other than the stables, it was the place that reminded her of him the most. Whenever he came home at night, he would sit here for hours, working on the bloodline registries or balancing the family finances in the ledger. She leaned back in the chair and closed her eyes, allowing herself to imagine for a moment that he was still here.

When Kate opened her eyes again, her gaze fell on the top edge of the painting that had hung behind the desk for as long as she could remember. She hadn't really looked at it since returning, but now it drew her in. It depicted a coastline with water an impossible shade of blue green, yet so clear that you could see the outline of rocks on the seafloor. Hovering in the distance, emerald-green mountains stretched toward a cloudless sky. Kate had been fascinated by the painting as a child. Although it was an imaginary landscape, existing only within the mind of the artist, Kate used to call it . . .

Fenmore.

Realization dawned bright as a new star in her mind, and Kate stood from the desk on trembling legs. *Go to Fenmore.* Was this what he meant? It seemed impossible, and yet she found herself running her hands over the painting's surface, searching it for some hidden message. Finding nothing, she lifted the painting off the wall, ready to rip the back of it open.

Instead she found a lockbox embedded in the wall behind it, hidden all this time. Her pulse began to race as she raised her hands to the handle and pulled. Surely it would be locked, but to her relief, it slid open without hindrance. Her father must not have seen reason to keep it locked when it was already so well hidden.

A book lay inside the small space, turned sideways to fit. Kate pulled it out, her imagination spinning visions of a diary with the latest entry an explanation of everything. But when she set it on the desk and opened the front cover, she discovered it was only a ledger, similar to the one her father had used to keep track of their finances.

Similar, but not the same. In the year before his death, Hale had begun to show his daughter a little of how to balance their money. He knew that his wife would never be up for the task, and he didn't believe in trusting a hired clerk to do it. Kate would've recognized that ledger immediately, and this was not it. That one he always kept in a desk drawer.

Why have two? She flipped through the pages, full of entries written in her father's untidy scrawl. She searched it all the way to the back, still hoping for a note but finding nothing. Yet she knew without doubt that this was what her father had wanted her to find. There could be only one reason why he would have a second book: to hide a secret.

One Kate was now determined to uncover for herself.

SHE WORKED LATE INTO THE night, not even stopping for dinner, despite Signe's protests when she returned later that evening. But her friend knew Kate well enough not to bang her head against such a wall of stubbornness. Especially once Kate explained the significance of the ledger.

Probing it for its secrets proved a long and difficult task. It contained records that appeared to date back to the three years before Hale's death. At first Kate struggled to make sense of it, many of the names unfamiliar. She wished she had the original ledger to compare it to, but memory would have to suffice—there was no sign of the other anywhere in the quarters.

Still, the longer she worked, the more she made sense of it, recognizing which entries were for upkeep on the house in the Glentrove district, which were payments to her tutors, the seamstress bill, weaponry, and so many other day-to-day, mundane expenses. The payees she didn't know, she wrote down on a separate piece of parchment, marking them off when any insight came to her later.

Her eyes began to burn and her head to ache as the hours stretched on, but finally she uncovered the only secret the ledger had to give. Of all the entries, there was only one she failed to recognize by the end—regular payments to an establishment called the Sacred Sword. Kate had no idea what sort of business it was, but guessed it must be a tavern or gaming house based on its location in the Burnside district. Either way, she was determined to find out why her father would spend such a regular and large amount of money and why he would've needed to keep it secret.

Maybe he had a gambling problem, Kate speculated. Two years ago she would've dismissed the idea as absurd; her father's only passion in life was his horses. *And his daughter.* But she was old enough now for the blinders of childhood to have been stripped away, to know that even good men sometimes fell victim to their own cravings, whether it was drink or game or some other debauchery.

She hoped she was wrong, but even if she wasn't, it couldn't be worse than not knowing. She wanted to head to this Sacred Sword right now, but she was too tired. *Tomorrow then,* she vowed.

Kate woke the next morning to a loud knock on the door. It was early, and she wasn't done sleeping yet. "Go away," she said, pulling a pillow over her face.

But the person only knocked again, louder this time.

Muttering a curse, Kate rolled out of bed and stumbled to the door in only her nightshift and bare feet. She cracked it open, ready to give the person a harsh dismissal, but her mind went blank when she saw Corwin standing there.

He blinked at her state of undress. "Apologies. I didn't realize you'd still be abed."

"I was up late." Kate wrapped her arms around her chest. "Is there something you wanted?"

He hesitated a moment, then seemed to recover his nerve. "Yes, to invite you for a ride. I've even brought another bribe." He held out his hand, revealing a stack of sweet rolls.

Kate bit her lip, wanting to say no. She had plans today, but the smell of the rolls was too good to resist after her late night and no supper. She opened the door.

"Come in while I get changed."

Five minutes later, Kate emerged from her bedroom dressed in a tunic, breeches, and overskirt, her black hair tied in a neat braid. A scent of roses hung about her thanks to the bath.

Corwin looked up from where he was sitting at her father's desk, the ledger still open to the last page in front of him. "Was this your father's? Where did you find it?"

Cursing herself for being so careless, she debated her answer. Then she remembered he had promised to help her uncover the truth. The only secret she needed to keep from Corwin was about her family's wilder magic. She doubted the Sacred Sword had anything to do with that, though.

"In a lockbox behind that painting." She gestured toward the wall. "I think it's what my father meant by 'go to Fenmore.' When I was little, I thought that painting was what Fenmore looked like. I'd forgotten until yesterday."

Corwin peered up at it, his mouth forming an O of surprise. "Do you know what it means?"

Kate stepped up to the desk and helped herself to a sweet roll. "Not yet. But for some reason my father was making payments to a place called the Sacred Sword that he didn't want anyone to know about."

Corwin made a choking sound and tried to hide it behind a

cough. "Yes, that makes sense. I'm sure your mother wouldn't have approved."

Kate tilted her head, frowning. "Why do you say that?"

Corwin dropped his gaze and made a show of wiping the crumbs from his tunic. "Because the Sacred Sword is . . . ah . . . a . . . brothel."

Kate stared dumbfounded for several seconds until the realization of this truth struck her. Was that all it was? He'd been visiting a brothel and wanted to keep it secret from his wife? *Well, yes, he would've wanted to keep it secret from Mother. Only—*

Kate bent toward the ledger and ran her finger down the entries until she reached the very last payment he'd made to the Sacred Sword. She motioned to Corwin, her finger still in place. "Is this the kind of money one spends in a brothel like that?"

Corwin turned bug-eyed at the question and coughed again. "Um, no. For that kind of money, he would have to be visiting twice a day, every day of the month if not more."

Kate tapped the toe of her boot against the marble floor. "It doesn't make sense. We both know there's no way he could've been visiting so often. Not unless he could be in two places at once. So why spend so much?"

"No idea." Corwin shrugged, then narrowed his gaze at Kate. "But please tell me you're not planning on going there to find out."

"Whyever not?"

Corwin ran a palm over his face. "It could be dangerous, Kate. The men who frequent that kind of place aren't the sort of people you should be around."

Kate rolled her eyes. "I can take care of myself, Corwin."

"I know, I know." He raised his hands in surrender. "But if you're going to go, then I should go with you."

Making a face, she shook her head. "It wouldn't work. If the secret my father is hiding there is connected to why he attacked the king, then it's doubtful anyone who knows anything is going to talk to you, *the high prince*, about it."

"They might not talk to you either. I mean, no one came forward when there was a chance to tell you before. And in a place like the Sacred Sword, you're bound to receive the same treatment as Master Cade gave you yesterday. Or worse."

Kate's face heated at the memory. "I don't know what—"

Corwin cut her off. "Don't try to deny it. I know what happened. Dal had stopped by the stables and saw you go into the office." He shook his head. "I'm so sorry, Kate. It seems you were right. My word counts for nothing. Only my presence matters, and barely at that."

Kate wanted to be annoyed with him but couldn't manage it with that look of misery on his face. "It's all right, and it's over. I didn't want to work for him anyhow."

Corwin stood up in a rush. "I couldn't agree more, but you still need something to do involving your beloved horses, and I have just the solution." He straightened to his full height as if to lend himself courage. "Come work for me, as the personal trainer to my new warhorse. I'm so busy right now with all the preparation for the uror, and I just don't have the time to give him what he deserves. And after yesterday, well, I no longer want Master Cade to have the training of him."

Kate thought it over, her first instinct to say no. She didn't want to be any more beholden to Corwin than she already was. On the other hand, she did need a job, and not riding was even more unbearable than she could've imagined. She would join the Relay here in Norgard, if she could, but she doubted they would take her. Besides, she didn't want to be away from the city for long periods of time with Bonner facing such scrutiny and danger every day. He'd finally managed to create a single workable mold, but no new firearms yet.

"I'll do it," she said. "It'll give me plenty of time to find out the truth about my father."

"I'm glad." He hesitated, worrying at his lower lip with his thumb. Then, as if realizing what he was doing, he dropped his hand away. "Only, I've got to know: What happens after you find what you're seeking? Will you go on training for me?"

Kate thought about it, memories of yesterday and Cade's treatment of her fresh in her mind. "I don't know," she answered at last. "Staying in Norgard doesn't seem wise. I doubt this place can ever be my home again." The admission hurt, but truth so often did.

Corwin slowly nodded, his expression guarded. Then he held out his arm to her. "Shall we ride then?"

Kate slid her arm around his, feeling the heat of his body and how it made hers tingle, and together they headed down to the stables.

Just before they went through the main gate, a voice called out to them.

"Your highness, a moment, if you please."

Corwin let out a sigh, the sound barely audible, but Kate heard the sudden tension in it, like a bow pulled taut. She couldn't blame him. He wouldn't know a moment's peace until the uror trial was over.

Corwin faced the caller, whom Kate vaguely recognized as Minister Rendborne, the master of trade. "Yes, of course, minister. What can I do for you?"

Rendborne came to a stop before them, then turned to Kate, offering her a quick bow. "Nice to see you again, Miss Brighton." A broad smile crossed his face, and she couldn't help but return it. He was pleasant to look at, his golden eyes mesmerizing.

"I've found something you might find useful, your highness." Rendborne reached into the pocket of his overcoat and pulled out a book bound in brown leather. He handed it to Corwin, the mage-stone on his right hand glowing dully.

Corwin accepted the book, turning it over to view the title, only to see there was none. "What is it?"

"Your grandfather's journal, written during the time of his own uror trial."

Corwin blinked, his mouth falling open in surprise. "Where did you get this?"

Rendborne waved the question off. "The ministry of trade keeps its own private archives. I stumbled upon it by chance and thought it might help with your upcoming trial."

Corwin hesitated a moment, then held the book out to Rendborne. "I can't take this. The high priestess said we're not to accept help from anyone."

"Indeed," Rendborne said, bobbing his head in agreement. "But you *are* permitted to read and research as much as you want. Consider me your humble librarian. You'll still need to do all the work plumbing it for its secrets."

"He's got a point, your highness," Kate said, not wanting to see his strict adherence to rules lose him this opportunity. She had heard the talk of the Errant Prince among the servants and courtiers—the favor Corwin once held for winning the uror was gone. His disappearance had created too much uncertainty.

He glanced at her, still doubtful, then turned back to Rendborne. "Why not give it to Edwin?"

"I prefer a fair game," Rendborne replied at once. "Your brother's known about the uror colt longer than you have. Perhaps this will level the playing field."

"I see." Corwin debated a moment longer, then pocketed the book. "Thank you, minister."

"Best of luck to you." Rendborne bowed, then disappeared as quickly as he'd come.

Corwin headed through the gate into the stable, and Kate followed close behind him, her nerves prickling to be back here again so soon. Fortunately, there was no sign of Alaistar Cade, and all the grooms and stable hands gave them a wide berth. Two horses were already saddled for them in the training yard: Corwin's new black stallion, Nightbringer, and a red chestnut mare with a white strip on her face and four white stockings.

"This is Firedancer," Corwin said, holding out the reins to her. "And she's yours."

"Excuse me?"

A slow smile spread over his lips. "I lied when I said I had a horse for you to train. What I meant is that I have two horses to occupy your time. Mine and yours." He held out the reins again.

Kate pressed her lips together. *This cannot be happening.* But it was. She read the sincerity in Corwin's gaze, and excitement trembled through her. "Why are you doing this?"

"Because Kate Brighton without a horse is like a bird without wings. You saved my life. It would take a lot more than one horse to pay you back." He shrugged. "Besides, I'm told she's temperamental and stubborn. A perfect match for you."

Kate snorted, then broke into a laugh, joy spilling over her astonishment. She reached up and planted a kiss on Corwin's cheek. She laughed again at his stunned expression. Then she took the reins and turned to the mare. *Firedancer.* Her horse. Taking a deep breath, she slid a foot into the stirrup and mounted. The mare stepped forward, ears pricked in her eagerness to be off.

Kate looked down at Corwin, appreciating her vantage in the saddle. "Thank you. She's going to be perfect."

It was even truer than Kate could've guessed. When she and Corwin left the city, riding out into the countryside, she risked using her magic to touch the mare's mind. The moment she sensed the bright glow of her essence—intelligent, willing, brave—she knew Firedancer was everything her father always sought in the horses he bred, the secret to his success as master of horse. Having her was like having a piece of him back.

Wordlessly, Kate and Corwin turned south and urged their mounts into a trot to warm up. They'd exited Norgard through the eastern gate, a decision made more out of old habit than conscious choice; the path from the castle to the gate was easiest and the least crowded. The southern road here led straight and flat in between fenced pastures. Before long, Kate let Firedancer break from the trot into a canter while Corwin did the same with Nightbringer. They rode side by side, varying the pace. They slowed when they needed to, allowing the horses to catch their breaths, only to start up again. Once they'd gone two miles, they turned back.

With the city gate in sight once more, Kate took a deep breath, unable to hide her disappointment that it was over already.

Corwin turned toward her and said, "Race you. First to the Wandering Woods wins." Without waiting for a response, he heeled Nightbringer into a gallop, straight toward the distant tree line.

"You cheater," Kate called after him, catching up a moment later. Their horses matched strides easily, both of them fighting to get ahead, with their competitive natures showing. In the end, neither won nor lost. Kate and Corwin slowed their mounts to a walk at the same time, just before the entrance to the woods.

"Well, that was fun." Corwin slapped Nightbringer's neck affectionately.

"I think I needed that," Kate said, breathless.

But she still wasn't ready to head back to the city. She turned her gaze onto the woods, with its slender, white-barked trees stacked in tight rows like spears on a weapon's rack. There was something haunting about their stark beauty.

Feeling suddenly mischievous, she arched an eyebrow at Corwin and inclined her head. "Shall we cool them down in there, out of the sun?"

Corwin laughed, the sound just shy of nervous. "I haven't been in there in years. Not since the last time we dared."

Kate wasn't surprised. Few ever ventured into the Wandering Woods. It was said to be haunted, cursed. According to the history books, one of the Hellgates—the portals that unleashed the night-drakes onto Rime—was hidden somewhere among those trees. Years ago, she and Corwin had dared each other to ride into the woods in search of the Hellgate. They didn't make it very far before turning back, their imaginations getting the better of them. The fear had been fun, creating a ready-made excuse for them to find comfort in each other's arms. The memory sent a flutter through Kate's chest.

Things would be different today. They were different people, braver and wiser. Not that the adventure of it had anything to do with why she suggested going in. No, the guaranteed privacy was the appeal today. Kate wanted the freedom to use her gift, to get to know Firedancer the best way she knew how. There'd be no risk of magists discovering her in there.

"Well, I'm game if you are," Corwin said, and he urged Night-bringer down the overgrown path.

Kate followed after him, closing her eyes and stretching out with her magic. A sense of completeness came over her as she joined with Firedancer, feeling the mare's tired excitement. She had enjoyed their ride. So had Nightbringer, Kate was pleased to learn when she touched his mind as well. She breathed in, savoring the feel of the magic inside her. She'd gone too long without using it. With Corwin leading the way, silent and inattentive, Kate stretched out even further with her gift, soon sensing the birds, foxes, squirrels, and other wild animals in the woods.

"The first of the uror trials is in two weeks," Corwin said a few minutes later, jarring Kate out of the trance she'd fallen under.

Withdrawing her magic, she cleared her throat. "Yes, I heard. I'm surprised they're starting so soon."

"That makes two of us. But the priestesses are in a hurry. Given how long they had to wait for the uror sign to finally appear, I don't blame them."

Kate winced at the bitterness in his voice. She expected it not to be there, not now that the uror was here. Then again, maybe it was just nerves. Historically, there were always three trials for the uror, three tests designed to prove the heirs' suitability to sit upon the Mirror Throne. Kate had no idea what the tests entailed, but it was common knowledge that participants sometimes died during them.

"Are you worried?" she asked.

"A little." He slowed Nightbringer, making room for her to ride next to him, the path just wide enough to allow for it. "But to be honest, I fear winning far more than losing. Or even dying for that matter."

Kate scoffed. "Don't be absurd. You will make a great king. Everyone always thought so when we were younger." Kate remembered it well, the way the servants, courtiers, and even the king himself treated Corwin as the heir apparent.

"Yes, I remember. I used to believe them, too. More's the pity." He grimaced, his gaze dropping to his bandaged right hand, where the uror brand lay hidden. But after a moment, Kate realized it wasn't the bandage that held his attention but the vambrace around his wrist. She'd noticed that he always wore it to hide the tattoo beneath.

"What happened to you?" Kate said, curiosity getting the better of her. "The Corwin I knew would've been eager to win and certain of victory even before it began. Like the one who challenged me to that race just now."

He barked a laugh. "If only ruling a kingdom was as simple, but I'm afraid that Corwin died on a battlefield in Endra."

Kate shot him a puzzled look. "Is that where you were these last few years? In Endra?"

He nodded, bending low to dodge a branch dangling across the path. "I joined the Shieldhawks for a time."

"The tattoo." Kate gasped, her mind making the connection at last. No wonder it had been so difficult. The Shieldhawks were a legendary mercenary company out of Endra, the last organization she would ever have associated with the high prince of Rime. It was downright scandalous.

"I'm sorry," Kate said, noticing Corwin's bemused look. "I saw it when you were injured but I couldn't place why it was familiar. But . . . why would you join the Shieldhawks?"

Corwin turned his gaze ahead and shrugged, the gesture at odds with the stiffness in his shoulders and back. "Oh, many reasons. Not the least of which was the uror. If I was never to be king, I wanted to do something that mattered, and the Shieldhawks are mostly concerned with stopping Seva from taking over the world. I can't imagine a more noble cause than that. For a while I thought I'd found my place and purpose among them. I was wrong."

An ache squeezed Kate's throat at the loss she sensed in him. Swallowing it down, she asked, "What happened?"

Corwin blew out a breath, one loud enough to make Nightbringer prick his ears back at him in alarm. "We were sent on a mission to disrupt a Sevan supply line. I'd just made captain. There were twelve men under my command. Only two of us made it back."

"You and Dal," Kate said, remembering the conversation she'd had with him that night by the Relay tower.

Tight-lipped, Corwin added, "If there was any doubt about my unworthiness to lead, I proved it then. Initiating the trials now is nothing but the gods mocking me."

Kate gaped, shocked by the strength of his conviction. She felt it like a slap. Only, she remembered Dal warning her to be skeptical when he told her this story. He'd called Corwin's actions heroic.

"You can't really believe what you're saying, Corwin."

He started to respond, but Nightbringer spooked without warning, stomping his front legs. Firedancer did too, the force of it jarring Kate's spine. She tightened her fingers around the reins automatically and pressed her heels down in the stirrups, braced for another spook.

"I wonder what's gotten into them?" Corwin said.

"No idea." Instinctively, Kate touched Firedancer's mind. The mare sensed something wrong ahead, a smell that filled her with fear. Kate reached out further with her magic, searching for the wild animals she'd sensed earlier. They were keeping their distance from this place, those nearest quiet and still from the same fear infecting the horses.

Expanding her search, Kate stumbled across the source of the fear—a creature she didn't recognize. It was predatory, its mind focused like a cat on the hunt, but there was something *oily* about its thoughts, as if they weren't completely contained. If she got too close to them, their substance might rub off on her. She couldn't sense that warm glow that was at the center of most animals either. Where it ought to have been, there was only emptiness. Stranger too was that she sensed multiple minds, as if there were several creatures wrapped inside one, thoughts garbled and overlapping, connected like threads in a web. It was impossible to tell where one ended and another began.

Kate pulled back from the sensation, her stomach writhing. "We should find out what it is." She thought she knew but didn't want it to be true.

She slid from the saddle. Corwin joined her a moment later, and they tethered the horses to a tree before moving forward, revolvers in hand. Like her, he'd taken to wearing the one Bonner had given him in Farhold all the time.

Sensing the creatures, Kate made her way toward them. Their presence grew stronger with each step, but when she broke through the brush into a wide clearing where she knew they ought to be, there was no sign of them. *This is wrong. They're here. But where?* She closed her eyes, trying to orient her mind to their physical location—

Just ahead. She stepped forward slowly, wary of a trap. Corwin kept pace beside her.

Scanning the ground, her eyes fell on a small stone partially hidden beneath the tall grass. It was halfway buried in the dirt, but she could see the glow on it. *A magestone.* She pointed. "Look at that."

Corwin bent toward it. "What in the three hells?"

"Don't—" Kate started to say, but Corwin had already picked it up. The air in front of them shimmered, like a wardstone shield going up. *Or down,* Kate realized, her breath catching. In front of them, a massive hole had appeared where only wild grass had been a moment before.

A foul stench rose up from the pit, and with it came the sound of growls and snapping jaws. *Drakes. But which kind?* Kate peered over the side. Several sets of eyes set in snarling faces stared back at her. It took her a moment to see them clearly, their black scales camouflaged against the shadow of the pit. There were four daydrakes in all, and when they saw Kate, they lunged at her, half climbing out of the pit. She lurched backward with a gasp. But they weren't able to get out. The hole was too deep for their flightless wings.

No, not a hole, she realized. *A cage.*

One warded with mage magic.

CORWIN STARED DOWN INTO THE pit, his heart galloping inside his chest.

"What do we do?" Kate asked from beside him.

"We kill them before they can be used for further harm." He pulled the revolver from his holster.

"Wait, Corwin." Kate touched his arm. "Someone put those drakes in there, caged them, and tried to hide them."

Brow furrowed, he stared back at her. "You think we might be able to catch whoever is behind this?" *The Rising, here in Norgard.* He didn't want to believe it, his city in danger. The wilder responsible for his mother's death had killed dozens of people—and he'd acted alone. Corwin didn't want to imagine the damage wilders could do banded together.

"Not if we kill the drakes." Kate peered around the clearing. "Whoever it is might hear the shots and be scared off."

Glancing up at the sky, Corwin guessed it was drawing toward noon. He'd already spent too long out here, and if he wasn't careful he would be late for yet another high council meeting. But there was no question that this discovery was more important.

He turned back to Kate. "All right, we stay here and see who comes to check on them."

They retreated the way they'd come and crouched down behind

the white trees, their slender trunks offering poor coverage. Neither spoke, and in their silence, the noise of the forest grew louder, each creak of a tree bough or snap of a twig ominous. The minutes marched by. Before long, Corwin's stomach began to growl loud enough to hear, and his body ached from sitting still so long. He knew Kate must be feeling the same next to him.

"Do you want to check the horses?" he whispered to her.

Relief broke over her face, and she nodded once, then stood and retreated as silently as a wild animal. Corwin watched her go before turning back to the clearing. The drakes had settled some, but every few minutes he would hear the snap of teeth or a growl. *Please, Noralah, let me catch those behind this and be done with it.* He touched a finger to his bandaged palm, feeling the brand beneath it.

It seemed for once that the goddess was listening, for on the far side of the clearing, a figure soon appeared. The man was plainly dressed, with nothing remarkable about his appearance. Nothing like the Andreas miner with his blue tattoos and ragged clothing. He might have been a clerk or a farmer or something equally inconspicuous. *A wilder rebel?*

Slowly, carefully, Corwin eased the pistol out of the holster as he watched the man approach the pit with a puzzled expression on his face. He circled the hole slowly.

Corwin braced, ready to subdue the man once his back was turned, but before he could, he heard the snap of a twig from behind, Kate returning. It was a slight sound, but enough to draw the stranger's attention. He spun toward Corwin with wide, startled eyes.

Corwin leaped up, pointing the revolver. "Don't move!"

The man ignored the command, his hand already pulling something out of his pocket.

"Watch out, Corwin!" Kate shouted, rushing forward as if she meant to shield him from the attack.

The man threw the object at them, unleashing a blinding white light. A ferocious bang echoed across the clearing, so loud Corwin felt his brains rattle inside his skull. It was a flash stone, like the kind Raith had used to escape the daydrakes.

Stunned and disoriented, Corwin fell to his knees, unable to stay upright. It was as if the solid ground had started to churn like the waves of the ocean.

"Kate!" he screamed, but he couldn't hear the sound of his own voice. Groping blindly, he reached out, soon feeling her body next to his.

As the white light faded, Corwin's senses slowly came back to him. He could see again, although a dreadful ringing remained in his ears. He turned to Kate and cupped her face, running his thumbs over her cheeks.

"Are you okay?"

She nodded and rolled away from him, lurching to her feet. She stumbled toward the path by which the man had first arrived.

Corwin grabbed her arm. "There's no point. He's long gone by now." He guessed he was shouting but couldn't help it. "We need help."

Kate turned back. Scowling, she placed her hands over her ears. "I can barely hear a thing."

"Me too." Corwin bent down and retrieved his revolver from

where he'd dropped it. "We need to hurry, but first—"

He broke off and headed for the pit, where the drakes were writhing about, in a frenzy over the commotion above them. Gritting his teeth, Corwin aimed the revolver into the pit. There was no sport in this sort of killing, but the foul creatures couldn't be allowed to live. One by one, he planted a bullet in their skulls, his aim deadly accurate at such a close distance. Once again, he thanked the gods for Bonner's revolver, more certain than ever that it was the key to vanquishing all the drakes that plagued Rime.

When it was done, Corwin hurried down the path after Kate toward the horses. Both Nightbringer and Firedancer pulled at their tethers, ready to be away from this place. Corwin and Kate climbed into the saddle, then raced out of the woods and down the road to Norgard's eastern gate.

They didn't slow down until they made it back to the castle. "Stay with the horses," Corwin said, doing a flying dismount in the courtyard. "I'll be back with help."

He turned and raced into the stables, shouting for Master Cade.

"He's still in the high council meeting, your highness," one of the stable hands said.

Corwin swung toward the man. "Have a squadron of cavalry horses saddled and send someone to muster their riders. I want everyone ready to leave at once."

With the order given, Corwin left the stables and raced all the way to the council chamber in the central wing. The guards standing outside the door stepped aside as he barged in. Seated at the large, round table, all the high councilmembers looked up at once with matching alarmed expressions.

All save Edwin, whose lips curled downward. "I would say you're late, Corwin, but that would be a gross understatement."

"There are daydrakes in the Wandering Woods." Corwin pulled the magestone from his pocket and held it out. "They were caged in a pit and hidden with magic." Placing the magestone on the table, he told them the rest.

"Very worrisome," Grand Master Storr said when Corwin finished. Storr picked up the magestone, examining it closely. "This stone had a concealment spell on it, the kind for sale in any of the brown-robe houses. It would be difficult to trace, to say the least."

Corwin gaped at him, dismayed. The concealment spells he knew of were for hiding simple things like blemishes on the skin or an unfortunately shaped nose, not a massive pit in the ground housing four deadly daydrakes. "But the browns deal in the small arts, vanity spells and the like. This was far bigger and more powerful." Corwin waved Storr off when he started to respond. "Later. For now we need to scour the woods to catch whoever put the drakes into that cage."

Minister Knox and Master Cade both stood at the same time. "My men can be ready to ride as soon as the horses are saddled," Knox said.

"I've already got the grooms saddling their horses," Corwin replied before Master Cade could respond. Then he turned to Storr. "But we will need magist support as well. There's no telling what other magic our enemies possess."

Storr bowed his head. "I'll have Maestra Vikas assemble her golds. They will be best for dealing with such rogue magic."

Corwin didn't argue. He didn't care so long as they hurried.

But nearly an hour passed before the troop of cavalry soldiers and golds were mounted and ready to go. Edwin and Corwin rode at the front of the troop, with Kate trailing just behind them. No one questioned her presence, although Corwin suspected they would later. The councilmembers who'd decided to come along all eyed her curiously. So did Grand Master Storr, although he was better at hiding it. Only Minister Rendborne seemed unconcerned with her presence, going so far as to exchange a few words with her as they rode along. Corwin cast the man a grateful nod.

They entered the white woods in a single file, the path too tangled and overgrown for anything else. Behind him, Corwin heard several of the men whisper oaths of protection against entering the cursed woods. Maestra Vikas soon barked an order for her golds to cast spells of protection.

Within minutes they arrived at the same clearing. At least, Corwin thought it was the same one, only there was no sign of the pit or the drakes. The clearing was undisturbed, as serene as if it hadn't been touched by human hands in a hundred years.

Corwin glanced at Kate, doubt making him uneasy. "Did we make a mistake?"

Biting her lip, she shook her head. "This is the place. Maybe they came back and hid it again?"

She dismounted and walked toward the center where the pit should've been. Corwin joined her, as did Grand Master Storr and Edwin. Visions of the ground giving way flashed through his mind, but nothing happened. They searched for hidden magestones in the grass, Vikas going so far as to use an illumination spell, but they found nothing. The pit and the dead drakes were gone, as if they'd never been there.

"It was here. I swear it." Corwin turned to where Edwin and Storr stood, Vikas and Rendborne joining them.

A glower colored Edwin's face. "If this has all been one of your ploys, Corwin, I'll—"

"What reason would I have to lie?" Corwin balled his hands into fists, ready to hit something in his frustration, even as an embarrassed flush threatened to rise in his cheeks. He felt twelve years old again, with his brother so ready to accuse him of seeking attention. "The daydrakes were real, Edwin, and so was that man with the flash stone."

Grand Master Storr cleared his throat. "If I may offer, your highness: Supposing it is true that these daydrakes are a tool of the Rising, then there's an easy explanation for what happened here."

"Yes," Maestra Vikas said, nodding. Like the grand master, she wore no mask, her skin pale as white silk. Equally pale hair framed her narrow face. It would've been an attractive face, with her gray eyes like storm clouds, if only her expression weren't always so austere, like a marble statue. "An earthist could've easily hidden evidence of the pit."

Corwin swore beneath his breath, seeing the insidious brilliance of it. He exchanged a look with Kate, hers more worried than angry. "It took us a long while to get back here. Surely enough time for a wilder to have come in and taken care of it."

Edwin looked doubtful, but he didn't argue. Instead he turned to the men crowding into the clearing. "We need to search the woods.

Overturn every leaf and stone. I want small groups heading in different directions, but there needs to be a gold in each one for safety."

"A wise plan, your highness," Storr said, sketching a bow.

While Edwin took charge of organizing the groups, Corwin drew Kate aside for a private word.

"You must be tired and hungry. Do you want me to have someone escort you to the castle?"

"I don't need an escort." She brushed back a strand of hair that had fallen loose from her braid. "But no, I'll stay and help. I might be of use."

Corwin held in a sigh. He didn't want her in these woods, not with wilders and drakes about, but he knew better than to try to order her home. Besides, a part of him was relieved she was staying. It was the same part that always seemed able to find her in a crowd. He wanted to take her hand, to lace her fingers with his, but he settled for a touch of her shoulder.

"I know you'll be of help. I don't think I would've found the pit in the first place without you."

Kate dropped her gaze, shrugging. "The horses told us more than anything."

"True. But if you're going to stay, I want you to ride with me." He hesitated, then added, "Please."

Kate looked up, her eyes bright and that secretive, sideways smile appearing on her face. "Of course. Where else would I go?"

Away, he thought, remembering Hale's ledger, *once this is all over.* But no, he shouldn't dwell on that now. It was a dangerous subject, leading him down a dark road to nowhere.

They searched the woods until dusk began to descend and Edwin called it off. They'd found nothing so far, but early the next morning they returned to search once more. Again, they found nothing. Hour after hour, path after path. Nothing. Not so much as a single claw mark in the mud.

"We didn't even find the Hellgate," Corwin said as the search party rode back to the city. "How is that possible?"

Although he hadn't directed the question at anyone in particular, Master Storr chose to answer. "People lie, your highness, sometimes even the ones who write the history books."

It was an unpleasant thought, but less so than the certainty that he'd come so close to uncovering the mystery behind the daydrakes and who might be controlling them, only to fail again.

IN THE WEEKS THAT FOLLOWED, there were no signs or rumors of any daydrakes near Norgard, but a steady string of reports came in of sightings and attacks in the west and north. Some half dozen caravans had been attacked on the southwestern roads, and in Thace, many of the farmers were too frightened to venture out, leaving crops and herds untended. The city leaders feared the coming winter and what would happen if this new menace wasn't stopped soon.

Corwin read each report desperately wishing he could do something to help—if only they'd captured the culprits in the woods. Even worse was that the reports themselves only served to deepen the mystery. Every time word of a new attack or sighting came in, Corwin marked the place on a map he kept in his chambers. He hoped to uncover a pattern, but so far there seemed to be none. If he hadn't seen those drakes in that pit, it would be impossible to believe there was someone controlling them, considering the vast scope and randomness of the sightings. *Either that or our foes are both widespread and powerful.* A disturbing thought.

But it wasn't one he had much time to dwell on, with the first uror trial looming. The morning it was due to start, Corwin sat alone at the desk in his room, reading his grandfather's journal, which Minister Rendborne had given him. He wasn't sure why he bothered given how maddeningly vague it was on the details. Borwin Tormane seemed far more interested in capturing his thoughts and feelings than offering advice for posterity. If anything, Borwin's account only served to rattle Corwin's already uncertain confidence.

> *When the first trial began, my brothers and I mounted the steps of Goddess Tor, all the way to the altar itself. Although we arrived together, I was separated from them the moment I stepped onto the stone. What happened next I cannot describe. I must not. But the test was greater than any I had ever faced before or even dared imagine. And yet the aftermath of it proved hardest of all, when they brought my brother Jorwen's body down from the altar, broken from the inside.*

The broken bit, Corwin knew, was his great-uncle's heart, which had given out during the trial. Whatever it involved had exposed this fundamental weakness inside him. Corwin placed his palm against his chest, feeling each steady beat beneath, strong and sure. *There is no such weakness in me,* he told himself. Then again, perhaps Jorwen had felt the same before going into the trial. But no, Corwin suspected his own weaknesses lay elsewhere.

Fatigued by so much reading, he idly turned the pages until he reached the end, where his grandfather had put down his thoughts on winning the trial. Interested despite himself, Corwin read:

> *I felt it before I knew it. A sense of power and completeness I had never known before or since. The mark on my palm grew*

*warm and began to glow. Like fire. Like the sun. Then all of
Norgard knew as I did—that I was to be the next king.*

Corwin glanced at his own uror mark, the raised red flesh still
tender and sore despite the work the green robes had done on it the
day before to accelerate the healing process. The high priestess told
him he should be grateful, that normally the uror mark was left to
heal on its own, but with the need to start the trials quickly, they had
decided to allow magists to assist. *I am to be whole in body when I
enter the trial today.* Corwin closed his fingers, hiding the mark.

Returning his gaze to the chronicle, he read the next paragraph.

> *But the greatest surprise, even more than winning and the
> lighting of the mark, is the uror sign itself. The bear has
> changed toward me and I toward it. Toward her. Jahara is her
> name. And I can hear her thoughts as she can hear mine. We
> are bonded now, as surely as Noralah with Niran and Nelek.*

Corwin read the last sentence several times, trying to make
sense of it. Was his grandfather being poetical? He did have that
tendency, and yet there was nothing flowery about this prose. Just
these simple sentences presented as fact.

Leaning back in his chair, Corwin traced his thumb over the
scar on his chin. In the other accounts he'd read, and indeed in
every lesson he'd attended about the uror trials, there'd been no
mention of this . . . goddess gift? He didn't know what to call it. It
sounded like magic, like the wilder Ralph Marcel and his influence
over animals.

With doubt churning in his mind, Corwin pictured his father's uror sign. The wolf called Murr had died when Corwin was just a boy. Still, he remembered his father's sadness over it, the way he mourned for weeks on end. Come to think of it, the relationship between them did have mystical properties. How else could you explain a tame wolf? Murr had followed his father everywhere, always at his side, like a shadow with teeth.

If only I could ask him about it now, Corwin thought. But there wasn't any point dwelling on what would never be. Even if he'd been allowed to ask, his father couldn't have answered.

A knock sounded on the door, and Corwin closed the journal before answering it. The priestess waiting beyond bowed her head, then motioned for him to follow. It was time for the trial to begin.

With his back rigid, Corwin stepped out into the corridor and pulled the door closed behind him. He'd been instructed to bring nothing with him, no armor, no weapons, only himself. Feeling surprisingly calm now that he was moving, he followed the priestess down to the courtyard, where a carriage waited. Edwin already sat inside it when Corwin entered. His brother acknowledged him with a single nod, then turned his gaze out the window.

Sitting down beside him, Corwin did the same, watching as the carriage left the courtyard for the city. People lined the streets, cheering as they passed. Before long they headed through the southern gates and out onto the open countryside beyond. Corwin caught a glimpse in the distance of Goddess Tor rising up from the fields, the craggy hill a massive green tower.

When the carriage pulled to a stop some time later, Corwin

climbed out first, followed by Edwin. Standing shoulder to shoulder, they both looked up at the steep, ragged stone steps carved into the hill before them. The Steps of Sorrows, they were called. The priestess who'd fetched Corwin from the castle headed up first, motioning for the princes to follow.

The climb proved long and arduous, a trial itself. The bright sun, unfettered by any clouds, bore down on them with relentless heat. Halfway through the climb, Corwin paused to wipe sweat from his brow and ease the ache in his legs. He glanced beneath him, taking in the sight of all the people assembled at the base of Goddess Tor, hundreds of peasants present for the trial. They wouldn't be able to see anything of what happened from so far away, but they would hear about it quickly.

Reaching the top at last, Corwin drew a deep breath and willed his heartbeat to slow. Easily a hundred more people had gathered up here on the wide plateau, noblemen and courtiers all. Dead center on the plateau sat the Asterion, the altar of the goddess. The massive stone table rested atop a dozen pillars, each one engraved with ancient symbols.

A canopy tent had been pitched not far from the altar stairs, with two smaller walled tents just outside of it. The high priestess, the grand master, and all the high council stood beneath the canopy, watching the princes as they approached. Corwin ran his gaze over the crowd, searching for Dal. To his surprise, he spotted him nearly at once. Even more surprising was that Signe, Bonner, and Kate were with him. *I wonder who he had to bribe to make that happen.* But however it was done, Corwin was glad to have familiar faces here. Kate smiled at him, and the gesture seemed to push air into his lungs. He wished he could talk to her, but instead he was ushered inside one of the walled tents, where two more priestesses waited.

They converged on him at once, removing his clothes. He bit down a protest, forcing himself to be still and supplicant. Once he was completely naked, even his socks removed, they wrapped a loincloth around his waist, securing it with a crude rope belt. Somehow he felt even more exposed with it on. Finally, one of the priestesses fastened the vambrace around his right arm once more, hiding the Shieldhawk tattoo. It seemed he would be able to keep that secret from the public, at least.

A moment later, Corwin found himself standing beneath the canopy in front of a ceremonial table set before the high priestess. Two chalices, golden and encrusted with precious gems, waited side by side on the table, both full of some dark-red liquid. Wine, Corwin hoped. He'd seen blood look that same color.

Beside him, Edwin also wore a flimsy loincloth around his waist, although there'd been no need to hide any tattoos on his body. The councilmembers, along with Grand Master Storr and Maestra Vikas, hovered to either side of the high priestess, watching silently. Corwin caught Minister Rendborne's gaze—so impossible to miss with the striking color of his eyes—and the man gave him a conspiratorial wink and flashed an encouraging smile.

Raising her hands, the high priestess said, "Today, you, the princes of Norgard, sons of Tormane, will be tested for your worthiness as heir." As in the opening ritual, she wore a headdress made of a horse's head and diaphanous ceremonial robes. "But first, you must drink of the blood of the goddess. It will give you both vision and sight."

There's a difference? Corwin wanted to say, but wisely he kept his mouth shut.

The high priestess picked up the cup on the right, the gold-coined bracelets around her wrists jangling with the movement, and raised it to Edwin's mouth, bidding him to drink. He did so, closing his eyes as the cup's golden edge touched his lips.

Corwin closed his eyes as well when the high priestess offered the second cup to him. For a moment, as the liquid touched his tongue, he tasted blood before it transformed into the familiar, rich flavor of gothberry wine. Even still, it left a strange, bitter aftertaste, and he felt the heat of it pool in his stomach.

When he emerged from beneath the canopy a few moments later, the sunshine stung his eyes. The high priestess herself led him and Edwin up the stone steps to the top of the Asterion. It was so high, it felt like the top of the world, the landscape below a distant blur. Corwin shivered as the wind nipped at his naked flesh and ran rough fingers through his hair. He had never been on top of the Asterion before, but he'd seen others make the ascent, the old and the infirm, giving themselves over to sacrifice. The evidence of that act remained in the dark stains covering the stone, scars of both blood and ash.

The high priestess stopped just before the threshold of the Asterion and turned to face them. "Once you cross, there is no returning until it's done," she said. Then she stepped aside and bade them enter.

As always, Edwin went first, although Corwin could see his trepidation in the rigid line of his spine. Corwin followed after, walking boldly at first, only to lose his nerve the moment he passed over the threshold. The sun, blinding a moment before, faded to gray as an unnatural mist rose up all around him. He blinked, his head swimming at the sudden change, but no matter how hard he tried, he couldn't see anything. It was as if he'd stepped off the earth and into the clouds. The crowd below, the fields and distant hills and woods, all was gone.

Corwin walked forward a few steps, searching for some sign of what to do. He didn't dare go too far, not with how little he could see. Although the altar was large enough to hold a hundred men standing in a circle with arms widespread, Corwin didn't want to be the first heir to plummet to his death by accident.

Seconds passed slowly, agonizingly, the mists swirling about him. He could still feel the wind from before, but despite its strength, it couldn't dispel the unnatural haze. *What now?* Corwin thought, turning in a slow circle. Then, as if in answer, he spotted a glint of something just ahead. But it disappeared just as quickly, and he waited for it to happen again.

When it did so a moment later, he moved toward it cautiously. The mists parted at his approach, revealing a large, old tree that he knew beyond doubt did not exist atop the Asterion. *It will give you both vision and sight,* the high priestess had said. *Visions.* He wondered if there'd been more than gothberry wine in that cup.

Three swords stuck out from the center of the tree's broad trunk, their blades halfway buried in the wood. The one on the right was his father's, the golden hilt carved into the likeness of Niran and Nelek. The one on the left was his own sword, the hilt wrapped in leather with a straight, unadorned cross guard above. A large sapphire imbedded in the pommel provided the only ornamentation. The sword in the middle he didn't know, but it was so striking he couldn't seem to pull his eyes away from it. Its blade was made of black steel and the hilt of ivory. Five gemstones of different colors adorned the pommel—blue, white, green, red, and brown.

Summoner, Corwin realized. The mythical lost sword once carried by Norgard's first king. He longed to touch it, but something inside him stayed his hand. He was in the midst of a trial, and this was surely a test, a choice. Did he take his father's sword, the sword of a king? Did he take *Summoner,* sword of myth and legend?

I am none of those things. With his decision made, Corwin wrapped both hands around the hilt of his own sword and yanked it free of the trunk. The moment he did so, the tree and the other two swords dissolved into mist. But the sword in his hand remained solid and real. He tightened his grip on it just as a loud keening sound reached him.

He spun in time to see the nightdrake charge him, leaping out of the mist like some kind of white wraith. The size of a bull, its thick-muscled body moved with powerful grace, quick and deadly. *This isn't real,* Corwin thought, *just a vision.* But his mind couldn't tell the difference and the instinct to protect himself took over.

Gripping the sword in both hands, he lunged toward it, stabbing at its neck. The drake dodged to the left, avoiding the blow by inches. It spun, twisting its body in midair, and charged him again, jaws snapping. Corwin leaned backward, just avoiding the teeth as he made another stab at it. This time he hooked the inside of the drake's jaw. The creature gave a scream and yanked its head back, opening the tear begun by Corwin's sword even farther. Blood seeped out between its fangs, and it snapped at Corwin again as it backed away. It disappeared into the mist, but Corwin could still sense it nearby. Circling, watching.

Hunting.

"Come on," he said. "Come at me one more time." He slowly pivoted, eyes searching the mists.

The nightdrake charged him from far to his left, its movement foretold in the smoky swirl. It leaped, wings fanned out behind, the whole force of its body in the motion. Corwin spun toward it, the instinct to strike strong inside him. He resisted, waiting for the right moment. Just before the drake reached him, he pivoted, letting the drake's head and neck get past him. Then he drove the sword down, spearing it in the soft place between the neck and shoulder. The creature screamed as it fell, sword buried half a foot into its body. Its claws raked against Corwin's bare leg as it convulsed, and Corwin yelped from the sudden pain. Definitely no mere vision. Leaning on the sword, he drove it further in, but the next moment, the creature dissolved into nothing.

Stumbling forward, Corwin just managed to catch himself before falling. He peered around, waiting for another drake to appear. A tremble slid through his body and down his legs, the right one already starting to burn from the drake's poison. He leaned to the left, keeping the weight off it as best he could. At least it wasn't deep, the bleeding slow and sluggish. But it was only going to worsen.

A glint in the corner of his eye caught his attention, and he turned toward it as the mists parted once more, this time to reveal a second tree, smaller and younger than the first, not much more than a sapling. Hanging from its branches were a morning star, a dirk, and a buckler. Another test, this one easier than the last. Corwin had never been one for two-handed fighting, and so he picked up the buckler and slid it on his left hand.

The moment he did so, a figure appeared from around the tree. The man wore peasant's garb, dirtied and patched, and he had ash smeared across his forehead and cheeks. Wary, Corwin retreated a step, resisting the urge to raise his sword.

"Who are—?"

The man flung out his hands, and a ball of fire appeared in his palms. Corwin had only a second to think *wilder* before the flames reached him. He raised the buckler just in time to deflect the fire. With a loud curse, the pyrist sidestepped and tried again. Corwin spun, following the movement and keeping the buckler in front of him. The pyrist let loose with his magic once more, this time a steady stream of fire. Corwin blocked for a few seconds, but the small shield wouldn't be able to stand such a blast for long.

With a shout of desperation, he spun away from the pyrist and pivoted around the young tree, his wounded leg throbbing with every step. A second later the tree burst into flames, the heat of it forcing Corwin back. The pyrist followed, lobbying volley after volley. Corwin blocked when he needed to and dodged whenever he could. Before long he was doing wild leaps and flips through the air, whatever he could to stay away from the flames. His right leg went blessedly numb, but he wouldn't be able to keep this up for long.

I've got to stop him. More than that, he *wanted* to stop him. To slay this pyrist, so like the one who had killed his mother.

There was only one way. Despite the danger—the risk of fire and the oppressive heat—Corwin circled closer to the man. Several flames caught him on the shoulder and one lashed across his cheek. He hissed in pain but didn't retreat. Instead he moved faster, leaping and spinning like an acrobat. He whispered a silent prayer of thanks for his Shieldhawk training, where he'd learned the art of the dodge and survival. Spin and leap, dodge and duck, spin again. All the while he kept his eyes on the pyrist, waiting for an opening. When it came, he took it without hesitation, burying his sword in the man's side. The pyrist cried out once before vanishing.

Panting, Corwin bent over and dropped the buckler to grip his wounded shoulder, already covered in blisters from the flames. He wouldn't be able to raise his arm, the pain strong enough to leave him dizzy. He needed this to end soon, but another figure appeared, this one bearing a sword and shield. He wore the traditional brigandine armor of Norgard, a lightweight piece that covered the torso but left the arms free for full movement. A helmet hid his face. No sooner had Corwin spotted him than the man attacked. The prince barely had time to grab the buckler from the ground and use it to block a downward, hacking swing. His opponent's sword screeched as it met the steel on the front of his buckler.

Wrenching free of the clash, Corwin retreated. He kept his sword out in front of him, but it shook in his sweaty hand, his arms weak from fighting and from the drake poison working its way through his body. He didn't want to fight this man, but the stranger gave him no choice. Wherever Corwin went, he followed, relentless. He swung and Corwin blocked. He thrust and Corwin parried. Each hit landed like a hammer, and Corwin knew either he must kill this foe or he would die himself.

It wasn't easy to kill a man in armor, especially not when you were wearing just a loincloth. Corwin pressed close, blocking more attacks than dodging them as he searched for openings to land his blade. For a while, he didn't think it would happen—the other fighter was too good, too careful. But then he made a mistake. Thrusting his sword at Corwin, he overextended, leaving an opening big enough for the most inexperienced of swordsmen to exploit. Corwin lunged toward it, sinking his sword through the man's shoulder and into his chest. A killing blow.

The man shrieked and fell to his knees. Sickened by the sound and the sight of the death he'd wrought, Corwin pulled his sword free. But the man didn't vanish as the others had done. Instead he raised a blood-soaked hand to his helmet, using the last of his strength to pull it free.

Corwin stared down into the face of his father. As he once had been, young and strong, not the wasted shell he was now.

"You are not worthy to wear my crown," Orwin said. "Not . . . worthy."

The words landed harder than any blow. *Oh goddess, let this end,* Corwin thought. A tremor struck his body, this one hard enough that he dropped his sword and shield both. He fell to his knees, succumbing to the pain and poison while across from him, the vision of his father vanished at last.

Another figure appeared a moment later, this one far smaller than the others but no less a threat. Corwin gaped at the boy, his gut twisting at the sight of him. He wore a flimsy breastplate of boiled leather, much too big for him, and he carried a rusted iron sword. The Sevan crest, a red bull in charge painted on the breast-plate, seemed to mock Corwin. Everything about the boy was a mockery, a reminder of his greatest failure and biggest regret.

Unbidden, a memory rose up in his mind of riding with the Shieldhawks toward the Sevan supply line they'd been sent to destroy. He'd taken a shortcut, going against his commander's orders. Ahead, he saw a boy dressed like a soldier. Only he couldn't be a soldier. He was too young and frail, eyes too wide and frightened.

"Kill him," Otto had said. "You've got to, Captain. He'll give us away, soon as he can."

But Corwin hadn't. In the end, he couldn't. The boy was just a child, someone's son. A slave given in tribute to the Godking who had conquered his lands. "Go home," Corwin told the boy. "Find your parents." And then he set the boy free—to betray him and his men to the Sevan forces.

Outrage and anguish ignited inside Corwin, the strength of it driving him to his feet just as the soldier boy attacked. Corwin dodged the blow, pivoting to the right. Then he turned and grabbed the boy by the wrist. With one hard squeeze, he forced the boy's hand open, making him drop the sword. With his other hand, Corwin grasped the boy by the back of his breastplate and hauled him off his feet. Even in his weakened state, overpowering him was easy. Still the boy fought him, kicking and snarling like a wild beast.

Corwin held him aloft as he bent to pick up his own fallen sword. One stab was all it would take, hardly more effort than swatting a fly. He raised the sword and the boy cried out, the sound as pathetic as a mewling kitten.

Kill him, a voice whispered from amid the mist. *Finish this. Prove yourself. Kill him.*

Corwin raised the sword again. His body trembled; sweat stung his eyes, blurred his vision.

Kill him! The voice seemed to strike him like a fist, demanding his compliance. *Kill him and this will end. Your suffering will be over. Kill him!*

"No," Corwin said. "I won't kill him. I won't do what you want." He would do what was right and just—mercy for a foe too weak to fight. Letting go of the boy's breastplate, he shoved him toward the mist. "Get out of here."

The boy vanished, and the next moment the mists parted, bright sunlight pouring over Corwin. He blinked against it, aware of a strange tingle spreading over his skin. Looking down, he saw his injuries had vanished. So had the sword. None of it had been real. And yet it had been. From far below, the cheers of the crowd reached him. He glanced at Edwin, standing on the other side of the altar. It seemed they'd both made it—one trial over and two more yet to come.

You're not worthy, Corwin heard his father say once more.

And no matter the cheers, he couldn't hear anything but those words.

FOR THE FIRST TIME IN her life, Kate regretted not being able to tell Corwin the truth about her magic. It had never seemed to matter before. Keeping her wilder abilities a secret was normal, expected, a promise she'd made to her father from the first moment she was old enough to understand that she was different.

"Does Mother know?" a seven-year-old Kate had asked him.

"No, Katie girl," Hale replied. "She doesn't. Not about you and not about me."

"Isn't that a lie?" Kate wrinkled her nose. "I'm not supposed to lie."

"It's not a lie when the truth would hurt the ones we love. Not telling them is a sacrifice we must make *for* them. Do you understand?"

"Yes, Daddy." Kate believed him completely, especially once he explained the consequences of being discovered a wilder. She never wanted to be taken away from her father by those masked people.

But what happens when not telling the truth might put them in more danger than telling them? Kate wondered. There'd been something wrong in the Wandering Woods that day when they'd returned to search for the drakes. The moment Kate stepped through the trees, she felt cut off from her magic. Not like at night, when it vanished completely, but as if there was something standing between her and it. Something blocking it. *Or someone.*

She longed to tell Corwin, but couldn't find a way to do so without revealing her secret. She didn't see how she could ever tell him she was a wilder, especially not now with the growing threat of the Rising. She'd never experienced such open hatred for wilders before. Fear, yes, but not hate. The risk of what Corwin would do—what he would be compelled to do—if he learned the truth about her seemed greater than ever, now that he might finally become the next king. Although there was no clear winner in the first uror trial, he had done well. She'd seen it, felt it. Everyone present had. Watching the two princes inside that unnatural mist had been strange, almost like watching a dream—their shapes and those they battled, indistinct and confused. But of the two, Corwin's image had been clearer somehow, almost brighter.

Still, the temptation to tell him kept getting stronger. In the two weeks since the first trial, Kate had spent nearly every morning with him. He kept showing up at her door with sweet rolls and an invitation to ride or sometimes just to walk in the gardens or along the ramparts. Even worse, she felt her instinct to stay away from him weakening each day. Instead, she found herself longing to see him. She savored every time he touched her, which he did often, always finding some excuse to place his fingers on her shoulder or back or to tug at her hand. And just yesterday, it even seemed for a moment that he was about to kiss her. The disappointment she felt afterward bothered her even now.

It has to end. She needed to uncover her father's secrets soon, before Norgard became too much like home again—and before she once more set her heart on someone who could never be hers.

If only she could figure out how. It wasn't like she could just march into the Sacred Sword and demand they tell her. She barely knew what questions to ask. And going inside to snoop wasn't going to be easy either. She'd spent enough time these last few weeks observing the comings and goings outside the brothel to know that she would stand out like a mule in a herd of warhorses. She was sure that she wouldn't seem as natural as the women she saw frequenting the place, and Kate doubted she would be able to score a job. She didn't have any of the skills such an establishment would require. Besides, even if she did, she was too recognizable. Not a day went by that she didn't hear whispers of *Traitor Kate* following her at every turn. Still, there must be some solution; she just needed to find it.

"How would you do it?" Kate asked Signe while they were out riding one morning. Corwin had been busy the last two days with high council business, and Kate enlisted Signe's help in taking the horses out for a much-needed hack in the countryside.

Signe cocked her head in consideration. "My mother says there are two ways to always get a garro to talk. Fear of pain or love of money."

"Garro?" Kate said, leaning forward to shoo a fly off Fire-dancer's neck.

"There is no exact word to translate. But it means anyone not born to the islands."

Kate looked over at her friend, grinning. She found the idea both absurd and slightly offensive. "Are you trying to say that no one from Esh would ever divulge a secret?"

Signe nodded, her expression solemn, and she seemed to sit up a little straighter in the saddle. "We call it Seerah. It is the holy silence. There is nothing more important to us than keeping it."

A dozen questions came to Kate, but she didn't get the chance to ask any of them, as she and Signe rode into the stable yard at Norgard castle to find Dal waiting for them. Well, waiting for Signe.

"How would you like to take a trip to Tyvald with me?" Dal asked her, a devilish grin spilling over his face. With him was his falcon, Lir, the bird hooded and perched on his shoulder. "Just for a few days. Corwin's asked me to look into a daydrake sighting."

Kate sighed at this news, her guilt over not telling Corwin what she'd sensed that day in the Wandering Woods prickling inside her. These daydrake attacks were getting worse, and Tyvald was close, only a day's journey away. She wondered why Corwin would want Dal to look into it in person, but could only guess it was something bad.

Signe regarded Dal coolly, although Kate knew it was just pretense. So did Dal, but he enjoyed the game.

"I can certainly spare a few days," Signe said drily, "but you must promise me excitement and adventure."

Kate closed her eyes as Signe's words reminded her of yet another worry. As it was, Signe could spare a lot more than a few days. There was little for her to do until Bonner finally succeeded in making his revolvers. In the month they'd been here, he'd produced only one. If he didn't start to make progress soon, Corwin and the high council were bound to start asking why. Bonner was already beginning to cave to the pressure, taking more and more risks with his magic. The increasing daydrake attacks only fueled his desperation.

"My sweet lady," Dal said, taking Signe's hand and kissing it, "I swear that you'll fight to catch your breath at every moment."

Signe giggled, an uncharacteristic sound that told Kate better than any words that her friend had strong feelings for Dal. She couldn't help the sharp stab of envy she felt at the knowledge. *Love is so easy for some.* Not that she begrudged Signe her happiness.

While Signe went off to pack, Kate dropped in on Bonner in his new workshop and was glad to see his father was there. Thomas Bonner was short and slight, all the stoutness he possessed from the hard life of a blacksmith withered away by the wasting disease. Although father and son looked nothing alike—to be expected, as Bonner was adopted—they were just alike in manner, sharing a kind and hopeful nature that Kate never failed to find refreshing.

"Ah, Miss Kate," Thomas said, brightening at the sight of her. He pulled her into a hug, squeezing her tight. Kate was glad to feel the strength in him. He'd been in Norgard only a week, but already she could see his health was improving thanks to green-robe magic. "I'd just come to fetch Tommy for lunch. He'd work himself to death if I didn't. Won't you join us?"

Kate stifled a grin at the look of annoyance that crossed Bonner's face whenever his father called him Tommy—the only person permitted to do so.

"I would love to," Kate said, kissing the man on the cheek. She could use the distraction from her troubles, if only for a little while. With Thomas there, she couldn't discuss any of her concerns about Bonner's use of his wilder magic. Thomas didn't know this truth about his adopted son, another lie kept to protect a loved one.

Still, all too soon, lunch was over and Kate found herself alone in her room, her doubts and worries pressing down on her harder than before. She couldn't do anything to help Bonner, but Signe's words about how to get someone to talk had given her an idea. All she needed was enough coin and the right disguise.

And enough courage to go through with it, Kate thought, looking at her image in the mirror the following night. It had taken her hours to assemble the disguise, and even now she wasn't quite certain she looked enough like a young man to get away with it. She wore her loosest-fitting breeches, tall boots, and a red velvet doublet that she'd found stowed in a trunk in Signe's room. Kate felt guilty about going through her things, but her need was too great not to, and the doublet far too perfect.

Although she didn't quite recognize the cut and pattern of the clothing, it had clearly been made for a grown man. He'd been taller than Kate but not much wider, which meant the jacket hung just past her hips, helping hide her feminine shape. Even more perfect, the buttons lining the front of it were made of rubies the size of her thumb, a fortune that had left Kate dumbstruck when she first spotted it. She longed to know the story of why Signe kept it, but doubted she would get the real one even if she asked. She worried about wearing it in public but in the end decided that if she was going to buy the information she needed, it was best to look wealthy enough to afford it.

I'll put it back when I'm done, and she'll never know, Kate silently swore as she slid a cowl on to hide the bulge of her hair, pinned to the back of her head.

Finally, she picked up her bag of coins and a jeweled dagger Corwin had given her a few days before—another gift for saving him—and tucked them into her belt. She had to wear the belt loose to avoid revealing too much, but after a moment's adjustment she was ready to go.

Walking, it took her nearly an hour to reach the Burnside district. She would've liked to ride, but she didn't want anyone in the castle seeing her like this. Sneaking out the servants' entrance was a lot easier than through the front gates, as she would have had to on horseback. Besides, she didn't like the idea of leaving Firedancer unattended in such a rough area.

At this time of night, the street out front of the Sacred Sword buzzed with people, mostly men coming in and out of the taverns, gaming houses, and other brothels. Kate supposed the crowd was one of the drawbacks of the high king's edict that all such establishments be kept to one district. People came from all over Norgard to indulge their sins here.

Doing her best to walk like a boy, Kate stepped onto the porch in front of the entrance and nodded at the guards. Above their heads hung a carved wooden sign bearing the brothel's name written beneath a sword being drawn from a sheath with a red rose entwined around it.

The guards ignored her, and she walked by with a sigh of relief. Beyond the door was an antechamber with three archways leading to interior rooms. Gauzy curtains covered the ones to the right and left. Through the center archway, Kate saw the tavern portion of the establishment, an assortment of tables in different sizes and shapes, most of them occupied. In the middle of the room stood a low platform where several musicians played while two scantily dressed women danced in slow, seductive circles.

Kate pulled her gaze away only to find two more such women

standing by a podium set between the archways. Both wore cropped bodices that left their midriffs bared, their moonbelts clearly visible. They eyed Kate with matching dubious expressions.

"Can I help you?"

Kate cleared her throat, then in the deepest voice she could manage said, "A table, please. For now." She waited, breath held as she braced to be turned away.

The woman on the left stepped around the podium. "Follow me."

Letting out her breath slowly, Kate followed the woman into the room. She felt eyes on her as she sat down at an empty table far in the corner. Resisting the urge to fidget with the doublet as it rode up too high on her neck, she surveyed the room. Any one of these people might have the information she needed.

The serving girl who arrived a few minutes later was easily the homeliest of the workers Kate had seen. Too thin, with lank brown hair and small breasts, she stared down at Kate with a pinched expression. "What can I bring you?"

Kate ordered the fish with mushrooms and roasted potatoes and a cup of the house wine. While she spoke, she made a show of removing her money purse and placing it on the table, coins jangling. Thank the gods she'd amassed enough valens since she'd started working as Corwin's horse trainer to make an impression. It helped that she had nothing to spend the money on, all her basic needs provided by the castle. The truth of this sat uncomfortably in her mind. She didn't want to be dependent on anyone, Corwin least of all.

When the serving girl returned, Kate paid her double the price of the food and drink. The girl scooped it up eagerly, her earlier annoyance tucked behind a veneer of greed.

"But come back often," Kate said before the girl walked away. "I will need more to drink." She held up the cup in emphasis, then took a long swallow. The bitter taste burned her throat, but she managed not to cough.

After weeks of meals prepared in the royal kitchens, she found the fish barely edible, too salty and dry. Kate ate it anyway, using the excuse of each bite to observe the activity in the room. She tried to picture her father in this place but failed at every turn. Most of the men were high on alcohol or sex or both. In some ways she thought she'd rather be facing a pack of drakes again.

When the serving girl returned to the table sometime later, Kate ordered more wine, again paying double for it.

"What is your name?" Kate said, handing over the coins.

The annoyance reappeared on the girl's face. "Janelle."

Sensing her resistance, Kate slid over another coin. "Have you been working here long, Janelle?"

The girl shrugged. She was younger than Kate first thought, her thinness and frown lines falsely aging her. "Few years."

Hoping she was telling the truth, Kate asked, "Do you remember a man who used to come here often about three years ago? Tall, with black hair and brown eyes."

Janelle huffed as she picked up the coin. "Sure, I remember him. He's just like that man over there or that one. They're all the same, don't you know." She pointed at several nearby tables, and it was all Kate could do to keep from grabbing the girl's arm and pulling it down, *the idiot.*

"This man was slight of build. A horseman. He worked at the royal stables."

The girl started to shake her head, but then understanding dawned on her face. "Do you mean Hale Brighton, the traitor?" She practically shouted the name.

"Yes." Kate gestured for the girl to lower her voice.

Janelle put her hands on her hips. "Why you want to know about him?"

Kate blinked, the question taking her by surprise. She'd been so focused on a convincing disguise, she'd forgotten to work out a convincing story.

"Uh . . . just . . . curiosity. I mean, he's famous. Or infamous, rather."

"I don't think so." Janelle turned and walked away.

Kate watched her go, her heartbeat pounding in her ears. Janelle headed to the front of the room and began speaking to a matronly woman standing by the door into the kitchens. She wore her gray hair piled on top of her head in an intricate coiffure, and not an inch of bare skin showed below her neck—the mistress here, Kate guessed.

In moments, she realized that her innocent question wasn't being taken so innocently. Everyone around her was whispering now. Some were pointing. The mistress started a slow, measured walk toward her. Kate reached for her wine, feeling an urge to fidget, but she held back, afraid she would spill it. It wasn't just fear rising up in her but anticipation. If anyone would know why her father was making such large payments to this place, surely it was the person in charge.

The woman stopped at Kate's table. "I am Madam Anise. Are you enjoying the wine? The food?"

Kate nodded, once, twice.

"Good, that's good." Anise folded her hands in front of her. "And will you be partaking in any of our other services this evening?"

With warmth spreading up her neck, Kate shook her head.

"I see. Then as soon as you're done with that wine, I can expect you to take your leave, yes?"

Kate gritted her teeth. This was not how it was supposed to go. With a defiant look she said, "I might have another, and another after that."

Anise leaned forward now, and Kate could see she was a tall woman, strong of body and even stronger of will. "I don't believe you shall."

Kate searched for a response, but before she could think of one, a man at a nearby table stood up and stumbled toward them. His long, bushy beard glistened with spilled wine, the smell of alcohol coming off him in nauseating waves.

"Who's this girl trying to pass for a boy? It's that Traitor Kate, ain't it, Anise?"

The madam turned a shriveling look on the man. "What she is, Boyle, is a paying customer. Now go back to your drink. Or would you like me to send for Kristiana?"

The man Boyle made a quick retreat, but it didn't matter. Others were approaching. Searching for a quick exit in case she needed one, Kate's eyes fell on a familiar face across the room. The sight of that red stain across the man's nose and cheeks, mark of the Shade Born, sent a clench of fear through her stomach. In the four weeks she'd been here, she hadn't forgotten Master Raith's threatening words to her. Now here he was sitting at a table a few yards away. For some reason he wasn't wearing his mask or robes, which was why she hadn't noticed him before. He'd seen her, too, but a second later, he passed out of view as Kate found herself surrounded by a group of hostile men.

"Get up, girl," Anise said, her voice brooking no argument.

Kate stood, and Anise took hold of her arm, escorting her past the men. Her grip felt like a vise. Kate tried to pull free but couldn't.

"Let me go," she said as they passed through the archway back into the entrance. "I have questions. I'm not leaving until I get answers."

"Be quiet, you stupid girl. Do you want every person in this place to learn why you're here?"

Kate's mouth fell open, outrage surging through her before reason asserted itself. She was making a scene, revealing her business to people who wished her harm. And that included Raith, a man who already knew her most dangerous secret. She clamped her mouth shut and stopped struggling. But Anise didn't let go. She dragged Kate through a narrow door into a small room Kate hadn't noticed when she first came in. It was a private office, barely big enough to hold the narrow desk and two chairs, one on each side.

"Sit." Anise pushed Kate toward the nearest chair. She closed the door behind them before swinging to face Kate again. "Why did you come here?"

Kate debated a lie but knew she only had this one chance to get what she wanted. "My father, Hale Brighton, made regular, large, and *secret* payments to this establishment during the last three years of his life. I want to know why."

Anise folded her arms over her chest. "How exactly do you know he did this?"

"A ledger. It's in his handwriting, and the Sacred Sword is clearly marked."

Anise's nostrils flared, and she looked ready to stab something. But when she spoke again, her voice was low and calm, another command. "Come back tomorrow morning. First thing. Don't tell anyone. Wear the cowl again, but not that ridiculous doublet, and make sure you aren't followed. Do you understand?"

"Yes," Kate said. "But—"

Anise silenced her with another look. Then she opened the door and called to one of the girls by the podium. "Escort our guest outside through the back."

Kate followed the girl down the hallway on the left, her head swimming over what had just happened. Doors lined one side of the hallway, most of them shut. One that wasn't revealed a small, lavishly decorated bedroom inside. Glimpsing it, Kate turned her gaze to the front and didn't look again into any of the other rooms.

The hallway ended in a door that led to a dark, litter-strewn alley. Once outside, Kate hesitated a moment, allowing her eyes to adjust, then turned left, in search of a way back to the main road.

Moments later, she stepped out onto the street not far from the entrance to the Sacred Sword. She took a deep breath, glancing at the doorway. Fear and anticipation coiled inside her like two snakes ready to strike. She would never be able to sleep tonight, when in just a few hours she would learn the truth about her father. Not even Raith's appearance could dampen her relief. *I'll run away if I have to, once I know—*

A group of men exited the Sacred Sword, some of those who had threatened her just moments before.

"There she is," one of them shouted, pointing. "There's that Traitor Kate."

Kate spun and hurried down the street, straightening the cowl over her hair. There was still a crowd, and she should be able to lose them in it. With their shouts chasing after her, Kate picked up the pace.

They will get tired of the game soon, she told herself. But the crowd was thinning out ahead, and still they followed. Spying an alley, Kate darted down it, breaking into a run. She would lose them easily now. The alley dumped her onto a quiet street, nearly deserted this time of night. The lamps in the streetlights were dim, the oil almost burned out, but the moon was full overhead, the silvery light glistening against the cobblestones.

Kate slowed to a jog, making sure of her location. She didn't want to get lost out here. This street seemed to run parallel to the one she'd left behind. If she followed it long enough, she could cross back over, then find her way to the castle.

Two men stepped out of the darkness at the intersection ahead, and Kate froze, recognizing their faces. They were huffing from the exertion of getting in front of her to cut her off. She spun around, only to find the other three were here now, too, cornering her on the narrow street. Drawing her dagger, Kate faced the first two. They would be easier to get past. She couldn't stand and fight, not with so many of them and her only weapon a dagger.

Steeling herself, Kate darted forward and made a quick slash with the dagger. She took the first man by surprise, slicing his forearm. He stumbled sideways, and she surged through the opening. But before she made it past, a hand seized her. The others had caught up, moving faster than she'd anticipated. Fingers closed around her upper arm, yanking her back. Kate lost her balance and the dagger flew from her hand. Spinning toward her attacker, she let fly a wild punch. It landed on the man's chest. He puffed out a breath but didn't let go. *Stupid, Kate. Aim higher. For the throat.*

She tried, but more hands seized her. She struggled but couldn't break free, not under such a coordinated attack, not against men whose purpose wasn't to fight but to subdue.

"Let me go!" Kate screamed. "Let me go!" She began to flail, throwing all her strength into it.

"Now, now, there's no point in fighting," one of them said. "We just want to see justice served. It's not right for a traitor's daughter to have such trinkets, even if you are favored by that fool Corwin. Good thing the Errant Prince isn't here to protect you now." The man grabbed at one of the ruby buttons on her doublet and pulled it off.

"You're a thief," Kate said. "This has nothing to do with my father." She kicked out, striking the man on the wrist. Yelping, he dropped the ruby, and Kate kicked again.

The man stepped back, out of reach. "Make her pay for that one, John."

A big man, easily the largest of the group, approached her, his right hand balled into a fist. Kate kicked out at him, struggling harder than ever to free herself. John deflected the kick with one hand and landed a punch with the other. It struck her belly, robbing her of the ability to breathe, let alone scream. She wanted to curl inward, to ease the pain rippling through her, but the cruel hands holding her kept her upright. The man called John struck her again, then stepped aside, letting the first man have a go at her. He kicked her in the side of her leg, and agony lit up her body all the way to her teeth. The next moment all of them were coming at her, raining down blows.

Kate felt her consciousness slipping but fought to stay awake. She had to keep fighting. These men wouldn't stop until they killed her. Forcing her eyes open, she saw moonlight spilling over her, bright as the day.

Summoning all the strength she possessed and more, Kate sucked air into her lungs, then screamed, "LET ME GO!"

More than just words filled the command. Somehow, impossibly, she invoked her wilder magic. It was the deepest part of her, the truest part—and it refused to surrender. The magic swept out from her like an explosion. The men holding her stumbled back, dazed and reeling.

Realizing she was free, Kate scrambled to her feet and ran.

PAIN LANCED THROUGH HER LEG with each step, but she barely felt it as she darted down the nearest alley. Straining to see in the darkness, she stumbled over litter and debris, feet slipping in the muck. She started to fall, only to have someone reach out and catch her.

"No!" she screamed, lashing out with her magic again. It answered the call, more sluggish than before, but still there, despite the presence of night.

The hand on her arm loosened but didn't let go. "I'm not going to hurt you, Kate."

Recognizing the voice, Kate felt an insane urge to laugh. Of all the people to find her now, why did it have to be Master Raith?

"But please, refrain from using your magic on me," the magist said. "It's very disorienting."

Kate gaped up at him, too stunned to respond.

"Let's be off before those men recover and give chase." Raith tugged her forward.

Dazedly, Kate followed the magist out of the alley and back onto the main street. She was afraid of Raith, but the threat posed by those other men was more immediate. The street wasn't as busy as before, and Raith stepped beside her, holding her arm as if he were her chaperone.

"Just be calm and act naturally. Hold the doublet closed as best you can," Raith said in a hushed voice.

Kate obeyed, grimacing at the state of the shirt, torn and dirty and with half the rubies missing. *Signe will murder me when she finds out.*

They walked on in silence for several minutes, and after a while, Kate felt the first small waves of relief slipping over her. With it came full awareness of her injuries. Her right leg was throbbing where the man had kicked her. She tried not to limp, but it was impossible.

Noticing it, Raith slid his hand into his pocket and withdrew a plain gray stone. He raised it to his mouth, the gesture disconcerting with the sight of his permanently blackened fingertips. He whispered a word of invocation, lips brushing against the stone, and a faint white light crawled across its surface as the spell activated. He handed it to her. "Hold this against your heart. It will ease the worst of your injuries."

Kate accepted the healing stone. With a grateful sigh, she held it cupped over her left breast. The magic worked at once, a tingly heat slowly spreading through her body. In moments she could walk without limping, although the ache remained, reminding her in visceral detail of what had happened. With the magic in the stone now spent, she handed it back to Raith.

"Why are you helping me?" Kate glanced up at him. In the weak light, his birthmark appeared as nothing more than an unusual shadow across his face.

"That's a rather strange question," Raith replied, not looking at her but keeping his gaze fixed ahead where the street began to bend. A leather worker's shop sat at the corner. "Why wouldn't I help you?"

She frowned, unsure if he was playing with her or being unintentionally obtuse. Either way she was too tired for games. "Because you threatened me the day we arrived at Norgard."

"Threatened?" Now Raith tilted his chin toward her, brows raised. "I don't recall threatening you."

Kate scowled and lowered her voice, even though the only person in view was still too far away to overhear them. "Yes you did. You said you know what I am."

"And what are you, Kate?"

The question caught her off guard. *But he knows!* Unable to answer, she turned her gaze ahead, concentrating on the road. The person soon drew near enough for Kate to see it was an elderly woman, her narrow shoulders stooped with age and her gaze fixed on the ground as if she feared tripping. A moment later, though, she looked up, glancing first at Kate, then Raith.

"Good evening," he said, nodding toward the woman.

She stared hard at his face, taking in the mark of the Shade Born. At once her eyes widened with fright. Then she made a warding gesture before deliberately turning away to walk on the other side of the road, his greeting left unanswered. Kate took in Raith's expression, expecting to see anger or annoyance at such rudeness. Instead he seemed as if he hadn't even noticed.

Once the woman had passed, Raith said, "You have nothing to fear from me, Kate Brighton. I've kept your secret all this time, and that will not change. But I wish you would have the courage to claim what you are. Your father never did, and that doesn't sit well with me."

"You knew my father?" The words came out more accusation than question.

Raith nodded as he stepped over a pile of trash left out in front of a dark doorway. "Yes, well enough to know what he was and about his ability to influence minds."

Kate held her breath, wanting to deny it, but there seemed no point. "You mean influence the minds of animals," she corrected.

Raith shook his head. "Animals were only the beginning of his power, easiest to touch and manipulate because of their simplicity. But as he grew in skill, he became capable of so much more. But surely you already know this, given the way you drove off those men."

My magic. I used it on a human! And at night. Shock made her stumble, and Raith grabbed her arm to keep her from falling. But no, it was impossible. Her magic didn't work that way. It only worked on animals. And yet . . .

"I didn't know," she said, voice barely a whisper. "That was the first time I've ever done such a thing."

Raith abruptly stopped walking, his eyes locked on something in the distance—a man on horseback, bearing down on them. No, not any man, but Corwin.

Raith turned his gaze on Kate and said hurriedly, "We need to talk more, once you've rested. I can help you, Kate. And more important, you can help me."

"With what?" She narrowed her eyes, a warning sounding in her head.

"To save Rime from its own destruction and finish the task your father started." Raith broke off, falling into a bow as Corwin reached them. "Your highness."

Corwin dismounted, his attention centered completely on Kate. "Oh gods, what happened?" He swept his gaze over her torn, dirtied clothes. Then he pulled her into his arms. "Are you all right?"

Kate sagged against him, relief leaving her weak. Raith's words still echoed through her mind, but she couldn't make sense of them right now. And with those warm, strong arms around her, she didn't want to.

Wait, what am I doing?

She pulled back from the embrace. "I'm fine. Just ran into some trouble."

"At the Sacred Sword?" Anger threaded Corwin's voice, a muscle ticking in his jaw.

Refusing to feel guilty, she said, "What are you doing out here, anyway?"

"I came to find you. When I saw you weren't in your rooms, I knew you were up to something foolish."

"It would be best to get her home quickly, your highness," Raith broke in as Kate started to argue. "Before any more trouble finds us."

"Yes, you're right." Corwin stooped as if to pick her up, but Kate stumbled back from him.

"What are you doing? I don't need you to carry me."

Jamming his hands on his hips, he muttered, "You are such a mule. Fine, get on the horse then." Corwin turned to Raith. "Thank you for helping her."

I helped myself, Kate almost pointed out but held back. She didn't want to answer any questions about what had really happened. Hiding a wince at her still-aching leg, she mounted Nightbringer.

Raith bowed his head. "Get her back to the castle safely, your highness. I will stop in to give you my report on the drakes tomorrow. I only just returned to the city this evening."

Corwin nodded absentmindedly, then turned and mounted Nightbringer behind Kate. His hands slid around her waist, and he pulled her back against his chest. She resisted a moment, then sank into his warmth and the firm support of his body against hers. They rode back to the castle without speaking.

When they entered the bailey, Corwin slid from the saddle, then helped her down next to him. He handed Nightbringer off to a groom and started to lead her into the castle.

She pulled out of his grip. "I can see myself from here."

"No, Kate. I'm going to get you safely to your room and make damn sure you really are all right and not just being stubborn."

Too tired for the battle it would take to change his mind, Kate pressed her lips shut and allowed him to walk beside her back to her quarters. At least once they were inside, he didn't argue when she went to her bedroom to change.

Leaving the ruined clothes piled in a corner, Kate unwound the cloth she'd wrapped around her breasts to flatten them and slipped into a clean shift. She pulled on a robe over it, barely feeling the press of her moonbelt against her hips as she tied the cord. She'd been wearing it so long, she hardly noticed it anymore.

When she returned to the front room, Corwin took her hand and guided her to the nearest sofa, pushing her down into it.

He knelt in front of her, concern furrowing his brow. "Do you need a healer? Where are you hurt?"

Kate shook her head, slumping back onto the chair. "I told you, I'm fine. Master Raith saw to it with a healing stone."

"You needed a *healing stone*?" Corwin's fingers curled into fists. "How badly were you hurt? Never mind. Do you know who attacked you? I'm going to hunt them down and kill them."

"No you aren't," Kate said with a sigh.

Corwin stood and started to pace. "Why did you go without me? Without anyone? I warned you, Kate. Why do you always have to be so reckless?"

Her temper sparked. "It wasn't reckless. I was disguised and careful. Things just went wrong. And I didn't take you for the same reason I said before. No one will tell secrets to the high prince of Rime."

"Oh yes, and they told you so much that they had to beat you black and blue."

With a disgusted noise, Kate stood and stepped away from Corwin; otherwise, she might have hit him. She paced around the room, anger driving off the fatigue. Only—it wasn't truly anger she was feeling, but lingering fear—the terrible sensation of being unable to escape those men who meant her harm, combined with the way she'd used her magic to drive them off. *Influence over minds—all minds, not just animals.*

Curious despite her doubt, she reached for her magic, wondering if it would work again, but it lay dormant inside her, as inaccessible as it always was during the night. Questions rose up in her mind, and she forced them away. She wouldn't find any answers here.

"I'm sorry, Kate," Corwin said from across the room. "That was uncalled for."

She faced him to see the sincerity of his apology in his expression. The color was fading from his cheeks, and a strange look had risen in his eyes.

"I know how important it is for you to learn the truth about your father, and I've done little enough to help," he continued. "Did you discover anything?"

Kate stared at him, taken off guard by the sudden shift in his attitude, yet another sign of how much he'd changed and grown. The old Corwin would never have let go of his possessive anger so easily.

"No," she finally answered, remembering Anise's warning. "You were right. They didn't want to talk to me." She took a deep breath and let it out slowly, her own temper slipping away. "And don't apologize. I know things have been difficult for you with the uror and the daydrakes. My father's secrets are my concern."

A tentative smile passed across Corwin's face. "May I make a confession then, a terrible, selfish one that you might not want to hear?"

The air seemed to thicken around them, surging with an unknown energy. Her heart quickened for no reason she could name other than the hungry, desperate way he was looking at her now. She recognized that look. It used to appear just before he kissed her. The idea that he might do so now sent tingles up her arms.

"What is it?" she said, barely able to get out the words.

Corwin took a step toward her. First one, then two, until he was standing close enough that she could feel the heat of his body. "A part of me is glad you didn't learn anything . . . because . . . I know that once you've learned the truth, that'll be one less thing keeping you in Norgard."

Kate looked up at him, confused.

"And I don't want you to leave again." He held her gaze, unflinching. There was a nakedness in his expression, his feelings bared for her to see—tenderness and doubt and desire.

A torrent of emotions surged through Kate in answer. The charge in the air between them increased, the sensation both terrifying and thrilling at once. She took a step closer to him. Corwin's hands rose to her face, tilting her head toward his. Then he brought his lips down on hers.

Heat exploded in her chest, traveled down into her belly, then farther still. She kissed him back, her lips opening to his while his tongue plunged into her mouth. She remembered his kisses from before, hesitant and soft. This was nothing like it. Those early ones had been a gentle rain. This was a storm, and she was caught in it. Kate closed her eyes in the onslaught of sensations pulsing through her body. She didn't feel the lingering ache of her injuries anymore, only the sweet, shivering tingles of his touch. She wanted this.

Sweet goddess, how much I want this.

She gripped his shoulders, and his hands left her face to hold her waist instead. When his fingers brushed against the moonbelt, his breath hitched, and he pulled her forward, crushing her body against his. Corwin lifted his mouth off hers to leave a trail of kisses over her cheek and down her neck. She shuddered, her body flinching at the torturous pleasure. She put a hand against his chest, feeling the corded muscle there as her fingers drifted lower, eager to explore him.

Corwin untied her robe to cup her breasts, loose in the shift. Kate moaned at the touch, and he captured the sound with his mouth. Then he bent down just enough to hoist her into his arms. She wrapped her legs around his waist. His hands gripped her thighs as he headed down the hall to her room and lowered her onto the bed.

Corwin kissed her again, longer and slower this time, savoring the taste. Then he moved on top of her, his weight pressing her into the mattress. Kate tried to draw a full breath but couldn't. She tried again, and this time a hint of panic rose up in her, bringing her back to her senses.

"Corwin." She pushed against his chest. "What are we doing?"

Groaning, he braced himself up far enough to stare down at her. "What do you mean?" He dipped his head again and nipped at her throat, playful. "Isn't it obvious?"

Yes, yes it was, she thought, her eyes slipping closed again. Her body knew exactly what it wanted even though she had never been here before. She bit her lip, fighting back the wave of desire his mouth stirred in her as the nip became a kiss.

"But what happens after?"

Corwin raised his head again, a devilish grin splayed over his lips. "Well, if it goes well tonight, we can do it again tomorrow. And the day after that and the day after that."

When he tried to kiss her again, she turned her head away before he could.

"What is it, Kate?" Corwin frowned down at her, a crease of

concern in his brow. His hand rested on her hip, one finger idly tracing a stone on the moonbelt.

Oh gods, the moonbelt! Understanding blazed into her mind, cooling the heat of her ardor in the span of a second. No wonder he was acting so boldly. He'd made an assumption, had probably made it weeks ago when she'd first dropped the moonbelt in front of him back at Farhold. He believed she was somebody different than who she was. Someone who had taken lovers for the mere pleasure of her body and with no concern of the consequences to her heart. But she didn't know how to separate the two. She might've taken to wearing the moonbelt, but she was the same Kate she'd always been.

Confusion clouded Corwin's face. "Is it assurance you need? Do you want me to ask you formally?"

Now it was her turn to look confused. "Ask what?"

"For you to be my paramour."

"Your what?" Kate sat up, shoving him off her with enough force that he grunted and fell back on the bed. She climbed to her feet, outrage thrumming through her now. "Your *paramour*?" Was that what this was about? He'd said he didn't want her to leave. Was this how he hoped to convince her to stay?

Corwin blinked. "Yes, surely you know what one is."

"Of course I do," she snapped. The practice was common among the nobility, where so many marriages were made for politics instead of love. Paramours occasionally held power and influence in their own right, sometimes even over the wife of the man to whom they were bound.

The wife.

For a second Kate thought she might be sick at the idea of

sharing Corwin with another woman. No. That would not be her. *Not ever.*

Kate pulled the robe back over her shoulders and fastened the belt once more. "The answer is no, Corwin. I won't be paramour to any man. You must not know me at all if you thought I could ever be that to you."

With a bewildered look on his face, Corwin rose from the bed, adjusting his own clothes. "I don't understand. You wanted this just as much as I did." He motioned to her helplessly.

She couldn't deny it. "Yes, I wanted it." *I still do,* her body screamed, and she was glad he couldn't hear it. Kate drew a deep breath and let it out slowly. "But it's not all I want. At least, I don't think it is. But what I do know is that I don't want to give you that part of myself if you're not willing to give the same to me."

Corwin's mouth fell open. "What are you talking about?"

"Your *wife*. The princess you're bound to marry someday." She put her hands on her hips. "Can't you understand? Would you be willing to share me with another man?"

"Absolutely not." He huffed, nostrils flaring.

"And there we are." Kate took a deep breath, reining in her temper. "I will not live a life that's not my own. Not even for you."

"I would never ask you to," Corwin said, defeat filling his gaze. "But you know I have no choice about who I will marry."

She did. Only . . . "You're the high prince and might be the high king. The world will answer to you, not the other way around."

"That's not fair, Kate. You know it's not so simple."

"But it could be," she said, indignant. "If you would just . . ." She trailed off, not even certain herself what she was saying. The disappointment she felt now was the same she'd felt years ago—when, once again, he had chosen the kingdom over her.

Corwin exhaled, his expression wounded. For a moment he was the boy he'd once been. "I thought we were becoming friends again . . . becoming like we were before."

Kate pressed her lips together, memories of the last few weeks rising up in her mind—of their morning rides in the countryside, the banter, and casual touches. Despite how much she'd tried to resist, she'd let him sneak back into her life, allowing herself to forget everything that stood between them.

He is the high prince, and he'll never be anything else.

She sighed and said in a soft voice, "We can never be like we were before, Corwin. Those days died with my father."

Flinching, Corwin dropped his gaze, guilt splayed across his features. Then he turned and walked out the door, leaving her in the dark silence of her room, alone with her pride and nothing more.

THE SACRED SWORD WAS A different place in the morning. Quiet and mostly deserted, Kate found it strangely welcoming. Golden sunshine filled the foyer from a tall, crystal glass window set above the entrance. It warmed the top of Kate's head as she stood waiting for Madam Anise. The girl who had greeted her when she arrived was different from the ones last night. Dressed in a plain skirt and modest bodice, she barely paid Kate any mind at all as she cleaned the wooden podium, wiping it down with an oil-soaked rag.

Kate craned her head to peer through the entrance to the tavern, hearing the distant clank of crockery. A pleasant smell wafted toward her, reminding her stomach that she'd neglected it this morning in her haste to depart her quarters before Corwin showed up at her door with more of his tantalizing sweet rolls. In hindsight, it was a silly act. Corwin wouldn't have come today. *Not after last night.* She supposed that might have been the real reason behind her hurry—avoiding the sting of Corwin's absence.

It's for the best, Kate reminded herself. She should never have let him get that close again. She always knew they could never be together, a truth more apparent now than ever.

Finally, the door to the small office opened and Madam Anise appeared. "Come in, Miss Brighton."

Kate hurried forward, her stomach starting to cartwheel. She'd half expected to be turned away again. The office was much the same as it had been the night before, small and dark, with no windows and only two candles burning. Anise motioned for Kate to sit, and she did so, folding her hands in her lap and pressing her lips together to keep in the questions bubbling up inside her. The woman sat at the opposite side of the desk, letting her forearms rest on it, hands clasped. Once again, she wore an austere dress, this one the dark gray of storm clouds.

"Before we go any further, I want to give you the chance to walk away from this while you still can."

Kate raised her eyebrows in surprise. *Was she kidding?* "No disrespect, madam, but I didn't come this far to turn back now."

"No, but you might never have started if you'd known where it would lead." Anise leaned back in the chair. "The answers you seek will change your life, Kate Brighton, in ways you can't even guess. You won't ever be able to unlearn what you learn. From what I've gathered, your life here in Norgard is somewhat comfortable. Prince Corwin seems to care for you, you're living in your family's old quarters, and there is little that you could want for."

Kate sat up straight, her nerves twitching at the sensitive subject. "My life in the castle is temporary. It always was. I came back to Norgard to learn the truth about my father."

Anise stared at her for several long seconds before nodding. "If you're sure, then let's get on with it." She pulled open a desk drawer and withdrew a large sapphire nearly the size of her thumb. Faint lines marked the magestone's shimmering blue surface. Kate recognized it at once from a visit she and Signe had made to the order houses just a few days before. They'd gone into each one, searching for a magestone for sale that might help Bonner create his revolvers without getting caught. The incident in the Wandering Woods had inspired the idea—if whoever was behind the daydrake attacks could use the common spells available in the order shops to hide them, then why couldn't Bonner? Only, the spells of any worth and power were embedded on precious gemstones and priced too high for the likes of Kate and Signe. *The doublet could've paid for it,* Kate thought, fretting once more as she pictured the state it was in now and dreading what Signe would say when she returned from Tyvald.

"This contains a binding spell." Anise set the sapphire on the desk. "A curse that will only activate if the person bound to it breaks their vow. Do that, and every inch of your body will be covered in boils and lesions, including your tongue, so that you will be unable to speak any more betrayals."

Kate shuddered, having no difficulty imagining how terrible it would be. Growing up, she remembered a young lord who'd incurred a similar curse, and he hadn't been able to sit a horse for weeks afterward until the spell finally faded. At the time, she thought it the worst punishment a person could endure.

"Before I will allow you to learn anything else," Anise continued, "you must accept the vow not to reveal these secrets. The truths you are determined to learn will put more than yourself at risk."

Kate swallowed, questions swirling in her mind. What was her father involved in for this woman to go to such drastic, expensive lengths to ensure her silence? For half a moment, she considered taking Anise up on the offer to walk away. But no. The truth was what she came for, and she would have it.

"I accept the vow."

"Very well. Hold out your hand." Anise scooped up the sapphire and placed it on Kate's outstretched palm. Then she slid her hand over Kate's, cupping the stone between them. Anise spoke the words of the incantation, and Kate saw the light seep out through their fingers as the spell in the stone activated. Heat began to spread over her body, making her itch and want to squirm, but she resisted until it was over.

Once done, Anise returned the sapphire to the drawer. The etchings of the spell had turned to brown blemishes on the jewel's surface, ruining its beauty and rendering it worthless. "Follow me," she said, rising from her chair.

She led the way out of the office and into the tavern portion of the brothel. The chairs were all set on top of the tables, the floor still wet in places from the morning's scrubbing. Anise stopped just beyond the door to the kitchens, and told Kate to wait, before going inside.

She reemerged a moment later with another woman joining her. Wearing an apron and with a kerchief wrapped around her head, the woman made for the most unlikely of cooks Kate had ever seen, especially inside a brothel. She was breathtakingly beautiful, with sea-green eyes and bright-blond hair that hung in a loose braid down to her waist. Although not young, the woman's body was thin and lithe as a dancer's. The only thing seemingly out of place was her scarred hands, covered in burn marks that ran from her fingers to her forearms before disappearing beneath the hems of her sleeves.

"This is Vianne." Anise motioned to the woman.

Stepping forward, Vianne grasped Kate's hand. "Welcome, Miss Kate. It's so good to meet you at last. I'm glad you've finally come."

Kate's eyes widened, her confusion growing by the second. "Who . . . who are you?"

"Not here," Anise said. Then she turned and strode from the room.

Vianne motioned for Kate to go first, and the two of them followed Anise out of the tavern and into the right-side hallway. Unlike the night before, all the doors were open this time, revealing the bedrooms within. Kate forced herself to look into each one, determined not to be embarrassed this time. She might have rejected Corwin's offer to be his paramour, but she understood that some of the issue resided with her inability to grow beyond the untested ideals of her childhood. Each room presented a different flavor and feel. One was dark and sultry, decorated with lacy black curtains, black silk sheets, and more than a dozen candles, unlit at the moment. Another was done all in red. Yet another all in white. *Whatever your pleasure,* Kate thought with a peculiar feeling in her stomach.

When they reached the end of the hallway, Anise paused, looking over her shoulder a moment, then turned and entered the last room, another bedroom and the most ostentatious of all Kate had seen. Decorated in the royal colors of Norgard, a massive bed, large enough to hold ten people, loomed in its center, while an equally large sofa occupied one whole side of the room. Mirrors hung from every wall and the ceiling.

As Vianne closed the door behind them, Anise approached the

mirror on the farthest wall. She grasped a knob at the top of the gilded frame and pulled. The mirror swung open to reveal a doorway beyond with stairs leading downward. Cool, damp air swept into the room, sending a flurry of chills over Kate's skin. A single lamp that hung on the wall just inside lit the way.

Anise headed down the steps, and moments later they emerged in a cramped, low-ceilinged room stuffed to the brim with a long table and chairs. Several more doors were placed around the walls, and Kate wondered if there was a secret passage leading down here from every room above.

"I'll let you take over," Anise said, sitting down in the one of the chairs and motioning to Vianne.

Wordlessly, Vianne crossed the room to the farthest door in the corner. She paused with her hand on the doorknob and said to Kate. "He's bound to be . . . excited. We don't get visitors often. Please be patient with him."

Who is behind that door? Kate thought, too bewildered to speak. She felt as if she were strapped to a runaway horse, incapable of doing anything but rush headlong into whatever danger awaited beyond.

Vianne pushed the door open and stepped inside. Kate noticed the warmth first, pleasant and welcome, a stark contrast to the room she'd been in. Four lamps hung from the walls, the flames inside them flickering and dancing playfully as if stirred by a breeze, one that couldn't possibly be blowing in this cave-like place.

A little boy came hurtling across the room toward Vianne. At a single glance, Kate understood that this was her son. They had the same bright-blond hair, and when the boy reached Vianne's opened arms, she picked him up and rained kisses down on his head while he laughed with delight.

"You're back!" the boy said. Kate couldn't quite place his age, although she guessed four or five, given his size. "That was fast. I'm—" The boy craned his head toward Kate. "Who is that?" He sounded at once both intrigued and frightened. His thin, small fingers tightened around Vianne's shoulders, the knuckles showing white.

"This, my little prince, is a very special guest." Vianne leaned down, forcibly returning the boy to his feet. She had to pry his hands from her shoulders, and even then he latched onto the folds of her skirt instead. Vianne turned to Kate. "This is my son, Kiran."

Kate stared back at the woman, her mind an utter blank. An explanation of why this woman would be introducing her son tried to assert itself into Kate's thoughts, but it was too impossible to allow. It couldn't. *It can't be*—

"He is your brother, Kate," Vianne said. "Kiran is Hale's son."

The world seemed to spin around Kate. She wanted something to hold on to, but the room was bare save for a table and chair and two narrow beds. Even the walls wouldn't have given her purchase. At first she'd thought they were made of stone, same as the rest of these underground chambers, but now she saw that they were a dull metal. Even the floor and ceiling were metal.

With a worried look, Vianne bent toward Kiran. "This is Kate. She is your sister."

The boy's eyes widened and his mouth gaped open, his surprise almost comical. That was when Kate saw the truth in his eyes. They were the same shape as her father's, the same shade of brown.

She sucked in a breath. "This is why my father was sending those payments? To support you and your . . . *his* . . . son?"

Vianne nodded. "I wasn't always a cook. Your father was one of my regular visitors. Until one day when he became something more."

Love? Kate wondered. *Did my father love you?* He must have, but even if he hadn't, Kate knew her father would've loved his son. She wanted to be angry, to feel betrayed at her father's deception, but that was the old Kate, the child who had not yet experienced the world beyond her sheltered life. Grown-up Kate understood that her parents' marriage had been cold and empty. She couldn't blame her father for finding comfort somewhere else.

More questions crowded into her mind. "Why does he live down—" Kate felt a small hand at her waist and looked down to see Kiran tugging on the end of her tunic. She squatted, putting herself at eye level with the child.

"Are you really my sister?" the boy asked, head cocked ever so slightly.

Kate nodded, marveling at how familiar he seemed, as if she'd known him all his life. He looked so much like her father. *Our father.* The fact that she hadn't known him before now sent a wrench through her chest.

The boy's answering smile seemed to swallow his whole face. "Want to see my toys?"

Without waiting for a response, Kiran grabbed her hand and tugged her toward the bed. Kate couldn't say no—it was impossible to deny this child. He seemed starved for human contact. *And the sun,* she noted at his alarming paleness. She could see the veins on his face like blue rivers crisscrossing his forehead and beneath his eyes. Did he live down here all the time? It didn't make sense.

One by one, Kiran pulled out the toys from beneath his bed, ragged, pathetic things, most broken and frayed. One of the dolls, a crude object made from old canvas with a painted-on face, was singed across the top of its head where Kate suspected yarn had once been sewn to make the hair.

"How old are you, Kiran?" Kate asked after a moment.

"Six," he said with an air of pride, as if this were a most impressive age. "I can count to a hundred. Want to hear? One . . . two . . ."

Six years old. Kate felt sick to her stomach. He was too small to be so old, but she should've guessed it already. Her father had been making those payments for three years before his death. The questions burned fresh in her mind, but she held them back, giving the boy the attention he craved while his mother watched them from the doorway, her eyes bright with emotion.

He is my brother. My father's secret. But there was more to the story, Kate was certain.

Eventually, Vianne crossed over to them and gave Kiran's head an affectionate pat. "I need to talk with Miss Kate, my little prince. Will you play on your own for a bit?"

Kiran nodded, although his lip threatened to curl into a pout. Guiltily, Kate followed Vianne out of the bedroom and back to where Anise sat, waiting for them.

"I know you have questions," Vianne said. "And we're ready to answer all we can."

Kate pulled out one of the chairs and sat down slowly. "Why do you keep him down here?" It seemed the most important of all the questions jockeying for position in her mind. She couldn't imagine a more miserable existence.

Vianne stole a furtive glance at Anise, who nodded. "Master Raith trusts her, and the binding spell will ensure her silence in everything she learns today."

"Raith? What does he have to do with this?" Kate asked, unconsciously leaning forward.

"We'll get to that," Anise replied. "Go ahead, Vianne."

The other woman let out a sigh, her scarred fingers drumming against the table. "Kiran is forced to live down here because, like your father and like you, he is a wilder."

Kate's jaw dropped to her chest. This woman knew? Her father had trusted her with his secret? Why?

"Then again, Hale is not solely to blame. I am a wilder, too." Vianne raised her hand and a small flame appeared on her palm.

A wilder. A pyrist. At once everything made sense—the metal walls, the burned toys, even the strange warmth. Only, it didn't make sense. Most wilders didn't come into their magic until adolescence.

"Kiran has his powers already? But he's so young."

"So were you—just seven if I remember right."

Kate swallowed, a strange resentment rising up in her over how much her father must've trusted this woman. *And yet he kept her secret from me.*

"Kiran's ability first appeared when he was just a baby," Vianne continued, giving a slight shudder. "We don't know why it came to him so early, but you can imagine how difficult it was to keep him hidden, and the danger he posed to others. That's why Hale had the room built for him. Kiran didn't know how to control his magic back then. How could he, being so young? He's much better now, though." Vianne nodded, as if to reassure herself of this truth.

"Then why keep him down here still?" Kate asked, and too late she realized how stupid the question was.

"The Inquisition, of course," a man's voice spoke as if from nowhere.

Kate jumped in surprise, her hand going to the revolver at her belt. After last night, she never wanted to be without it. But she didn't pull it out as Master Raith slid from the shadows by the stairs and approached them. Once again, he wasn't wearing his mask or robes. Anise and Vianne both greeted him warmly, and a moment later, Kiran came bolting out of his room to leap into Raith's arms. To Kate's growing shock, the master magist hugged the boy, then tickled his sides, coaxing a giggle. *Who is this man?* She stared at him, taking in the birthmark on his face and the permanent black stains on his fingertips.

Raith set Kiran back down a moment later with a promise to come play with him once he was done out here. Kate watched it all, feeling as if she'd stepped into some strange, unknown world where right was left and up was down.

Once Kiran had retreated, Raith said, "Now, where were we? Oh yes, the Inquisition. As you know, Kate, the Inquisition gives the gold order the power to actively hunt for wilders, regardless of age or suspected guilt. Kiran was just three years old when the high king sanctioned it. But your father tried to stop it from happening altogether."

At once Kate remembered what Corwin had told her about how

her father and the king had been arguing about the Inquisition before the attack.

"It's why he went to the king's chambers that morning," Raith continued, "to change Orwin's mind. Hale knew you would not be in danger from it. You are, or were, a part of the gentry and so, for the most part, exempt from the gold's reach."

"But not Kiran," Kate said, anger starting to simmer inside her at the injustice of it.

"No," Vianne agreed, her voice sharp and bitter. "Not the bastard son of a prostitute."

Kate winced, pity mixing with the anger now. She understood without doubt that her father would've done anything to protect Kiran and his mother. Of course he would have. They were family. *I have a brother.* The thought tugged hard on her tear ducts, and she forced it away.

"Is that what happened then?" Kate asked. "Was the attack on King Orwin just an argument that escalated into a fight?"

"I doubt it," said Raith with a sad shake of his head. "But I'm afraid we don't exactly know what happened. That was a secret Hale took with him to the next life. He went there not to assassinate the king but to persuade him, with the help of his magic if need be."

"His magic?"

"Yes, his magic—and yours—can influence the minds of living creatures. It's called sway. It's a rare and powerful spirit gift."

Suddenly Kate remembered just who she was talking to. "But I don't understand. You're a magist, and yet you were friends with my father, and you know about Vianne and Kiran and me."

"Oh, and me, let us not forget," Anise said, the hint of a smirk on her face. She held out her hand and a gush of water rose up from her palm, bubbling over on itself like a miniature fountain.

Kate gaped. "You're a wilder, too?"

Anise flashed a pleased, proud smile.

"We all are here," Raith said, and when Kate swung back to him, he added, "Magists are no different from wilders. The ability to imbue inanimate objects with spells is just a form of spirit magic, similar to what enables you to touch minds. We're even bound by the same laws. Did you know that when wilder magic and magist magic meet directly, they will cancel each other out?" He nodded at her frown. "It's true. All magic flows from the same source. It's all connected. When it meets itself, it simply stops."

Kate's frowned deepened. "I don't understand."

He gestured to the revolver on her belt. "It's like what would happen if two bullets were to meet in the air, both of them rendered powerless at the impact."

Slowly, Kate nodded, although her doubt remained.

"Magist magic doesn't work at night either," Raith went on. "We can't create new spells any more than a pyrist can summon fire or an aerist wind. Everything we might need at night, we must prepare in the day."

Now Kate openly gaped in astonishment. She'd never heard this before, and it seemed a secret the Mage League wouldn't want divulged. But she was glad to learn it, to know the magists weren't as all-powerful as they seemed.

Then another question rose up in her mind. "Do you know why I was able to use my magic last night?"

Raith shrugged. "Who can say? Magic is a fickle thing, as unpredictable as the weather, at times. But I would venture to guess it was because the moon was full and you were standing in its light. No one knows exactly how it all works, but magic in Rime is connected to the light. Moonlight is usually too weak to make much of a difference, but it's not unheard of. Of course, if you want to know more, you'd have to ask a white robe. As for myself, I've never been preoccupied with magical theory. Not when there's a world that needs fixing."

Kate started to ask him more, but he cut her off with a raised hand. "The point here, Kate, is that we were all the same once, some three hundred years ago, before the War of Three divided us into wilders and magists. Back then all the cities in the three fronts employed magic wielders in their armies—magicians, as we were called then. They used all the magic available to them to try to destroy their enemies. Including, as the legend goes, unleashing the nightdrakes."

"I always thought that was just myth," Kate said.

"Some of it might be. We don't really know what happened, other than that magic was involved." Raith scratched at his chin, his blackened fingers noticeably stiff. She wondered how they'd gotten that way, imagining some spell gone wrong.

"But we do know the consequences," Raith continued. "After the war ended, thanks entirely to the destructive force of those same nightdrakes, the laying of blame began. Magicians with active gifts, like those of fire and earth, were held responsible for the devastation by both the city leaders and the magicians with more passive spirit gifts, like what the magists possess today. Our magic could be contained. It's more easily restricted and was thereby considered safe, while the other forms of magic were deemed too unpredictable and too powerful to be allowed. And so the lines were drawn."

He paused and drew a weary sigh. "But I and some others in my order believe it's time for those lines to be erased, for wilders and magists to be united again. That is what your father ultimately wanted when he decided to do all he could to convince the king to stop the Inquisition, and it's why I asked Vianne to tell you the truth about your father even though Hale didn't want you to become involved."

"I don't understand," Kate said, feeling as if she were standing on the narrowest edge of a precipice, an inevitable fall looming. She remembered Anise's earlier warning, and dread began to pulse in her temples. "What exactly is going on here?"

"This," Raith said, gesturing to the room, "is the headquarters of the Rising, and you are here because we want you to take your father's place among our ranks." He paused, then added with a wry smile, "And before you ask, Corwin's theory about us is wrong. We have nothing to do with the daydrakes. On the contrary, we're doing everything we can to stop them."

CORWIN STARED INTO THE DARK pit before him, and a tremor of fear passed over him from head to toes. *The high priestess expects me to jump into this?*

Last night, he'd finally finished reading his grandfather's account of his uror trials, and although much of it remained vague and pointless, the section concerning the third trial had been specific enough to give Corwin worry.

I jumped into the Well of the World and passed out of this life entirely. At least for a time, Borwin Tormane had written.

The Well of the World. Corwin leaned nearer the pit, one so deep it was said to have no end. It seemed to snarl at him like a black mouth. Although the pit was called the Well of the World, the underground cave that housed it was called the Vault of Souls—in part, Corwin suspected, because of the way it echoed. A single voice speaking a single word easily became a thousand hushed whispers against the uneven rock walls and stalactite-strewn ceiling. Located beneath Mirror Castle, this was a holy place, one he'd rarely been allowed to visit before. Even today, he'd had to ask the high priestess for permission. She'd granted it without comment, although she'd sent two of her priestesses to escort him. They stood watch by the single narrow door behind him.

Corwin stretched out the torch he held as far over the pit as he dared. Nothing. There was nothing inside it to give reflection. Just a dark hole in the ground. He tried to imagine jumping into it. He couldn't. Even though he still had the second trial to get through first, he felt ready to quit right now just to avoid thinking about taking that leap even for a moment. It made him dizzy and sick to his stomach.

"Please tell me you're not going to jump," a voice called behind him, and Corwin gave a start. He spun around, the torch hissing at the motion.

"Dal, you idiot," Corwin said, spying his friend standing across the way. "You nearly scared me to death."

"Not my normal effect on people, I'll admit," Dal replied, glib as usual. "But do you mind coming out of there? These beautiful ladies won't let me go any farther, and you know how shouting gives me a headache."

Resisting a grin, Corwin strode across the vault toward the entryway. Silently the priestesses let him pass, and he and Dal headed up the long, narrow stairs single file, arriving in the throne room a few minutes later.

The vast hall, columned along both sides, stood empty this time of day. With rain battering the long, arched windows, it was as dark and somber as a tomb. The door to the Vault of Souls rested a mere six feet from the back of the Mirror Throne, close enough that the light from Corwin's torch was refracted a thousand times over in the reflective surface. As its name suggested, the throne was made entirely of mirrors, symbolizing the need for the king to both see and be seen at all times, honest and true. Corwin saw his face shining in it and looked away.

He turned and clapped Dal on the shoulder. "I expected you back days ago." More than a week had passed since Dal and Signe left for Tyvald.

Dal wrinkled his nose, stepping aside to make room for the priestesses, who had stopped to seal the vault and lock it with a large key. "The morning we were set to leave, the city went on lockdown. More daydrakes sighted in the area. Took three hells' worth of convincing the magists to leave as soon as we did."

Corwin ran a thumb over the scar on his chin, feeling a knot clench in his stomach. The situation was worsening every day, and yet he was no closer to an answer. Depositing his torch in the empty cradle beside the vault door, he turned and headed for the nearest exit, motioning for Dal to follow. He was due in a council meeting in the next few minutes.

"What did you discover?" Corwin asked as they stepped into the corridor.

"Very little we don't already know, about the daydrakes at least. The packs kept coming in waves, their behavior the same as nightdrakes. But Signe and I did meet a woman who claimed she saw another escaped wilder in the city the day before the first attack."

"Another one escaped from the golds?"

Shrugging, Dal brushed the arms of his tunic, sending up a cloud of road dust. It seemed he'd made it inside before the rain started. "She wasn't certain. The wilder had been just a boy when the golds took him nearly two years ago, and by her own account he looked much changed from when she'd known him."

"I see," Corwin said, doing his best to keep the disappointment from his voice. He'd hoped for more, although he should have been used to disappointment by now. He'd felt the same after hearing Master Raith's report. The attacks were random, difficult to trace, and with few signs of human involvement, wilder or otherwise. Raith had even gone so far as to speculate that perhaps the Rising wasn't behind the attacks at all, but Corwin remained skeptical. If not they, then who? There seemed no answer. He'd finally received a reply from the gold order in Andreas. They didn't deny or confirm anything about Ralph Marcel. Instead, the letter stated that such records were private, protected by the rules set down in the League Accords. There was nothing Corwin could do about it, high prince or no.

"What were you doing down at the Well of the World, anyway?" Dal asked, drawing Corwin out of his reverie. "That place gives me a chill that has nothing to do with how cold it is down there."

"Actually, the hole itself seemed quite warm," Corwin said. "But I was merely contemplating the third trial." This wasn't entirely the truth. He'd come down today in particular to avoid seeing Kate. His rooms where he'd been reading overlooked the cavalry fields, and he'd spotted her through the window. Before he knew it, he'd wasted a full ten minutes watching her take Firedancer through her paces and was soon fighting the urge to go down and speak to her. He'd been fighting that urge all week, actually, ever since their disastrous interlude. He wished it had never happened, that he'd never allowed himself to taste what he couldn't possess. The memory of it was bound to drive him mad.

"The third trial?" Dal asked as they turned left, down another, narrower corridor. "Don't you think you're getting ahead of yourself? We haven't even gotten to the second trial yet."

"True, but the second is only four weeks away and the third soon to follow," Corwin replied. Then, trying to change the subject, he added, "The high priestess has determined the second will take place during the War Games. She says that all of Rime should have a chance to witness the uror." He had been looking forward to the War Games, an annual festival celebrating the unification of Rime, but now he dreaded its approach.

"All hail the high king," Dal said, rolling his eyes.

Hearing an unusual noise ahead, they both slowed down as they approached an alcove. "Is someone there?" Corwin called.

There was the sound of rustling fabric, then Minister Rendborne appeared at the base of the alcove, his golden eyes overly bright. He rubbed his hands together nervously, the glow of his magestone ring winking.

"Your highness, forgive me. But yes. We were just, uh . . ."

Corwin covered his mouth to keep from laughing as he spotted Maestra Vikas standing just behind the minister of trade. He didn't need to see the red flush around her lips to understand the two had been enjoying a secret tryst.

"No need to explain," Corwin said. "I'll, uh, see you at the meeting."

Rendborne bowed his head, and Corwin and Dal moved on, neither speaking until they rounded another corner.

"Well, that was strange." Dal made a face. "I didn't think magists enjoyed that sort of thing."

Corwin snorted. "They're still human, you know." Although the match did surprise him. He pictured the charismatic Rendborne with someone more interesting, and certainly more fun, than

Vikas. Then again, perhaps opposites did attract.

"Yes, but making love to that cold lady would be like sleeping on a bed of ice," Dal said, giving a shiver.

Laughing, Corwin clapped Dal on the shoulder again. "I'm glad you're back."

"Me too, although what in the three hells have you done to Kate in my absence?"

Corwin tried to hide his wince but failed. "Nothing . . . why do you say that?"

"I saw her on the way in just now, and she barely spoke to me. If her eyes were daggers, I believe she would've speared me through the heart."

Corwin huffed, wishing he could deflect the question, but this was Dal. He wouldn't give up until he got the full story.

"Corwin, what did you *do*?"

"I might've asked her to be my paramour," he began, and quickly filled Dal in on the rest, leaving out the more intimate details of the encounter.

When Corwin finished, Dal shook his head, puffing out his cheeks. "That's a tough blow, my friend, although not too surprising she would react that way. Paramours usually come after the marriage, not before. And if you ask me, why bother tying yourself down like that already? It seems you've been tied down enough with all this uror business. We haven't had a bit of fun in weeks." Dal paused; then a sly smile slid across his face. "Well, you haven't, anyway."

"The kitchens are that way, if you want to drop in and grab some salt to pour on my wounds while you're at it." Corwin pointed behind him.

"I'll pass just now." Dal's expression turned serious. "I'm truly sorry, my friend. I don't envy you, and I wish things could go back to the way they were before we left on that damn tour."

Me too, Corwin thought. In the six months he'd been home from Endra and his sojourn with the Shieldhawks, he'd had no responsibilities and even fewer cares, aside from avoiding memories. But it was a little boy's wish, a little boy's dream—one that could never come true. *And if I hadn't gone, I never would've found Kate again.* Even now, with the pain of her rejection still smarting inside him, he couldn't regret that.

Corwin shook his head. "The tour wasn't all bad. You seem to be enjoying Signe's presence."

"How could I not?" Dal grinned. "It's a shame Kate isn't more like her friend. But give her time. Maybe she'll come round eventually. If not, some other girl will catch your fancy sooner or later. They always do."

Corwin nodded faintly. Only it wasn't true. No other girl had ever held his attention like Kate. Those others had been distractions, ways to pass the time. Kate made time stand still. It had been that way ever since they were children.

Coming to a stop, Corwin faced Dal. "What if . . . I'm in love with her?"

A stunned look crossed Dal's face, his eyebrows climbing his forehead. Corwin couldn't blame him for the reaction—they never discussed matters of the heart.

Dal cleared his throat. "If that's the case, then I've no advice to give. As for myself, I don't believe there is such a thing as love. At least not the kind the poets write about. Two people devoted to each other without fail, for all their lives? It doesn't exist. People wander in their hearts even if they don't with their bodies."

"That's a little cynical, don't you think?" Corwin turned and resumed walking, although he kept the pace slow, not eager to arrive at the council chambers.

"I have only my parents to test the theory against, but believe me, their marriage confirms it many times over."

Corwin held back a reply, sensing the underlying bitterness in Dal's tone. Although they'd never discussed it outright, Corwin knew his friend's parents were the reason he'd joined the Shieldhawks. Their marriage was rife with such scandal that Thornewall's lord and lady were often the center of gossip in the highest circles, despite their lower-rung status among Rime's nobility. The version Corwin heard was that both the baron and baroness played a regular game of trying to best each other over who could claim the youngest, most attractive lover. It was said that of the six Thornewall children, only the eldest two brothers could claim certain legitimacy. The rest were all supposed offspring of Lady Thornewall's various lovers. Including Dal. *If the rumors are true.* Corwin didn't know, and he didn't plan on asking.

Still, despite how difficult it must have been for Dal, Corwin couldn't accept his conclusion that love didn't exist. His own parents had loved each other deeply. Even now he felt certain his father would still mourn his mother, if he had wits enough to do so. Then again, Corwin thought, such a love could exist only when it was felt by both involved, like a flower needing both sunlight and water to thrive. He didn't know if Kate ever truly loved him. He'd seen her kiss Edwin that day, with an enthusiasm he thought only for him.

The memory soured his stomach.

"I'm not sure if I hope you're right or wrong," Corwin said. "All I do know is that Kate won't come around to Signe's way of thinking. Kate Brighton changes her mind about as well as I can ride a horse standing on my head."

"I'd like to see that," Dal said, grinning. "But for now, I need to wash off the dirt from the road."

"Enjoy yourself. I'll be stuck in another thrilling high council meeting."

Dal clapped him on the back. "Stay resolute, my friend. I'll come visit you this evening. Let's have a night out, see if we can't get you past your heartache with some overdue diversions."

Corwin gave a halfhearted nod, then watched Dal retreat down the corridor, his mind reeling with an unreasonable jealousy. What he wouldn't give to trade places with Dallin Thorne, sixth-born son of a minor house. If only for a day. Or ten.

Or maybe the rest of my life.

Corwin supposed his biggest problem with the high council meetings was the way they discussed the same agenda items over and over again while rarely making any true decisions. It felt like being a ribbon tied to a wagon wheel, both dizzying and wearisome.

Today they were discussing the limited availability of moonbelts to the peasantry for at least the third time. Corwin would've given anything to skip this one, as his mind kept replaying the events with Kate over and over again—the way it had felt to kiss her, to touch her. He hadn't been truly aware of how many assumptions he'd made about her wearing a moonbelt until she reacted the way she did. That he was wrong in assuming, he understood, but he hadn't yet worked up the nerve to apologize. It didn't help that she was avoiding him as much as he was her. Every day for the past week she'd been heading out into the city and staying away for hours at a time. He'd asked the guard-tower captain to make note of her comings and goings—for her safety as well as his peace of mind—but he couldn't help but wonder what exactly she was doing out there, without him.

Tomorrow, he told himself. *I will go to her in the morning and beg forgiveness.* But even as he thought it, doubt pressed in. What could he say to make things right between them? What could he do?

"You're the high prince and might be the high king," he heard Kate saying once more. "The world will answer to you. . . ." How he wanted to believe it.

"It's a population issue, ultimately," Minister Fletcher was saying as Corwin forced his attention back on the discussion. The master of the hearth was easily the youngest of the high councilmembers, a thin man with skin the dark brown of driftwood and curly black hair. Corwin knew him least well of the councilmembers, as he'd been appointed to the position less than a year ago. "The peasantry have three times the number of babies as the gentry each year."

"Of course they do," Minister Porter replied. The master of coin seemed Fletcher's opposite in every way—old and rotund, his skin a ruddy pink and hair a pasty yellow, a color achieved with help from a magist tonic, Corwin suspected. "Each child who lives past infancy is another valuable worker. That's quite the incentive for the common people. Whereas for the highborn, more children mean more dowries and inheritance concerns."

Fletcher tapped an impatient finger on the table, not intimidated by the older man in the slightest. "Yes, but many peasant women, especially those who are aging or have suffered difficult pregnancies, would stop having babies altogether if only they had access to a moonbelt."

"But they do have access." Porter's tone was heating already, as it often did in these meetings. "They're for sale in every green-robe shop in Rime."

Fletcher barked a laugh. "Oh, to be sure. They can visit those shops and stare longingly at the merchandise, but most of these families either can't afford to purchase one or choose to spend that much-needed money elsewhere. Like feeding their other children."

"What are you suggesting then, Minister Fletcher?" Porter sneered, jowls quivering. "That the high king *buy* the moonbelts for them out of the royal coffers? For I can assure you the League is not going to start handing them out for free."

"That's exactly what I'm proposing," Fletcher replied, puffing out his chest as far as it would go, which unfortunately wasn't far enough to impress anyone. "If we don't curtail the population, we will soon outgrow our housing capabilities, not to mention the food stocks for the winter. People will be living on the streets, begging at our doors, starving to death."

Porter huffed. "Overpopulation is nothing new, and we should deal with it the way we always have. Encourage the elderly and infirm to give themselves over to the gods in sacrifice. We could even lower the age of sacrifice if need be, or allow families to submit entreaties on behalf of the crippled and those unwell in mind, regardless of age." He paused and raised his hands skyward in a gesture of honor to the gods. "Life is a wheel and so it must turn."

Corwin shifted in his seat, remembering all too clearly the ash and blood stains atop the Asterion. It was a cold, frightening way to die.

"You act as if it is an easy thing for someone to volunteer for death, Minister Porter," Corwin said, unable to stop himself. "Peasant or no, these people love and value their family members as much as the gentry do theirs."

Porter snorted through his broad, flat nose. "Not to offend, your highness, but such a sentimental attitude has no place at this table. We must make decisions based on reason and facts, not feelings."

Corwin leaned forward, wanting to pummel the man. *I will show him a world governed by feelings.* . . .

But as always, Edwin was there, ready to step in and smooth things over. "My lords, this is a much simpler issue than you would have us make it. Either we find a way to stop the peasants from having so many children or we build more homes." Edwin motioned to Nell, the master builder, who was seated directly across from him. "What do you say, Minister Nell—which would impact the royal coffers more favorably, moonbelts or new buildings?"

Nell hid a laugh behind a cough. "The moonbelts, your highness. No question. Short of moving the walls of Norgard, there will be no more houses built in this city. The buildings in the poorer districts are already as tall as possible. Any higher and they will start to topple."

"And there you have it," Edwin said.

Why not build a new city? Corwin thought. But as always the same old problem to this solution reared its head—the matter of who would pay for it. No one wanted to. At least, none of those who actually could.

"But Prince Edwin, how will we afford such an expense?" Porter said, wringing his hands. "We simply cannot raise taxes. Not if you hope to avoid the starving-children scenario Minister Fletcher so eloquently warned us about. Not to mention the increasing cost of these damnable Rising attacks."

Edwin turned to Grand Master Storr. "Do you have a solution to offer, Master Storr? Is there a way for the crown to purchase these moonbelts at a reduced cost?"

Storr ran a hand over his short, perfectly trimmed beard, as if considering the question carefully. "I'm sure we can come to some sort of arrangement, your highness. The League is always open to trade, of course, and we ask for so little in return."

The hells you do, Corwin thought. That was one of the lessons he'd learned these last few weeks—the impartial, noninterfering League he'd been brought up to believe in was a myth. In every high council meeting Corwin had attended, Grand Master Storr exerted the League's power whenever the opportunity presented itself. And to Corwin's disgruntlement, those opportunities were on the rise as more and more reports of daydrake attacks came in. Despite Master Raith's speculation that the Rising might not be involved, given the absence of the sun lion, the people were blaming wilders just the same. Their demand for more golds to seek them out must be filling the League's coffers, while the cities were feeling the strain all across Rime. The cost of grain and coal had nearly doubled as the shipments were either slowed or didn't arrive at all.

"This trade you speak of," said Minister Rendborne, his golden, eagle eyes fixed on the grand master. "Do you mean your proposal that the high king require all the governing bodies in Rime to include a master magist as part of their ruling councils in exchange for a reduced price on wardstones and other defensive magics?"

Storr inclined his head. "The very same, although the high council must choose which is more important, a reduced cost in moonbelts or a reduced rate in defensive services. The League will accept either, but we cannot afford both."

Of course not. Corwin folded his hands in his lap, fingers clenched. Gods forbid the League, already wealthy beyond measure, cut into its profit for the good of Rime. *Next the League will offer the crown a loan to pay for their very same services.* It was ludicrous, incestuous. *The wheel spinning on indeed.*

"It seems to me that both might come at a higher price than the kingdom ought to pay," Rendborne replied, and Corwin felt his affection for the master of trade increase tenfold. Not only had he tried to help Corwin with the gift of his grandfather's journal, but now Corwin saw him as a possible ally, a reasonable voice in a chorus of madness. Nothing could be worse, in Corwin's mind, than giving the League more power than it already held.

"Regardless, there is no question which is more important," Minister Porter said, ignoring Rendborne's comment completely. "We need to protect the caravans from the drakes."

"Yes, I would agree," Master Storr said. "Defense is more critical than ever before. But if I recall, the high council decided that the revolvers were to be the solution to the drake problem—and not more magic." Storr turned an innocuous gaze on Corwin. "Is that not still the case, your highness? Has Master Bonner finally succeeded in his task?"

Corwin didn't miss the slight in Storr's words, and for at least the hundredth time that day, he wished he'd skipped this stupid meeting. He had no answer to give. Despite the time Bonner had been here, overseeing the blacksmiths day in and day out, they'd produced a meager handful of revolvers so far, most of them plagued with problems like misfiring or jamming. The only ones that did work were the ones Bonner assembled personally. Corwin couldn't understand it, but he knew it was time to start pressing for an answer. No matter how much he liked Bonner, the man had to hold up his end of the bargain.

Edwin cleared his throat, somehow commanding the floor with the simple sound. "The discussion of the revolvers and the ineptitude of my brother's gunsmith is beyond the scope of this meeting. The council will take the League's offer into consideration before deciding which trade is in our best interest."

And just like that the argument was over. Corwin caught himself glaring at Edwin from across the table. *My brother's gunsmith.* The words dug at Corwin. Edwin's slights were so common these days, he should be used to them by now. At every turn Edwin took the opportunity to point out how much more fit he was to rule. Corwin didn't know why it bothered him. He agreed—Edwin was the better choice. Corwin was too rash, too easily led by emotions rather than reason and too likely to misjudge the wicked, giving people more credit than they deserved. And as much as Corwin questioned some of the decisions Edwin made, at least his brother had been here to make the decisions. Unlike him, the Errant Prince.

If he'd been with Mother that day, she might still be alive.

Pushing these troubling thoughts to the back of his mind, Corwin forced his attention to the meeting once more. The subject of moonbelts and overpopulation had given way to marriage alliances— *Sweet goddess smite me now and end my misery.*

"Lord Jedrek of Kilbarrow," Minister Rendborne was saying, "has requested the marriage contract between his daughter, Princess Sabine Esborne, and High Prince Edwin be modified. It seems that with the arrival of the uror, he wants the agreement of marriage to be between his daughter and whichever prince is chosen as the heir."

Corwin's stomach tied itself into a knot at this news. A marriage contract. Between the princess and whichever brother won. *Edwin or me.* At once images of Kate from that night flooded Corwin's mind, and it was all he could do to stay still in his seat. *Your wife,* she had said, objecting to the idea of sharing Corwin with some stranger. She was right to object. He didn't like it any more than she did.

"Jedrek's request is not surprising," Edwin said, making a note on the parchment in front of him. His knuckles shone white around the pen, the only sign of his annoyance with the subject. "Proceed with modifying the contract. The Esbornes will not be satisfied until they have a daughter as high queen, and their bloodline as part of—"

The door to the council chamber burst open and a man stumbled in with two royal guards half carrying him.

"Pardon the interruption, my lords," one of the guards said, "but this man insisted on seeing you."

Corwin got to his feet along with the rest of the council. Murmurs of alarm echoed around the room. The stranger's face and arms were bleeding, his tunic dyed crimson in patches. He looked dazed and feverish, barely able to hold his head up. Corwin didn't recognize the man, and he wore no insignia, although the expensive cut of his clothes marked him a highborn.

"You're addressing the high princes of Rime, sir. Speak your piece," the guard said, giving the man a shake.

"Stop that," Corwin said, stepping forward. "Can't you see he's half dead?" Corwin glared at the guard a moment, then turned to the injured stranger. "What happened?" A foul, familiar stench was coming off him. "Were you attacked by daydrakes?"

The man nodded, and he sagged against the arms holding him up. "Our freeholding. It's surrounded by them. We haven't been able to go in or out for days. I only just made it through."

"Where?" Corwin said. "Which freeholding?"

But the man sank to his knees in a faint.

"Get the healers," Edwin shouted, and one of the guards hurried out the door.

"Did he say where he came from?" Corwin asked the remaining guard, but the man shook his head.

"He might've told when he first got here," the guard replied. "I'll go check. The magist who rode with him is dead, but someone must know."

"I know," a new voice said from the doorway.

Corwin glanced up to see a freshly washed and dressed Dal

standing there, a bewildered look on his face. "You do? Where? Who is he?"

"Thornewall Castle," Dal replied, sounding strangely far-off. "I saw him through my window. Couldn't quite believe it."

"Dal," Corwin said, his alarm building by the second, "who is this man?"

Dal looked up, his eyes not quite focusing. "He's my brother."

CORWIN HAD NEVER SEEN DAL in such a state. His sarcastic, carefree friend had been quiet for nearly an hour now, not uttering so much as a word while they waited outside the door where the healers were seeing to his brother. Lir perched on Dal's arm, and he ran a hand down the falcon's back over and over again. Dal cared for the bird like nothing else. *Except maybe his brother.*

There'd been no updates in the hour since the man arrived. Corwin hoped that was a good thing. If the green robes were still working their healing magic, then there was a life still to be saved.

After a while, Corwin couldn't bear the tension any longer. "Is there anything I can do, Dal? Anything you need?"

Dal's hand stilled on the falcon, and he looked up at Corwin. "My family. You heard what my brother said. We have to help them."

Corwin squeezed his shoulder. "Help is coming. The high council is arguing it now—how many men we'll send, how quickly we can respond."

Dal grimaced. "They're taking an awful long time of it. I wish you'd stayed in the meeting, Corwin. I don't think . . ." He hesitated, his teeth worrying at his bottom lip. "We both know that Thornewall doesn't matter enough for them to hurry. It offers no significant trade. The only things anyone even knows about us are the scandals my parents so happily provide."

"That's not—"

"It is." Dal raised a hand, cutting him off. "But I care about my brothers. They're good people, worth saving."

No mention of your mother and father, though, Corwin thought, guessing the rumors were indeed true, that Dal was the son of someone other than Baron Thorne. "I know you care about them. Of course you do. And we will mount a force to purge the day-drakes. There is no other option."

Dal looked doubtful still, and he resumed stroking the falcon.

"You've got a point, though," Corwin said. "They are being slow about it. I'll find out what's going on."

With a promise to return with news, Corwin headed back to the council chamber. When he reached the hallway, he saw that the guards normally stationed at the door when a meeting was in session were nowhere in sight. Annoyed that no one had bothered to tell him the outcome, Corwin was about to march off in search of his brother when he heard voices coming from within the room.

He approached the door. His brother's voice was raised in anger. "You're pushing it too far. It's too bold."

Corwin listened for the response but could hear nothing.

Then his brother said, "Yes, I want it, but I have to weigh the risk against—"

The sound of footsteps approaching made Corwin jump guiltily. He shouldn't eavesdrop, no matter the circumstance. *And I've more pressing matters at hand,* he thought, and pushed open the door.

Edward's outraged glare greeted him. "Corwin, when will you

ever learn to stop barging in like a child?"

"I thought the meeting was over," Corwin said, his brother's insult sliding off him for once. He glanced around the room, mildly surprised to see Storr was here as well. It seemed that more often of late, Corwin found his brother sharing some confidence with the grand master.

As always Storr looked perfectly at ease, as if he hadn't just been holding one half of an argument. He offered Corwin a polite smile.

Corwin ignored it and glanced back at Edwin. "And it seems that it is over. What has the council decided about Thornewall?"

Edwin turned his attention to the table and started collecting his papers. "We will send out a small scouting party tomorrow morning."

"A small scouting party?" Corwin gaped, incredulous. "That's all?"

Edwin looked up, his gaze sharp. "Yes, that's all. Baron Thorne and his freeholding is the least of Norgard's concerns. We have no idea how many drakes there are or how dire the situation truly is. Hence, a scouting party."

"Oh, it's dire," Corwin said. "You saw Dal's brother. You heard him."

"What I heard is that they've been trapped. That's very little to go on. A scouting party will be able to survey how many of the beasts there are, where they are, and what threat they pose beyond this small freeholding." Edwin paused to give a dramatic sigh. "I realize that your primary tactic is to rush into battle and ask tactical questions later, but the stakes with this new threat are too great, brother. We have to be smarter here."

Heat surged into Corwin's face, some of it shame but more of it anger this time. He never should've told Edwin what had happened in Endra with that Sevan soldier boy. Through gritted teeth, he said, "It's a three-day ride to Thornewall from here. Three days back. That's nearly a week that Dal's family will have to endure."

"It will take longer than that, I'm afraid," Master Storr said, helpful as always. "With the threat of daydrakes certain, the entire scouting party must be warded for the journey. That will take all the wardstones we can spare right now, and your brother has rightly concluded the crown simply can't afford the cost required to create the additional stones at speed."

Corwin closed his eyes and counted to ten, trying to talk himself out of an explosion and into seeing things Edwin's way—erring on the side of caution, practicality.

Practicality be damned. Edwin hadn't witnessed Dal's suffering. These men on the high council never considered the human cost in the games of politics and finances they played. Once before Corwin had sat back and ignored the hurt and desperation of someone he cared about; he'd listened when they said Hale Brighton couldn't be given the mercy of exile, that letting a traitor live would only weaken the high king's authority. He'd stood by and done nothing.

Not this time.

Lowering his hands to his sides, Corwin said, "We will not send just a scouting party, but also food and supplies. If the magists can keep the scouts safe, they can do the same for a caravan. We will absorb the cost this time. We *can* afford it, if we choose. And in this case there is no other choice."

"Absolutely not, Corwin. The high council has already determined—"

"The last I checked, the high council does not rule Norgard or Rime. Their purpose is to advise the king, not make the decisions for him."

"Yes, but you are not the king," Edwin said.

"Neither are you, *brother*." Corwin held up his right hand, palm out so that his uror mark was clearly visible. "But this says I might be, one day. And that is all the authority I need."

With that, Corwin turned on his heel and strode from the meeting room, not giving either man the chance to argue.

Once Corwin had made up his mind to act, the decision as to what to do next came surprisingly easily. He went to Minister Fletcher first and ordered two supply wagons be prepared. Then he went to Minister Knox to start selecting his most capable soldiers for the mission. Finally, he sought out Bonner. He needed to know just how many revolvers were fieldworthy before he talked to the blue robes about providing defensive magic.

Corwin headed to the forge and found several blacksmiths still hard at work, their faces red and their tunics sweat soaked, and Bonner not among them. Feeling his irritation growing, he crossed the forge toward Bonner's private workroom in the back. The door was closed, but he heard voices inside.

Corwin resisted the urge to barge in and knocked on the door instead. "Bonner, it's Corwin. I need to speak with you."

The door opened a few seconds later, Bonner's face peering out at him with a look of sheepish surprise. "Come in, your highness. Had no idea you'd be coming by today."

"Neither did—" The words died on Corwin's lips as his eyes

fell on Kate. She was in the far corner of the room, her arms folded tightly around her waist. She met his gaze for a second, then looked away, a hint of red in her cheeks.

She wasn't Bonner's only visitor. Signe was there, and so was Master Raith. *You again,* Corwin thought, remembering how the magist had come to Kate's aid the night she'd visited the brothel. That made twice now he'd found the magist in close proximity to Kate when all reason said he shouldn't be.

"What are you doing here, Master Raith?" Corwin asked.

Raith, who'd been leaning against one of the worktables, straightened up and adjusted his blue robes across his shoulders. "I wanted to see how the revolver making was going, your highness. My order has a keen interest in seeing it succeed."

I doubt the grand master would agree with you, Corwin thought. *He's wanted them to fail from the beginning, more concerned with maintaining his profit than solving Rime's problems.* Still, he was glad to have Raith's support at least.

"I see. Well, I'm glad you're here. I've need of your blue robes once more." He launched into the story about Dal's brother and the attack on Thornewall. Without meaning to, his gaze kept drifting toward Kate as he spoke.

By the time he reached the end of the story, her face had clouded over with worry. "What are you going to do?"

Corwin scowled and ran a hand through his hair. "Edwin planned to send a scouting party, but it's not enough. I mean to lead a supply caravan and make sure it gets there safely. Dal's brother said the people are starving. There's no telling how long they've been trapped." Thornewall was isolated and difficult to reach, located among the cliffs that covered the farthest eastern point of Rime. *Which is why it was so easy to pen them in,* Corwin realized—only why would the Rising attack Thornewall? It had no strategic value to the high king, unlike some of the other sites of the attacks. Dal and Edwin were right on that account—the barony mattered little to the power of Norgard.

Corwin turned to Raith. "Will you help me, Master Raith?"

"Of course," Raith said without hesitation. He ran a blackened finger over his nose and cheeks, unconsciously tracing the lines of the Shade Born on his face. It was the first time Corwin had seen the man do such a thing. "But even more important than getting the supplies there, this might be just the opportunity we need to finally discover what—or who—is behind these drake attacks."

"How do you mean?" Corwin asked, not daring to hope after so many failures.

Raith's gaze wandered across the room, briefly lingering on Kate before he turned back to Corwin. "If I remember the geography of Thornewall correctly, the only path to the castle is through a narrow pass with sheer cliff walls on either side. That limits where someone controlling the drakes could be. If we position scouts out of view of the caravan, we might be able to catch them."

"But won't we be attacked?" Signe said, stepping forward.

Corwin arched an eyebrow at her. "We?"

She gave him a haughty look. "I'm coming. You're going to need all the help you can get to save Dal's family."

Corwin nodded, grateful for the offer and what it would mean to Dal.

"I have devised a new shield spell," Raith said. "It should protect against a drake without the need for a dedicated wardstone, long enough, at least, for our scouts to get back to the caravan and the safety of the main wardstone barrier."

Corwin addressed Bonner. "We'll need all the revolvers you can provide." He paused, then added, "And are safe to use."

Bonner nodded, a pink tinge coming to his ears. "I've six or seven now, but if I get to work right away I might be able to finish up two more."

"Whatever you can manage." Corwin thumped him on the back, praying for a miracle. He turned to Raith. "We'll need flash stones as well and any other combative spells that might help." Corwin could practically hear Minister Porter complaining about the cost already, but he didn't care.

"I'm coming, too," Kate said, moving to stand next to Signe.

Corwin opened his mouth to argue, then closed it, knowing there was no point. She did not belong to him; she was not his to shelter.

"Good," he forced himself to say. "You're the best shot with the revolver. That will come in handy."

Kate's face was unreadable. "When do we leave?"

"At dawn." Corwin turned to go, his mind racing with all he needed to do yet, but he froze as a figure appeared in the doorway. It was Dal, but Corwin barely recognized him—the look on his face like that of a ghost, pale and devoid of all emotion.

"We're leaving for Thornewall in the morning?" Dal asked, his voice low and inflectionless.

"Yes," Corwin said, "but you should stay here and see to your brother."

Dal shook his head. "There's no point. My brother is dead."

KATE HAD NEVER BEFORE BEEN plagued with such doubt. Not even in those terrible days after her father's arrest. She'd been in a daze all week since first meeting Kiran and learning the truth about why her father had been in King Orwin's chambers that morning. She still didn't know why he'd attacked the king when he had only gone there to influence his decision about the Inquisition, but she was closer than ever before to understanding.

The Rising. It seemed impossible. Her father had never expressed concerns over other wilders to her, not even to acknowledge their existence. It was always just him and Kate, father and daughter, two wilders in hiding against the world. But maybe Hale's attitude had changed and Kate had never noticed. She couldn't deny things were different after Queen Imogen was killed by that wilder. Perhaps it had an impact. Or maybe it was Vianne and Kiran who opened her father's eyes to the larger world. If so, she understood, given the cruel living conditions Kiran was forced to endure.

She would never know for sure, but in the last few days she couldn't deny Hale's involvement with the Rising. Just last night she'd attended a secret meeting in the basement of the Sacred Sword. More than half of the people there had spoken to her about her father—some to offer condolences and others criticisms of his failure.

It seemed to her that the Rising was divided in all things, opinions on her father included. For more than an hour she listened to Raith arguing that they needed to be cautious, to explore every avenue to end the Inquisition without bloodshed. But another leader in the rebellion, an earthist named Francis, argued the opposite.

"The time to strike is now. Rime is already in turmoil," Francis had said, his voice teetering toward a shout. "Whoever is behind these daydrakes will continue to lay the blame on us until nowhere is safe. We need to defend ourselves before it's too late. The plan is already in place. We just need to act."

The plan, it seemed, was to seize control of Farhold, the only city in Rime capable of being fully self-sustaining. The Rising would claim the city for themselves and use it to force the high king to end the persecution.

Afterward Kate had asked Raith, "Won't many innocent people in Farhold die during the siege?"

A grave look crossed his face. "If it comes to war, then yes. Violence is an inevitable consequence. But I would ask you, what is worse? A handful of people dying in this siege, or hundreds of innocent wilders being kidnapped and executed, one at a time, for years to come?" He faced her then, placing a hand on her arm, his voice tremulous with emotion. "This is why I so desperately need your help, Kate. You've a strong influence with Corwin, and goddess be good, he will win the uror over his brother. If you can help him see the truth about us, then maybe he will use his authority as high king to end the Inquisition before any blood is shed."

"You don't know Corwin very well," Kate said, feeling a knot in her throat. *I have no influence over him.* She might've if she'd agreed to be his paramour, but she'd closed that door and had no intention of opening it again. Unwilling to discuss such matters with Raith, though, she said instead, "He hates wilders."

"I'm not certain that's true. Though even if it is, his feelings are nothing compared to those of his brother, and his high council." Raith made a look of disgust. "Edwin appears evenhanded, but Master Storr has told me that the hatred in him runs deep. In his mind every wilder must pay for his mother's death. Since taking over for his father, he's done everything he can to expand the Inquisition's power and refocus the League's priorities on capturing wilders. Did you know Maestra Vikas allows him to attend the Purgings in Norgard?"

Kate thought she might be sick. It was one thing to fear wilders or even to suspect them all capable of the same harm that caused Queen Imogen's death, but to want to watch them die? That was something else.

"Corwin cares for you," Raith continued. "That's plain for anyone to see. And I believe he's wise enough to see past his prejudices against wilders, if given the chance. He only needs to realize that wilders are equally as capable of good as of evil. The man who set the fire that killed his mother wasn't part of the Rising—we never had the chance to recruit him. So many slip through our fingers. The Rising works hard to keep wilders from ever using their powers to harm, although we don't always succeed. Such is the result of a country in which prejudice divides us, forces us into hiding, threatens our families. Corwin might be able to see this truth; he just needs to be shown by someone he trusts."

Kate didn't reply, although she wanted to believe him—that the

Rising didn't want to spread fear and violence, that their only cause was to win the freedom to live in peace. At her silence, Raith had attempted a new tactic to convince her, by offering her a way to keep Bonner's magic hidden from the League and to allow him to finally make his revolvers. Once she'd gotten over her shock at how much the master magist knew, she'd agreed to his plan. It was for that very reason they'd been in Bonner's workshop when Corwin had appeared a short time before with news of the attack on Dal's home.

And now Raith's convinced me to use my powers to try to find whoever is behind the daydrake attacks. I must be mad.

Kate shook her head, wishing she could dislodge these worries from her mind by force.

"Are you all right?" Bonner said. It was just the two of them in his workshop now. Signe was off somewhere with Dal, and Raith had left shortly after Corwin with a promise to return so as to help Kate continue to develop her ability to use her magic on humans—a skill she would need to track down whoever was controlling the daydrakes. But she didn't want to do it, no matter how important. All her life, her magic had been simple: a way to talk to animals, to influence them. Innocent, harmless. But using it on humans? That made it infinitely more powerful—and dangerous.

Realizing she'd been silent too long, Kate glanced at Bonner, a weak smile coming to her lips. "I'll be fine. It's just a lot to take in."

"I know how you feel." Bonner grimaced, the expression out of place on him. He held up the magestone necklace Raith had given him before departing. A diamond the size of a marble hung from a leather cord. "Do you really think this will shield my magic from the magists?"

Fortunately, Raith had also told Bonner about the Rising and his part in it, thereby allowing Kate to discuss it without the risk of activating the binding curse. "I don't see why Raith would lie about it, or even give it to us for that matter if it weren't going to work. That diamond must cost more money than either of us will ever have in both our lifetimes combined."

"Good point." Bonner fastened it around his neck, then spoke the incantation, activating the spell within. The cord was long enough that the diamond hung halfway down his chest. He tucked it into his tunic, out of sight. Then he picked up one of the half dozen revolvers lying on the worktable. These were the rejects, the ones with too many imperfections to work properly. Balancing the gun on one hand, he placed his other on top of it.

Hesitating, he looked at Kate. "This feels wrong."

"You don't have to do it." She walked over to him, cupping his hands with hers. "You could tell Corwin that this was all a mistake and leave Norgard. Go back to Farhold and live out your life without these troubles."

"Would you come with me?" Bonner fixed a penetrating stare on her.

A week ago she could've said yes. But not now. Not with Kiran. Every day she'd gone to see him, trying to catch up on all the years stolen from her. He was the only family she had left. She wasn't about to give him up now that she'd found him.

She shook her head and dropped her hands from Bonner's. "I can't leave Kiran. He's living in a *cage*, Bonner. It's awful. Something must be done."

"I know. And that's why I'm going to stay too. If I can finally make enough revolvers, and Corwin can eliminate the drakes, I will have saved the world. Then maybe afterward he'll be so grateful that I can tell him the truth about my gift."

Remembering Raith's words from last night, Kate slowly nodded.

Bonner adjusted his grip on the gun and closed his eyes. Although Kate couldn't sense anything, she understood that he was probing the metal with his magic, purging it of dents and impurities, smoothing out the places it had gone wrong.

"Done," he said a moment later. They both waited, half expecting a gold robe to come bursting through the door to arrest them. When several moments went by and nothing happened, Bonner shrugged and said, "I guess it worked." He set down the revolver and picked up the next one.

"Wait, Bonner." Kate touched his arm. "You can't make too many at once. The reason why Raith knew what you are is because of the questions people are asking about why only your revolvers work and no one else's."

With a huff, Bonner nodded. "You're right. I'll fix two more. Then tomorrow when the rest of the smiths start working, I'll correct each gun as needed once it's made. That way, it'll look like the smiths are managing to do it on their own."

"Good plan, but keep the diamond hidden. If any magists spy it, they'll wonder what it's for. Raith says the spell is unsanctioned."

"I'll be careful." Bonner patted the front of his tunic where the diamond lay hidden beneath it. "You were wrong, though."

Kate frowned. "About what?"

"I couldn't leave Norgard now any more than you. My father wouldn't survive the trip."

"I don't understand. He's doing so much better." They'd had supper together only yesterday, Thomas warm and welcoming like always. It was true that he remained too thin, his appetite small as a bird's, but his spirits were high. He'd even teased Bonner about finally finding a wife and settling down. *"Someone as beautiful and kind as our Kate here,"* he'd said, winking. *"I think you mean fierce, Pa,"* Bonner had replied, and they'd all laughed.

Bonner didn't meet her gaze now. "Yes, he is, but it's conditional. I spoke to the greens about it just this morning." He glanced up, far too much emotion in his face. "They can't cure what's wrong with him. All they can do is keep the sickness at bay with magestones. His body is burning through two a day at least. But if he stops wearing them, he'll regress back to how he was before, and eventually . . . he'll die. I could never afford so many magestones without this position."

Love is a cage, too, Kate thought, miserable for her friend, *one that has caught us both.* She slid her arms around his massive frame. It was like hugging a boulder. "Then let's make sure you succeed in giving Corwin his revolvers."

Raith returned an hour later. He brought a second diamond magestone with him and gave it to Kate. "You're going to need this."

Kate accepted it and put it around her neck. "Does everyone in the Rising wear these?"

Raith snorted a laugh. "We could only dream of such fortune.

But no. Just like the rest of Rime, we can only buy or steal such precious gems. Most of the wilders have to settle for lesser stones that have the power to prevent them from being discovered if a gold tests them for magic like they do when someone is arrested by the Inquisition. But it doesn't enable them to use their gifts at will without fear." He pointed a blackened finger at Kate, then at Bonner. "Don't either of you lose them and don't let anyone take them. A thief would do almost anything to steal one."

Nodding, Kate said, "What now?"

Raith put his hands on his hips and fixed a determined gaze on her. "Now we teach you how to attune your gift to humans, and let's pray to Noralah that you're a quicker study than your father."

"You taught my father how to do this?"

Raith walked over to the nearest chair and sat down, motioning for Kate to take the one opposite. "*Taught* is not the right word for it. There is no teaching someone with wilder magic, not like the study magists are put through at the League Academy. All you can do is learn through trial and error. I assisted your father by volunteering to be the subject of his attempts. I'll do the same for you now. Your first task will be to glean a single image from my mind. I'm going to focus on the image with all my concentration. That should make it easier."

Kate doubted it. She didn't have the faintest idea how to adapt her magic for a human, much less what precision was needed to read a mind, but she sat down across from the magist anyway. "Okay, where do I start?"

Raith scratched the stubble on his chin. "Just do whatever it is you do when you listen to animals, but try to attune it to me."

"That's somewhat less than helpful, but I'll give it a go." Kate closed her eyes and reached out with her magic same as she would if she were searching for wild animals in the forest.

In moments she began to detect the various animals in the castle, several cats and an alarming number of mice. She even sensed Lir in Dal's rooms, the falcon anxious in response to her master's dark mood. Finding these animal minds was easy, but when she tried to home in on Raith's thoughts, nothing happened. She might as well be trying to teach horses to fly for all the good it did.

She opened her eyes and glared at Raith. "This isn't going to work. I have no idea what I'm doing."

Raith leaned back in the chair, regarding her with a narrowed gaze. "How did it work on those thieves that night?"

"I don't know. I was scared and angry. I did it without meaning to."

Raith nodded. "An emotional trigger. It's not uncommon. But how can we re-create one now?"

Kate shook her head. At the moment all she felt was tired and uncertain, utterly spent from the last few days.

"I have an idea." Bonner set down the gun he'd been cleaning and approached them.

Kate looked up in time to see him make a grab for her, one arm pinning her while he started tickling her sides with his free hand. With a shriek, she struggled to get herself free, but she couldn't keep herself from laughing.

"Stop!" she tried to shout, unable to draw a full breath.

Bonner only tickled her harder, relentless.

"Stop!" she said again, starting to panic at the ache in her stomach. It soon sparked into anger. "Stop, I said!" This time, she put the force of her magic behind it, and Bonner stumbled backward, releasing her at once.

"That was . . . unsettling." Bonner touched his forehead. "It was like I felt you inside here."

Kate glared at him. "Now is hardly the time for tickling, Tom Bonner."

Raith waved at her. "Never mind that. Channel the emotion, Kate. Try to glean my thoughts."

Still angry, Kate closed her eyes and reached out again. Moments later she sensed two separate thoughts—the first an image of a gleaming red apple. The second was: *Gods, I'm going to pay for that later.*

Kate opened her eyes, gaping. "It worked, I think." She pointed at Raith. "You're thinking about a red apple. And you"—she swung her finger at Bonner, wielding it like a dagger—"are worried about what I'm going to do to pay you back for that."

Bonner let out a nervous laugh. "That's . . . a little frightening, knowing you heard what I'm thinking."

Kate's stomach did a flip. It was frightening. And *wrong.* She cut her eyes to Raith, who was nodding his approval. "If I learn to do this, will it happen all the time? Will I start hearing everyone's thoughts, whether I want to or not?"

"I don't believe so. Your father never spoke of such at least." Raith cocked his head, expression curious. "Do you sense the thoughts of animals all the time without meaning to?"

Kate considered the question before answering. "No, not unless their emotions are strong, like the horses that night in Jade Forest during the fire."

"There you have it, then." Raith clapped his hands once. "There's no reason why humans would be any different, I wouldn't think. If you don't want to listen in, then you don't have to."

Kate nodded, swearing silently that she would never listen in on someone's thoughts unless absolutely necessary. "So what's the point here? When we head to Thornewall, I'm supposed to listen for whoever is in hiding or something? So we can catch them?"

"You should do more if you can," Raith replied. "Their thoughts might reveal all manner of important information, and once they're caught, we can't be certain they won't kill themselves like Ralph Marcel at the Gregors' house."

Kate shook her head, unable to imagine what could make a person desperate enough to willingly walk into death.

We must uncover the reason, she realized, remembering Dal's heartbroken expression at his brother's death. *Whoever is doing this must be stopped.* It was up to her. She took a deep breath, wishing the gods had laid a different task at her feet. Why couldn't she have to win a horse race, or some mounted trial? Anything other than stealing into someone's mind.

Because the gods want to be entertained, Kate thought, reminded of this truth by the mark of the Shade Born on Raith's face. *They don't want anything to be easy.*

Sighing, she said, "Let's try again." She shook her finger at Bonner. "But no more tickling. I've got to learn to do it when I'm calm."

Bonner grinned. "Never again, I swear."

Hours passed before Kate managed it again. After a while she began to think of it like singing. That was the best analogy she could come up with. The thoughts of animals were on a different part of the scale. They were lower, in easier reach. Human thoughts resided on a much higher scale, one you had to stretch for. All she needed to do was attune her magic to the different plane. Easier said than done, after a lifetime of training her magic only to reach one level. But she kept at it until she was able to do it several times in a row.

She began to understand that attuning herself to the different scale was the hardest part of the challenge. The rest of it, the actual listening in part, was much the same, though the human mind was larger, more complex, like a massive vault full of thoughts and memories. Without meaning too, Kate caught glimpses of Raith's past, of the life he'd endured as a child—fear and hate directed at him for no other reason than the different way his skin had been marked. But at his center, he possessed the same glowing flame, his essence as bright and beautiful as any she'd sensed before.

In the end she found that using her magic on humans was actually easier, especially when it came to communicating back. After all, with humans, she spoke the same language. But the ease was also the biggest danger, Kate realized when she accidentally sent a thought directly into Raith's mind.

He winced and rubbed his forehead. "You'll want to be careful about doing that, Kate. You'll give yourself away at once. Those diamonds will only prevent the detection stones from going off. They won't do anything to hide proof of magic happening. Also, there's no need to shout."

"Sorry," Kate said, sagging back on the chair. She felt drained to the point of passing out, the well of her magic like an empty hole inside her. Never before had she used it so much at one time. "I didn't mean to do it. I'll be more careful."

"Good." Raith stood and glanced out the window, where the last rays of the sunset were casting faint orange streamers over the horizon. "I'm afraid that's all we have time for. We'll practice again on the road and when we stop to camp. If we're lucky, the time it takes us to get to Thornewall will be enough for you to master the skill."

Kate nodded, ignoring the doubt that remained. Mastery or not, she would do the best she could and could only hope it would be enough.

THE CARAVAN WAS READY TO leave at dawn the next day. When Kate spotted Corwin in the courtyard, he looked exhausted. Dark smudges circled his eyes, and he moved with a jerky sort of weariness as he mounted Nightbringer. Kate supposed the effort of organizing a group this large so quickly must've kept him up half the night. There were twelve blue robes, all handpicked by Raith, and ten Norgard cavalrymen on warhorses, with two more driving the supply wagons.

Everyone bore arms—swords and daggers, as well as ranged weapons, either bow or revolver. There were ten working revolvers in all, carried by Corwin, Signe, Kate, Dal, and six of the cavalrymen. Stuffed in everyone's pockets and saddlebags were a vast amount of flash stones and the shield stones Raith had promised. Kate felt as if she were riding off to war rather than a rescue mission.

They traveled at a quick, steady pace that first day, the wagons rolling along easily on the smooth, even road. By the second day, they reached rougher ground, the road getting rockier by the mile and the hills more frequent. Although Corwin hoped they would make it there in three days, it soon became clear that four was the best they could manage—unless they wanted to enter the cliffs surrounding Thornewall at dusk and risk the threat of nightdrakes.

Kate passed the time in the saddle practicing her sway. It was difficult at first, her instincts protesting the danger of wielding her magic so openly—and in front of a dozen magists as well, each of them carrying the required detection stone in their maces and only half of them sympathetic to the Rising. But after a while she grew to enjoy the freedom of it. While they were still in open country, she practiced stretching out as far as she could, listening for the minds of humans. Twice she was able to sense the approach of other travelers ahead before they came into view. Best of all though, Dal had brought Lir with him, and she occasionally joined with the falcon's mind while it flew above the caravan, giving herself the ability to see far and wide and to savor the sensation of flying itself. She could get used to such freedom.

When they made camp each evening, she would join Raith in his tent, and the two of them would discuss in low voices her accomplishments that day. Then they would spend the last hour before nightfall practicing as they had at Norgard, with Kate trying to uncover thoughts while Raith now actively tried to hide from her.

When they stopped for the third day, Corwin called them all together to discuss plans for the morrow. They gathered in the center of camp, where he and Dal had drawn a crude map on the ground using rocks and sticks.

"In the morning," Corwin said, "we will send out the scouts as planned. Some will go ahead and others will follow behind. However, Lord Dallin believes that if there is to be an ambush, it will happen as we reach this point here." Corwin indicated a place on the map where the trail became its narrowest. Stacks of large rocks had been laid side by side to indicate the bottleneck.

"It's called the Serpent's Pass," Dal said, sweeping his gaze over the group. "Both because of the way it twists and because of how deadly it can be. In the spring, summer, and fall, there's always the chance of rockslides. In the winter, avalanche. The horses won't be able to go much faster than a walk. The ground is too rocky."

"If there hasn't been any sign of daydrakes or their handlers by the time we reach this point," Corwin said, "we will purposefully delay. We don't want to meet them in the Serpent's Pass. We'll stage one of the wagons to appear broken down. Whoever is watching will see us as easy prey, but we won't be."

There were murmurs among the men as they digested this news. Corwin allowed them a few moments, then raised his hands for silence. "Now, we need to decide on the scouts." He began listing the names. Kate waited for hers to be called, but it wasn't, and upon reaching the end of the roster, Corwin said, "The rest of us will stay with the wagons to defend the supplies and to take down any drakes that come into range."

Signe leaned toward Kate and said with a hiss, "Does he think we're mere decorations? I don't want to guard the wagon."

"Neither do I," Kate said. What was worse, it would make it harder for her to detect the drakes' handlers. She needed isolation to hear clearly with her magic.

When the meeting ended, Raith approached Kate. "We need to change Corwin's mind," he whispered.

"Yes, but how, without telling him the truth?"

Raith glanced around the camp as if searching for the answer. "I have an idea. Come with me."

Kate followed Raith to where Corwin and Dal were spreading

out their bedrolls. Despite the crisp air, they'd decided there would be no fires this evening, so as not to tip off any potential enemies.

"Your highness." Master Raith bowed his head in greeting. "We need to discuss the scouts."

Corwin looked up, his expression at first surprised, then annoyed, as his eyes fell on Kate before shifting back to the magist. "In what way, Master Raith?"

"I believe Miss Kate would make the best scout. Her skills will be wasted guarding the wagons."

"So will mine," said Signe, who, predictably, had come with them.

Dal fixed a stare at Signe. Although he'd pretended to be his usual, lighthearted self these last few days, everyone who knew him could feel the change in him. It was as if he'd been weighed down by an invisible cloak, his jokes slower to come than before, his smiles less liable to linger. Kate hadn't heard him laugh at all.

"I would prefer," Dal said, his gaze sliding off Signe's face to land somewhere near his feet, "that you stay near me."

Signe openly gaped in response, and Kate cringed at her lack of finesse. Then, to her surprise, Signe closed her mouth and nodded. "If that is what you want."

Dal looked up, his expression intense. "It is."

"Good, now that's settled," Raith said with a touch of impatience. "But what about Kate? She is the best rider here and should be the first scout. To be honest, she might be the only scout we need. One rider is less liable to be spotted and raise an alarm. Also, with the path so treacherous, no one else has a better chance of getting back to us unscathed if there's an ambush ahead."

Corwin stared at the magist, his lips pressed tight together and every muscle in his body rigid.

"He makes a fair point," Dal said, nodding at Corwin. "Not to mention one scout will mean more here at the ready to join in the fight."

Kate braced for an angry refusal as Corwin cut his gaze to her. His blue eyes were like ice, coaxing a shiver down her spine.

"Is that what you want, Kate? To ride ahead?" A muscle ticked in Corwin's jaw as he awaited her response.

She nodded, not trusting herself to speak. The air between them felt charged as if from an approaching storm. The tension caused a flood of memories to rush into her mind of the last time they'd faced each other like this. An ache of desire pulsed through her. She couldn't help it. When it came to Corwin, her body was its own creature. She looked away first.

"So be it," she heard Corwin say. "I will discuss it with the others."

Kate watched him go for a moment, then forcibly pulled her gaze away.

Raith stepped up to her and said, "Go get something to eat and turn in early. There's not enough daylight left to train, and you need to be rested for the morning."

With a grateful sigh, she told him thanks, then headed off to find a place to lay down her bedroll. They had stopped for the night less than a furlong from the cliffs, and there were several large boulders scattered throughout the camp. Kate selected a place near one of the biggest, hoping it would shield her from the noise of the soldiers, who she suspected would be up late, too restless for sleep with what waited for them tomorrow.

She untied the bedding and flung it out before her. Bending to straighten it, she froze as a voice said, "Is there something between you and Master Raith?"

Looking up, she saw Corwin leaning against the boulder, his face half hidden in shadow. She slowly rose, letting the full meaning of his question settle in her mind.

"Something *between* us?" She put her hands on her hips, uncertain if she felt like laughing or hitting him. A little of both, most like.

He nodded, his gaze locked on her face. "I know it's none of my business, but . . . I can't keep my head straight around you, and perhaps knowing that you have moved on might . . ." He didn't finish. He didn't need to.

Might let me move on, too. For a brief moment she considered giving him a lie to put him out of his misery. But she was tired of lies. They seemed to be growing all around these days like invasive vines, strangling her at every turn. Instead she longed to tell him about herself and about Kiran and what she hoped to accomplish tomorrow. She longed to do what Raith asked of her—to convince him to help bring an end to the Inquisition. The diamond mage-stone felt like a manacle around her neck.

Carefully, she shook her head. "No, there is nothing like that between Raith and me." She searched for an explanation, realizing too late that she should've anticipated this. Corwin was bound to wonder about what she and Raith were doing all that time they spent together. "We've been discussing the drakes and the best way to handle them. That's all."

Doubt clouded Corwin's expression, and he shifted his weight from one foot to the other.

Before she knew what she was doing, Kate said, "There's never been anyone but you, Corwin." Her bottled-up emotions threatened to burst inside her, and she held them back with a hard swallow.

His eyebrows rose on his forehead. "Never?"

"Not one, not on purpose anyway."

He seemed to mull this over. "You mean that kiss with Edwin." Jealousy rang clear in his voice, despite his obvious effort to hide it.

She took pity on him, remembering that she never had offered an explanation. "I thought he was you. I even said your name. I wouldn't have kissed him otherwise. But you do look alike, and it was dark. I never would've hurt you willingly. Edwin tricked me. He tricked us both."

Corwin gritted his teeth, a muscle flicking in his jaw. "He's always hated me, hasn't he?"

Kate started to agree, then stopped. "I think it's more complicated than that. He loves you, too, but you were never allowed to be mere brothers. The uror made you rivals from the beginning, and your father's favoritism didn't help."

It was strange how the years had given her such clarity, and she felt an unexpected wave of pity for the older Tormane brother, almost enough to make her understand the man he'd become now. She recalled the subtle way Edwin demeaned Corwin at every turn—snide, biting comments about his character, his looks, everything. They'd often been said in jest, but jealousy fueled them. Then after Queen Imogen died, he'd had even more fuel to feed his resentment.

Corwin slowly nodded. "It makes you wonder if there isn't a better way than the uror." For a second his gaze turned far away, the look of a man wandering lost in his own thoughts. Then he shook his head and came back to her. "I'm sorry, Kate. I know you would never have hurt me on purpose. I've always known. I just let the events of that night cloud my feelings. I suppose I'm always doing that. Even now, it's easier to think Edwin simply hates me without cause than to admit the cruel circumstances between us. But I suppose I should look for the good in him as well."

Kate bit her lip, fighting the urge to step closer to Corwin, to comfort him with a touch. Or maybe it was herself she sought comfort for.

His gaze dropped to the rocky ground between them. "I need to stop judging by appearance alone, with just my gut feeling on the matter. Like the way I misjudged you. The assumptions I made about . . ." He trailed off, his eyes flicking to her waist for a moment. The moonbelt wasn't visible, but they both knew she still wore it. He raised his gaze to hers. "I'm sorry for making that callous offer. I never meant to hurt you. I hope you know that."

"I do," she said, unable to look away, even though she should—before she did something foolish. She pressed her lips together as the temptation to tell him the truth rose up even stronger inside her.

Corwin broke the connection first. "Good. Be careful tomorrow," he said, and then he disappeared behind the rock.

Regret pricked at her. What a hypocrite she was. How could he not misjudge her when she'd been lying to him for years, keeping her secret? She used to think it was harmless, for his own good, but now she wondered if she hadn't created the problems between them by her deception, as if by holding herself back she had ensured that they would never truly stand on the same ground. Or maybe the gods were just punishing her for the lie. In the end, neither possibility brought her any comfort.

Kate was distracted the next morning when she rode out ahead of the caravan, her thoughts still on Corwin and their exchange the night before. She believed his apology, but it didn't change things, as much as she might want it to. He was still the high prince and she the traitor's daughter.

The wilder.

Should I tell him? Is Raith right? Will it make a difference?

She didn't know, and she couldn't stop the questions from cycling through her head. Not until Firedancer gave a sudden spook, nearly jarring her out the saddle. She gasped, heart racing. Then, recovering quickly, she glanced around, looking for the source of the noise that had so startled her horse, only to find nothing.

For Shades' sake, Kate, what's wrong with you? She forced thoughts of Corwin from her mind and reached out with her magic. Something must've caused the noise, a falling rock perhaps. Only what had made it fall? She swept for the presence of someone else, either human or animal, but found nothing. Perhaps it was the wind. Even now it moaned high above the cliffs that rose up on either side of her.

At least the shock had put her mind back on the task at hand: finding the drakes and their handlers. Urging Firedancer forward, Kate stretched out with her magic again, doing it in sweeps, to the front, the sides, even behind, where she could just make out Corwin and the others.

There were few animals around—a mountain cat, some squirrels, and birds, of course. But nothing else. Not for nearly twenty minutes as she rode along, keeping Firedancer at a walk. Then finally, she sensed it: that oily, multiple-minded presence just ahead. But—it was impossible. There was nowhere for the drakes to be. Nothing but cliff face on both sides and an empty path stretching straight onward. Even still, she slowed Firedancer to a halting walk, her magic telling her one thing and her eyes telling her something else.

When she drew parallel with the drakes, her magic unequivocal, Kate reined Firedancer to a halt. She craned her head back, trying to see if they were above, or if they might be on the other side of the cliff, in a different pass. Yet she couldn't see how. This was the only path. All the maps said so. She scanned the left wall, searching the cliff face for some explanation of why she could sense them there.

Then she saw the line running down the height of the rock wall, far too straight and precise to be natural. Dismounting, she gave Firedancer a command to stay put. Then she approached the cliff, stretching her hand out toward the line. When her fingers should've met stone, all she felt was air. *It's an illusion,* Kate realized, her eyes finally making out the lie. There was a passageway hidden here, easily large enough for a horse—or a drake—to pass through.

Pulling out the revolver from the holster at her side, she stepped into the opening. Her heartbeat quickened with each footfall, the drake presence growing stronger. Seeing the end of the passage ahead, she stopped, aware of the mistake she was making. It wasn't the drakes she was after but the people controlling them. She'd let them distract her with their multiple-minded presence. Pulling away from them, Kate closed her eyes and raised the tenor of her magic, attuning it to that higher, human plane.

Nothing. All she could sense was the distant minds in the caravan. Guessing the drakes must be caged here, as they'd been in the Wandering Woods, she steeled her courage and rounded the corner.

Her breath caught in her throat, awestruck fear rising up in her. Ahead more than fifty daydrakes were crammed into a small gorge cut into the cliffs. There was nothing visibly restraining them, but even when they caught her scent, they didn't move toward her. Something held them caged in the gorge, which wasn't a natural formation but a perfect circle as precise as a bullet in shape. Only wilder magic could've carved it.

Needing to warn the others, Kate turned around but froze at the sight of a man blocking the path. Short and slight, hardly bigger than herself, he carried a pistol in one hand and a sword in the other. Around his throat shone a black magestone, the magic pulsating dully.

Kate raised her hands in surrender, but the man aimed his pistol, his intent clear. Knowing she had no chance of avoiding the shot at this close range, she seized the only weapon left to her and turned her magic on him. She entered his mind easily, but a moment later, she felt her consciousness flung from his thoughts. She stared at him, dazedly, realizing he had the gift of sway, too.

"Nice try, my little wilder girl," the man said, and she recognized the slight lilt to his words—he was a native of Penlocke, the port city south of Norgard. "But your skill ain't close to as strong as mine."

Maybe not, Kate thought, *but I've more than one trick to play.*

Kate called to Firedancer with her magic, urging the horse into a run as she coaxed her into the hidden passageway. The man pulled back the hammer, ready to fire, but he swung around at the sound of hoofbeats. Kate couldn't use the revolver, afraid of hitting the horse, and so as Firedancer came charging toward them, she pulled a flash stone from her pocket and flung it at the man. The stone exploded in a bright burst, the effect of the magic not affecting her, the one who cast the spell.

The man jumped in alarm, pulling the trigger by accident, but he didn't fall. He wasn't even blinded. Somehow he was shielded from the flash stone's magic. As he turned back to her, Kate saw that the magestone around his throat glowed brighter now. She suddenly remembered what Raith had said—how magics met directly will cancel each other out.

With his only bullet now wasted, the man dropped the pistol and raised his sword. Kate urged Firedancer to safety, quelling the mare's panic over the flash stone's effects, while she raised her revolver. Not wanting to kill the man, she aimed for his shoulder and fired. The bullet flew true, and the man dropped the sword as the shot severed his grip. He shrieked in pain, rage flashing in his eyes.

When he lunged for her, Kate fired again. The bullet struck him in the side, but he had too much momentum. He barreled into her, knocking her to the ground. The revolver fell out of her hand and went off, discharging another shot into the air.

The man's body pressed down on Kate, and she felt the hot stickiness of his blood pooling over her from the wounds in his side and shoulder. He would bleed out soon, but somehow he still had strength enough to wrap his uninjured hand around her throat. Kate tried to pry him off but couldn't. Panic began to roar inside her, driving away her ability to think. Desperately, she reached for the magestone around his neck and began to twist, hoping to choke him. Terror filled his gaze as he struggled to pull her off. She sensed his emotions now, rage and pain like a tempest inside him.

Aware that he was weakening, Kate focused the strength of her magic and screamed into his mind, *Get off me!*

He froze, his fingers slackening. It was the moment she needed to free herself enough to reach the gun. But the man recovered all too soon, pushing her out of his mind as he grabbed for the gun as well. They struggled, hands grasping for control of the weapon. It went off with a bang so loud Kate felt it in her teeth. By pure chance, the bullet struck his throat, and blood began to gush from the wound like water from a pump.

He was dying fast—and taking his secrets with him. Desperately, Kate plunged into his thoughts, fighting off the horror of what she was doing. Images flooded her mind, faces of loved ones, regrets, and a terrible soul-deep fear of what was happening to him, his inability to *stay* when he could feel the life leaving him. Through it all though, she managed to glean a recurring memory at the front of his mind: that he had been arrested by the Inquisition for being a wilder.

And then he was slipping away. . . .

With a cry, Kate pulled back from his thoughts, terrified of what she would feel when the last of his life fled his body. She scrambled out from underneath the dead man and rolled onto her stomach, ready to be sick, then froze in terror at the sight of the drakes moving toward her.

They were free. The man must've been controlling them, and now he was dead, his magic broken.

Lurching to her feet, Kate called for Firedancer. She leaped into the saddle, and they raced through the passageway back to the main pass. The drakes surged behind them, their screeching wails loud as rolling thunder.

Kate still had the revolver, two bullets left in the cylinder, but it wouldn't matter against fifty drakes. She pulled a handful of flash stones out of the pouch on her saddle and flung them behind her, slowing down the first wave of drakes, but the second kept coming. They would be on them soon. Firedancer was galloping, hooves slipping on the loose rocks, but they couldn't slow down. Kate needed to warn the others.

Reaching out with her magic, she searched for Raith but couldn't distinguish him among so many, not over such a distance. It didn't matter though. Their thoughts buzzed with alarm, and she guessed they'd heard the gunfire. Wanting to be sure, Kate raised the pistol overhead and fired off the last two shots. Then she holstered the gun and pulled out the shield stone, activating it with a single word.

She saw the shimmer of magic spread around her, but doubted it would hold against so many drakes. She had to find a way to slow them down before they overtook her. If she could reach the caravan, she would be safe behind the ward. Then the answer came to her—one so simple she'd overlooked it. Her magic. If that other wilder could hold them, so could she. Somehow. But there were so many. More than she had ever tried to control before.

Shoving the doubt away, she focused on the drakes nearest. If she could get them to slow, there might be a ripple effect. She could clog the pass with drakes piling up on one another, maybe even force them to start attacking each other. Grasping hold of those oily, multiple minds, she sent out the command.

Something strange happened. The drakes obeyed her will, but it wasn't only the ones she touched. She sensed her command echoing over and over again, spreading through the minds of the other drakes like an infection. Stunned, she realized she didn't have to control them all. If she could reach one, the rest would follow, their will bound together.

A thrill of victory went through Kate. She could end the threat right here, with a single thought. But then the complication of the situation struck her. She couldn't do that and still keep her secret.

Seeing no other choice, Kate decided to make a ruse of it, a performance with the daydrakes as the actors. She formed the behavior she wanted from them in her mind and sent it out as a command. The drakes sensed and obeyed, the pack racing after her but not attacking, just flashing their fangs and claws, screaming their wails. Their poor, dumb collective minds couldn't sense the trap waiting for them, didn't know that the force guiding them was leading them to their deaths.

But the moment Kate charged to safety past the waiting caravan, Corwin and the others opened fire, and one by one the daydrakes fell, unwilling sacrifices on the altar.

CORWIN SURVEYED THE CARNAGE. FIFTY dead drakes. He should've been pleased, but disappointment plagued him. The drakes were dead, not a hint of them anywhere else in the pass. Their handler was dead as well, leaving few clues about who he had been and no hints at all about his service to the Rising.

"You're sure he was from Penlocke?" Corwin asked Kate when she led them to the strange, circular gorge where the daydrakes had been caged.

"Yes," she said, arms wrapped around her waist. Although dirty and bloodstained, she appeared otherwise unharmed.

Even now, Corwin could barely contain his relief. When he first heard those gunshots, he felt his heart seize in his chest, fearing the worst. He'd lain awake all last night, regretting the things that had come between them. That he'd *let* come between them. And wishing for some way to make it right. There had to be one, even though he still couldn't see it. But at least she lived and there would be time. He clung to that hope.

Raith was stooped over the man, searching his body for distinguishing marks. They'd stripped him naked but found nothing so far. Not so much as a scar or an unusual mole. It seemed impossible that they would ever find out who he was among the vast citizenship of Penlocke.

A moment later though, Raith stood up, nodding. "This man has been treated by the green robes for an illness sometime within the last year."

Corwin frowned. "How can you tell?"

Stooping over the body again, Raith motioned for Corwin to join him. "Do you see these fine white lines?"

Corwin focused his gaze where Raith pointed, but it took him a while to make out the blemishes on the man's skin, as fine as a spider's webbing. "Barely. What are they?"

"The result of a drawing spell, the kind used to purge the body of poison and certain diseases."

"Interesting, I suppose, but I don't see how it will help us." Corwin stood again, hands on hips.

Raith rose as well. "The greens keep records of everyone they treat. It's possible I might learn his name from them. Once we are done with our business at Thornewall, I will travel to Penlocke to find out more."

Corwin thought about the golds' denial of ever having caught Ralph Marcel. Perhaps Raith would have better luck with the greens. "Please leave as soon as you're ready. We have more than enough magists with us now that the daydrakes are dead."

"Thank you, your highness." Raith glanced at Kate, and Corwin braced for him to say Kate would be coming with him. Corwin had accepted that there was nothing romantic between them, but there was still *something* between them. But Raith only said, "I will leave tomorrow, once you've settled at Thornewall."

Beneath a gray, twilight-dim sky, they at last arrived at Thornewall Castle. To Corwin's eyes, however, it was more of a fortress. Like the one at Andreas, the wall here was built into the surrounding cliffs. The stone edifice loomed high above them, impregnable and unwelcoming, while its lower surface bore the scars of claw marks. Several bodies of dead, decaying daydrakes surrounded it, those the freeholding had managed to fell from atop the wall.

The moment the guards on the bailey saw the royal banner, the people inside burst to life, welcoming them in with great pomp and excitement. Baron Thorne greeted Corwin with fumbling relief. He kept bowing and thanking him for their rescue, all the while ignoring his youngest son. Worse still was the way the baron hardly even reacted to the news that his second-youngest son had perished.

Seeing for himself that the rumors about Dal's sordid family were true made Corwin feel ill. These people were undeserving of Dal, unworthy of his love and the risk he'd taken coming here to save them. Still, as distasteful as Dal's parents turned out to be— his mother not much better, although she at least wept at the news of her son's death—the rest of the people who lived at Thornewall mattered more. Their relief and joy at being rescued made the risk and all the expense worth it.

I should defy the high council more often. It was a dangerous thought, very much like one the Corwin who had once been a captain in the Shieldhawks would've had, and yet he couldn't help smiling to himself.

True to his word, Master Raith left the morning after their arrival, taking two of his blues with him. Corwin and the rest stayed a week. The soldiers helped with the arduous process of burning the bodies of the dead drakes. They also ran sweeps through the pass and surrounding areas, searching for more of the creatures, but not finding a single one. It seemed the threat to Thornewall truly was over. Why the freeholding had been targeted in the first place remained a mystery. Corwin could only hope Raith would uncover answers in Penlocke.

On the sixth day of their stay, a caravan from Norgard arrived bearing Dal's brother, his body already prepared for the holy burning by the priestesses of Noralah. That evening they held the death ceremony, but it was Lady Thorne who lit the pyre instead of her husband as was tradition.

Afterward, Corwin walked along the ramparts of the castle with Dal. Neither spoke for a long time, both lost in their own reflections while a chill, damp breeze blew in their faces.

When they reached the section of wall overlooking the Penlaurel River, they came to a stop and leaned against the edge, peering out at the dark water, the expanse so wide they couldn't see the far shoreline.

"It's strange, but Robert and I never got along," Dal said, breaking the silence at last. "When we were children, we were always forced to do things together because of our closeness in age. I hated it. He used to steal my dessert and break my toys. Yet all I can think of now is how much I'll miss his irritations."

Corwin nodded, understanding the sense of loss completely. There were days he missed the way his mother used to scold him nearly as much as he missed the way she would hold him close and stroke his head when he was hurt or scared.

"Of course," Dal continued, "none of us really got along except for Matthew and Lucas, the eldest brothers." A bitter laugh escaped Dal's throat, the wind doing its best to steal the sound away. "But I suppose that makes sense. Can't have the purebreds mingling with the mongrels."

Feeling an ache in his chest at his friend's misery, Corwin searched for something to say but could think of nothing aside from empty platitudes.

Dal brushed hair back from his face, nodding to himself. "It's the cruelest part of this life, I think, that we don't get to choose the families and situations we're born into."

Corwin turned his gaze on the water lapping against the rocks below, his thoughts on Edwin and the rivalry of the uror that had divided them from the beginning. And on Kate, how he would've picked her over anyone. "You're right about that. Gods know I would've chosen differently." He hesitated, doubt nagging him. "Then again, who's to say we would be happier if we did choose? I imagine most of us would get it wrong either way."

"At least we would have chosen our own misery," Dal said. "But some would do all right. I imagine most wilders would choose families from Endra or Rhoswen or even Esh if such were possible. Every time I feel sorry for myself, I remember that poor woman in Andreas trying to save her son. The gods are cruel to have given them such a fate."

The memory rushed into Corwin's mind unbidden. It wasn't the first time Dal had mentioned it. The arrest of that child in Andreas seemed to haunt his friend—that and Signe's continued criticism of the Inquisition. Then again, now that he'd met Dal's mother, Corwin wondered if that might be part of it—the effect of witnessing the fierce love of a parent ready to do anything to save her child. It was something Dal never had. Lady Thorne was too self-absorbed to put anyone else's needs above her own.

With thoughts of his own mother pressing on his mind, Corwin cleared his throat. "I'm surprised you're still sympathetic, given it was a wilder controlling the drakes that threatened Thornewall and killed your brother."

Dal cast Corwin a sharp look. "Don't be ridiculous, Corwin. They're two different people. As far we know that woman in Andreas never hurt anyone until they tried to take away her son. Who's to say she wouldn't have lived all her life in peace if her hand hadn't been forced? Wilder or no, they're still human. They make choices good and bad, same as the rest of us."

"Yes, but for most of us those choices don't result in people's blood being drawn from their body." *Or raging fires that cause stampedes.*

"No, the rest of us merely use swords and guns and call it justice." Dal scowled into the distance, then turned a skeptical look onto Corwin. "And let's not forget kings and high councilmembers. They often make decisions that result in the pain and suffering of others—usually without them having to witness it. They speak a word and their will is done." He snapped his fingers, then paused. "Not unlike your brother refusing to send help."

Corwin ran his tongue over his teeth, disliking the way he saw Dal's point. Kings did wield the kind of power that affected hundreds of faceless people, like the peasant women in need of moonbelts or the sick and infirm forced to give themselves over in sacrifice to make room inside the city.

And the gods know how well I understand bad choices.

Dal leaned down, braced against the top of the ramparts as he rested his chin in his hands. "What's more, people hate wilders even though they can't help how they're born any better than I can help being my mother's bastard. My father despises me for something I had no part in, and there's no changing his mind about it. Believe me, I've tried." Dal sighed. "You know the worst of it though? I don't even know who my real father is. None of us do. My mother refuses to tell so that we can never confirm the rumors to the rest of the world."

Corwin blew out a breath, unable to fathom what that must've been like.

When Dal fell silent again, Corwin thumped him on the back. "Let's look on the bright side. By not knowing, you can make him something special. He could be a great war hero."

Standing up from the rampart, Dal snorted. "Or a court jester." Then he laughed, the first real one Corwin had heard from him in days. "One thing is certain, though. I got my dashing good looks from him, thank the gods."

Corwin laughed, too, picturing the balding, sagging Baron Thorne. "I believe you're right about that."

"Come to think of it," Dal said, "maybe he was a pirate, like the men who built this fortress."

"This place was built by pirates?" Corwin asked, delighted more by the lightness he sensed in Dal than the novelty of such a history.

"That's the legend, although some of it is indeed fact. Do you see those rocks down there?" Dal pointed over the ledge.

Glancing down, Corwin noticed the rocks at once. They seemed out of place, too straight and even to have formed naturally. "What is that?"

"My ancestor built them there to block the smuggling caves. This place is full of them." Dal pulled back from the wall with a sigh. "It's a shame those caves aren't open now. Everyone could've escaped that way, and Robert would still be alive."

"I'm sorry," Corwin said, crestfallen at how easily Dal had slipped back into his melancholy mood. "If I had the power to change it, I would."

Dal didn't respond, not for several long moments. "No one can change the past." He hesitated, running a hand over the stubble on his chin. "But you might be able to change the future."

Corwin shifted his weight, unsure he liked this sudden turn in the conversation.

Dal narrowed his eyes at him, expression earnest. "Do you remember what I said back in Norgard about wishing things could go back to the way they were before we left on the tour?"

"Yes. . . ."

"Well, I was wrong. I don't wish that."

A confused smile turned up the edges of Corwin's mouth. "Why do you say so?"

Dal drew a deep breath. "Because you should be king. There's no one better suited."

"We both know that isn't true. No matter how many times you say otherwise." Unconsciously, Corwin's eyes shifted to the unnaturally smooth side of Dal's face. Underneath lay a visceral reminder of all the reasons why he wasn't fit to wield such power.

."Why, because of this?" Reaching up, Dal pulled the magestone out of his ear. His features blurred for a moment before settling once more into Dal's true face—the left side a scarred, craterous ruin. Even now, nearly a year later, Corwin could still feel the explosion responsible. One that had killed half his men in a single blow.

Corwin looked away, his stomach a hard knot in his center.

"Don't turn away, Corwin," Dal said, scolding him like a child. "What happened to me, to our shield brothers, was unavoidable. You led us true. You stayed to fight and defend those of us who fell, even when others would've run away. You saved *me*."

"Yes, but we never should've approached from that direction in the first place. If I'd just followed orders, we wouldn't have found that boy. And if we'd never found him, I'd never have let him go, and we never would've been ambushed." Corwin's fingers curled into fists, the memory of the soldier boy's face fresh in his mind after the first uror trial.

Dal shook his head, the slight movement exaggerated by the way the shadows splayed across the ruined side of his face. "You don't know the boy betrayed us. We never saw him again, remember? It's only your guilt assuming so. But I know better. I saw the look in that kid's eyes when you told him to go home. It was the same way I felt when I learned you decided to come here to rescue my family despite the high council's wishes. Your willingness to act quickly—to do what must be done despite the risk, the *cost*—*that* makes you the king Rime needs. We need someone who puts the people first and not the position. Someone who leads with his heart. A good heart."

Corwin opened his mouth to protest, then closed it again at the fierce look in Dal's eyes. There was no getting past that.

Forcing a smile to his lips, Corwin put an arm around Dal's

shoulder and squeezed. "I appreciate the vote of confidence." Then, wanting to change the subject, he added, "And now I think it best we head for home. We've stayed in this miserable place long enough."

"I couldn't agree with you more," Dal replied, sliding the mage-stone back into his ear. "Norgard is truly my home now."

"I'm glad you think so," Corwin said. *You will always have a place there, my friend,* he thought. But he didn't say it aloud. Some things just didn't need to be said.

IN THE WEEKS THAT FOLLOWED their return from Thornewall, Kate enjoyed a stretch of peace unlike any she had ever experienced before. Thanks to the power of Raith's magestone diamond, all of Bonner's troubles had disappeared. Kate couldn't be happier for him or more relieved that she didn't have to worry any longer.

Bonner was the toast of the court, the object of glory among the Norgard soldiers, and the focus of fascination and wonder among the peasantry. The newspapers were printing articles about him, wealthy merchants with unwed daughters were sending him marriage contracts with massive dowries attached, and most of the gentry were vying to purchase something made by him personally. Best of all, though, Bonner had secured his future in Norgard, and the guarantee that his father could live out the rest of his life receiving the treatments he needed from the greens.

The only one not celebrating Bonner's success was Grand Master Storr. He'd written a letter for the *Royal Gazette* cautioning the public from putting too much faith in machines over magic, but for the most part, no one seemed to be heeding him.

Kate was glad of it, all her worries far away. Even the trouble with daydrakes and her uncertainty about her place in the Rising didn't worry her, with Master Raith still in Penlocke and not here to pressure her into telling Corwin the truth about her magic.

Her life soon fell into a comfortable routine. Although Corwin no longer brought her sweet rolls in the mornings, he did start training with her on Nightbringer again a few times a week. Both of them avoided speaking of the past, the resulting lulls in conversation occasionally awkward but more bearable than picking at old wounds. Kate sensed a change in Corwin, a confidence that hadn't been there before. Part of it was no doubt his recent victories—both saving Thornewall and Bonner's success with the revolvers. But part of it was something deeper, as if he was finally able to see himself the way the rest of Norgard seemed to see him now—as a worthy heir. She wasn't hearing him called the Errant Prince anymore. *What if he wins?* It was a question she tried not to dwell on.

Yet the best parts of Kate's days quickly became her visits with Kiran. At first she would come by the Sacred Sword and spend a few hours with him down in his secret underground home. But it didn't take long before her loathing of the dark, miserable place drove her to insist she be allowed to take him outside.

Vianne had refused at first. "It's too risky, Kate. What if someone sees you with him? They'll want to know who he is, where he came from. We can't risk it."

"I'll wear my cowl. No one will pay attention in the middle of the day. There are hundreds of children in Norgard."

Vianne scoffed, hands on hips. "What if he loses control of his magic? If that happens even for a second—"

Anise, who made a habit of coming down too whenever Kate visited, waved her hand at the other woman. "You can't use that excuse forever, Vianne. Sooner or later, the boy must learn to control it in places other than this dingy hole in the ground."

"You agree with her?" Vianne spun toward Anise, her expression a mixture of shock and outrage, as if the woman had just betrayed her to the golds.

Anise rolled her eyes. "I've been telling you the same thing for months now. The boy is ready. It's not healthy for him to be down here all the time. Children need fresh air and sunshine to grow."

"What do you know about children?" Vianne said, but Kate could see right away she regretted her words.

"More than you will ever know." Anise sounded perfectly calm, which only made her anger seem all the more dangerous.

Vianne let out a heavy sigh and turned back to Kate. "All right. You may take him out once. For a single hour—then you bring him right back. No one can see you."

Kate wanted to argue that an hour was hardly worth it, but she held back. It was a small victory. "I'll return for him tomorrow. We'll go for a ride in the countryside."

Vianne's eyes seemed to widen to the size of teacups. "Outside the city?"

"There's nothing to fear out there," Kate said, remembering how she'd swayed the daydrakes to do her bidding. "Besides, if he were to have a mishap with his magic, it's less likely anyone would see. We'll avoid the main roads and the bigger fields."

The next day Kate arrived earlier than usual. At first she thought the plan wasn't going to work. Kiran's excitement over the adventure was coming off him in visible sparks. Kate started to cancel their plans, but the moment Kiran sensed her doubt, he broke down crying. It wasn't a tantrum like she'd seen other children have. This was abject heartbreak so pitiful that Kate almost descended into tears herself.

Vianne, no less susceptible to her son's despair, knelt before the boy and took his hands into her scarred ones. "You've got to keep it under control, Kiran. Do you understand? If you let off so much as a single spark, you will never get to do this again."

Kiran's lower lip quivered as he fought back tears. The vivid flush on his face only emphasized the overall paleness of him. He slowly nodded.

Vianne turned Kiran's hands over, exposing his palms. "Now show me a single flame." The boy responded, a single steady flame appearing above his right hand. "Show me two." A second flame appeared. "Show me three sparks in a row."

On and on it went, Vianne testing Kiran on his ability to control his magic. He performed beautifully, exhibiting a control far above what Kate would've expected from a six-year-old. Then again, she didn't have anything to compare it to, since she'd known no other wilders first coming into their power.

Finally, Vianne pronounced him ready, and she let Kate lead him up the stairs and out into the back alley where she'd left Firedancer tied to a post. Kiran let out a burst of excited laughter at the sight of the horse.

When he tried to rush up to the mare, Vianne hauled him back. "Be careful. Horses can kick and bite, my little prince, and that's a warhorse. They're trained to do it on command."

"It's fine." Kate motioned Kiran forward. "She will never hurt you. I promise." Kate climbed into the saddle, then reached down to help pull Kiran up while Vianne lifted him. Kate settled the boy in front of her, holding him tight around the waist.

"Be back in an hour!" Vianne called after them as they started to ride away.

Kate took them out the western gate toward Jade Forest. As she went, she instructed Kiran on the basics of riding. It was his first time on a horse, but he showed no fear.

"Our father was master of horse, you know," Kate said once they were outside the city and free from the chance of someone overhearing. "You will be a natural."

"Will you teach me every day?" Kiran said, practically shouting in his excitement.

She gently shushed him. "Not every day. But as much as I can. We'll start this morning." Kate rode to an isolated spot between two fields, a place she and Corwin had often visited when they were younger. Normally, she wouldn't have allowed a child so young to ride a warhorse alone, but with the diamond around her neck, ensuring her secrets, she wasn't worried—she could control Firedancer with a single thought.

Kiran struggled with riding, but that was to be expected. There was nothing natural or easy about the skill. What mattered was that he was brave and tenacious, willing to learn.

"Well done," she said when he brought Firedancer to a halt. "You will be riding like a master in no time at all."

Kiran beamed at her. "I want to go again!" Kate indulged the boy, unable to tell him no with his enjoyment so palpable.

When they returned to the Sacred Sword nearly an hour past due, they were greeted by a livid Vianne. Kate braced, expecting a tirade, but within moments Kiran's infectious joy over the outing had cooled his mother's wrath. *Glad I'm not the only one bewitched by this child,* Kate thought. Then again, she couldn't imagine anyone not liking him.

And yet the gold robes would put him to death if they knew. It was a thought she tried not to dwell on, but it kept coming back to her time and time again.

After that first successful outing, Vianne began to relax, allowing them more time. The benefit to Kiran outweighed her reservations. Soon Kate was taking him out two or three times a week. Kiran quickly lost some of his paleness, until he finally looked more like a normal boy and less like a ghost. He started gaining weight and muscle, too, able to ride the trot for longer intervals without stopping to rest.

One day, Signe decided to come with them, needing a break from the castle and her chores making the black powder. Kate was glad to have her. When they'd first returned from Thornewall, Kate had finally had a chance to explain about the ruined doublet. It hadn't gone well. Rather than shout or rage, Signe had instead gone utterly, completely silent, as cold as the water in a frozen river. Kate apologized over and over again, realizing the doublet must've had some deep importance to her friend, but for more than a week Signe barely spoke to her. Slowly, though, it seemed time was healing the wound, as it did most.

"It's good to be out," Signe said as they rode along. "These revolvers are eating up all my time for fun."

"Why don't you just share the secret of how to make the black powder?"

Signe gave her a look sharp enough to cut glass. "Because of Seerah, Kate."

"The holy silence?" she asked, remembering the word.

With her lips pinched in a grim expression, Signe gave a solemn nod. "The secret of the black powder is the most important of any secret I hold. I will never share it. To die would be better."

Kate frowned. "How did you learn it in the first place? We both know you're not one of the Furen Mag."

Signe gave her a look that seemed to say, *Are you sure?* "Perhaps I stole it. To protect myself. There is no greater weapon than knowledge."

Kate glanced at her friend, suspecting another tall tale. "Protect from what?"

Signe flashed a smile, one full of teeth. "From the hobgoblins, of course." She turned her eyes on Kiran, who was listening intently from where he sat in front of Kate in the saddle. "They come at night to steal you from your bed, but if you can ask them a riddle they cannot solve, then they will spend all night trying to figure it out before vanishing at the first light of dawn."

"Hobgoblins?" Kiran said, sounding both scared and excited. "My ma says they're not real. Just stories."

"Oh yes, they're real. As real as the drakes of Rime," replied Signe.

Kate rolled her eyes. "Don't you believe her, Kiran. Signe likes making up stories."

Signe grinned. "Not everything I say is a story. But I like hiding the truth in embellishments. It's a skill we have perfected in the islands."

"I don't doubt it." Kate pointed a finger at her. "But someday I will get the truth out of you. It's only fair."

"I hope so. For it means we will still be friends when we are both old and covered in wrinkles, with gray hairs poking out on our chins."

Kiran made a noise of disgust at this, and both girls laughed.

Afterward, once they'd brought Kiran home and were heading back to Mirror Castle, Signe turned to Kate and said, "Something needs to be done for that boy. It is no kind of life he's living."

Swallowing, Kate dropped her gaze. She focused on the narrow space between Firedancer's ears, finding comfort in the view. "I know." It was a truth she was finding harder and harder to ignore with each passing day. Although Kiran was improving thanks to their rides, he needed more. So much more. Like friends his own age, and a chance to run and play, scrape his knees, and cause mischief.

"You should tell Corwin the truth, Kate, as Master Raith says."

Kate glanced at Signe, a thrill of nerves shooting down her legs at the idea. Still she resisted, the fear of how he would react holding her back, as always.

"The truth of what I am, Signe, it's like my version of your Seerah."

"I know." Signe gestured toward the sky with an upraised palm. "Better than you may guess." She swallowed, the cords in her throat flexing. "I once told a secret to a man I loved. One I thought loved me as well."

Kate went still, shocked to realize that Signe was telling her something about her past. Something true. She forced her mouth closed and waited for her to go on.

A wry smile crested Signe's lips for a moment. "It was the same man who once wore the doublet you took. I don't know why I kept it, other than to never forget the mistake I made."

And to never forget him, Kate guessed. She knew a thing or two about how hard it was to stop loving someone even when you should.

"I don't understand, though," Kate said. "If telling him the secret was a mistake, then why do you say I should risk the same with Corwin?"

"Because Corwin is a different man altogether," Signe said, regret and hurt shining in her pale eyes. "He knows what it means to lose someone. He knows what it means to regret. He will under-stand, or at least try to. He is loyal to those he loves. Like Dal. And like you, too. You just need to give him a chance."

"When he's had the chance to choose between me and his duty, I haven't fared so well."

Signe shot her a hard look. "He might not have earned your honesty, that's true. But sharing the secret of our true selves with another is always a risk, wilder or no. He might reject you, yes. But if he doesn't, then you will get to be yourself with him at last. You can't tell me that wouldn't be worth it." She paused long enough to shrug. "Besides, Kiran deserves a better life, and it's in Corwin's power to make it happen. That alone makes the risk worth taking. Take it for your brother, if not yourself."

"Bonner deserves better, too," Kate said. An ache went through her chest, a mixture of fear and hope. Could she do it? Did she dare?

"You deserve better, as well, Kate," Signe said, her expression now fierce. "You must be brave enough to take it."

ON THE MORNING OF THE second uror trial, Corwin woke early and made his way down to the stables. He'd barely slept all week, not since the start of the War Games. Dozens of dignitaries from all twelve Rimish cities were in the castle, keeping his presence in constant demand. He spent his days observing the games—mock battles, tournaments at arms, horse races, and so many other events, all done to celebrate the unification of Rime fifty years ago. It used to be his favorite time of year, and he wished more than ever that the high priestess had chosen to keep the games and the uror trial separate, if only so he could participate in the activities like he used to. By the end of each day, his mind was so overwrought that it took him hours to settle his thoughts enough to sleep, his body not tired enough to force the issue. Last night, however, had been the worst by far. What sleep he did get had been restless, full of strange dreams. Most of them involving an impossible black and white horse.

The uror colt nickered when Corwin arrived outside his stall door the following morning. He peered in at him, and he peered back, neck arched and ears pricked forward. Corwin stepped inside, and the colt retreated to the back of the stall, tossing his head and prancing in place. He'd had little handling, most of the grooms too afraid to do much more than lead him outside to graze.

Corwin cooed at the colt, slowly holding out his hand. "Easy, good fellow. What are you so nervous about this morning?"

The colt tossed his head again before reaching his long neck toward Corwin. His nostrils flared, and he snorted once. Corwin held still, letting the horse inspect him. A moment later, the soft, velvety muzzle brushed against his fingertips. Tingles slid up Corwin's arm at the touch. It might've been his imagination, but he didn't think so. Although the animal acted like an ordinary horse, he was anything but ordinary. Corwin stepped closer to the colt, running his hands down the sleek, muscled neck—the black side of him, although some of the white of his mane spilled over the top in striking contrast.

For a moment, Corwin remembered his dream. In it, he'd been riding the uror horse into battle, the two of them in perfect unity and focus as they faced a shadowy, unknown foe—thousands of faceless soldiers spilling onto the Rimish shore from red-sailed boats. Astride the uror stallion, though, he hadn't been afraid. Just determined, exhilarated at the fight and the victory waiting within his grasp.

Nothing at all like he felt right now, with the second trial looming. Yesterday, he'd been given a glimpse of what it would entail—a maze. A maze in the sky.

It didn't resemble the second trial his grandfather had gone through in the slightest. That seemed easy by contrast—a hunt through Jade Forest after some mythical creature Borwin never quite got around to describing. *Even if it had been invisible, it would've been easier than this,* Corwin thought when he first saw those raised stone platforms. His eyes hadn't been able to make sense of it. It shouldn't be possible. More than a hundred boulders hung suspended over the training field, some close together and others far apart. There were stones with stairs leading up, some with stairs leading down, some spiraled and some straight. There were stones with holes in their centers, ones that slowly revolved. At the very top, on a narrow platform, rested a jeweled crown on a mirrored pedestal. The goal was simple: reach the top and seize the crown.

Getting there, however, would be anything but simple.

Sighing, Corwin ran his hand down the uror colt's nose. "If I only knew how to fly, it would be easy," he said.

"Is his highness worried about the trial?"

The voice gave both Corwin and the colt a start. The horse stamped all four feet on the ground, just missing Corwin's toes before he wheeled around, retreating to the far corner of the enclosure again.

Taking a breath to calm his racing heart, Corwin stepped out of the stall and gave the newcomer a stiff smile, surprised but not disappointed to see it was Minister Rendborne. Corwin cleared his throat. "That depends. Are you bearing another helpful journal, one with a map to the top perhaps?"

The master of trade let out a theatrical sigh. "I'm afraid not. I did see a drawing for a flying contraption inside one of my books, but it was written by a man called Melchor the Mad. I didn't think you would find such a person worthy of trust."

"You're probably right. I don't believe mortal man was ever meant to ascend such heights, mad or otherwise."

Rendborne laughed, and the sound immediately set Corwin at

ease. "Too right you are, but that is why there are gods involved."

"Gods or magic?" Corwin asked, arching an eyebrow. Dal had planted the idea in his mind when the two of them first saw the hanging stones. *"Looks like something a wilder could do, doesn't it?"* Dal had said. *"An earthist or an aerist. Maybe both."*

Although Corwin had meant the question to be rhetorical, Rendborne replied, "Is there any difference?" He gestured with his right hand, palm up so that the glow from his magestone ring shone against the floor.

Corwin blinked, taken aback. It sounded like blasphemy, except the man had a point. Of all the things he'd seen since the uror began, nearly all of it could've been accomplished by magic, both wilder and magist. The mist atop the Asterion could've been a water gift. The illusions, nothing more than magist spells. He supposed even the visions of his father and the Sevan soldier could've been summoned with some form of spirit magic. He glanced back at the stall. *All known magic except for the uror sign.*

Rendborne seemed to be thinking along the same lines, for he said, "Did you know that my predecessor once received an offer to buy your father's uror sign?"

Corwin swung his gaze back to the man. "You're joking."

"Indeed not." A look of disgust crossed Rendborne's face. "It was a wealthy merchant from Endra. He offered a king's ransom in gold and jewels."

"But why?" Corwin pictured Murr, trying to fathom what someone would do with a live wolf, one who obeyed only his father.

"I expect it was for the same reason my clerks receive ten missives a day from foreign merchants requesting permission to trade with the League for their spells and trinkets. There's an entire world out there, and yet all the magic resides in Rime." Rendborne motioned to the horse. "And that animal there is pure magic. There are people who would kill for it."

The thought chilled Corwin. He didn't see what possessing an uror would do for anyone, but he could see a dozen reasons why the enemies of Rime would want it dead, the Godking of Seva most of all. It was a sign, a symbol of Norgard's power and might. The thought brought a new and troubling possibility to mind. "I wonder what would happen if an uror sign died before the trial ended."

"It's happened once before," Rendborne replied, matter-of-fact. "But in that case, it was an heir who killed it, making the outcome obvious. The innocent brother was named king and the killer became the Nameless One."

Corwin inhaled his shock. "I've never heard that before. About the killing, I mean. But you must be talking about the brother of Morwen, son of Rowan. My great-great-granduncle." The title was used in all the texts he'd read about the two brothers.

"The very same. I'm not surprised you haven't heard it before." Rendborne made a dismissive gesture. "I only know the story because I've an obscene fondness of reading. The master of trade's private archives are half the reason I petitioned for the job. But I doubt it's a tale the high priestess wants told. Especially not to the heirs during the uror trial."

"Yes, I suppose that's prudent." Corwin glanced at the uror sign, somewhat unsurprised to find the horse watching him. He'd never seen anything more beautiful. The idea of someone killing him turned his stomach. Forcing his gaze back to Rendborne, Corwin decided it was time to change the subject.

"What brings you down to the stables this morning?" he asked. "If not to offer me more books."

Rendborne rolled his golden eyes. "I need to speak to Master Cade. It seems Lord Nevan of Andreas wishes to make a trade for a dozen warhorses."

"I see." Corwin pressed his lips together, holding back a grin. "And here I'd thought maybe Maestra Vikas was lurking about."

"Yes, well, not this time." Rendborne gave a fake cough, his hand rising unconsciously to the necklace of talons he wore, eight of them hung from a silver chain around his neck. "Thank you for your discretion on that matter. It's . . . ah . . . appreciated."

Corwin grinned in earnest now, amused by the man's discomfort, but in a friendly way. "Of course. What's life without a few secrets?"

Rendborne returned the grin. "Indeed. But I must be off. Good luck today, your highness."

Corwin watched him go, then returned his attention to the uror colt. He debated lingering awhile longer with him, then decided he'd rather find Kate. But when he arrived at Firedancer's stall, there was no sign of her. It didn't surprise him, not with how busy and crowded the castle had been all week, but he couldn't help the disappointment he felt.

A few minutes later, a page arrived, summoning him to the training field. Today marked the last of day of the War Games, comprised of individual event finals—archery, tent pegging, rings, and mounted swordplay. Corwin's presence was required on the main stage, not to witness the winners but to be ready to start the uror trial once the trophies had been given. The high priestess had decided the trial would make for a memorable way to end the event. If not for the uror, Corwin would've been out on the field right now competing instead of watching.

As it was, he found the rounds not half as interesting as when Kate had done her Relay trial back in Farhold. Instead, his gaze kept drifting to the stone maze hovering above the training field. He did his best to study it, trying to visualize the path he would take to reach the top. Sitting beside him on the stage, he saw Edwin doing the same, neither brother speaking as the hours wore on toward midday and the start of the trial.

Finally, the competition concluded, and the priestesses arrived to escort Corwin and Edwin onto the training field, where two small tents had been erected near the maze. With a crowd of courtiers and nobles from all the twelve cities gathered around, the high priestess spoke to the princes briefly, then waved them each into a tent with a suggestion that they spend the remaining time in prayer.

At least I get to stay clothed this time, Corwin told himself, but that offered little comfort in the isolation inside the tent. He did make a feeble attempt to pray, but the sound of voices outside kept interfering. Giving up, he sat down to wait it out, only to surge to his feet a moment later when the back side of the tent rose up and a figure slid beneath it.

"Kate," he said, surprise raising the tenor of his voice. He lowered it at once, taking in her nervous look. "What are you doing here?"

She crossed her arms in front of her, then dropped them to her sides. "I just wanted to wish you good luck."

"Will you be watching, then?" The question was absurd, and he knew it as soon as he said it.

A slow smile crossed her face. "Someone has to heckle you. Who better than me?"

He grinned at that, remembering the game of insults they used to play during their many races and mock battles.

Kate pressed her lips together. "Will you . . . meet me in my quarters afterward? There's something I need to tell you."

Curiosity at what it could be sent a flutter through Corwin's stomach. "Of course. That is, if I survive the climb." He forced a smile, but Kate didn't return it.

"You will win this day," she said, holding him with a fierce gaze. "The uror selects only the worthy, and you are worthy, Corwin."

Before he could reply, Kate turned and disappeared beneath the tent, leaving him alone once more. But her words lingered. *You will win.*

He didn't know if that was true, but for the first time he thought maybe he wanted it to be.

Mounting the first platform was easy, but with a single glance sky-ward, Corwin knew it would be the only one that was. He could see Edwin far across from him, standing on his own platform, head tilted back toward the maze above.

The two princes waited for the horn blast that would signal the start. Corwin flinched at the loud noise when it came, the nervous energy inside him igniting like oil in a torch. Channeling it, he ran toward the nearest platform above and jumped, just making it. *One down, a million to go.*

Or so it seemed. The next two were much the same as the first, but from there, several options awaited his selection. He chose the nearest one—the obvious choice—but the moment he jumped onto the platform, it immediately began to drop toward the ground. Cursing, Corwin spun and leaped back to the one he'd been on before, just barely making it across. The sinking stone continued falling all the way to the ground, landing with a soft thud against the grass. Below him, the crowd let out a collective murmur of surprise.

Wiping his brow, Corwin studied the remaining two options, both within reach but farther away than the sinking stone had been. He decided on the harder one this time, assuming that had been the point of his failure with the last one. He leaped for it, barely managing to grab the edge, but at least the stone held true this time.

Moving on, he was more careful in his decisions, not automatically selecting the easiest path. The one time he did, the platform shifted out of place the moment he stepped on it, forcing him to retreat once more.

But the choices weren't always so obvious. A short while later he selected a platform that began to spin the moment he touched down on it, moving with such force that he was thrown off his feet.

By the time he managed to stand, he was so dizzy he could barely see where to go next, until finally he leaped for another platform at random. This one thankfully didn't move. It had a single spiraling staircase rising up out of its center. He climbed it, painfully aware of how far down the ground now was.

Reaching the top, he took a moment to gain his bearings. Far across from him, he saw Edwin standing several feet above him, farther along in the maze. Corwin needed to hurry. But when he surveyed his options, he discovered the only way up was to go down, first to a small, circular platform and then up to a larger one shaped like the head of an ax. He went for it, doing his best to ignore Edwin's progress, lest it goad him into making a mistake.

The higher Corwin went, the harder and stranger the maze became. Halfway to the top, all the stones began to move. Some of them rose, some sank. Others spun in circles while yet others would randomly appear, then disappear. He spent several minutes watching the stones, searching for a pattern in their movement. There was one, but it was so complicated he had a hard time keeping it straight in his mind as he jumped.

Two moves later, he forgot the pattern entirely when he stepped onto a stationary platform only to have the world flip upside down. Or maybe he flipped upside down. He couldn't be sure. All he knew was the ground was above him and the sky below. He stood there, unable to move for the certainty that the power holding him would break and he would fall to his death. His breath came in hard pants and sweat ran up his face into his hair.

Far, far below him, he saw the people still standing on the training field. He heard their shouts, muffled and distant.

"You've got to move, Corwin," he said aloud. The wind pulled at his words. "You've got to *move*," he repeated, more firmly. Then, closing his eyes, he forced a single foot forward. He didn't fall, just stepped nearer the edge of the platform, although he remained upside down.

Leaving his eyes open this time, he stepped again. To his surprise, the movement felt normal despite the view, and before long he was able to reach the edge. At first there seemed nowhere to go. He couldn't be sure the nearest platform would be upside down like this one. What if it was right side up?

This is a leap of faith, he realized. A test sure as any other.

Holding his breath, Corwin jumped. The world righted as he flew through the air, and he shouted in alarm, jarred by the movement. He clenched, drawing his legs to his chest instead of reaching out to grab the platform ahead. Realizing his mistake, he tried to correct it but was too late. His fingers brushed the edge but found no purchase. Air rushed around him as he fell, too terrified to scream.

A moment later he was saved by mere chance when one of the disappearing stones reappeared beneath him. He scrambled up at once, guessing he had only seconds before the stone disappeared again. He raced to the edge and leaped to the next just in time to avoid another fall.

He ended up farther down than when he'd started and was forced to do the entire sequence again. At least it was easier this time. When it came to jumping off the inverted platform, Corwin forced himself to commit fully to the jump and managed to grab the other platform with relative ease.

He continued on, growing more confident despite the challenges. This was a test of the mind as much as the body. He just needed to remember that.

When he finally reached the top, he turned in a circle, searching for the platform with the crown. To his surprise, it hovered below him, a few dozen feet away, with half a dozen stones in between. Far across from him, he saw Edwin pull himself up onto a platform of similar height—his brother must've encountered his own set of troubles. They stared at one another, both sizing up the distance between them and the crown—a single crown, for a single winner.

For a moment, Corwin hesitated, all the reasons he should let Edwin win tumbling through his mind. But then he heard Kate's parting words once more: *You are worthy.*

A rush soared through him, spurring him onward. He raced forward, leaping across the stones without thought or speculation. Some of the stones fell the moment his foot pressed down on them, but he had enough force to clear the edge and make it to the next one.

The crown platform waited just below, and Corwin launched himself toward it, falling into a tumble as he landed to soften the impact. Edwin appeared on the opposite side, half a second behind. But that was all the time Corwin needed to get there first. His hands closed around the crown, and a moment later he slid it onto his head.

The moment it was in place, all the stones save the one the princes stood on vanished. For a moment, it was just the two of them in all the world, suspended in the air—one a victor and one not. Then, slowly, the platform began to lower toward the ground. Edwin watched Corwin the entire time, his gaze severe and his lips set in a thin line like the sharp edge of a razor.

When they reached the ground, Edwin bowed his head. "Enjoy your triumph while it lasts, brother. For I promise that in the end, you will not wear the crown."

The bitterness in Edwin's tone made Corwin flinch. He was accustomed to his brother's jealousy and resentment, but this felt like something more. The uror mark on Corwin's palm began to prickle, and he resisted the urge to rub the scarred skin.

Before he could respond, the crowd converged around them. The people were shouting Corwin's name. They reached out to touch him, to lift him up. Corwin searched the crowd, looking for Kate. As always, he found her. She watched him from afar, one hand lingering near her lips, as if the smile she wore needed to be contained. He remembered his promise to meet her afterward. *I have something to tell you,* she had said.

I have something to tell you, too, he thought, remembering the words she'd said that night in her room: *You're the high prince and might be the high king. The world will answer to you.*

It was something he should've said a long time ago, but he'd been too afraid. Not now. Now he thought he might be brave enough to say it to the entire world.

KATE WAITED IN THE MAIN room of her quarters, her heart beating somewhere near her throat. It had been that way ever since she'd snuck into Corwin's tent and asked him to meet her here. In the hour she'd been waiting for him, she'd considered disappearing at least half a dozen times. She resisted, willing herself to be brave. After seeing what Corwin had gone through during the trial, she felt she could do it. Even if sitting here, waiting to tell him the truth about her magic, felt harder than climbing an impossible maze in the sky.

As the minutes slid by, she reminded herself of all the reasons why she had to tell him the truth. She had to do it for Kiran and for Bonner, for Vianne and Anise, and for the wilders who met at the Sacred Sword, all of them restless with the need for change.

I must do it for myself. That, more than anything, gave her the strength to see it through. She was tired of hiding, tired of lies and secrets. Yes, she was a wilder, but that didn't make her less. It didn't make her deserving of such fear and hate. She deserved to be who she was meant to be without judgment and condemnation.

When the knock finally sounded, Kate jumped out of her chair with a jerky movement. Fumbling, she reached for the door and pulled it open. Corwin waited beyond, a nervous smile on his lips.

"May I come in?" he asked after a moment.

Realizing she'd been silent and staring, she stepped back and motioned him through. The moment she pulled the door closed behind her, Corwin took her hand in his. He ran a thumb over the top of her hand, his eyes lowered to the place where their skin met. She froze, uncertain about the touch and the intimacy in his gaze.

"I know you have something to tell me, Kate," he said in a voice not much more than a whisper, "but there's something I must tell you first."

Her breath turned shallow. "What is it?"

Slowly, he raised his eyes to hers, ice like always, and yet blazing. She wanted to step back, frightened by the intensity of his stare, but tension threaded the air between them like strands in a web, holding her in place.

He exhaled and said, "I love you, Kate."

The words hung in the air, as if caught by the same webbing. Kate stared back at him, too stunned to speak or move at all. They weren't empty words. This was truth, naked and heavy and free.

"I always have," he continued, holding her gaze with his, unwavering. "Since we were kids, and even more now that you've come back into my life. You've refused to be my paramour, and rightly so. I was a fool for even thinking it. You deserve better. You deserve everything you want and more. And I want to give it to you. I finally see the truth you tried to tell me from the start, that the choice is in my grasp. For a while I convinced myself that to be right I had to always follow the path set before me. But I'm learning that's not true. There is a time to obey, yes, but also a time to make our own rules."

He paused, as if aware he was starting to ramble. Then he gripped her hand tighter and said, "If I win the uror, I will become king and will decree my own fate. If I lose, I will choose it. Either way, I will choose you. Always." He paused. "That is, if you'll have me."

Kate felt her mouth fall open. She hadn't expected this. She might've wished for it, both back then and maybe even now, but she never expected it. She wondered at the change she'd sensed in him these last few weeks. Perhaps this was the outcome, a slow awakening to the truth. She didn't know, and at the moment she didn't care.

She took a step nearer to him, her heart and body demanding a response. She started to reach for him—then pulled back, remembering her own purpose here, the truth that remained veiled between them. She couldn't be certain he would still feel this way once he knew. All the harsh, stark memories of how he'd reacted to his mother's death pressed against her thoughts now, and a shiver raced down her spine.

At her silence, Corwin's hopeful smile faded away, the pain of rejection filling his gaze. "Have you nothing to say?" he asked gently.

She cleared her throat, weighing her words carefully. "I'm glad you're seeing the truth, but I still haven't told you what I need to. It might have some bearing."

"What is it, Kate?"

"Perhaps . . . perhaps you should sit." She motioned to the chair in front of her father's desk.

Corwin frowned, worry furrowing his brow. "Why are you afraid?"

"Please, Corwin. Sit down. It will be easier. For me."

His frown deepened as he sank onto the chair. She gazed at him for several seconds, battling her fear. *If he reacts badly, I can use my sway on him,* she told herself, but the idea repulsed her. *Sweet goddess, don't let it come to that.*

"What I'm about to tell you might be . . . shocking, to say the least," she began. "It's a secret I've kept all my life, trusting it only to a very few. And now I'm going to trust it to you."

Corwin leaned forward, his body tense and his expression mixed. She saw curiosity there, but also hurt. "What is it?"

"First, will you swear not to react right away, but to think about it with an open mind?" This would be the truest test to see if the change in him was real—if he truly believed that sometimes new rules needed to be made and old ones broken.

In answer, Corwin reached for her hands, folding them in his. She felt the scar of his uror mark, warm against her skin. "I swear it on both hands."

Kate nodded, but still she couldn't go through with it, the years of secrecy working against her. But then she fixed Kiran's face in her mind, drawing the strength she needed from it.

"I'm a wilder, Corwin. I have a spirit gift."

He went still. Utterly. Completely. Even his breathing halted. Kate felt her own breath double, her heart racing. Desperately she wished to take it back, but there was no doing that now.

Corwin let go of her hands and leaned back in the chair. Kate braced, already feeling the pain of his rejection. Slowly, he turned his head toward the window. A faraway look crossed his face, the expression of a man lost in thoughts and memories.

Then just as slowly he turned back to her, not quite meeting her gaze. "It's animals, isn't it? You can speak to them, control them."

"Yes," Kate said, barely able to respond for the coldness in his voice. "How . . . how do you know?"

He raised a finger to his chin, tracing the scar there. "I saw you use it." He nodded again, answering his own question. "On the road to Andreas when you saved me from the daydrakes. I didn't remember until now, but your horse did things no horse should do. It listened to your commands almost as if it were human."

"Yes, that's right," Kate said, trying to find reassurance that so far he was keeping his promise not to react. He seemed calm enough and hadn't yet shouted for the gold robes to come arrest her. She saw no reason not to go on with the rest of it. He might not be able to love her as a wilder, but at least he would know the truth of who she was. She refused to settle for less now.

In a steadier voice, she said, "My gift allows me to speak mind to mind with animals and even with people. Although I didn't know about that last part until recently."

Corwin's gaze sharpened, and for a second she saw fear there—and also the old hate, like she'd seen hundreds of times after his mother's death. She couldn't blame him the fear. She feared her power too, both what she could do with it if she chose and what someone else with the same gift could do to her—if they chose.

It's always a choice, to do right or wrong, no matter the power.

Emboldened by this truth, Kate said, "What I can do isn't evil, Corwin. I've never hurt anyone and I never will. It's simply a part of me. An ability I've always had. Ever since I was a child." For a second she considered expanding the argument, to tell him that no wilder was evil by birth. That it was always either choice or circumstance. But she didn't think it wise to press him.

Several seconds passed, the silence oppressive. Then finally, a wry, uncertain smile crossed his lips. "No wonder you were always so much better with the horses than me."

Kate didn't know what to think now, uncertain if he was teasing or being sarcastic. She hoped for the former. She wrinkled her nose, trying to keep things light. "I'll admit, I did use it to my advantage from time to time."

"Why didn't you tell me before now?" Corwin said, and this time she heard the bite in his tone.

She let go a weary sigh. "Can you really not guess my reasons? Wilders have always been hated and feared, even before the Inquisition. My father made me swear never to tell anyone. From the first moment I learned what I could do, he warned me of the risk." She paused, sensing the uncertainty in Corwin now. He seemed to be walking a tightrope, teetering between acceptance and rejection. Desperately, she reached for a way to push him where she needed him to go. *Remember Kiran,* she told herself.

"I've wanted to tell you the truth for weeks now," she went on, "ever since we found those drakes in the Wandering Woods."

Confusion furrowed Corwin's brow. "Why only then, when you had so much time before?"

She ignored the underlying accusation in his words. "Something was wrong that day, Corwin." She launched into the story, telling him everything: about how her magic had been sealed off, then later how she'd used her ability to control the drakes at Thornewall. If he could just see the usefulness of wilder magic. The ways it could be used for good, if given the chance.

Corwin took it all in with an expression that wavered between disbelief and awe. "You controlled all the drakes?"

"Yes, but only because of how their minds work. I've never felt anything like it before," Kate replied. "But then again, up until a few weeks ago I used my magic on horses only, and only when it was certain no one would be able to tell. My father ingrained that lesson in my mind so deeply, I didn't think I would ever be able to break it."

"Your father." Corwin's eyes widened. "He had the same ability, didn't he?"

"Yes," Kate said, and she flinched backward as Corwin suddenly rose to his feet in a jerky motion.

Again she braced for an explosion, but he only wheeled about and walked over to the window, bracing himself against the frame. She waited where she was, giving him time to sort through his feelings.

At last, Corwin faced her once more, his eyes bright. "You said this magic works on people, too. Does that mean your father might've used it on mine? That he caused his illness with his sway?"

Kate felt the color drain from her cheeks at the thought. A few weeks ago she would've denied it, would've been furious at the insinuation. But now, after all that had happened—both what she herself had learned to do and what she had experienced with that wilder in Thornewall—she couldn't deny it so easily.

"I don't know, Corwin," she said finally. "I don't think he would've done anything like that, and even if he had, I don't know how it would've worked."

Corwin nodded, one finger worrying at the scar on his chin again.

Kate took a step toward him, her muscles so tense she thought they might snap at every movement. "But I did find out what he was doing at the Sacred Sword."

"You did? What was it?"

"He—" She stopped herself just in time, feeling a flicker of heat pass over her skin. The curse. It was still on her. She couldn't tell him about Kiran or the Rising or anything else she'd learned that day.

Kate shook her head. "I'm sorry, but I can't tell you. There's magic involved. I was sworn to secrecy with a magist curse."

Corwin pressed his lips together, hands curling into fists.

"Believe me, Corwin, I want to tell you, but I can't. Not now. Master Raith will have to—"

"Raith is involved?" Corwin's body went rigid. "Of course he is."

Kate raised her hands, trying to calm him. "Yes, but he'll be able to tell you everything once he's back from Penlocke."

Corwin glared down at her, his anger finally arriving, if in a different form than she'd anticipated. "Does this secret concern what happened to my father?"

Kate bit her lip, unsure how to respond, how much was safe to share. She'd never expected the conversation to turn this way. "I can't answer that, but you've got to trust me when I say that no one knows what happened that night between my father and yours. Not me and not Raith either. I wish we did, but we don't."

A muscle ticked in Corwin's jaw. "How can I trust you, Kate? When you've kept such things from me all this time?"

"That's not fair, Corwin. You know it's not. Wilders are put to death just for being who we are. We're hunted like animals." Tears burned in her eyes, all the agony she felt for Kiran and Bonner, for herself, rising to the surface. "But wilder or no, I'm still the same Kate I've always been. I'm still me."

Corwin dropped his gaze, as if he couldn't bear the sight of her. He examined the uror mark on his palm, tracing it with a finger. Then, finally, he looked up again, the anger gone from his gaze, his expression solemn.

"You're right. I can see you had no choice. But you've got to understand how this looks, knowing your father could do what you can. There's no telling what—" Corwin broke off, his features slackening into surprise. Then a wild, eager look rose in his eyes. "But what you're saying isn't true. Someone does know what happened."

"Who?"

"My father. He was there. He saw everything."

"Well, yes, Corwin," Kate said, uncertain, "but King Orwin's not well in the mind. You said it yourself."

"Yes, I did." He gestured at her. "But you've the power to enter minds. To read the thoughts of people."

The realization struck Kate like lightning, too shocking to fully comprehend.

"Can you do it?" Corwin said, his reservations about what she could do forgotten for the moment.

"I don't know." Her mind spun, just as caught up in the idea. Could it really be that simple? The key to unlocking the mystery, nothing more than using her magic? She nodded to herself, hope filling her like air. "But I'm willing to try."

"All right," Corwin said, a slight tremor in his voice and his blue eyes suddenly ablaze. "Let's do it, then. Maybe we can put this mystery to rest once and forever."

"Yes," Kate said, telling herself not to mistake his willingness here as acceptance. But perhaps it was a start. Even if it wasn't, even if he turned on her later, at least she had this chance to find the truth at last. That made the risk worth it.

THE KING'S CHAMBERS REEKED OF his sickness, a cloying, putrid smell that Kate could almost taste on the back of her tongue. The king himself sat in a cushioned armchair next to the window, his dull gaze fixed on some random point outside. Pale light beyond heralded the approach of night. She would have to hurry before her magic faded and they lost the chance. As it was, her nerves crackled beneath her skin with the worry that they would be discovered at any moment.

Or that Corwin might suddenly change his mind and call for the golds. In the long walk over here, they'd shared only silence, and he'd not touched her once, not even an accidental brush of his arm against hers as they moved side by side down the corridors.

"Good evening, father," Corwin said, coming to stand just behind the king.

When Orwin didn't respond, he motioned to Kate. "Do . . . whatever it is you need to do. We've only a few minutes before the servants come with his supper and before I must make an appearance at the banquet."

Kate nodded, too tense to speak. It wasn't just the idea of invading the king's mind, but also of letting Corwin watch. She felt as if she stood here naked, all of her laid bare before him for the first time, and without the reassurance of the love he'd confessed earlier. His acceptance now was uneasy at best.

Carefully not looking at Corwin, Kate reached out to King Orwin, her stomach clenched in both pity and revulsion at the worn, sickly look of him. This was not the man she'd known. She'd once thought Corwin's description of his illness was a son's despairing exaggeration, but she could see now it wasn't. Not at all. *Something is wrong here.* She felt it, the same way she'd felt the wrongness in the Wandering Woods that day, in the minds of the drakes.

Steeling her courage, Kate laid her palm against the king's shoulder. Then she closed her eyes and reached out to him with her magic. The moment she touched his mind, she knew it was a mistake. She felt the spell close in around her, a trap that had been set for her—or others like her.

Like my father.

She opened her eyes just long enough to see the brightening glow on the magestone around King Orwin's neck, the way it pulsed a warning—sending out an alarm to whoever had created the spell in it and given it to the king.

Kate tried to break away, but it was too late. The magic held her in its grasp. Then against her will she felt thoughts and memories and feelings pouring into her, like a floodgate at the moment of breaking. It was too much, too strong, King Orwin's mind a broken vessel. She felt her own mind being drawn into his until she was seeing the world through his eyes and the slant of his memory. Corwin and the room vanished away as time slowed and Kate slipped into the past. . . .

IT'S EARLY, DAWN just breaking over the horizon. Orwin lies in his bed, wakeful still as he has been all night. Sleep rarely comes for him anymore. Not now that he sleeps alone, his wife dead for nearly a year.

He hears the footsteps long before the knock sounds on the door. It's Hale. He knows it before he calls for entrance. Hale has come to continue the argument from last night, to try to plead against the Inquisition, but Orwin won't hear of it. The Inquisition is right. It's just. The wilders must be stopped. It is as Master Storr claims—the crown must protect the people from the dangers wilders pose. Even children can do great harm. The wilder who set the fire in the market that day was just a boy, and yet he was responsible for so much destruction, pain, and suffering— all of it inflicted on the innocent, those incapable of defending themselves against such power.

Like his poor Imogen. Even now he hears the sound of her death cries, the pitiful, labored breathing. It haunts his sleep, his soul.

Hale enters, bowing before his king and friend. "Please, Orwin. You must reconsider. This isn't right. Too much can go wrong. It gives the League too much power, which is just what Storr wants."

"I am not concerned with Storr and his ambitions," Orwin says. "In this, he and I are agreed. We are determined to eradicate this wild magic from our land once and for all. Only then can we live in peace, knowing our children, our wives, are safe."

"What about those who never do harm? Who want to live in peace as well? There are innocents among them."

Orwin grits his teeth, refusing to hear. "But they still possess a power that no shield can block, no sword cut down."

"Pistols can't be stopped with a shield or armor either. Yet we allow them."

"Those weapons can be taken away. These cannot."

"Yes, but we don't take them away until they've been used for harm. Not before."

Orwin answers with a glare, done with words.

Hale looks away, shaking his head reluctantly in defeat. When he raises his gaze, Orwin feels a pressure building in his temple. It's foreign, alien, an outside force, like the power of a mage spell.

"I'm sorry, my king," Hale says, and his voice seems to be inside Orwin's head. "I can't let this happen. Please forgive me. I would never force your will if there were any other choice."

"What do you—"

Hale raises his hand and touches Orwin's forehead. Pain explodes inside Orwin's skull, and he screams, feeling ripped asunder.

Hale stumbles backward, and his expression turns fearful. He gapes in horror. "What magic is this?"

Orwin doesn't answer. Stooped over, he cradles his

aching skull. Hands touch his shoulders, pushing him upright.

Hale grabs for the king's neck, and his fingers close around the glowing stone at Orwin's throat. "Where did you get this?"

Orwin doesn't answer. He has no memory of the stone or its purpose.

Cursing, Hale yanks the stone free of Orwin's neck. But he grips it too hard, breaking the stone. The magic oozes out from it in a gray, oily mist. It slithers upward, sliding into Orwin's nose, his mouth, his ears. Hale cries out, trying to stop it, but such formless power can't be stopped.

Orwin feels the magic inside him, writhing like something alive. It's in his head, the pressure building. He claws at the sides of his face now. But then his mind shatters, his vision fragmented, like staring into a broken mirror.

"My king, my king," Hale says, trying in vain to help. "What have I done? I didn't know. I didn't. I would—"

Senseless and no longer in control, a murderous rage explodes inside Orwin. Screaming, he lunges for the dagger at Hale's side. Pulling it free, Orwin moves to strike, but Hale raises his hands in time to stop the blow. The two men struggle. A small part of Orwin understands what's happening—that he's no longer in control of himself. Something has pushed him aside and taken over. He can't stop it, even though he wants to. The rest of him is determined to kill the man before him.

But Hale has always been stronger. He gains control of the dagger, but Orwin is frantic with the rage pulsing inside him. The dagger shifts, the blade turning downward. And then it plunges, sinking deep into Orwin's thigh.

"Oh gods, Orwin," Hale says.

Orwin screams again just as the door opens and Corwin rushes inside. "Father!" . . .

Without warning, the memory broke and Kate was hurled from Orwin's mind back into her own. Gasping, she bent over and grabbed her head, the inside of her skull aching with the memory of what Orwin had suffered. What he suffered still.

"Kate? Are you all right? What happened?" Corwin's hands slid around her shoulders, warm and steadying.

"Magic," she said. "The magestone around his neck. It was a trap." She looked up at Corwin, the truth expanding in her mind like clouds parting to reveal the sky. "Someone knew what my father was going to try, only the magic went wrong. It infected your father and—" She broke off, her gaze flicking to the magestone King Orwin wore. She remembered the alarm she'd sensed when she first touched his mind. She turned back to Corwin. "We've got to get out—"

The door across from them burst open, and three people rushed inside—Maestra Vikas, Prince Edwin, and Grand Master Storr.

"You!" Kate screamed, the king's memory fresh in her mind. Storr had planted the idea in Orwin's head, nurtured it. He was the most powerful magist in the kingdom. "You did this. You killed my father." He might not have wielded the ax, but he'd set the trap.

"What's going on here?" Edwin demanded, his gaze flashing from Kate to Master Storr, then to Corwin.

"Wilder!" Maestra Vikas cried. "Just like I said."

The maestra raised her mace toward Kate, a magestone starting to glow. The spell erupted out from it, soared through the air, and struck Kate with the force of a battering ram. It lifted her off her feet and threw her down. Her head cracked against the floor and a starburst lit her vision, blinding her. Then darkness set in, absolute and inescapable.

PART THREE

The Rising

"KATE!" CORWIN CRIED, RUSHING TO where she'd fallen. He glared over at Maestra Vikas. "What did you do?"

"Step away from her, your highness," Vikas replied coolly. "She is a wilder, I'm certain of it."

It was true, Corwin knew it beyond doubt, and yet this woman was head of the gold order. He couldn't just hand Kate over to her. "What are you talking about? This is madness."

"Is it?" Vikas approached and reached toward Kate. Corwin tried to push her away, but the maestra moved as quickly as a snake striking. She pulled on the leather cord Kate had been wearing about her neck, revealing the glowing diamond that had been hidden beneath her shirt.

Vikas stood and held up the magestone necklace for all to see. "Then how do you explain this?"

"It's a magestone," Corwin said, scowling. "Made with mage magic, not a wilder's."

Ignoring him, Vikas turned to Storr. "This is what I warned you about, grand master. It's a spell designed to *hide* wilder magic."

Storr stared at it, frowning. Corwin remembered Kate's shouted accusation that the grand master had killed her father. *Someone set a trap,* she'd also said. Someone had known Hale would try to use his sway to change King Orwin's mind about the Inquisition—and

Storr had been behind it from the beginning. *But would he go so far as to manipulate my father?*

Yes. A hundred times yes.

And yet Corwin couldn't understand it. What did the grand master gain by the Inquisition? There had to be something. Corwin had never seen Storr do anything that wasn't politically motivated.

"I've never seen a spell like this," Storr said, taking the magestone from Vikas and examining it. He sounded genuinely puzzled—vexed even. He glanced at Corwin, then turned to Edwin, his expression now grave. "It's treason to harbor a wilder, your highness."

Corwin drew a sharp breath. *Treason.* The notion was absurd, ridiculous—and yet true, according to the law.

Edwin stared at the grand master, his expression torn. His eyes flicked to Kate, then up to Corwin. "Did you know it, brother? What she *is*?"

A chill crept down Corwin's spine at the disbelief in Edwin's voice and the betrayal already rising in his expression. "Kate isn't a criminal, Edwin. No matter what they say."

Anger steadied Edwin's voice. "I didn't ask if she is a criminal but if she is a wilder. And if you *knew*."

"She's not a wilder," Corwin said, embracing the lie to protect Kate from the hatred he sensed in Edwin. One that had been there since the day their mother died. "She is innocent."

"You're lying, Corwin. You forget how well I know you. You can't lie to me." Edwin cut his eyes to Master Storr. "What happens now?"

"Knowingly harboring a wilder is treason, as I said."

Corwin's hands clenched into fists. "You can't be serious. I'm the high prince and nothing happened here." He gestured to his father, who had remained as still and silent as ever.

Vikas shook her head, a cold glint in her gray eyes. "Your rank doesn't matter, your highness. Not here. Not in this." She took a step toward him. "You are under arrest, Prince Corwin, for willfully harboring a wilder and allowing that wilder to use magic against the high king."

Corwin held his ground, his gaze fixed on the mace in the maestra's hands. "We're in the middle of an uror." He waved at Edwin. "Help me. I'm your brother. You can't let them do this."

For a second, doubt flicked across Edwin's face. But just as quickly it was gone. He folded his arms over his chest and shook his head. "As you said, Corwin, I'm not the high king. Not yet."

Corwin flinched at having his words thrown back at him. For a moment, he considered fighting his way free. But he'd brought no weapons with him, and he'd already seen how effective Vikas could be with her mace. He couldn't fight this. Not here. Not yet. *The charges won't stand,* he told himself, *not once the council and the high priestess have their say.* The uror trial must be completed—the laws of man could not interfere with the laws of the gods.

Corwin raised his hands in surrender and stepped away from Kate. A few minutes later, he was being escorted back to his quarters by a pair of guards and a gold robe Vikas had summoned.

"What will happen to Kate?" Corwin asked the gold master magist.

"The same that happens to all wilders, once caught," the man replied. Although the full mask he wore hid his expression, there was no mistaking the satisfaction in his voice. Flakes of ice seemed to slither down Corwin's back. The golds would take her to their house outside the city to perform the Purging, same as they did with any wilder. He didn't know what all it involved, but the word conjured gruesome images in his mind. Afterward, the golds would put her to death and bury her body in an unmarked grave as a final act of condemnation.

With panic bubbling up inside his chest, Corwin eyed the pistol hanging on the belt of the guard in front of him. It wasn't a revolver, but the single shot might be enough for him to escape. Only once again he remembered the power Maestra Vikas had demonstrated. The gold carried his mace in hand, ready to use at the first sign of resistance.

Taking a deep breath, Corwin pushed the urge to fight aside. The time would come to escape. He just needed to wait for it.

And wait he did. For two whole days.

The silence and isolation proved maddening. For hours on end, Corwin spoke to no one and did nothing other than pace his rooms and search in vain for an escape. There was only the one door, guarded now and with the lock on it reversed. Several large windows offered pleasant views, but the drop to the ground would cripple even the strongest man. There was no making a rope either. After the guards led him in, the gold combed through the rooms, removing any possible weapon or tool. Corwin was left all the comforts he could want—clothes, a soft bed, hot running water—but the place was no less a prison.

Even worse was that no one had been allowed in to see him, save the servants who brought him his meals. Dal tried at least twice, arguing loudly with both the guards and the golds, but to no avail.

Worst of all, Corwin worried for Kate. Where was she? How long did she have before they began the Purging? He didn't know. He'd willfully kept himself in ignorance about the Inquisition and its ways, choosing not to question too closely, nor to think too deeply. In hindsight it seemed obvious that he'd always understood that imprisoning people who had committed no crime was wrong, despite what they might do. *Might or might never.* How many innocents had been put to death already?

Kate could be the next. *Oh gods, let me out of here!* But the gods seemed unconcerned with his troubles.

Finally, desperate to do something besides wait, Corwin went to his desk and sat down. The map of the daydrake attacks he'd been keeping lay open before him. He stared at it, suddenly remembering Ralph Marcel. He'd been caught by the Inquisition, same as Kate, yet he'd escaped somehow. And that woman in Tyvald had claimed to Dal that she'd spotted another captured wilder running free.

Could there really be two? Corwin had seen enough of the gold-order houses from the outside to guess that escape wouldn't be easy. The golds were like highly trained soldiers, fervent in their handling of wilders, and once collared, the wilders couldn't use their magic, as he'd seen with that boy in Andreas. Even the boy's mother had failed to harm the other magists when she attacked them. Kate's chances of escape seemed impossible.

Then how had those others done it? Corwin opened the desk drawer where he'd stowed the letter from the golds in Andreas. He wasn't sure why he'd kept it, useless as it was, but now he read over it again, carefully studying it. It didn't tell him anything new, except, when he examined the golds' official seal, he saw it bore the outline of the grand master's profile.

The arrogance. There could be no doubt Storr was the champion behind the Inquisition. Was there no limit to the man's ambition? Did he think himself a king?

Yes, Corwin thought, answering his own question. Then a terrible truth dawned in his mind—perhaps Ralph Marcel and the others hadn't escaped the golds at all. What if instead, the golds—led by the grand master—were using their powers for their own gain? *Controlling the daydrakes . . .*

The idea seemed absurd at first, but then Corwin saw the brilliance of it. Everything that had happened since the appearance of the daydrakes and the attack on the Gregors' manor had only served to increase the League's power. It had given Storr more and more leverage in high council meetings and had surely fattened the League's coffers. Corwin examined the map of the attacks. The League's involvement would explain how widespread they'd been, as well.

Corwin crumpled up the letter, venting his frustration. Something had to be done, but he was stuck in here. A prisoner—all thanks to Storr.

The sound of a key rattling pulled Corwin out of his angry reverie. He turned in time to see the door swing open and Edwin step inside.

"Edwin, thank the gods you're here." Corwin rose from the desk, his anger at his brother momentarily forgotten in his need for answers. "I think—" He broke off at one look at Edwin's cold expression. Only then did he remember how close his brother had become with the grand master. They were confidants. Friends.

He won't believe me without proof. Especially now that he thinks I'm a traitor. Anger surged inside Corwin. *He ought to believe me first, though. We're brothers.*

And yet they weren't. Thanks to the uror. Dal was more a brother to him.

Wordlessly, Edwin crossed the room to the table where the remnants of Corwin's meal sat mostly uneaten. He poured a fresh cup of wine and took a deep drink before facing Corwin once more.

"Do you remember what it sounded like? Every time she took a breath?"

At once, Corwin's anger went cold inside him, knowing exactly which *she* his brother referred to. Of course he remembered. It was a sound he would never forget, each in and out of her lungs a strained, wheezing rattle. For days after the trampling his mother lingered, fighting to live, to breathe.

"I remember."

Edwin set down the cup hard, some of the wine sloshing over the side. "Do you truly? I find it hard to believe when you dishonor her memory so easily."

Corwin glanced out the window, guilt prickling down his skin. His brother had always been good at making him feel wrong, even when he wasn't. He pictured his mother's face. The people had called her Queen Imogen the Gentle. He blamed himself for her death, but he also knew deep inside that she would've forgiven him for what happened. To let Edwin use her as a weapon against him now seemed the true dishonoring of her memory.

Corwin turned back to his brother. "My business with Kate has nothing to do with what happened to Mother."

"She's a *wilder*," Edwin said. "And you *knew*. You've probably always known."

Corwin fought to remain calm. "So what if I did? Kate hasn't done anything wrong."

"Perhaps not yet. But what happens when she does? What excuses will you give the innocents harmed by her powers?"

"Kate would never—"

Edwin cut him off with a raised hand. "She is still dangerous. All wilders are. Their magic has been outlawed these last two hundred years. We can't make exceptions now."

Two hundred years is a long time, Corwin thought. He saw Kate as she'd looked when she told him the truth about her magic at last, her wariness, her hope. *It's simply a part of me,* she had said. She'd been born with this ability. Condemned at birth. *All because of the law.*

"Kate is not dangerous, wilder or no," Corwin said, resolute. "She doesn't deserve to be condemned for something she's never done."

Scorn twisted Edwin's features. "And will you make the same exception for all the wilders?"

Corwin didn't answer. He didn't know. It was like the Sevan soldier he'd let go free. If Dal was right, the boy had simply fled, embracing his freedom. Corwin couldn't be certain of what he hadn't witnessed. But he also couldn't deny that the version he believed was equally possible. It was the same with the other wilders. They did pose a danger; they *might* cause harm. He shook his head, incapable of knowing the right answer to such a complicated problem. In the end all he knew for certain was that he loved Kate, no matter what she was.

And Storr must be stopped. The League held too much power, just as Kate had claimed that night in Jade Forest.

"The wilders we condemn," Corwin said, "they are born citizens of Rime, same as you and me."

Edwin swore. "I hope you lose the uror, Corwin. You don't deserve to win. Not if you believe that." Hatred black as coal and hot as fire sizzled in his words, and Corwin took an involuntary step backward, stunned by the depth of it.

"How can you hate so . . . so expansively?" Corwin said on a gasp.

"How can you not?"

All the ways Corwin could respond, all the arguments he could make, came and went through his mind. There was no arguing with this sort of belief. It was a battle that could only be fought from within. He'd learned it firsthand, in the months after his mother died as his own hate raged inside him until he finally realized he had to let it go or it would consume him forever. Pity rose up in Corwin at what it must be like for his brother to have lived with such hate for so long, to let it burn him up from the inside out.

He sighed in defeat. "Why are you here, Edwin?"

Scowling, Edwin swore again, then said through clenched teeth, "You have been granted a reprieve. It seems that despite your actions, you are bound by the goddess to complete the uror." He paused, a cold smile passing quickly over his face now. "I suppose it's for the best. When you fail, then the whole kingdom will know for certain which of us deserves to be king."

Corwin didn't reply, refusing to take the bait.

"You are allowed to resume your normal duties," Edwin continued, assuming a civil tone, the kind he reserved for speaking to the public or the high council. "But you've been assigned a gold-robe guard. He's waiting outside. He's to stay with you wherever you go to make sure you don't conspire further with any more wilders."

Corwin balled his hands into fists, despising the idea of a guard, as if he were a child in need of a nanny. "I didn't conspire to do anything."

"It's too late for your lies, Corwin. Besides, I should probably thank you for the damage you've done. The courtiers are already cursing your name."

"What? Why?"

That cold smile flashed again. "Because with the discovery of the high prince aiding a wilder, the gold robes have been conducting an extensive search for more guilty parties here in the castle."

"That's ridiculous."

Edwin rolled his eyes. "Hardly. Maestra Vikas has exposed Bonner as a wilder as well. He's been wearing the same diamond magestone we found on Kate to disguise the fact that he's an earthist."

Corwin gaped, disbelief pounding in his temple. *No, it couldn't be.*

A smug look rose in Edwin's gaze. "Apparently, his power allows him to manipulate metals. That's how he's been making the revolvers."

The truth struck Corwin like a fist to the gut. It made too much sense, explained why only the revolvers he'd forged personally had worked in the beginning. "I didn't know Bonner was a wilder."

"I suppose you didn't know that Kate is a part of the Rising either?" Edwin bared his teeth in a sneer. "Yes, that's right. They've been headquartered right here in Norgard all this time, in the basement of a brothel, of all places. The golds arrested more than twenty yesterday and killed several more during the raid."

Corwin's mind spun at this news, his insides stinging at the betrayal of it. He couldn't believe it. No wonder Kate had been bound to secrecy over what she'd discovered there. He didn't have to ask the name of the brothel to know it was the Sacred Sword. And yet Raith must have been the one to cast that spell, which meant he was a part of the Rising, too.

"Although, ironically, we have you to thank for the discovery," Edwin said. "If you hadn't asked the guard-tower captain to record Kate's comings and goings, the golds might never have found them."

What have I done? Corwin's stomach clenched.

"Did you plan it?" Edwin said, his narrowed gaze sharp as a knife. "Did you and your wilder friends create the daydrake threat just to give you the opportunity to solve it with your conjured revolvers? Was it all a ruse to win the uror?"

Corwin would've laughed at his brother's insecurity even now, but there was nothing funny about the accusation. Despite the absurdity that he would ever do such a thing, the notion of an heir trying to win the uror by earning the adoration of the people wasn't farfetched. There were several texts that made the claim that it was this very force—the will of the people—that mattered most in determining the winner. But there was nothing he could say to convince Edwin of his innocence. Not now, not yet. Corwin needed answers, and although the sting of learning Kate was part of the Rising still lanced through him, he refused to give in to it until he learned her reasons. He trusted Kate. Loved her. There had to be an explanation for all of this.

Clearing his throat, Corwin said, "You've delivered your message. We have nothing more to discuss." He motioned to the door, holding his arm out until Edwin left.

Once alone, Corwin took a moment to decide what to do next. He needed to find Master Raith. The man was a magist, which meant he might be loyal to Storr, but he also was connected to the Rising. Either way, he would have some of the answers Corwin needed.

TO CORWIN'S RELIEF, THE GOLD-ROBE guard assigned to him was just a journeyman. He might stand a chance of overpowering him, if it came to it. But first, he needed to find out about Kate. To do that, he would need help from someone he could trust, perhaps the only person he could trust right now.

Doubtful of his chances of finding Dal in his quarters at this time of day, Corwin nevertheless decided to check there first. To his surprise, though, Dal was inside—with Master Raith. The magist wore his blue robe but not his mask.

"Corwin," Dal said, opening the door. "Thank the gods they finally let you free."

"Not exactly." Corwin stepped into the room and the gold made to follow.

"No you don't." Dal held up his hand to the man. "These are my quarters, and you're not welcome."

The gold glared at him through the mask that covered only half his face. "I'm under orders to stay with his highness at all times."

"I don't care if you're the incarnation of the goddess herself, you're not coming in here."

"Lord Dallin," Raith said, approaching the door, "it's all right. Let him in."

Dal's teeth clacked together in disapproval, but he stepped aside and permitted the gold entry. Corwin crossed the room to the window, putting as much distance between himself and the gold as the space allowed.

Dal yanked the door closed and faced Master Raith. "I don't see how we're—"

Raith spoke an incantation and a flash of magic erupted from out of his drawn mace. The spell soared outward and struck the gold in the chest. With a gasp of surprise the man slumped to the ground.

"Oh, well, never mind then." Dal grinned and brushed off his hands. "That's one problem solved."

"What did you do to him?" Corwin said, too leery of Raith to be relieved. The magist was both dangerous and unpredictable.

"He's just asleep." Raith bent toward the gold, grabbed the man by the shoulder, and pulled him onto his back. "He'll wake in a few hours." Rising, Raith turned to Corwin. "We've much to tell you, your highness, and little time."

"Where's Kate?" Corwin said, hands on hips.

"As far as we know she's still alive. That's part of what we need to discuss, if you'll just listen."

Reluctantly, Corwin pressed his lips together.

Raith reached into his robes and withdrew a sapphire magestone. "Before I can tell you anything, I must bind you to secrecy."

Corwin took a step backward, his fisted hands rising up. "So it's true. You are part of the Rising." He glared at Raith, then at Dal. "Are you a part of this, too?"

Dal returned his glare. "I'm playing catch-up here, same as you. I'm just a step or two ahead is all."

Corwin started to respond, but Raith cut him off.

"You have many questions and doubts, and I can give you answers, but only if you agree to this." Raith held out the sapphire. "There are more lives than Kate's at stake here, your highness, and I have vowed to protect as many as I can."

Corwin glanced at Dal again. He stood leaning against a sofa in an attitude of boredom, but Corwin could see the tension running through his friend from the crease in his brow to the way his toe tapped slowly against the floor. "Did you take this vow?"

Dal nodded. "With no hesitation, especially not after the questioning the golds put me through. They are out for blood. It's not just Kate and Bonner. I think they've taken Signe, too. She's missing."

"Missing?"

"Your highness," Raith said with a hint of impatience in his voice. "The answers lie here." He held up the sapphire once more.

Corwin regarded the magist, the weight of this decision pressing down on him. It was one thing to accept Kate as a wilder, but quite another to condone the Rising. Those wilders had caused destruction and death, like the Gregor family, massacred in their home. *Kate trusts him, though,* a voice argued in his mind.

"All right. I agree to keep the secret, but that does not mean I agree with the Rising's actions."

"Yes, understood." Raith took a step toward him. "All we ever ask is a chance to explain ourselves."

Corwin held out his hand and remained silent as Raith engaged the spell.

"Now that's done," Raith said, returning the ruined gem to his pocket, "it will be easiest if I start at the beginning."

He launched into the tale, and Corwin listened, both rapt and incredulous as the master magist told him about his part in the Rising, and about Kate's half brother, the very reason why Hale had attempted to stop Orwin from enacting the Inquisition that night. He described the way Kiran had grown up, hidden in the basement of the Sacred Sword. Hearing the story, it didn't take long for Corwin to understand Kate's reasons for all she'd done. *She has a brother.* She would've done anything to protect him.

Finally, Raith claimed that someone else had been making it look as if the Rising were behind the daydrakes. "But we're not, your highness. Faking our sun lion symbol is an easy thing."

Corwin remembered the variations in the drawings. Was this the reason for them?

"I swear it's true. On my life, I swear it." Raith placed a hand over his heart. "I knew Marcus Gregor personally. He was a wilder and a member of the Rising. All of his family had magic. That is why he withdrew support for your father once King Orwin enacted the Inquisition. We never would've attacked one of our own."

This truth stunned Corwin, but it also made sense. He slowly nodded, remembering his suspicions about Storr and the Inquisition. "I believe you. On this point at least." Despite Raith's words that the Rising worked to keep rogue wilders from causing harm, they were still guilty of some violence.

But there were more pressing concerns just now. "Kate claimed that Storr was responsible for what happened to Hale," Corwin said. "That he'd laid some kind of magical trap inside my father to catch him. But I wonder if Storr's not responsible for even more."

He quickly told them about the conclusions he'd drawn earlier.

Raith listened, without speaking, until Corwin finished. "I don't want to believe it's true," Raith said, his expression troubled, "that such corruption exists in the League, but I can't deny it's possible. I was unable to identify the man controlling the drakes at Thornewall on my trip to Penlocke, but I already knew he'd been caught by the Inquisition. Kate heard it in his thoughts before he died."

A thrill of unease slid through Corwin at this revelation. What a power it was, to read men's minds.

He shook the feeling off. "That makes three wilders involved who'd been caught by the League—that is, if we count what that woman in Tyvald told Dal. That's too many to be a coincidence."

"You're right," said Raith. "Though I don't believe all the orders are involved. The blues most certainly aren't. But the golds must be. Storr created the order himself at the start of the Inquisition. He would've picked magists loyal to him. And Kate and Bonner aren't at their order house. I stole a look at the ledger yesterday. There are a few of the wilders captured during the raid on the Sacred Sword being held there, but not all of them."

"What about Kiran?" Corwin asked, his gut clenched as he realized that if something happened to the boy, he was responsible. He never should've spied on Kate.

"Neither Kiran nor his mother is there," Raith replied, distractedly. He nodded to himself. "It would seem the golds are being selective as to which wilders they take, leaving just enough for the Purging to avoid suspicion from the other orders."

Corwin grimaced, seeing the brilliance behind it. Never before had he realized how separate the League's orders were, even though he should have. What with their different-colored robes, individual houses. They were like children, siblings caught up in their own quest for autonomy.

Then the awful truth of what Raith was saying struck him, and he felt himself pale. "If Kate isn't being held at the gold-order house, then where is she?"

"I don't know. She and the others aren't in the city. My people have been searching for them. Our only hope is to find proof of what they're doing. It's no good approaching Storr. He's too well insulated. Perhaps we can force a confession out of Maestra Vikas. She was appointed by Storr, after all."

Corwin slowly nodded, a sick feeling in his stomach.

"There's only one thing that doesn't make sense," Dal said, standing up. "Why would the golds take Signe? She isn't a wilder."

"No," Corwin agreed. "But she does have the secret to making her black powder. Combined with Bonner's revolvers, that's the key to a great power." *They might just kill her,* Corwin thought with a glance at Dal, but he kept it to himself. He could guess Dal had already considered the possibility—he knew as well as Corwin did how much the revolvers threatened the League's power. Storr had made his feelings on the matter clear with that letter in the *Royal Gazette*.

Deciding at last to fully believe Raith's claims, Corwin returned his gaze to the magist. "Are you sure you've looked everywhere for them? What if we enlist more people to help?"

"It won't make a difference," Raith said. "We've combed every inch of the city already, and we've used searching spells and other magic. They are not here."

"Yes, but what about outside the city? Jade Forest or . . . the Wandering Woods!" He clapped his hand together, remembering what Kate had told him. "Kate said there was something strange that day we went back to find the daydrakes. She said she felt cut off from her magic. It sounded to me like the way the collars work that the League uses on captured wilders."

Raith's brow furrowed. "She never mentioned it to me . . . but if the golds were trying to hide and imprison wilders, that would be a way to do it."

"That settles it then," Dal said with an eager clap of his hands. He walked over to the wardrobe next to the door and swung it open to reveal the cache of weapons inside. He pulled out a sword, revolver, buckler, and belt and handed them to Corwin.

"You're going to need these."

Corwin grinned, pleased to see that Dal had had the foresight to gather his weapons from the armory. He accepted them with a grateful nod.

"If there is a shield spell active in the woods," Raith said, "we're going to need more than common weapons." He turned to Dal. "I need three gemstones, rubies or emeralds. Something of that value."

Wordlessly, Dal turned back to the wardrobe and withdrew a gold-hilted dagger, encrusted with rubies. A family heirloom, Corwin knew, the only one he possessed and likely ever would.

Dal handed Raith the dagger. "Do whatever you need to it."

Raith took the dagger, turned to the nearest table, and proceeded to pry out three of the rubies with the tip of his knife. Once done, he held the rubies in his hand and spoke the words of an incantation. The lines of the spell spread across the glistening red surfaces.

"Here, keep these with you when you enter the woods." Raith handed one each to Corwin and Dal, keeping the third for himself. "The spell will allow you to see through magical disguises."

"You're not coming with us?" Dal cocked an eyebrow.

"If there is something in the Wandering Woods, we will need help," replied Raith. "I will meet you there as soon as I can." He pointed a finger at Corwin and Dal in turn. "But if you find anything, stay hidden until I arrive."

"We'll wait as long as we can," Corwin said, "but hurry." He wouldn't promise not to act, though. If there was a chance of finding Kate, he doubted any danger would be great enough to keep him in place long.

KATE WOKE TO DARKNESS AND a strange pressure at her throat. Disoriented and confused, she raised her hands to her neck and gasped as her fingers brushed cold, hard metal. A mage collar. At once the memory of what had happened flooded into her mind—of visiting King Orwin and being attacked by Maestra Vikas. Now here she was, imprisoned by the Inquisition.

She tried to sit up only to whack her head against something hard above her. Raising her hands, she felt the wooden lid. She was inside a box of some kind, a crate—one that was moving. The motion was the familiar chaotic bounce of a wagon.

Kate pounded on the lid with the side of her fist. "Let me out of here!"

"Be quiet," a voice shouted back, followed by a violent thud against the top of the crate. Powerless to do anything, including bend her knees or shift onto her side, Kate lay there and listened, fear simmering inside her. She thought about Corwin, wondering how he'd reacted when she'd been attacked, if he'd simply stood aside and let her be taken. She didn't know. But either way she couldn't count on his help now.

Sometime later, the wagon came to a stop and she heard the creak of wood as someone pried off the lid. She blinked against the sudden light in her eyes, the man who appeared over her nothing more than a shadow.

"Get up," he said.

She struggled to her feet, swallowing words of protest as she saw the three gold robes, all with maces at the ready. She stood no chance of escaping. Her only weapon was her magic, but the collar at her throat blocked her from it as surely as if it were night.

The nearest gold grabbed her arm and hauled her off the back of the wagon. With her eyes finally adjusted, she realized it was late, almost night, but she didn't think it was the same night.

"Kate! Are you all right?"

She looked up, her heart lurching into her throat as she spotted Bonner on the other side of the wagon. He too wore a mage collar. "What happened?"

"Be quiet." The gold shoved her forward. "Move along, both of you."

Bonner fell into step beside her and took her hand, squeezing her fingers with a tremulous grip. The sharp scent of fear-laced sweat hung in the air around him.

Glancing about, Kate took in the sight of an unfamiliar keep ahead of her, a massive towering fortress. Rounded like an amphitheater, it seemed to be made of a single continuous piece of stone with no visible sign of mortar or blocks. It had no towers and no windows, as if it were meant to keep everyone and everything out—or to keep something else within. By contrast, however, the battlements surrounding the keep looked incapable of protecting anything. Huge gaps in the wall left by crumbling stone made the place feel ancient and ruinous.

Where are we? Kate craned her head to look behind her. The answer stole the breath from her throat when she spotted slender, white-barked trees through a hole in the battlements. The Wandering Woods. Which could only mean this was—

"The Hellgate," she whispered aloud, and saw Bonner jerk his head at her in alarm. She shared the feeling. They should've been at the gold house, awaiting the Purging, not here, in a place of myth and legend.

The magists led them through the opened door into the fortress. Despite its size, it was simply constructed, with a single outer corridor surrounding the vast main hall at its center. Dozens of platforms rose up around the room all the way to the ceiling. But instead of seats like in a true amphitheater, the platforms held cages with daydrakes trapped inside. Kate shrank back from the sight. The drakes' black scales glistened in the light of the torches hung from the walls. There were enough of them in here to raze an entire city.

"It's the gold robes," Kate said, and Bonner nodded solemnly. "They must be behind the attacks." *On Storr's orders*, she felt certain.

The golds stopped in front of a row of empty cages on the ground floor and forced Kate and Bonner inside two of them, locking them in. Then they walked away, leaving them alone in the dark, damp space.

"Is this really the Hellgate?" Bonner asked, peering around.

Kate pointed at the dropped floor just beyond the cages. Instead of stone, iron bars crisscrossed over a wide, deep hole. She could feel the warm air seeping out from it like the exhaled breath of some slumbering giant in its depths.

Bonner shuddered, but couldn't do much more than that. The

cages were clearly made for animals, long but too short even for Kate to stand up in.

"No one will ever find us here," Bonner said.

Kate didn't reply. It was pure chance that she and Corwin had stumbled across the drakes that day in the Wandering Woods, and magist magic must've kept them from finding more when they came back with the search party. Not that the golds needed magic to keep this place hidden. Belief in the Hellgate had fallen into myth, its true existence forgotten except in stories. But centuries ago people feared it. They stayed away, allowing the land surrounding it to grow wild, to swallow it up until the golds freed it from its own wasting death, a ready-made secret fortress.

"How were you discovered?" asked Bonner, pulling her from her thoughts.

Kate told the story quickly, stating how when she'd visited the king she'd set off some sort of magist trap, one she guessed had been left by Storr, same as he must've done to her father before. "But how did they find out about you?"

Bonner grunted. "Once you were taken, the golds rounded up everyone for questioning. They found the diamond magestone. It didn't take them long to guess I'd been using it to hide my magic making revolvers."

"I'm so sorry, Bonner. I didn't know what would happen."

"How could you have?" He waved her off, then raised his hands to the collar. "If we could just find a way to get this off, I could bend these bars open."

For several minutes both of them tried to loosen the collars, to no avail. They needed a key. Then they searched the cages, probing them for weaknesses but finding only pebbles and dirt. Wearied by hopelessness, Kate sagged against the back of the cage. There was nothing to do but wait for what would happen next.

Eventually the golds returned, herding more people into the cages. When Kate saw Vianne and Kiran, she cried out, "No! Let them go!" She grasped the bars in front of her, wishing she had the strength to pull them apart.

The golds shoved Vianne and Kiran into the cage next to Kate's, and it was all Vianne could do to calm the boy. She pulled him onto her lap, muffling his sobs against her shoulder.

Kate turned away, tears pricking her own eyes. Surveying the other captives, she realized they were all members of the Rising, including Anise.

When the magists had gone, Kate learned the story of what happened, the golds raiding the Sacred Sword without warning or provocation.

"It's my fault," Kate said, struggling to keep her emotions under control. "I never should have visited so often."

"You couldn't have known you'd be found out," Anise said. "It's a risk we all take."

Vianne ran her hands down the back of Kiran's head, saying nothing. He lay quiet at last, perhaps asleep.

"Is he all right?" asked Kate.

"For now, but what are they going to do with us?" Vianne spoke the question loud enough for the others to hear, but no one answered. It was like waiting to wake up from a nightmare—that feeling that maybe you never would.

The golds returned again sometime later—hours, it seemed, with Kate's legs and back aching from lying on the hard floor. Her throat and mouth felt stuffed with wool. Maestra Vikas came with them. Kate screamed at her, demanding an answer for why they were here.

"Silence," Vikas said, and spoke an incantation.

Kate saw the glow of magic beneath her throat as one of the magestones in the collar activated.

The maestra knelt before her cage, a smug look on her austere face. "There now. That's better. But tell me, Kate, how did you like my trap, the one you stepped into when you tried to sway King Orwin?"

It was you! Kate tried to respond, but the spell stopped her.

Vikas smiled. "Yes, that's what I thought. Your father didn't care for it much either."

What did you do to him? Kate tried to scream, but again nothing came out.

Vikas stood, silencing anyone else who dared talk.

Helplessly, Kate watched as Vikas conferred with the other golds.

"Prepare these three for shipping, but take this one off for testing." Vikas indicated several of the wilders. Then she moved farther down the line, sorting the rest of them like sheep. What they were being sorted for, Kate couldn't guess.

"These two are to stay for now." Vikas pointed first at Bonner, then Kate. "The Lord Ascender has plans for them, but the mother and child I want on the road by nightfall. Any later and they will miss the ship." She waved a dismissive hand at Vianne and Kiran.

"Isn't the boy too young to make the journey?" one of the golds asked.

Vikas smiled. "From what I hear, he's older than he looks."

Kate tried to scream, her anger like a wild beast inside her chest. She slammed her body against the bars, but Vikas only gave her another smile, sickly sweet and triumphant.

She left a few minutes later, but the golds remained to do her bidding. Kate watched, powerless as the magists unlocked Vianne's cage and pulled her and Kiran out. The boy thrashed and screamed until one of the golds invoked the spell for silence on his small collar.

The stillness afterward pressed down on Kate like a boulder atop her chest. She closed her eyes and willed sleep to come for her, but it refused, her mind too strained by fear and dread. They were taking Kiran and Vianne to a ship, but a ship to where? How would she ever find them again? She couldn't lose Kiran now, after so many years apart already.

Time trudged by. It might've been days or weeks, although she feared it was only hours. There was no way to account for the passing, nothing to ground her to reality. The light in the Hellgate never changed, and the only noise was the sound of the daydrakes' restless pacing and the strange way they called to one another in their wailing snarls and growls.

At some point, Kate must've finally drifted off, because the next thing she knew, two golds were pulling her free of the cage.

"Come now," Maestra Vikas said, standing behind them. "The Lord Ascender is asking for you."

The Lord Ascender? Was Storr giving himself new titles now?

In the cage next to her, Bonner pounded his fists against the bars, but the golds ignored him, their masked faces hiding any reaction at all.

With no other choice, Kate followed the golds without protest as they led her to a room in the main corridor.

The maestra paused outside the door and regarded Kate with her pale, icy gaze. "The honor of seeing the Lord Ascender is one granted to only a few. Above all else, you will show him respect."

Kate blinked at her, confused. She'd met Storr before.

"And if you're wise, you will heed his words. He is the Lord Ascender. A god on earth. He possesses more knowledge than anyone alive, who has ever lived. I could spend a thousand years by his side and still not learn all he has to share." There was naked awe in her voice, and Kate wondered if she wasn't quite sane. Before becoming the head of the golds, Vikas had been one of the whites, an order whose members were sometimes plagued by madness, a side effect of their area of focus. The whites pursued magical knowledge over everything else, and they studied the high arts, dangerous and arcane magic.

Her speech over, the maestra waved a hand, undoing the silencing spell. Before Kate could talk, Vikas stepped into the room first, then moved aside, motioning Kate forward. The two golds remained in the hall as Vikas shut the door behind Kate.

The sight of the room beyond took her breath away. Tapestries woven of spun gold studded with glistening gemstones hung from every wall, transforming the plain, ancient stone into a space fit for a king. *Or a god, as Vikas claims.* A plush carpet, the color of blood, spilled down the center of the room, leading to an ornate chair carved from crystal. Sconces placed on either side of the chair set the crystal ablaze until it looked like a glowing throne, almost like the Mirror Throne itself.

A man sat upon it, leaning back against the indigo pillows with both his hands curled around the armrests. Kate's heart thumped against her breastbone as she realized it wasn't Storr sitting there. She'd seen this man often in the castle, but never like this. He wore a silver circlet and a cloak made of white and black feathers.

"Welcome, Kate Brighton," he said, his golden eyes glistening nearly as bright as the throne he sat on. "We meet as our true selves, at last."

Kate stared at Minister Rendborne, sense escaping her. "I thought Storr was behind this."

Rendborne nodded. "He does make for a good scapegoat, but no. Storr is merely a vain, greedy man. Such are easy to manipulate. But I must say, that wasn't the first response I expected from you." He waved to the area next to him.

Kate followed the motion, at last seeing what the splendor in the room had kept hidden—a second chair, this one occupied by Signe. She was strapped into it by ropes tied around her arms, waist, and chest. Her legs remained free, except for the spiked wooden screw around her right foot—the two pieces of board compressed together by an iron vise. One that had pressed so hard it had crushed the foot beneath.

"Signe!" Kate dashed toward her, only to be thrown backward by a blast of magic. It had come from Rendborne, right out of his outstretched hand. "You're a magist?"

"Oh, no, dear child. I am so much more. As are you, wilder." He stood from the crystal chair with a terrifying aspect.

Kate pulled her eyes off him, surprised by how hard it was. A part of her wanted to watch him, mesmerized by his presence, as if he were a flame and she the moth. She got to her feet, gaze fixed on Signe unconscious on the chair with her chin resting on her chest. "Why do this to her?"

Rendborne walked over to Signe. "Are you familiar with the Eshian notion of Seerah?"

"The holy silence," Kate said on an exhale.

Smiling, Rendborne motioned to Signe. "This one holds fast to that vow. She is a credit to her people." Cupping Signe's chin with one hand, he raised her head off her chest and turned her face toward Kate, revealing the thick gash from her brow line to her chin. Blood still oozed out from it, running down her neck like a red river.

Kate choked on a gasp.

"It's a difficult thing, breaking a person," Rendborne said in a detached, clinical tone. "You have to find out what matters most to them, where their heart lies. This one I thought might've been vanity, but I was wrong. She didn't fear the scar this will leave behind at all. Impressive."

Vomit climbed Kate's throat, and she sucked in a breath. She needed to stay calm, keep her wits about her. "Why are you doing this? She's done nothing to you."

Rendborne continued on as if she hadn't spoken. "Then I thought perhaps the threat of crippling her would work. She's so fierce and independent. Surely the idea of never walking again would have broken her. But you know what happened?" Rendborne dropped

Signe's face and turned to Kate. "She still refused to divulge her secrets. Isn't that fascinating?"

Kate shook her head. It wasn't if you knew Signe.

"Yes, fascinating." Rendborne raised his hand to touch the necklace of talons strung around his neck. "But frustrating. I need to know how to make the black powder. Since she refuses to tell me, you are going to fetch it for me instead."

Several seconds passed before Kate fully understood what he was saying. Her stomach recoiled at the idea. "You want me to steal the secret out of her mind?"

"We both know you have the ability." Rendborne motioned to the glass jars on the workbench. "These are the elements she uses. I recognize them all, save this one." He picked up a jar. "It seems to be a substance found only in the islands. But the proportions elude me, and the trial and error it would require to work out the recipe would take an age. Time I don't have. I need you to use that gift of yours and find out from this one."

"I won't do it."

Rendborne smirked. "Believe me, child, you are not my first choice. But I've only two wilders left with your ability, after you killed poor William in Thornewall, and neither is available at the moment. I need it done now and quickly. You *will* do it for me, Kate Brighton, willingly or not."

She opened her mouth to argue, but then an idea occurred to her. For her to use her sway, he would have to remove the collar.

Worried he would suspect something if she agreed too quickly, Kate said, "What happens if I refuse?"

"Suffering and death, of course." Rendborne rolled his eyes as if the subject bored him. "I'm afraid I know your character too well to bother trying to bribe you instead. Proud and honorable like your father. Now, before I remove your collar, you should know that any attempt to use your gift on me will fail." He touched his chest, where a crystal full of a dark-red liquid lay beneath the necklace of talons. "This magestone shields me. The magic was woven from your father's blood."

Kate inhaled sharply. "You're lying."

"It's gruesome, I know, but of all the gifts I possess—control over fire, water, earth, air, and even most of spirit—the gift of sway still eludes me." Envy rang clear in his voice, his eyes a golden smolder as he stared at her.

"No one man has that much magic," Kate said, her gaze fixed on the crystal, still disbelieving his claim that it was her father's.

"I told you. He is no man, but a *god*." Vikas spoke from behind Kate. She'd almost forgotten the maestra was there. Vikas stared at Rendborne with raw desire on her face.

Rendborne beckoned Vikas forward, and when she reached him, he bent his head toward her and kissed her full on the mouth. Breaking the kiss, he stared down at her with genuine affection. "And you will soon be the goddess who rules Rime next to me." He turned his gaze to Kate. "I have Isla here to thank for discovering the spell to create this." He picked up the crystal and shook it, stirring the tenebrous contents.

Beside him, Vikas reached into her robe to reveal an identical crystal. She held it up, examining it with a fond gaze. "Magic resides in the blood. Even after death, the power remains—that is, if the blood is extracted from a still living host. In the end, your father gave me every last drop before the executioner took his head."

Kate gritted her teeth so hard, pain shot through her jaw as she fought to hold in a scream. She remembered the way he'd looked that day, when they led him to the executioner's block. Pale and emaciated, a man drained of all the life and hope left in him.

"He never spoke a word," Vikas said, "not even to cry out."

Kate closed her eyes, hatred expanding inside her like air drawn into a bellows. She understood at last why it was her father had refused to see her. Why he'd left his message in code. The meaning had been double—find Kiran and leave Rime, get away from this evil.

"Let's begin then," Rendborne said. "Once I remove the collar, you will enter your friend's mind to find out how she mixes the black powder. If you do it successfully, she will live and not suffer any more abuse. If you refuse or attempt to escape in any way, there will be death to pay."

Kate stared at the man, trying to know his thoughts without her sway. The death he spoke of wouldn't be Signe's, she decided. The secret she possessed was worth too much for him to kill her outright. *But I'm expendable.* That was all right. Kate would rather die than let this man control her. If she failed, her death would buy Signe time. But first Signe needed to be freed.

"I understand," Kate said at last.

Satisfied, Rendborne waved his hand, and she felt the collar loosen around her neck. It fell to the ground, and when she glanced at it, she saw the lock on it was still intact but the metal to either side had been pulled apart. *With magic.* It seemed Rendborne had been telling the truth about his powers; he had the magic of both air and earth, that she'd seen so far.

Kate breathed in, stretching out with her sway. Gently, she probed both Vikas and Rendborne. As they claimed, she couldn't reach either of them. But behind her, just through the door, she sensed the two golds, neither of them protected from her magic.

Kate made a show of turning toward Signe. Her friend was awake now, her eyes squeezed shut against the pain. *I'm sorry, Signe,* Kate thought as she approached the chair.

"Hurry," Rendborne said. "If you're successful, I will heal her pain myself."

Kate placed her palm against Signe's forehead. Physical touch made connecting with another mind easier, but this was all for show while she reached out with her magic to the two golds. The moment she sensed them, she grasped hold and forced them to her will.

Their minds folded to her power at once, bending like stalks in the wind. *Kill the Lord Ascender!* she commanded, and both men obeyed, bursting through the door with maces raised. Their spells soared toward Rendborne, and he raised his hand like a shield before him. The magic fizzled and died as it reached him, and in the next moment he summoned lightning in the palm of the same hand and cast it at both the golds. Still attached to their minds, Kate felt the pain tear through them. She shrieked and let go.

Turning toward her, Rendborne cast another spell. The magic hit Kate like a strong wind, and she fell to the ground, paralyzed.

"You really should not have done that." Rendborne retrieved the collar. He placed it around Kate's neck, melding the broken pieces together with his magic.

"Kill me now," Kate said. "I won't do what you want. Not ever."

He smiled coldly. "I wasn't ever threatening to kill *you*, Kate. Your death has no value. Only your abilities do." Rendborne turned to the golds, who were just now recovering from the attack. "Go and fetch Bonner . . . and his father."

Chills erupted down Kate's skin, and she struggled in vain to break free of the spell. *Why is his father here?*

The golds returned all too quickly, dragging in the Bonners, both of them in chains. Thomas visibly trembled with fear.

The moment Bonner spotted Kate and Signe, he began to struggle. "What are you doing? Let them go!"

For a second it was all the golds could do to keep control of him, but then Rendborne froze him in place with his magic—a vortex of air surrounding him.

"Don't struggle, son," Thomas said, his voice kind and gentle as ever. "It won't change anything." Although his words were strong, Thomas seemed to sag beneath the weight of them.

Rendborne drew a knife from his belt and approached father and son standing side by side. "I warned you, Kate, there would be a death to pay if you disobeyed me." Rendborne raised the knife to Bonner's throat.

"NO!" Kate screamed, terror robbing her of reason. "Don't hurt him! Please, I'll do whatever you want." Rendborne was right; everyone had a breaking point, and he had found hers.

"Yes, I know you will do what I want now," Rendborne said. "But still, the consequences of your disobedience must be paid." He pressed the knife to Bonner's throat, a sliver of blood appearing beneath the blade.

"Don't hurt my boy," Thomas sobbed. "Take me instead."

Rendborne glanced at the old man. "Very well," he said, and before anyone could react, he pivoted toward Thomas and sliced his throat. The man let out a single, liquid gasp, then crumpled to the floor.

Bonner's scream was loud enough to shake the walls. The agony in the sound ripped through Kate. She could see him struggling against the magic that held him, mad with the need to kill the man before him, to do anything to save his father.

"Settle him down," Rendborne said, releasing the vortex of air around Bonner. At once, the golds turned their maces on him. Bonner fell to the ground as they beat him over the head, neck, back, legs, arms, everywhere. Kate cried for them to stop, but it made no difference. She was still paralyzed by Rendborne's magic, helpless to act. They continued on until all the fight went out of Bonner, and he slumped against the floor, his face pressed into the ever-expanding pool of his father's blood.

Rendborne turned back to Kate. "This was the punishment for the first disobedience, Kate. I recommend you do not try a second one." He pointed his hand at her and released her from the paralysis.

"Why are you doing this?" Kate said, tears making her voice thick. "Who are you?" She couldn't pull her eyes off Bonner. He was still conscious, but only just. Thomas, she couldn't bear to look at, heartsick with memories of laughter shared over meals, his gentle teasing that his son should find a wife like her.

Rendborne bent toward Kate, removing the magestone on his right hand. The skin on his palm blurred for a moment, then cleared, revealing the raised, branded flesh there, a faded eight-spoked wheel set inside the holy triangle. *An uror mark?* Seeing it only added to her confusion. He cupped her chin, raising her face to his.

"Who are you?" she said again. She peered into his golden eyes, feeling the weight of age in them. He seemed both old and young at the same time. A god, Vikas called him. A god in human form.

"You will know me in time. But for now, do as I command, Kate, and the suffering will end." Rendborne released her.

She felt the fight ebbing away from her. She could not defeat this man. But Bonner and Signe still lived. She needed to do whatever it took to keep them from further harm.

"Don't do it, Kate." Bonner raised his bruised and blood-smeared face toward her. "I'd rather die."

"I can't let you." Kate climbed to her feet, then turned and walked over to Signe, defeat bowing her spine until she felt she might break in two. *I am Traitor Kate,* she thought. Betrayer of her prince, her kingdom, and her friends.

THE HELLGATE WAS BOTH LESS frightening than Corwin had imagined it would be and yet far more impressive. Or maybe the reality of finding it, of learning that the mythical place existed, just hadn't yet sunk in. They'd found it so easily this time. With Raith's magestones he and Dal had spotted a well-worn path shortly after entering. They followed it as it snaked between the skeletal white trees until they reached the crumbling battlements of an ancient fortress.

At first they thought the fortress was abandoned, but after tethering the horses a safe distance away, they approached one of the gaping holes in the wall and spotted movement beyond, the distinctive flash of a gold robe in the fading sun. *Kate must be here,* Corwin thought, watching the activity near the keep. For a moment the urge to rush in headlong nearly overwhelmed him, but he pushed it back down again. Deciding to remain outside had nothing to do with Raith's warning and everything to do with instinct. He'd spent too long studying military strategy, both with his tutors at Norgard and with the Shieldhawks, to do something so reckless as to charge a fortress like this, one with a single door and no windows. He and Dal had made certain of it, doing a sweep of the perimeter to make sure.

Now, with night fast approaching, they'd returned to the spot nearest the path that had brought them here, taking cover close to the wall to observe the comings and goings. They watched as golds came in and out of the fortress, often carrying crates, of the sort they used to transport their magestones from city to city, which they loaded onto wagons. When a group of them later carried out a cage, Corwin's chest gave a lurch at the sight of the daydrake inside it. It seemed his hunch was true—the golds were behind the vile creatures.

"How many golds do you think are in there?" Dal said.

"I've counted thirty, maybe more," Corwin replied, keeping his voice at a whisper. "But we can't be certain."

"They don't seem concerned with intruders."

Corwin nodded. They hadn't spotted a single sentry. He supposed these magists didn't fear discovery, not with the magical shield hiding them.

A rustling noise drew Corwin's attention, and he peered behind him to see Raith approaching on foot with his mace drawn. Corwin waved to him, a finger pressed against his lips.

"What have you found?" Raith whispered, reaching them. He peered through the gap where two golds loitered in the bailey out front of the opened door into the fortress. Corwin quickly told him everything they'd seen so far, and Raith listened without comment, nodding at turns.

"What do we do now?" Dal said, addressing the question to Raith.

The magist traced a finger over the birthmark on his face. "We need to capture one of the golds for questioning."

"Yes, but how, without alerting the others?"

Raith thought for a moment. Then he motioned to the ward-stone embrasure just visible from where they crouched in the underbrush. "In a few minutes they will need to set the shield. The embrasures toward the back might allow us to capture one out of sight of the others."

Dal frowned. "What about the barrier? If it doesn't go up . . ."

"I'll complete the spell," Raith said. "They'll never know. But we should get into place now. We'll need to get behind our own ward-stone barrier soon after. My people are waiting not far from here."

"How many did you bring?" Corwin asked as they slowly retreated from the wall, moving toward the rear.

"Twenty-six," Raith answered.

"So few?" Corwin glanced at the man.

Raith's expression was impassive. "There would've been more, if not for the raid. But they're all wilder or magist, and they are all willing to fight, which will have to be enough."

Yes, it would. Corwin's mind whirled with plans and possibilities, working out scenarios of how they could get inside, get to Kate and the others, and get back out again. It wasn't going to be easy. *First make sure she is indeed inside,* he told himself.

Reaching an isolated wardstone, they had to take up position well away from the wall, the only place with enough cover to shield them.

"I will take the gold down the moment he reaches the embrasures," Raith said. "But be ready to move him as soon as I finish the spell."

Dal raised his hand. "One problem. Won't they notice when one of them doesn't come back?"

Raith shook his head. "Not at first. By the time they do notice, it'll be too dark to venture out."

With that settled, they hunched down to wait. It didn't take long before a gold appeared, carrying a glowing wardstone between his palms. Corwin sank down even lower, breathing shallowly. The sweet smell of the everweeps covering the ground filled his nose, a strange, pleasant comfort in this tense moment. He needn't have worried; the gold was oblivious to his surroundings. Clearly he'd performed this task so often, he'd become indifferent to danger.

Just before the gold reached the embrasure, Raith rose from his hiding place, uttered a spell, then raced forward as the gold collapsed. Picking up the stone, he whispered a few words, invoking the warding once more, and slid the wardstone into its place. Corwin and Dal rushed toward the gold and picked him up by the arms, dragging him away as quickly and quietly as they could manage.

In moments, they were well away from the Hellgate. They stopped to get the horses, all three of them. When Corwin and Dal left Norgard, Corwin had brought Firedancer with them, saddled and ready for Kate. Dal had brought Lir as well. The falcon remained perched on the front of his saddle, a hood over her head. They tossed the unconscious gold over Nightbringer's back, then headed for the encampment.

Raith led the way. Unlike the golds at the Hellgate, sentries guarded the perimeter of the wilder encampment, three blues standing watch near the wardstones. The camp inside the magic shield was still and quiet, the people huddled in groups on the ground or standing watch. They stirred at the sight of Corwin and the others, hushed whispers breaking out like a wind gust.

Corwin eyed the people, his heart sinking at the sight of so many women and children among the men. Some of the youngest were barely old enough to be left unattended, let alone go into battle. Several of the women had infants with them. Another looked ready to give birth at any moment, her belly swollen and heavy with child. *How will we ever take the fortress with such a small group?* For surely the pregnant women and the children couldn't be put in such danger as they would soon face. Then again, Corwin reminded himself, this was Raith's army to command, not his.

That became clear within minutes of their joining the camp. Raith issued orders, selecting several of the men to help interrogate the prisoner while sending the rest as far away as the barrier would allow. Corwin understood. There was nothing pleasant about forcing a person to divulge secrets. They laid the gold on the ground inside a cluster of trees, the best buffer to muffle his screams.

Retreating as far as he dared, Corwin leaned against a tree to watch and listen. Raith did most of the work, using the spells in his magestones to inflict pain, while a wilder named Francis held the gold up, arms pinned behind his back. To Corwin's relief it didn't take long, such was the power of Raith's magic. Corwin closed his eyes during the worst of it, the man's screams like the crack of a whip. But finally, at last, the gold began to talk, and Corwin moved in closer to hear.

"Yes, the wilders are inside," the man said, panting. "Some of them."

Behind him, Francis slowly lowered the gold to the ground, then retreated a step, wiping the sweat from his brow with the back of one meaty arm. Even still his face glistened in the light of the torches nearby.

"Who?" Raith said, squatting in front of the gold, who seemed barely able to remain upright by his own strength.

"Kate Brighton, the gunsmith Bonner. That's all."

Standing opposite Corwin, Dal took a step forward, fist clenched. "What about Signe?"

The gold glanced up at him and nodded once. "The Eshian's there, too."

Francis stooped toward the gold, and the man cowered away from him. "And the others taken during the raid on the Sacred Sword?"

The gold covered his face, his words muffled behind his hands. "They were here but they're gone."

"Where?" Francis wrapped a large hand around the man's shoulder, right at the base of the neck, and squeezed.

"They're on a ship from Penlocke, on the way to Seva."

Corwin's spine stiffened at the news. He stepped nearer the gold. "Why Seva?"

The gold raised his gaze to Corwin, the whites of his eyes smeared with blood from whatever Raith had done to him. "Weapons for the Godking's army."

"An army of wilders," Raith said, rising to his feet. He glanced at Corwin, fear etched across his face.

Corwin felt the same fear echo through him. He didn't know what he'd expected, but surely never this. The golds were serving Magnar Fane? Despite his incredulity, it wasn't impossible to believe that Seva was involved. The Godking had been a young man when he sent his army to invade Rime all those years ago. It was his first taste of failure, a defeat he'd never gotten over. It was only a matter of time before he tried again. And now thanks to the golds, he would have magic to help him.

"The daydrake attacks," Corwin said, his mind making a new connection. He turned to Raith. "Most of them were near rivers and waterways, allowing easy transport to Seva." He'd missed the pattern all along, but now it seemed obvious.

"That explains why they would attack Thornewall, as well," Dal said. "The smuggling caves lead right to the river. With wilder magic it would be easy to open them again."

"And he has Signe and Bonner, too," Corwin said. "All he needs to give Seva the revolvers." Again, he felt as if the pieces of the puzzle were sliding into place. All except for the most important one. Corwin knelt before the gold as Raith had done a moment before. "Who leads you? Is it Grand Master Storr?"

The man laughed, his lips parting to reveal bloody teeth. "Storr is just a pawn in the game of a god."

Francis grabbed the man around the neck again. "Leave the riddles out of this."

"Who then?" Corwin stared into the gold's eyes, desperate for the answer.

"I serve the Lord Ascender. He is god made flesh."

Worried the pain might've driven the man mad, Corwin said, "Even gods have names. What is his?"

"He was once the Nameless One," the gold replied. Then he laughed again. "But he's had many names. Too many to count."

Fear pulsed inside Corwin, electrifying his nerves. *The Nameless*

One. "The only man with that title is long dead. He would've died years ago."

The gold shook his head, his expression emphatic now. "He lives. He lives forever. God made flesh."

With a grunt of disgust, Francis grabbed the gold by the shoulders and hoisted him into the air. "What's his name now?" Francis began to squeeze, as if he meant to crush the man with his bare hands.

The gold cried out, head thrown backward, the cords in his neck popping out. "Rendborne," he said, gasping. "Minister Rendborne."

Francis dropped the man, letting him hit the ground hard. Francis turned to Raith and Corwin, eying them both. "Do you think he says the truth?"

Neither spoke. Corwin couldn't make the idea fit inside his head, incapable of reconciling the Rendborne he knew as the minister of trade—charming, forthright, a man of the people—as the traitor responsible for the daydrake attacks and sending wilders to Seva. That was until he remembered Rendborne telling him that the Nameless One had killed his own uror sign. He claimed he'd read about it, *but what if . . . ?*

A shiver clawed down Corwin's spine. *The uror sign is pure magic,* Rendborne had said. What happened to the person who killed one? Did the magic release? Could it be captured somehow like the way the magists embedded spells on stones? Corwin wanted to ask Raith but didn't dare in front of so many people. Not when there was a living, breathing uror in the castle stables right this moment.

Instead he said, "I've reason to believe it might be true." He gestured at Dal. "We know Rendborne's also close with Maestra Vikas. Dal and I saw them having a secret tryst."

"Very well," said Raith, shocked resignation in his voice. "We now have a name for our enemy. But we need more."

Corwin stepped back, letting Raith resume the interrogation. His thoughts remained on Rendborne. The truth brought no satisfaction—not when he couldn't understand the why. If Rendborne was the Nameless One, brother of Morwen, son of Rowan, then he was a Tormane, Corwin's ancestor. Why would he betray Rime to Seva? How could he still be alive? *Unless he truly is a god.* But no, Corwin refused to believe it.

Knowing there would be no answers to his questions tonight, Corwin returned his attention to the interrogation. Raith was pressing the gold for details about the fortress itself, ways in and out, where they were keeping Kate and the others, and where Rendborne was likely to be.

"What do we do with him now?" Dal asked once they'd wrung the last bit of information from the gold.

"We take him back to Norgard as our prisoner," Raith said. "He's proof of the golds' treachery, and of Rendborne's."

Ready to voice his agreement, Corwin stopped short as across from him, Francis drew the sword at his hip and thrust it straight through the gold's heart. The man let out a liquid gasp, then fell to the ground. Corwin stared at Francis, shock thrumming through him at such cold violence.

"We aren't going back to Norgard." Francis fixed a defiant gaze on Raith. "The Rising is done waiting and hiding. We don't need proof—we're here to fight, to end this threat."

"This is the high prince." Raith motioned to Corwin with a vigorous shake of his hand. "He can end the threat of the Inquisition diplomatically, without the need for fighting and more death. There's been enough already."

"The Errant Prince will never be king now, not when he's joined with us." Francis jammed his hands down on his hips. "We must bring about our own change. It's time to fight."

I haven't joined with you, Corwin thought. *Not yet.* But the man's fury stirred something inside him. This was different from Edwin's hate. This was the result of suffering and subjugation.

Raith gave a resigned sigh. "First we must succeed in rescuing Kate, Bonner, and Signe before Rendborne can use them to arm himself and Seva. That's the immediate threat. Once they're all safe, we will decide what to do next."

Corwin held his breath, expecting Francis to argue, but the big man remained silent. Even still, tension seemed to hum in the air around him and Raith. Feeling it, Corwin guessed that this wasn't the first time the two had clashed like this.

A moment later, Raith asked Corwin for a private word. They retreated to where the horses were tethered, the only place with no one near enough to overhear.

"Will you help me in this, your highness?" Raith said.

"With what? If you mean the Rising, I—"

"No, not that." Raith cut him off with an upraised hand. "I've no idea how we get into the fortress tomorrow and out again. And as you can see, there are many lives to protect." He gestured to the camp, which was louder now than before, the people whispering about what had happened as they spread out bedrolls or passed around bread and salted meat or flasks of wine.

Corwin traced the scar on his chin, feeling a quake in his belly. "You want me to lead?"

Raith nodded. "You're better suited than I. You know strategy, and my strength is to defend, not attack."

"But you heard Francis. All they see in me is the Errant Prince."

Raith fixed a fierce gaze on him. "Then you must show them you are something more."

"How?" Corwin said, frustration and doubt making him want to pace. He turned to Nightbringer instead, finding comfort in the horse's presence, something steadfast in this upheaving world around him.

"By showing that you hear them, your highness. That's the only way to lead." Raith sighed, and when Corwin turned toward the sound, he found the magist examining his blackened fingertips.

Raith looked up, his expression dark with some unknown emotion. "You can't let others define who you should be. That's a lesson I've been learning since birth." Raith gestured to the mark of the Shade Born on his face. "When people see this, they see something they should fear. My parents believed in the superstition so much that they took me outside the city wall when I was just a babe and left me in the snow to die. I almost did." Raith waggled his fingers, and Corwin realized frostbite must have turned them that color.

Swallowing the hard knot of pity in his throat, he said, "What happened?"

"A magist found me. A master healer, one skilled enough that I managed not to lose all my fingers and toes." Raith smiled, a wet sheen in his eyes. "Master Janus brought me to an orphanage. They took me in, but only because he was a magist and insisted. Every year afterward, he checked in on me to make sure I was being treated fairly. I wasn't, of course. But Janus told me repeatedly that the only way for me to be more than what the gods had marked me for was to stay true to who I was. To make my own fate by making my own decisions. And here I am." Raith motioned to the camp. "A magist helping wilders. That lesson is why I've risked all that I have to make a better life for these people. Wilders can be more than the power they are born with, if we are willing to hear their words, see them for who they are—what they do, not what they *can* do. And you, Prince Corwin, can be more than your title. You just have to rise up and become it. Lead us."

All the reasons he should say no flooded Corwin's mind. He saw the faces of his Shieldhawk brothers, heard their names whispered in his ear. He saw the Sevan soldier boy, for once remembering him clearly, without the fog of his feelings. Maybe Dal had been right—maybe the boy hadn't betrayed them. Maybe there'd been no way to avoid what happened that night. It was a lesson he'd been taught often by his tutors and even his father: battles can only be fought and won or fought and lost. It was a risk you took every time you went in.

"Do you really believe they will follow me?" Corwin asked.

"If you show them that you understand them, and take the first step, they will take the second," Raith said. "Tomorrow they will watch you risk your life to save wilders. You will become more than the Errant Prince in their eyes. You will become *our* prince. And one day you will be our king. Rime will never be whole when we stand so divided, wilder against magist. But you have the power to unite us."

Corwin heard his unspoken words—be the king who sets the wilders free, who ends their suffering. *Who makes Rime whole again.*

He glanced at his tingling palm, the uror brand clear and striking. He lowered his hand, resting it on the revolver belted at his waist.

"We'll need to work fast," Corwin said. "We attack at dawn."

RENDBORNE PROVED TRUE TO HIS word. Once Kate retrieved the secret of the black-powder formula from Signe's mind, he healed most of her wounds. Those that could be healed, that was. Kate knew without asking that Signe would bear the scar on her face forever, and no magic could put back the shattered bones in her foot completely.

While Rendborne worked on Signe, the golds returned Kate and Bonner to their cages. Neither spoke. Bonner seemed beyond words. Even though Kate couldn't hear his thoughts with the collar back in place, she still sensed something vital inside him had broken with his father's death. He seemed ready to lie down and let go. Kate understood the urge. It was her fault Bonner's father was dead, her defiance that had cost her friend so much.

She fought the feeling back. This was not the end of all things. So long as she could breathe and think and act, there was a chance to survive. She had Signe to thank for the hope still left alive inside her. When Kate invaded her friend's mind, she found herself being welcomed in, the bright glow of her essence mesmerizing even through her pain. At first Signe's pain overwhelmed Kate, but then she managed to bear it, and soon she found herself sharing it. It hurt, but the relief she sensed in Signe gave her the strength to endure.

I'm so sorry, Kate thought, sending the words right into Signe's mind.

Don't be, her answer came back at once. *We must be strong. We must fight.*

Signe's resilience, even now, after all she had suffered, lent Kate strength.

But it was quickly waning—even more so when two golds appeared, carrying Signe between them. Her foot had been bandaged with enough wraps that it looked twice its normal size. Signe seemed to have fainted again, her head lolling. The golds deposited her in the empty cage next to Kate's, dropping her like a sack of grain. Kate clamped her mouth shut to keep from screaming at them.

Once they were gone, Kate scooted to the edge of her cage. "Signe, are you okay?"

No answer.

Kate pressed her face against the bars, the metal like cold, dull teeth against her skin. "Signe, please be okay."

"I'm not," Signe replied, her voice low and sluggish. "But I will be. Once we're out of here."

How? Kate bit her lip to keep from saying it aloud, afraid of letting Signe hear her despair.

"This might help us do it." Signe scooted toward her and held out a key, the kind that would unlock their collars.

Kate's breath caught, and for a second she was too stunned to move. "Where did you get that?"

"Rendborne is an arrogant fool. He should've broken my hand instead of my foot."

Then Kate understood. "You stole it off the gold just now?"

"Easy as juggling a knife."

"Signe, I could kiss you," Kate said.

"Later. We need to get out of here first."

With shaking hands, Kate took the key from Signe's fingers. She raised it to the back of her neck and prodded until she found the keyhole. The key slid in with some resistance, but when she turned it, she heard the click of the mechanism unlocking. The collar loosened at her throat and almost fell. She grabbed it and held it in place while beyond the cage a gold walked by. Once he was gone, she lowered the collar, savoring the freedom from its weight. She could sense her magic again, although it was dormant with the late hour. Come morning, though, she would be able to use it again.

Giddy with hope, Kate refastened the collar so no one walking by would notice. Then she edged to the other side of the cage and called for Bonner. He was lying down, his head away from her, face hidden in his arms.

When he didn't answer, she called again, her voice cracking. "Bonner, Signe stole a collar key. We can escape, but we need your help."

Still no answer.

"Please, Bonner. We can't do it without you. Please."

Bonner drew a loud breath, then slowly sat up. "What do you want me to do?"

The sound of his voice made Kate flinch. This wasn't her ever-hopeful, ever-optimistic friend but a dark, forlorn creature, alien and unknowable. Ignoring the ache beneath her breastbone, she slid the key through the bars to him. For a second she feared he wouldn't take it, but then he reached out and grasped it between his rough fingers. A moment later, he pulled the collar from around his neck.

"Will you be able to bend the bars come morning?" Kate said.

"Yes, but we need to think this through. We can't fight our way free with so many golds, and Signe isn't walking out of here on her own."

Kate sat back, her mind racing. Bonner was right. They would never make it out fighting, and the going would be slow with one of them carrying Signe. They needed a way to distract the golds while they escaped. If only Vianne were still here. She could set the place on fire, but she and Kiran must be far away by now.

Blowing out a breath, Kate gazed around the room, trying to come up with a solution. Then her eyes fell on some of the drakes slumbering in their cages, and hope burst inside her.

"The drakes," she said, struggling to maintain a whisper.

"What about them?" Bonner replied from where he leaned against the side of the cage, eyes closed.

"If you can get their cages open, I can make them attack the golds."

His eyes flitted open, and she saw the wet redness in them. "Are you sure?"

"Yes. It'll be just like at Thornewall." She was certain of it.

"Very well," he said, closing his eyes once more. "Come morning, we go. And never come back."

Kate winced, wishing she had some way to ease his pain. "We should try to get some sleep now while we can."

Bonner mumbled an acknowledgment, then fell silent. Kate

scooted to the back of her cage and lay down. Despite her fatigue, sleep was slow to come. Her mind kept replaying the day's events. She saw Bonner's father cut down without a thought. She saw the vial of her father's blood around Rendborne's neck, and heard Vikas's gleeful words at the memory of draining his life, and her boast of setting the trap in King Orwin's mind. Hatred burned within Kate. Yet after a while her thoughts eased enough that she began to drift in and out of consciousness.

But as the hours slid by, she fell into a deeper sleep, only to be hurled out of it by the sound of an explosion. It was like lightning striking a cliff face. The walls of her cage shook, bits of stone and dirt showering her as she lurched upward from her prone position.

"What's happening?" Kate crawled to the front of her cage.

In the cage next to her, she heard Signe laugh. "I imagine Rendborne just tested his black powder. If my calculations were correct, it didn't go very well."

Kate's eyebrows climbed her forehead. "You lied about the mixture? To me?"

Signe shifted nearer the bars, her scarred, puffy face coming into view. "I told you. I would die before revealing the secret to anyone. Such is the power of Seerah." She shrugged. "Besides, here is our diversion."

Kate gaped at her in awe.

"Let's go," Bonner said, his hand already at the back of his collar, inserting the key. Several golds rushed by, on their way toward the explosion.

Once free of the collar, Bonner used his magic to pull apart the shackles at his wrists and feet. With another flick of his hand, he bent back the bars on his cage, making an opening. He climbed out, then did the same to Kate's cage and undid her shackles and collar. She crawled through the bent bars and immediately turned to help Bonner with Signe.

"We need to get her on my back," Bonner said, gently easing Signe toward Kate, who held out her arms to accept her. Signe sagged hard against Kate, one arm flung around her shoulders. Bonner turned his back to them and crouched low. Kate guided Signe forward, each step a painful shuffle. Then she helped Signe climb onto his back, pushing and shoving as best she could.

"Are you sure you can keep her up there?" Kate said. Signe's injuries had robbed her of strength, if not will.

"I'll manage." Bonner hoisted her higher, his bruise-covered arms wrapped around her legs. "Hold on as best you can, Sig."

Signe nodded, her face scrunched against the pain as she tightened her arms around his shoulders. Bending forward, Bonner raised his hand toward the nearest daydrake cages.

Another explosion sounded, making them all duck for cover. Only this one was different, coming from outside the structure. More explosions followed it, sending a fresh shower of rocks down on their heads.

"Get us out of here," Signe cried, unable to protect herself while clinging to Bonner.

They rushed toward the nearest exit, the drakes forgotten. They didn't need any more diversions. Whatever was hitting the fortress was enough. Already the golds were racing toward the exit, shouting about an attack.

Another explosion struck just as they reached the door to the corridor, this one closer and louder. Part of the ceiling came down behind them, sending up a cloud of dust and smashing a row of cages. The drakes inside them shrieked before being silenced by the crush of rock.

Bonner picked up the pace, jogging now. Signe gasped in pain with each step he took, but she held on. Kate followed after them, worried how they would get out with so many golds rushing for the only exit. But once in the corridor, she saw half a dozen giant holes had been blasted into the outer wall. Too many for the golds to defend or block. The sight of those holes sent a surge of hope through Kate. Only wilder magic could've done it.

"Bonner!" Kate called. "Through there." She pointed to the largest of the holes, one big enough to pass through. Pale morning light shone just beyond. Bonner headed through it first, ducking into a crouch to give Signe clearance. Kate hurried after, sucking in a breath of cool, fresh air.

They emerged inside the bailey of the Hellgate, surrounded by the crumbling battlements—and chaos. A battle raged before them, golds and wilders. The Rising was here.

So was Corwin.

Kate's heart lurched into her throat when she spotted him in the midst of the fray. *He came for me.* And he was fighting with the Rising, arm in arm with wilders. He had a sword in one hand and a buckler in the other. The small, round shield glowed with magist magic. Kate watched as he used it to deflect a spell. Then he turned toward his attacker and cut him down with the swipe of his sword.

Next to him, Raith let fly a spell at a gold while behind him a hydrist sent out huge blasts of water. Other wilders hurled fireballs and lightning while still others fought with wind or the very earth itself. This latter was the source of the explosions, massive rocks being uprooted from the ground and hurled at the battlements. The golds were fighting back, tossing spells or moving in for hand-to-hand combat, mace to sword or spear.

Watching the fight, Kate saw again that what Raith had once told her about wilder and magist magic was true. Whenever a stream of lightning or wind or fire met a mage spell, the two powers dissipated, fading into nothing. Only indirect attacks stood any chance at working. As it was, most of the fighters were switching to hand-to-hand combat.

"Kate!" Corwin shouted, spotting her at last. He started toward her, Dal following half a moment later, his gaze fixed on Signe.

A gold rushed toward Corwin, mace raised. Realizing he didn't see it, Kate raised her hand and stretched out with her sway, seizing the gold's mind. *Sleep,* she thought, and he slumped to the ground as if struck dead.

Reaching her, Corwin turned and called for a retreat. The other wilders heard the order and passed it along, shouting it to one another. To her shock, Kate saw that many of them were young, barely more than children. She tried not to look at the ones who had fallen. Not all of the dead and dying on the field were golds.

Dal took Signe from Bonner, hoisting her into his arms while Bonner, Kate, and Corwin formed a circle around her. Then they began to slowly edge toward the battlements where Kate could sense the horses waiting. They were almost there, but the golds were moving to surround them. They were so many and the wilders too few. *We'll never make it.*

A wrongness filled Kate's mind, a warning sounding inside her. *Daydrakes.* No sooner had she thought it than a stream of them came rushing through the broken fortress wall onto the field. For a moment she couldn't think from the fear, but then reason broke through and she reached out toward the nearest drakes with her sway. The message she gave them was simple—attack anything gold that moved. The drakes heard and obeyed. A moment later, the golds' press on the wilders slackened as they were forced to deal with this new threat.

Kate stopped in the retreat long enough to pick up a fallen sword. Like Corwin's buckler, its blade glowed with magist magic. She held it crossways in front of her, ready to deflect any incoming attacks. She ran her gaze over the golds, focused on shielding Dal and Signe. The golds were distracted, but they were cutting down the daydrakes far too quickly. It seemed they had spells designed to fell the beasts.

Hurry, Kate thought, wishing she could run. Then the urge to flee died inside her as she caught sight of Maestra Vikas fighting off a drake just a few feet away. Around the maestra's neck hung the crystal with Kate's father's blood inside it. All reason fled from Kate, all worry and concern about her friends rendered meaningless. All she could see and feel was blind hate, as red as the crystal's contents.

"Kate!" Corwin shouted behind her. "What are you doing?"

She could hear his words, but they were like the shadow of a memory, nothing compared with what she was feeling. With her eyes fixed on Vikas, Kate charged forward. Vikas saw her coming and raised her mace. She let fly a spell, and Kate swiped at it with the sword. The spell fizzled and died as it struck the blade, but so did some of the magic on the sword. She wouldn't be able to defend herself with it for long.

Kate reached out and touched the mind of the nearest daydrake. Its oily, infectious nature made her want to recoil as she summoned the drake to her. It and all the others left alive obeyed, nearly a dozen swarming in front of her like a pack of well-trained guard dogs.

Leaning to one side, Kate could just see around one of the drakes' shoulders. Vikas's expression had changed, the cold confidence of a moment before sliding away. *Yes, be afraid,* Kate thought. *I am coming for you.* Then, touching the drakes' mind once more, she commanded they kill the maestra.

The drakes obeyed, surging forward, their wails like lightning cracking in the air around them.

"Golds to me!" Vikas screamed as she killed the nearest drake with a spell. The golds converged around her, killing more drakes as they went.

But then Kate sensed the others pressing in behind her, coming to help. The golds turned to confront this threat while Kate continued on to Vikas. *He gave me every last drop before he died,* Kate heard her saying once more. She remembered the pleasure, the pride the maestra took in it. *Your precious Lord Ascender isn't here to save you,* Kate thought. There'd been no sign of Rendborne anywhere. She supposed a god couldn't be bothered with such trivial things as a battle. Or maybe he'd been hurt in the explosion. She could only hope.

Vikas cast another spell, and once again Kate deflected it with the sword. The glow was gone completely, but it didn't matter. In another step she would be in striking range. All the hours she'd spent training at the Relay, all the years spent honing her body, came back to her now. To this one fight: to avenge her father's torturer, the woman who had set the trap for him, who had harnessed his blood, enslaving him even in death.

Once Kate was close enough, Vikas didn't have room for her magic anymore and was forced to wield her mace like a true weapon. Kate raised her sword and stabbed for Vikas's belly. The maestra swiped the strike aside, then countered with an upward blow. Kate caught it and thrust down, sparks flying as the metal of their weapons met. Kate had never fought an opponent wielding a mace, but it didn't matter. The objective was the same—kill or be killed. She stabbed again, higher this time, and the tip of the blade pricked Vikas in the shoulder before the magist could counter. Shrieking, the woman leaped backward, out of striking range. Red bloomed through the gold of her robe.

Kate charged forward, swinging her blade from the left this time. But it was just a feint, and as Vikas moved to block, Kate whipped back to the right and struck the maestra in the side. Screaming, the woman fell sideways, but she swung back at Kate, catching her arm with the head of the mace. Pain tore through Kate, blinding her for a moment. She nearly dropped the sword in her need to grab her injured arm. Then she saw the crystal at Vikas's neck again, and the pain retreated in the wake of her fury. She raised the sword once more and swung at Vikas in a sloppy, chopping motion. Vikas rolled out of the way, then scrambled back to her feet, one hand clutched to her bleeding side.

Kate swung at her again, first left, then right, then from

underneath and above. Relentlessly she pursued the maestra, hatred lending her strength and foresight. Vikas fought back, sweat matting her pale hair to her face, her cheeks flushed. But she was weakening, blood ebbing from her side and shoulder, her muscles tiring. Kate knew she should be feeling the same, and yet she felt stronger than before, renewed with each blow. She could do this forever. Whatever it took.

With a scream of fury, Kate swung again, putting all her strength behind it. The blow landed across Vikas's wrist, just above where her hand held the mace. The blade sliced through skin and bone both, lopping off the maestra's hand entirely. Vikas fell to her knees, soundless, her remaining hand clamped around the stump of her other arm.

Kate bent toward the maestra and grasped the blood crystal around her neck by its leather cord. She yanked, pulling it free. Then without thinking, without even knowing what she planned to do, Kate plunged into Vikas's mind. Panic, pain, and terror enveloped her. For a second it was so much, Kate almost lost herself in it. She fought back the emotion, gleaning memories in the process, glimpses into this woman's life, the way Vikas's lust for knowledge had been there from the start, driving her to do unspeakable things. She'd tortured animals first, both ordinary creatures and night-drakes. She studied the power in their blood and then turned her aims on humans, experimenting on wilders. All the while she justified her actions by the value of the knowledge she gained. Long before Rendborne, Vikas had pushed boundaries no moral person would ever dare.

For a second, Kate almost withdrew in disgust, but then she

forced herself deeper, drawing strength from the maestra's fear. Kate amplified those feelings with her magic, pushing them to their extremes. Vikas trembled, eyes wide and jaw slack at the onslaught.

In full control now, Kate searched for Vikas's center, that glowing, vibrant flame, the essence of who she was, her very life force. Kate found it and seized it with her magic. *This is for Signe and Bonner. For everyone you've ever hurt. This is for my father.* Kate sent the words directly into Vikas's mind so that she would understand, taking the judgment with her as she crossed over into death. Then with all Kate had inside her, she extinguished Vikas's glow like blowing out a candle. Vikas made a single noise, a gasp of surprise almost, then fell and lay there silent and still.

Trembling, Kate stood, unable to think or feel from the shock of what she'd done and the heady power coursing through her. She felt like a storm, a force of nature ready to sweep in and destroy anything that dared step into her path.

A cry of fury filled the air around her. Kate turned in time to see Rendborne rushing toward her. Anger twisted his features, his gold eyes flashing in the sun. As before, Kate felt caught by his presence, enthralled. Her own sense of power, of purpose, fled from her. There was nothing she could do but yield to the man, this god made flesh. Helpless, she sank to her knees.

Vaguely, she was aware that the fighting had stopped, the golds retreating at the appearance of their master. Corwin, Bonner, Raith, and the wilders still left alive crowded in around Kate as if they meant to defend her from this man.

Seeing them, Rendborne raised his right arm and swung it right, then left. Magic exploded from his fingertips, the force of it knocking down everyone still standing. Out of the corner of her eye, Kate saw Corwin go flying backward, landing hard on his back with a groan of pain.

"What have you done?" Rendborne said, reaching Kate. She could see burns on his hands and face, marks of Signe's deception, but it brought her no satisfaction.

Rendborne stared down at Vikas's dead face, something like sorrow in his eyes. It seemed the monster was capable of love, whatever that meant to him. Kate was glad to see it, glad to know she had caused him pain, this man responsible for so much death and suffering. Around his neck, the blood crystal seemed to mock her, but there was nothing she could do about it. Rendborne was an unstoppable force.

As if to prove it, some of the wilders who had been farthest away attacked him now. He caught each attempt with a simple wave of his hand, as if he were swatting flies. Then he returned the magic in kind. The pyrist who dared cast fire at him, he set ablaze. The hydrist who tried to pull the water from his blood, he drowned in a gush of water he sent streaming over her head from out of his hands. The aerist suffocated inside a vortex of wind.

When it was done, Rendborne turned to Kate. "I see now how your friends love you, Kate Brighton. They are willing to die for you," Rendborne said. "And now they shall. All of them."

Rendborne retreated a few steps, bringing all his victims into reach. Then he raised his hands, cupping the right with the left. Kate saw the glow between his fingers, magic building around his uror mark. Then he raised his hand and unleashed the full force of his abilities, right at her. Right at them all.

CORWIN LOOKED UP FROM WHERE he'd fallen to the ground, his eyes still disbelieving the sight of the man before him. Rendborne. A Tormane. Yet as he looked, he could see a hint of it in the man's features, a vague familiarity. *This is the Nameless One.* God made flesh. For a moment Corwin believed it might be true. Never before had he seen such power. With a single flick of his wrist this man could level armies. There seemed no stopping him. Nothing to do but lie still and wait for the end to come.

No. One look at Kate was all he needed to know he couldn't be still. Couldn't let this happen. Corwin raised his head, seeing the magic building inside Rendborne's cupped hands. The man's right palm still bore an uror mark. Corwin couldn't see it, but he felt it. Felt it in the burning in his own palm, as if like called to like.

Rendborne raised his right hand. Corwin lurched to his feet and leaped, arm outstretched as if he meant to catch the spell like a thrown spear. Magic, white and bright as the sun, burst out from Rendborne's palm, his uror mark ablaze. With an instinct that didn't belong to him, Corwin reached toward the magic and caught it with his own hand, his own mark.

Agony lit through his body, his mind, his soul. He felt the magic burn through every fiber of his being, a force trying to tear him asunder. He screamed, the sound swallowed up by the magic.

Images ripped through his mind, of places he had never been, faces he had never known. Memories that didn't belong to him. He saw Rendborne as a young man, a young prince and heir. He saw the uror sign, a grand eagle feathered in black and white. He felt Rendborne's hatred and fear of the creature and all it meant, all it could mean. He doubted himself, resenting the way the sign made him feel less. He wanted an out, and killing it seemed the only way. But he didn't know what would happen. He didn't know the magic would react—that it would go into him, claiming him as its new vessel, its nature perverted.

The magic's corruption was slow at first, a festering disease. The high priestess banished him for his treachery, his brother named heir. They erased his name from all records. He wandered, lost in isolation as the magic ate away at him. Until at last it sundered him in two. He died, but the magic wouldn't let go. It needed its vessel. It put him together again, broken and wrong and yet more powerful than any man should be.

He learned to live again, but that wrongness consumed him even as it kept him alive, year after year, his power growing instead of waning. His hatred building until all he wanted was to see Rime and its people fall, to suffer and be subjugated, his to control and command at last. As it should have been.

He worked for years, laying his plans while a new Tormane ascended the throne, then another. But the corruption taught him patience. Until he formed the alliances he needed with Magnar Fane, the Godking, Maestra Vikas, those like him. He drew anyone he needed, his magic making these tasks simple. When the new uror sign appeared, he knew it was time to act. He tried to kill the colt but couldn't. No matter what he did, he couldn't touch it. Something protected the creature from him. The princes, too, were beyond his reach. Even his daydrakes failed to kill them. But the magic that protected them wouldn't last forever. Only he would last forever. He would outlive them all. Nothing could stop him. *Nothing.*

No, Corwin thought. *I will stop you. You will not win.*

A scream filled Corwin's ears, and belatedly he realized it wasn't his scream but Rendborne's. The magic had reverberated, forced back by the power in Corwin's uror brand. His mark glowed, brightly burning, pulsating with magic. Blinking through the haze of pain, Corwin looked up to see Rendborne crouched over, his right hand clutched to his stomach, the fingers blackened husks, like twigs charred in a fire.

With an outraged scream, Rendborne turned and fled, calling for his golds to follow and protect him.

Slowly, trembling all over, Corwin lowered his hand, the glow already fading from his palm. It was over, and somehow, he was still alive. So were the others. He got to his feet and reached for Kate, helping her to stand. Across from him, Dal picked up Signe once more, Bonner aiding him.

"Let's go," Corwin said, "before he comes back." He didn't think he could face Rendborne a second time. Not now.

With his arm around Kate's shoulder and her arm around his waist, they hobbled toward the gate, leaning on each other. Long before they reached it, men on horseback came charging through the gate toward them—Norgard cavalry, with Edwin riding at their head and Grand Master Storr and Captain Jaol beside him. They halted, and Edwin surveyed the scene, taking in the sight of dead wilders and golds, drakes, and the crumbling ruin of the Hellgate.

Then finally Edwin turned his gaze on Corwin. "Traitor."

Corwin flinched at the hatred in his brother's voice, the condemnation in his eyes. "Edwin, if you'll just listen. Rendborne has been sending wilders to Seva, to the Godking. He's gotten away, but if—"

"I let you go and you do this." Edwin gestured to the carnage. "You join your wilder friends."

"Why aren't you listening to me?" Corwin dropped his arm from Kate's shoulder, shuffling her behind him, to shield her from anything his brother might try.

"We will deal with Rendborne," Grand Master Storr said. At least one of them had been listening. "This corruption in the Inquisition will not stand."

"Yes," agreed Edwin. "Now step away, Corwin, while we deal with these wilders."

Captain Jaol raised his hands and the soldiers drew their revolvers.

Corwin stared at the weapons. Each one would fire six rounds, and unlike the battle between magist and wilder, there was no way to cancel out the destruction here.

"Edwin, just listen. This is wrong. The wilders aren't our enemies; we need—"

"The wilders are a threat. They always have been. Nothing will ever change that." Edwin turned to the soldiers. "Shoot around my brother if you must."

"Wait!" Corwin held up his hands and took a step closer. "I am your prince and I say to put your weapons away."

The soldiers hesitated, torn between the two heirs.

"Don't listen to him," Edwin shouted. He tugged on his horse's reins, wheeling the bay about. "He's a traitor. Kill the wilders!"

Again the soldiers hesitated. Even Captain Jaol looked uncertain. Furious, Edwin drew the revolver at his hip and cocked the hammer, the barrel pointed at Francis, the wilder nearest him. Francis stared back, hands flexed at his sides and his chin thrust out in defiance. Edwin raised the gun, his finger tensed on the trigger.

The gun split in two.

Edwin flinched, watching the broken pieces fall to the ground.

"Those were never meant to kill humans," Bonner said, hand outstretched. He waved his arm, and the other revolvers broke in half as well. Corwin took a relieved breath. He glanced at Bonner, seeing the weariness in his face. How much more magic could he wield? *Not enough.* Not with so many swords. All the wilders were drained from battle, ill prepared for this fight.

"This is your last chance," Edwin said through gritted teeth. A vein pulsed in his forehead, his cheeks flushed with anger. "You must choose, Corwin. The wilders who killed our mother. Or your family, Norgard, your birthright."

Time seemed to slow around Corwin as he weighed the choices in his mind, feeling the burden of them, the absolute finality. He glanced behind him at Kate and the others. Then he glanced down at the brand on his palm, remembering the way it had glowed and burned a moment before, pulsing with magic, with promise. In that moment he understood—Edwin couldn't take this from him. He could label him traitor, make whatever claims he wanted, spread whatever lies he wished—but he couldn't deny the uror. The third trial waited for them both. No power short of the gods' could stop it.

Slowly, Corwin stretched out his hand behind him, fingers reaching for Kate. A moment later, he felt her hand slip into his. "I choose them, Edwin. I choose the hundreds who have lived under the shadow of the Inquisition long enough. They are just as much people of Rime as you or I. And I am their prince as well."

Edwin drew his sword, and all around him the soldiers did the same. The hesitation they'd shown with the revolvers was gone now. Swords meant a fair battle, an honorable death instead of slaughter. *So be it,* Corwin thought, reaching for his own sword.

Something spooked the horses. Almost at once they all reared and spun, unseating their riders, men unprepared to hold on with the awkward balance of the swords in their hands. Edwin and Storr both fell while Jaol's horse carried him away into the woods, the man clinging to her neck. The other horses followed.

Edwin recovered quickly, sword raised once more. "Attack!" he screamed.

The remaining soldiers rushed forward, one pace, two.

"STOP!" The scream came from behind Corwin. He felt the power in the voice, the pressure in his mind. It rendered him still, incapable of moving, of doing anything besides listen. He watched Kate step around him to face Edwin and the soldiers—all of them frozen in place like living statues. She was doing this, same as she had sent the horses flying a moment before. Controlling them all with her magic.

The look on her face sent a shudder arching down his spine. Murder gleamed in her eyes. There was too much white in them, her teeth bared in a feral snarl.

"Kate," Corwin whispered, remembering the way she'd struck down Vikas with her magic. That was the only explanation for the way the woman had died, so sudden, like a candle snuffed by the wind. "Don't . . ." *Don't kill them,* he thought but couldn't say. The reality that she could sent a tremble through him. But it wasn't what she *could* do, only what she would do. A choice. Not yet made. *Spare them, Kate,* he thought. *Have mercy.*

Seconds passed, the forest still and silent. Tension crackled in the air, all of the men aware that they balanced on the edge of a knifepoint, death a mere thought away.

Finally, at last, Kate waved her hand. "Sleep," she said. Instantly, the soldiers slumped to the ground, Grand Master Storr and Edwin with them. The latter crumpled to his knees, a look of defiance in his expression, even to the last.

When it was over Kate turned to the others, a strange glow on her face, a distance in her gaze.

"Let's go," she said. "I don't know how long they'll stay under." She held out her hand to Corwin.

He hesitated half a moment before taking it. Her fingers felt cold in his palm as they walked side by side past the sleeping soldiers. Corwin glanced down at Edwin just once, regret squeezing his chest. But there was nothing he could do for his brother now. His choice was made.

THEY FLED WEST INTO JADE Forest, going as far and as fast as the horses and their injuries would allow. Kate rode without speaking, without thinking. Finally, with night descending, they made camp in a gorge at the base of the Cobalt Mountains. A narrow passage, barely wide enough for two horses abreast, led into the gorge, making it easily defensible should the golds or Edwin's forces find them. Kate doubted they would. Despite what she'd said, she didn't think the soldiers were likely to wake soon. The thought turned her insides cold, reminding her how close she had come to killing them all, as she had Maestra Vikas.

It had been so easy. The power of a god. *No wonder Rendborne desires it so much,* she thought, remembering the envy she had sensed in him. The gods were merciful to deny him the power of sway. With it, he would be even more unstoppable than he already was. *But what does it make me?*

A monster, a voice whispered in her mind, over and over again. She had used her magic to kill, and the sense of power it had given her had made her want to do it again, seductive as it was. Now, with the feeling gone, it didn't matter that Vikas deserved it. Didn't matter that it was righteous vengeance. The act left her hollowed out—and changed forever. She wondered if the others could sense the change in her, too, and she couldn't look at any of them as they rode. Especially Corwin. She had seen his hesitation afterward, how he had feared touching her.

Once inside the gorge, they made camp beneath the cliff at its base, a wide, circular outcropping. The sandy ground would make for soft bedding, and despite the steady fall of water from the stream above, it remained dry and warm. Raith and two of his blues hurriedly set the wardstone barrier while the rest gathered firewood and began tending the injured.

Kate threw herself into the work, despite her exhaustion. It was better than facing Corwin or Signe or Bonner. Better than facing herself. She tended the horses, unsaddling them, checking for injuries, then rubbing them down. She lingered longest with Firedancer, savoring the comfort of the horse's mind against her own. The fact that Corwin had brought the horse for her out of Norgard seemed to ease her fear a little. He cared for her, she knew. But how long could that care last now that he knew what she could do? Now that they both did.

He has magic, too, though, she tried to tell herself, remembering the way he'd protected them with his uror mark. She didn't understand how it had worked, what he'd done exactly, but she was glad for it. He had been the shield to protect them all. *His is only for good.*

Yes, and you chose for the good, a voice argued in her mind, *that is the same.*

Corwin, too, kept busy, doing what he could to help the magists work their healing magic before nightfall and helping to build additional shelters for the weak and the children who were with them. Most had been spared from the fighting, ordered to tend the horses during the battle. Most, but not all. One of the wilder boys had lost an eye in the fight. Kate spotted him lying on a bedroll near the fire, his head wrapped in a torn strip of cloth. They needed fresh supplies and to find permanent shelter. But where? They were all outlaws now.

Once she finished with the horses, Kate wandered through the camp, searching for other ways to be useful. She felt eyes watching her as she moved, and she couldn't help the guilt twisting in her gut. It was her fault these people were here. Only the more she looked into those faces, the more her guilt became anger. Yes, she'd contributed to the golds finding out about the Rising's headquarters, but that wasn't what had made these people a target in the first place. *It doesn't matter what we've done. We are hunted because of who we are.*

A hard resolve rose up in Kate. It needed to end. The hatred, the suspicion. The wilders had allowed it to go on for too long. *We all allowed it by our hiding.* By living in secret, they had let the world perceive them as it wanted to and not as they were. The Rising, which she had blamed for the oppression of people like her, wasn't even fully real. It was a ruse, conjured to keep the people of Rime—wilder or no—afraid.

I am done with hiding, Kate thought. *No matter what the others think.* This, at least, she could be sure of.

Realizing there wasn't any work left to do, Kate headed to the stream to clean up. She soaked her hands, scrubbing away at the dirt. Then she washed her face. She undid her plait, combed her fingers through it, then redid the braid. At last she stood and ran her hands down her clothes, trying to smooth out the wrinkles. Feeling something in her pocket, she reached inside it and withdrew the blood crystal. She examined it for several minutes, unsure what to do with it. Then, finally, she tied it around her neck. The crystal warmed against her chest. It was strange, almost perverse, knowing her father's blood resided inside it, and yet, it was right, too. Here he was, protecting her once more as he'd always done before. *I will give it to Kiran,* she silently swore. *Once I find him.*

Kate made her way to Signe, lying on a bedroll in front of a fire with her injured foot propped up on a saddle. Kate sat down beside her. Signe reached over and took her hand, squeezing her fingers.

"You did well," Signe said. "In the end, you saved us all."

Kate bit her lip, uncertain how to reply. She knew better than to deny it, not to Signe, but she didn't want to accept the praise either.

"How about you? Are you going to be okay?"

Signe nodded, meeting her gaze with no hesitation. She raised a hand to the scar on her face. "Does it make me look a fierce warrior?"

Kate smiled. "The fiercest of fierce."

"Good. It's nice that my outsides finally match my insides. Now whenever I tell people about how I am a slayer of giants and a tormentor of hobgoblins, they will know it's true."

"We already knew, Sig. No one could ever doubt." Kate slid an arm around her shoulder and hugged her tight for a moment.

"Careful now," Dal said, walking up to them and sitting on Signe's other side. "Or you'll make me jealous."

Grinning, he reached up and removed the magestone in his ear. The left side of his face went blurry for a moment as the spell dissipated. Once it was clear, Kate saw the scars, a mountain ridge of divots running from his brow to his chin. He tossed the magestone into the stream without comment.

Bonner joined them next, sitting beside Kate. He sat close, his shoulder pressing against hers. She leaned into him, drawing comfort by his nearness, his quiet acceptance.

Soon others joined them, making a large circle around the fire. To Kate's surprise, several of the wilders thanked her for what she'd done by putting Edwin and the soldiers to sleep. She accepted the thanks with a single nod, her lips pressed together.

Kate searched the gorge for Corwin, finally spying him across the way talking privately with Raith and Francis. In moments they stopped speaking and the three of them walked over to the fire. All eyes turned to them. It was as if the entire camp held its breath.

Raith raised his hands in an unneeded call for silence. Then he cleared his throat and said, "Tomorrow we journey to Carden to join the wilder forces there. Before we left Norgard, I sent out missives to our contacts in each of the twelve cities. The time for the Rising to move is finally here."

Applause broke out at this, and Kate cut her eyes to Corwin, shocked that he would condone this course of action. His gaze was fixed on the ground before him, his arms crossed over his chest.

"But the fight ahead isn't one we ever planned," Raith continued once the applause died down. "While the Inquisition and its supporters remain our enemy, the biggest threat is Seva. The Godking Magnar Fane, with the help of Rendborne—the Nameless One— has imprisoned our friends and loved ones. We must see them free. Prince Corwin has volunteered to lead the search party into Seva to find where the wilders are being kept. He will leave as soon as he is able."

Kate stared at him, wondering at his motivations. The Godking in possession of wilders was an undeniable threat, but Dal had told her everything that had happened while she was imprisoned in the Hellgate. Corwin knew about Kiran. *He knows everything about me now.*

Corwin stepped up next to Raith. Then he ran his eyes over the crowd, meeting each face. Even Kate's. His eyes lingered on her longer than the others, and when he moved on, she became aware of the ragged beat of her heart beneath her breastbone.

"I swear on my title, on my blood, and on my honor that I will do whatever I can to free the wilders and to defeat the Nameless One. But even more than that, I swear that we will reclaim Rime as a land for both wilder and magist and everyone in between. All of us together are what make Rime great. When we are done, all will live in peace and live as they are without hiding or fear."

Tears pricked Kate's eyes as she listened, and when the others applauded she joined in, mouth closed to keep her emotions from spilling out from her.

Raith raised his hands for silence again, and this time it was necessary. "Prince Corwin will need help. The trip to Seva will be perilous at every turn. He will need the best of us to aid him."

"I will go," Dal said at once. He shot Corwin a glare, one made fiercer by the scars on his face. "I can't believe you didn't tell me already."

Corwin shrugged, a smile teasing his lips. "I know better than to speak for you, my friend."

"I'm going, too," Bonner said, rising to his feet.

Kate glanced up at him, feeling a wave of fear for him. He wasn't made for war. He was meant to create, not destroy. But there was a hardness to him now that had never been there before. Perhaps it would be enough to see him safely through.

Kate stood up beside him and said, "Me as well. I will go." There was no question about it. It was already her plan, to find Kiran and Vianne.

She turned her gaze on Corwin, their eyes locking. As always, something moved between them, a force like lightning and thunder.

When the meeting ended, Corwin approached Kate. Wordlessly, he took her by the hand and led her to where a small band of trees grew on the side of the gorge. It offered the only privacy there was to find in the camp.

Corwin stopped and faced her. "I'm sorry for all the things I didn't do, Kate," he began. She opened her mouth in protest, but he placed a gentle finger against her mouth. "Please, let me finish. Then you can scream at me all you want. I will stand here and savor every minute of the abuse."

With a blush heating her face, Kate pressed her lips together and waited.

"You were right. I should've done everything I could to let your father go into exile. I should've believed you when you said he was innocent. I was blinded by the idea that to be king was to obey. That the laws were some fixed, holy thing, unchangeable, irrefutable in their wisdom. But they aren't. The world changes, the wheel spins, and so we must change as well. That is what it means to lead—finding the wisdom to bring change when it's needed and to hold fast when it's not. Thank you for helping me learn this truth."

The world is black and white and all the shades of gray in between, Kate thought. She held her breath, his confession sliding over her like stepping into a warm pool of water, soothing and welcome. She remembered that moment when he begged her not to use her power to kill Edwin and the others, how close she'd come. But he pulled her back despite his doubt and fear. He lifted her up. *Or maybe we lifted each other.*

"You never answered my question, though," Corwin said, pulling her out of her thoughts.

"What question?" she asked, breathless.

"Whether or not you'll have me." He stepped closer, their bodies nearly touching. "I love you, Kate Brighton. I always have. I'm yours however you want. As prince or pauper, husband or paramour. That power belongs to you and only you."

Kate stared up at him, her mouth falling open. She could see he meant every word. And there was a deeper meaning behind his words, one she sensed as clearly as if he'd spoken them aloud: that he accepted her in the same way—as she was, without question. Traitor, wilder, woman.

Kate. Just Kate.

With no words to offer him in return, she answered him the only way she knew how.

With a kiss.

The first of many, as long as their perilous future would allow.

ACKNOWLEDGMENTS

THIS IS THE HARDEST BOOK I've written to date, and I owe so many thanks for it that mere words won't be enough. Still, I'll give it a try. First, to my editor, Jordan Brown, for taking a chance on this book even though it was only halfway done. Your faith in the story, and in me, made all the difference. As did your brilliant insight.

To the wonderful team at Balzer + Bray for allowing me the privilege to once again call this place my publishing home and for believing in this girl called Kate, armed with magic and a moonbelt: Alessandra Balzer, Donna Bray, Tiara Kittrell, Renée Cafiero, Caroline Sun, Bess Brasswell, and Tyler Breitfeller. And extra-special thanks to the magicians behind the gorgeous cover: art director Alison Donalty, designer David Curtis, and artist Santi Zoraidez. Thank you for making Kate and Corwin look so good.

As always, thanks to my agent, Suzie Townsend, my first and

last champion. And to the rest of the New Leaf crew who helped give this story a place in the world: Sarah Stricker, Joanna Volpe, Kathleen Ortiz, Mia Roman, Veronica Grijalva, Pouya Shahbazian, and Jaida Temperly.

To my early readers and cheerleaders: Sarah Goldberg, Amanda and Jay Sharritt, Susan Dennard, Natalie D. Richards, Lorie Langdon, Liz Coley, Kristina McBride, Maria Pilar Albarran Ruiz, and Erin Rupert.

Extra-special thanks to my critique partner, Lori M. Lee. Thank you for riding out these publishing storms with me. And to Kristen Simmons—thanks for talking me down off ledges and up out of those pits of despair.

To my riding coach, Lori Miller, a true wilder at heart—thanks for the equine advice and guidance.

Thanks to the rest of my family not yet mentioned: Adam, Inara, Tanner, Betty, Phil, Debra, Krystal, and Vicki. And thanks to God, who makes all things possible.

And finally, thanks to you, dear reader. I hope you enjoyed the ride.

Keep reading for a sneak peek
at the sequel to ONYX & IVORY:

SHADOW & FLAME

PROLOGUE ⁓ KATE

NO ONE DARED APPROACH THE gate of the prison—not by choice, at any rate. Even the guards preparing for their watches regarded the Mistfold with wariness, like conscripts heading into battle. Not their first one, but their fifth or sixth, enough experience to make them fully aware of the hardships in store and the likelihood of death.

Kate Brighton couldn't blame them for it. The fortress was as foreboding as any she'd seen. Its red mudbrick wall, the color of dirt mixed with blood, stood more than thirty feet high, the top hidden by the thick, undulating mist that gave the prison its name. That mist was as vast and imposing as the sea, obscuring everything beyond it, even sunlight. Not that there was much of that to be seen yet, only a vague brightening from black to gray. Another dawn was here, and yet again Kate hadn't sensed it, her magic, once stirring to life with the rising of the sun, dead inside her. She pushed away the reminder and the wave of homesickness it brought.

Almost time, she thought, raising one hand to touch the revolver belted at her right side. A sword hung from her left, hidden by her long cloak. It was a heavier, more impressive weapon at a glance, but far less deadly. If fighting broke out, the revolver was all she would need. *When* it broke out. Despite their planning, violence seemed inevitable. There was too much they didn't know about what awaited them beyond the wall and beneath that unnatural mist. The only thing she knew for certain was that her little brother was being held in there, along with dozens of her fellow wilders.

"It's almost time." Corwin spoke from beside her, and hearing him echo her thoughts sent a trickle of warmth through her, easing the tight knot in her chest.

Craving a glimpse of his face, Kate turned to him, only to be met with disappointment. Although the voice was Corwin's, the face staring at her from the shadows belonged to a stranger. It was a plain face with features so unremarkable that Kate's brain was incapable of remembering it. But that had been the point when Harue fashioned the disguise. The magestone she'd made was perched in Corwin's left ear, the telltale glow of its magic hidden behind a gold plate. Fortunately, Harue had the foresight to create it before they'd left Rime a few weeks ago. The very next morning after setting sail for this gods-forsaken country, her magic had vanished, same as Kate's and the others'. It stopped Harue from making new magestones, but at least the ones she'd already made had retained their normal level of power and duration. An advantage of magist magic over wilders', it seemed.

"Yes," Kate replied, glancing away from that unfamiliar face. She wished Harue were a little less skillful at her craft. The magist might've left some trace of Corwin in the masklike glamour. Then again, such precautions were warranted. Corwin Tormane, high prince of Rime, was a wanted man. Both at home, where his older brother had labeled him traitor, and especially here, in Seva, the longstanding enemy of Rime. King Magnar Fane of Seva would sacrifice six of his seven sons to capture him.

"You hate this face, don't you?" Corwin said, a tease in his voice.

Despite herself, Kate smiled. Here was her Corwin, for certain—the one who could always see her hidden truths. "Not at all. It's better than your regular face, honestly."

"Well, in that case, I will make sure Harue remains in my employ indefinitely so that I might wear it for you each night."

"Moderation, my love." She patted his cheek. "Once a week at most, otherwise I'll surely grow bored with it."

"Is that so?" He arched an eyebrow, or at least tried to, but this face wasn't made for the gesture and so both brows rose, making him look surprised instead of playful. "Does that mean you'll grow bored of me as well?"

A smirk lifted one half of her mouth. "Let's survive this rescue first and discuss the rest of our lives later."

Corwin grinned back at her, a hint of himself flashing in those false, dark eyes. "Tonight then. Soon as we're on the ship for home."

Home. Kate longed for it. Despite the troubles waiting for them in Rime, she missed the land itself with a physical ache. The rolling hills of Norgard, covered in lush green grass and everweep flowers, the towering trees of Aldervale, the blue skies over gray mountains in Farhold, and the crystalline waters of the Penlaurel River. The life and color of Rime made Seva seem a withering wasteland by comparison. And her magic, of course. She missed that most of all. Even though she'd always heard that magic didn't exist outside of Rime, it had been a shock to discover her abilities were so conditional to her location.

She returned her attention to the gate where the change of guard was just finishing. Although she admired Corwin's absolute certainty about the outcome of this rescue, she didn't share it. Too much of their plan relied on luck and chance, both in short supply. If only she were able to use her ability to influence the minds of others; then they could get in and out of the prison with relative ease. Without it they were forced to rely on stealth and tricks like ordinary bandits.

Remembering those tricks, Kate reached into her pocket and pulled out two small pieces of cork, which she gently slid into her nostrils.

"Good luck." Corwin handed her a small glass vial.

She accepted it with a quick nod, hiding its smoky contents from view with her clasped fingers. Then, stepping out from the alley, she approached the two guards standing by the gate.

The one on the left looked up at the sound of her footsteps and raised a hand to the hilt of his sword. "What goes here?"

Kate smiled warmly, counting on these men misjudging her based on her size and sex. "Pardon me, but I seem to have lost my way." Her voice sounded strange with the cork in her nose, but neither guard seemed to notice. "Would you be able to tell me how to get to Merum?"

At the mention of the nearby pleasure district, both men's expressions shifted, and Kate seized her chance. Before either could respond, she took a quick step forward, squeezing her mouth shut as she flicked off the stopper on the glass vial, setting its smoky contents loose. The poison rose up in a thick cloud, enveloping the guards. The one on the left tried to cry out, but the smoke filled his mouth, rendering him silent. A moment later, they both fell to the ground, unconscious.

Kate dispersed the remnants with her hand, then beckoned behind her. Corwin and the others appeared in the courtyard, stepping out from their hiding places in the alleys surrounding the Mistfold. The prison was located on the farthest northern point of Luxana, the capital city of Seva. A strange place for a prison, although rumor claimed it had been a temple long ago.

There were eight of them in all, counting herself and Corwin, a small but deadly band. Dallin Thorne and Tira Salomon appeared first, both of them former mercenaries: Dal from the legendary company known as the Shieldhawks and Tira from their sister unit, the Shieldcrows. Dal flashed a grin at Kate, teeth bared in his eagerness for battle. The cavernous scars on the left side of his face gave the expression a sinister edge. Next to him, Tira yawned broadly, as if bored. Kate supposed she might well be. In the four months Kate had known the woman, she'd never seen anything faze her. She greeted every danger with the same unflappable indifference.

Walking a few steps behind them, Tom Bonner appeared more subdued and somehow far more dangerous than either of the mercenaries. Given his ability to manipulate metal, there wasn't any doubt of his potential for deadliness, at least when they were at home, but still Kate didn't like thinking of him that way. His countenance these days made her more uncomfortable than Corwin with his stranger's mask. She missed the old Bonner, gentle and optimistic, but that version of her friend seemed to have died along with his father, the elder Bonner murdered nearly half a year ago now by the same man responsible for putting the prisoners inside these walls.

The remaining three were wilders, too: Yvonne, an aerist, with control over air; Vander, a pyrist, with control over fire; and Francis, another earthist like Bonner. Only unlike him, Francis had a greater affinity for stone than metal. If he'd had access to his magic, Francis could've torn a hole in the Mistfold's wall and given them entry that way.

Remembering her own weakened state, Kate brought her focus back to the task at hand and stooped toward the nearest guard, relieving him of the ring of keys belted at his waist. Then she turned to the manway door off to the side of the gate and unlocked it. Dal and Tira headed in first, weapons drawn, while Bonner and Francis picked up the sleeping guards and hauled them inside.

Corwin, Yvonne, and Vander followed with Kate coming last, shutting the door behind her. She turned in time to see Tira bend toward the guards and slit their throats, one after the other, as easy as if she were harvesting wheat with a scythe.

"Dammit, Tira," Kate said. "What's the point of putting them to sleep if you're just going to kill them?"

Corwin touched her shoulder. "They are our enemies, Kate, and we couldn't be certain how long the sleep would last."

She shrugged him off and turned away, trying to regain her composure. Corwin was right, of course. These were Sevan soldiers, oath-bound to a king who'd been trying to conquer Rime for years and was now closer than ever to accomplishing that goal—that could be the only reason why he'd been imprisoning wilders, to use them against Rime in some way, magic or no. Though surely their magic would return once they came home. Yvonne, who had visited Seva as a child, claimed it would. *And these people are holding Kiran prisoner.* The thought of her little brother was all it took for Kate to steel herself against the guilt.

Quickly, the group discarded their cloaks, revealing the Sevan uniforms beneath, each one painstakingly acquired these last few weeks. Kate freed the helmet from the strap on her back and slid it over her head. The nose guard and cheek pieces hung too low, half obscuring her vision from all sides, but at least they would hide her face from onlookers. She was less certain about the uniform. The last time she'd tried to pass herself off as a man, it hadn't gone well.

"Yvonne," Corwin said, inclining his stranger's face toward the aerist, "you stay here and silence anyone who comes this way."

"With pleasure," Yvonne replied, her eyes bright with anticipation. She was one of the few wilders with them who didn't have a loved one caged somewhere here, but her mother had been killed by Gold Robes, the magist order that had been secretly kidnapping wilders and sending them to Seva. Rescuing those wilders was Yvonne's chosen method of vengeance. Kate often wondered what kind of person Yvonne would've been if it had never happened. She seemed born to be an assassin. Even without her magic, which she could use to squeeze the breath from a man's lungs with a single, silent thought, she was just as deadly, her knives more like extensions of her hands.

Corwin addressed the others. "The rest of us will move on in groups, staggering our approach. Try to blend in as much as possible. Our goal is to free as many wilders as we can without discovery." He turned and headed down the corridor searching for the nearest exit out of the gatehouse and into the prison itself. They'd been able to gather ample information about the gatehouse, but little about what lay beyond it, other than that the wilders were being housed in an area called "the pit." The dreadful name had kept Kate up late at night, especially the thought that her six-year-old brother was imprisoned there. No—Kiran would be seven by now. She clenched her jaw at the realization.

They reached the exit without incident, and Corwin opened the door and stepped outside onto a dusty, sunlit field encircled by the prison's walls. Kate blinked, her eyes slow to adjust to the sudden change. She hadn't expected this. From outside the mist seemed to enfold the entire prison like a dome, but glancing up she saw clear sky. The mist was still there, but it went no deeper than the wall itself. *Magic*. Only, Kate couldn't see how it was possible. No wilder could do this, not in Seva.

Lowering her gaze, she scanned the rest of the field, searching for prison barracks, but there were no structures in view. Instead, a massive hole sat in the middle of the field. *The pit.*

Kate and Corwin approached it quickly, hoping they appeared like nothing more than two guards going about their duty with the others following some distance behind. But when they reached the edge, Kate forgot her role completely.

"How?" she gasped, eyes drawn downward into the pit.

This place couldn't be. It was like looking through a window that opened onto another world. The bottom lay several hundred feet below, over a sheer vertical edge. Grass so green it was almost blue covered the pit floor, even though Seva was an arid place, water scarce and the flora rough and colorless.

But the grass wasn't the only thing that didn't belong. There were everweeps, too, thousands of them scattered across the floor thick as a garden. The sight of those flowers, with their perpetually dew-drenched petals of every color, sent an ache of homesickness through Kate, as if Rime itself waited for her below. "What is this?" Kate said. It didn't look like a prison at all, despite the presence of several structures down below. There were few walls and even fewer guards.

Corwin shook the question off. "Come on. There's a stairway down." He hurried toward it, and Kate followed half a beat later.

She swept her gaze over the pit as they descended the steep, narrow steps carved into the cliff's side, still trying to make sense of it all. More than a dozen long, low-ceilinged buildings squatted in a pentagonal formation in the middle of the circular pit. At their center was an arena-like structure formed by a short, crumbling wall. It might've been the ruins of an amphitheater. *Or a temple*, Kate thought, as her mind at last made sense of the most startling object in the pit, one so incongruous that her eyes had at first slid right over it.

A massive stone face lay in the center of the arena, the head of some long-decapitated statue. The statue rested on its side, part of it buried in the grass so that only a single eye and ear remained visible. That and half of the crown encircling its brow, fashioned in the shape of a serpent or perhaps a dragon. Kate supposed if the statue had a body to go with it, it would've reached the top of the pit and then some.

Although they descended the stairs as quickly as they could, it still took several long minutes to reach the bottom. Kate did her best not to think of how hard the climb back out would be. At least she wasn't tired. Just the opposite. She felt more awake, more alive, than she had in days.

Given the early hour, there was little activity in the pit, only a handful of guards walking scattered patrols. When one of the nearest spotted them, Kate instinctively reached out with her magic. *Go away*, she thought. *You don't see us.*

To her surprise, she sensed the man's mind clearly, and the sudden desire he had to turn back around again. Her magic. It was back! She nearly swayed on her feet at the realization.

"What happened?" Corwin grabbed her arm, steadying her.

"My magic. I can use it again."

"How?"

"I don't know." She peered around, prickles running down her skin. Some of it from the joy of having her magic again, but more of it from fear. Fear of this unnatural place, and the certainty that if she could access her magic again, so could everyone else. Including all the wilders imprisoned here. What was Magnar doing with them?

"There's no time to speculate," Corwin said. "Come on. Let's count our blessings while they come." He made for the nearest building, testing the door and finding it locked.

Kate reached for the keys, which she'd belted at her waist, but Corwin stopped her. "There's no need for that." He turned and waved to Bonner and Francis, who'd been following closest behind them. "Is your magic back, too?" Corwin asked Bonner.

Bonner started to frown, then stopped, a shocked look spreading across his face. "It is. I don't understand how—"

Corwin cut him off. "Can you take care of this lock?"

Pressing his lips together, Bonner raised his hand toward the look, melting it open with his magic. Corwin clapped him once on the back, then stepped inside.

Kate followed, the smell of too many bodies in too small a place enveloping her. She peered around at the murky darkness, her eyes making out the human shapes covering the floor. For a second, she thought they were dead, but a simple sweep of her magic told her they were only sleeping—and that Kiran wasn't among them.

She and Corwin began waking them one by one, soon helped by the others joining them. Sluggishly, the wilders stirred. Although they looked well fed, and there was no visible sign of abuse, they remained dazed long after waking, men, women, and children alike staring up at their would-be saviors with expressionless gazes.

Kate motioned Bonner over to her. "Can you remove this woman's collar?" She indicated the nearest wilder, who'd managed to sit up but hadn't yet tried to stand. She wore a collar studded with glowing magestones designed to stop a wilder from using their magic. Bonner waved his hand at the woman's neck, and the metal melted away like ice.

"I can't believe this is happening," Kate said, encouraged by how easily he'd performed the magic.

"I know. I feel nearly myself again," Bonner replied, unsmiling.

If only that were true, Kate thought, watching as he removed the next collar, and the next.

She turned back to the woman. "Can you use your magic?"

"Magic?" The woman stumbled over the word, as if Kate had spoken in a foreign language. But then she glanced down at her palm, and water appeared as if she cupped a miniature fountain in her hand.

"Good, you're going to need it." Kate closed the woman's fingers, and the water disappeared. "How long have you been here?"

She blinked slowly. "How . . . long?"

Dismayed, Kate plunged into the woman's mind. A small, quiet voice in the back of her head admonished her for the invasive act. Once, not long ago, she never would've combed through someone's mind like this, as if she had a right to these memories, these thoughts and feelings. But there was no time to consider the morality of what she was doing—her desperate need to find Kiran outweighed everything.

The woman's thoughts were dull and hazy, as if she'd been drinking. The effect was so powerful that for a second, Kate nearly forgot herself. Then she pushed through the haze to find what she needed. This woman had only been here some four weeks, and she hadn't been out of this room much at all. She hadn't seen any young boys who looked like Kiran. Kate withdrew, impatient to move on with her search.

Corwin approached her. "Everyone's free of the collars, but we're having a hard time making them understand what they need to do. They must be drugged or something. Can you help?"

Kate nodded, knowing at once what he wanted her to do. A few moments before, it would've been impossible, but now her magic swelled inside her, making her feel both full and light and complete all at once. Closing her eyes, she stretched out with her sway, pulling all the minds toward her like kites on a string. In an instant she conveyed the plan—that they were all to wait here, silent and still, and when the time came to leave they needed to be ready to use their magic on the guards.

She withdrew a moment later. "It's done."

Leaving Tira and Dal to stay with this group, Corwin and the rest moved on to the next house. Instead of a single, large room, this one held a long hallway lined with doors on each side, locked and windowless. Individual cells, Kate guessed. They wasted no time opening the first few doors, Bonner using his magic with careless ease.

When one of the doors opened to reveal Kiran inside, Kate couldn't stop the shout of joy that escaped her throat. She dashed into the room, reaching for him.

With a startled look, Kiran jumped back from her, fists raised to defend himself. Then recognition lit his face. "Kate!"

She pulled him into her arms, hugging him so tight he gave a grunt. Her mind reeled from the shock of how different he looked, how much older, bigger.

"Come on," Kate said, loosening her grip. "We've got to get out of here."

"No," said a voice from the other side of the room. Kate looked up to see Vianne, Kiran's mother, standing in the far corner and watching Kate with blood-shot eyes. Her face was bruised with fatigue.

"What do you mean, no? We're getting all of you out of here."

Biting his lip, Kiran took a step back from Kate and shook his head.

"We can't leave, Kate," Vianne said. "You don't understand—"

She broke off at the sound of a commotion outside, voices raised in anger. Kate turned to the door as Francis stepped through it, dragging a woman behind him—Anise, one of the wilders captured at the same time as Vianne and Kiran.

"Kate!" Francis said through gritted teeth. "Make her stop fighting me. Make her come."

"Let go of me, Francis." Anise tried to jerk free of his grasp, her face purpled with anger. "I'm staying. Let go!"

Kate gaped, confused that Anise, Vianne, and Kiran would refuse to be saved. What was going on? She began to ask, only to be silenced by the sound of gunfire. She and Francis exchanged a startled look. It could only be one of their people—revolvers were as rare as magic outside of Rime.

"Let's go." Kate grabbed her brother by the arm. He pulled back, but Kate didn't let go. Not until Vianne stepped forward and sunk her nails into Kate's forearm.

Anger cut through her disbelief, and without a second thought, Kate reached into Vianne's mind, grabbed hold of her thoughts, and forced her will into submission. A moment later she did the same to Kiran and Anise. She didn't understand what made them want to stay, but she wasn't going to wait around to find out with armed guards on the way.

Kate stepped out into the hallway, dragging her wards behind her. She felt them fighting against her at each step, their minds like eels, slippery in the hands of her magic.

Corwin dashed down the hallway toward them. "Go . . . go . . . go!"

"What about the rest?" Kate ran her gaze over all the open doors.

"They won't come," Bonner said, joining them. "Can you make them?"

Kate reached toward the other wilders, sensing them, but the moment she tried to engage, she almost lost her grip on Kiran, Vianne, and Anise. They fought her so relentlessly it took all her concentration and strength to hold them. She shook her head.

"Watch out," Corwin said, as several Sevan guards came through the doorway. He pulled out his revolver, but before he could fire, Bonner crushed the guards' swords with his magic, rendering them useless. Then he and Corwin mowed them down.

Turning away from the carnage, Kate moved toward the exit with her captives in tow. Outside, Tira and Dal were leading the first set of prisoners out of the house. As before, the wilders remained sluggish and dull-witted, only a couple of them using their magic against the attacking guards.

The entire prison was aware of their presence by now. Still, with the help of their revolvers, they were able to keep the danger at bay until they reached the steps. Dal led the way up with the wilders following behind him. Vander went next with Tira quick on his heels. Behind her, Francis dragged Anise along by the arm. Reaching the steps, Kate sent Vianne and Kiran up first. Corwin and Bonner brought up the rear behind her. Bonner paused several feet up the stairs and turned around long enough to destroy the stone steps with his magic, preventing the guards from following that way.

They climbed as fast as they could, the stairs steep and treacherous. On the ground below, a dozen Sevan guardsmen had formed a line, bows in hand. They nocked arrows and drew back to fire.

"Bonner!" Kate shouted. "Stop them!"

Bonner raised his hand as the guards loosed the arrows. They took flight, only to be halted by Bonner's magic. But already the bowmen were drawing again, even as more guards swelled their numbers. It seemed if they couldn't prevent the prisoners from escaping, they would kill them instead.

"I can't stop them all!" Bonner shouted, his face contorted from the effort.

A loud crack echoed over Kate's head, the sound like lightning striking the ground. She looked up to see a huge chunk of the pit wall being wrenched away. Another glance showed her it was Francis, his arms outstretched as he guided it, his face strained with the same effort Bonner had shown. The huge slab of stone hovered beside them as a shield.

"Keep going," Francis yelled through gritted teeth.

They charged onward, their steps punctuated by the sound of arrows bouncing harmlessly off the stone. Kate's legs began to burn, and her breathing grew labored. The top loomed far above them, an eternity away. But they only needed to get out of reach of the arrows.

"Kate," Tira called from ahead of her. "You've got to kill those guards before they kill us."

"I can't!" She didn't have the breath to explain how Kiran, Anise, and Vianne struggled against her even now, worse than before. Kate could feel their panic—their terror—at leaving the pit. If she let go, she didn't know what they would do.

"Please, Kate," Francis said, his face purpled from the effort of holding the stone.

Glancing down at the guards below, she knew she could kill them with her sway, easily and quickly, and likely not risk losing the wilders' minds completely. But she didn't want to. She'd killed that way only once before and it haunted her still. She could just put them to sleep instead, but that would take longer. Indecision taunted her. *They are our enemies*, she heard Corwin saying to her once again.

Reaching the limits of his magic, Francis let out a strangled cry and stumbled to his knees, arms dropping to his sides. The stone slab fell as he did and struck the side of the steps with a noise like a mountain being rent in two. Below, the guardsmen seized their chance, bows raised for another volley. At once, Kate reached out with her magic to subdue them, but she was slowed by the strain of holding Kiran, Vianne, and Anise. Before she could reach them all, one guard let loose an arrow. It flew toward Kate, so fast it was almost invisible. A heartbeat later, she felt the pain tear through her mind, realizing too late that it wasn't her pain.

But Kiran's.

Turning, Kate saw the arrow protruding from his chest, his features already slackening, his body going limp.

"NO!" She reached for him, but her hands found only air as he slid off the edge. It was over in a moment, his body crashing to the floor below. Before Kate could even scream, she watched another body plummeting to the ground after Kiran. In Kate's distraction she'd let go of her other wards, and Vianne had jumped, compelled both by her son and whatever force had been working so hard to draw her back to the pit. With a sickening lurch in her stomach, Kate turned to see that Anise too was trying to leap off the edge, held back only by Francis's tight grip on her.

"Stop her, Kate." The muscles in his arms rippled from the effort to hold her.

Kate grabbed Anise's mind with her magic. As before, the woman fought her, but Kate wrestled her under control. All the while the terrible truth beat in her brain—*Kiran is dead. Kiran is dead*. She hadn't saved him. She'd hesitated and he'd fallen. *Oh gods*.

"Move!" Corwin shouted from below Kate. His voice cut through her thoughts, reminding her there were other lives at stake.

Staving off her grief, she renewed the climb with the others.

They didn't make it far before there was another crack like lightning hitting ground. A violent tremble rocked the stairs, throwing Kate forward onto her hands and knees. The crack sounded again, louder and nearer than before. She glanced behind her toward the source of the noise and saw Corwin and Bonner were on their knees as well, but farther away then they'd been. A rift had appeared in the steps, dividing her from them.

"Corwin! Bonner!" she screamed. "Jump!"

Corwin scrambled to his feet, but before he could make the leap, there was a third crack, and this time the rest of the stairs beneath Corwin and Bonner fell away, a landslide of stone and dirt that dragged them both down, slowly at first, then faster, until they both plummeted toward the ground as Kiran and Vianne had done moments before.

Kate lost sight of them in the cloud of dust and didn't know where they'd fallen. But she didn't need to. She'd seen Kiran's. It was a fall no one could survive, and the truth of it made the world shatter around her, her heart seizing in her chest.

"Come on, Kate." Hands grabbed her shoulders, pulling her up, forcing her to stand.

"No," she said, reaching for her love and her friend, as if she could will them alive by her mind alone. She stretched out with her magic as far as she could, but she couldn't sense either Corwin or Bonner down below.

Dal knelt beside her, mouth to her ear. "They're gone, Kate, but Corwin would want you to survive." Dal's voice was like steel, hiding his own pain beneath it. Corwin had been his best friend for years, same as Bonner had been hers.

Dead dead dead. The truth filled her mind, overwhelming her until nothing else existed.

"Come on," Dal said, hauling her forward now. "You can't give up, Kate. Signe is counting on us."

At the sound of her name, Signe's face appeared in Kate's mind, through the black of her despair. Signe, another close friend, someone she loved. If Kate died here, Signe would feel the same pain Kate felt now. Dal was right. They needed to escape, alive.

Blinded by tears, Kate finished the climb. Once up, they crossed the field back to the wall and out into the city, sneaking their way down alleys and side streets until they reached the harbor where Signe waited on the ship to carry them back to Rime.

Home. Just as Corwin had promised.

Only he'd been wrong. He wasn't there to tease her with his stranger's face as she lay down for sleep that night. She was alone. And when the ship reached Rime's shores at last, she stepped onto her home soil feeling like a person rent in two. For a part of her remained in Seva, lying dead in that pit with Kiran, Bonner, and Corwin. Three parts of her heart, torn asunder.